THE WOLVES

Paddy Kelly

THE WOLVES OF CALABRIA

FICTION4ALL

A FICTION4ALL PAPERBACK

© Paddy Kelly 2019
All Rights Reserved.

The right of Paddy Kelly to be identified as the author of this work has been asserted by him in accordance with the Copyright, Designs and Patents Act of 1988.

All rights reserved.

No part of this publication may be reproduced, stored in or introduced into a retrieval system, or transmitted, in any form, or by any means electronic, mechanical, photocopying, recording or otherwise, without the prior permission of the copyright holder.

Any person who commits any unauthorised act in relation to this publication may be liable to criminal prosecution and civil claims for damages in accordance with the Copyright Act of 1956 (as amended).

ISBN   987-1-78695-206-6

This Edition Published 2019 by Fiction4All
https://fiction4all.com

Cover Design by: Paddy Kelly
Graphics by: Pedro Sperandio

Edited by
Katherine Mary Kennedy

The Wolves of Calabria

This work is dedicated to:

A devoute husband, father & former member of the New York Mafia who passed these stories down through the family.

My maternal grandfather,

Giuseppe M. Cavallo

Paddy Kelly

The Wolves of Calabria

✝

The Italian Wolf, also known as the Apennine Wolf, was in 1921 originally described as subspecies *Canis lupus italicus* by Italian zoologist Joseph Altobello. However, following WWII it was believed to be extinct.

It was not.

In actuality the wolves had spread north, northwest from Sicily to the island of Corsica then on to Southern France and finally across the Atlantic into New York City.

By 1946 the wolves, led by a cunning and ruthless leader, Charlie 'Lucky' Luciano, were planning to devour the youth and disenfranchised of the entire United States.

✝

Paddy Kelly

PROLOGUE

In February of 1942, by setting fire to the *T.L.S. Normandie* in New York Harbor, the crude but clever ruse by the Mafia worked as planned and duped the NYC authorities into believing there were German saboteurs roaming the city waterfront. The nation erupted into hysteria over the apparent sneak attack of imaginary infiltrators and gave birth to "Operation Underworld", the hiring of the New York Mafia by Naval Intelligence to guard the NYC waterfront against further acts of sabotage.

Within months Charlie 'Lucky' Luciano and la Costa Nostra were once again in control.

However, despite the mobilization of hundreds of F.B.I. and Naval Intelligence agents along the New York City and New Jersey waterfronts, and the cooperation of the New York Mob by September of the same year, save for a half dozen ex-German prisoners given the choice to infiltrate the U.S. and cause trouble or be executed, no saboteurs had been found.

These would be German saboteurs were captured in June immediately after landing when one of them struck up a conversation with a local out for an evening stroll with his dog. Predictably J. Edgar Hoover falsely took credit for the discovery and arrests, promised the Germans prison sentences in lieu of death for cooperation then, after they had cooperated, had them executed. He followed up his song and dance by submitting a falsified report to FDR.

After the authorities slowly came to the realization that there were no saboteurs regularly landing in New York City a hasty conversion of the expensive and labor intensive *Operation Underworld* to an intelligence gathering mission ensued. This time in support of the upcoming invasion of Sicily dubbed *Operation Husky*.

With Commander Charles Haffenden again in charge it was quickly and quietly achieved.

Meanwhile, Charlie Luciano, Meyer Lansky and Frankie Costello, not content to wait for events to take shape of their accord, were deep in the midst of planning the establishment of what would later become to be called . . . the International Drug Cartel.

†

✝

"In a world where everyone is guilty,
the only crime is getting caught."

- Anonymous

✝

Paddy Kelly

CHAPTER I

Villalba, Foothills of the Monti Erei
27 Miles North of Gela, Sicily
06:35, 27 June, 1943

☦

Now mercilessly pulsating the sun had long ago burned away the morning mist and the scenic but rugged hills of Villa Alba now stood indomitable against the blue-grey sky of the green western Mediterranean. Despite the early hour thirty-seven degree heat rained down on the rustic settlements between Gela and Licata.

Salvatore Lucania, alias Charlie 'Lucky' Luciano, had been born less than fifteen miles from here in Lercara Fridi, where his relatives still worked for the most influential Mafioso in Sicily, Don Calò Vizzini.

Above the settlements, tucked away, high in the foothills, the folds and crevices were peppered with sentries.

In their traditional white collarless shirts, black waistcoats and brandishing sawn off shot guns, the Mafiosi guards, perched high up on cliffs and ledges were there to watch, record and report all Nazi troop and equipment movements. Working in pairs one slept while the other stood watch. They had been there since the invasion two years ago and would be there as long as the most hated conqueror in their country's history remained.

Tucked away in one fold of a rock outcropping a man, barely a teen, sat in the shade tossing pebbles into a small circle drawn in the dirt a couple of meters away when a distant noise caught his attention. He sat up and listened more intently.

"Ehi! Veglia!" The young lookout nudged his sleeping mate with his foot. "Ehi! Veglia!"

"CHE?" Rubbing the sleep from his eyes he looked up from his blanket roll just as the hum of a small aircraft engine came into earshot. Both scrambled and took cover in a large crevice of rock as they turned their eyes and ears to the sky.

"Dove è?"

"Chiudere!" Seconds later a U.S. Army, O.D. green, Piper Cub appeared lazily gliding over the peaks. The two sentries raced into the open area and waved wildly. The scout plane dove to 100 feet and buzzed their position. On the pull up he dipped his wings signaling he had seen them. The plane flew out another half mile or so, looped around and headed back in towards the peak, flying considerably lower this time. The pilot opened his window, banked left and dropped a weighted piece of cloth through the opening then faded into the distance back south and out over the sea.

In an unintended competition the two dashed to where the cloth had landed, retrieved it, removed the stone and unfurled it.

It was a bright yellow scarf emblazoned with an embroidered, red upper case "L". The older sentry handed it to his partner with a broad smile and, in a barely restrained whisper ordered, "Andare! They come!"

With shotgun in hand and stuffing the scarf into his shirt, the younger Sicilian half hustled half stumbled down the mountain, vaulted into the saddle of his horse and in a cloud of dust vanished down the winding mountain pass.

Twenty minutes later, still at a gallop, the young rider arrived at a small chicken farm on the northern outskirts of the small village of Villalba. Abandoning his horse and out of breath he ran around back of the main house but saw no one. A young woman opened a first floor window and yelled down at him. He removed his hat before addressing her.

"Senorina, where is Don Vizzini?"

"In the hen house!" She ducked back in then stuck her head back out again. "If you come in the house wipe your feet!" She vanished into the window and the teen messenger double timed across the yard to a long narrow wooden building which was in an advanced state of disrepair.

There at the far end stood a very tall, pear shaped, elderly man. Surrounded by squawking chickens he was casually splashing feed across the floor. Again the youth removed his cap before he addressed the elder.

In ancient times The Village of White was

legendary in far off lands throughout the Mediterranean. By the time the United States was 100 years old, Villalba was celebrating its first millennium. Now, in a farmhouse that was 150 years older than the U. S. Capital building itself, in the heart of the village, a special message was about to be delivered.

Even bent with age the defacto Capo di Tutti of Sicily, Don Calogero Vizzini, stood six foot four and weighed in at 275 pounds. His oversized spectacles added rather than detracted from the imposition of his person. Vizzini had what's known in theatrical circles as 'absolute presence'.

The Calogero's worn, brown shoes had seen better days, his ballooned, grey trousers rendered his lower frame featureless and over his short sleeved, yellowed-white dress shirt his suspenders were forced to detour around the sides of his rotund abdomen.

This was the man who could be counted on to correct the recurring injustices of the law. The man all knew that no starving peasant ever came to his door and went away empty handed. If you were of his cosca, his clan, you feared no outsider.

"Don Vizzini?" The old man slowly turned and looked down his thick, horn rimmed glasses.

"Si Michael?"

The kid approached and held out the folded yellow scarf.

"Definitely Americani!" The boy added. The old man set the feed basket aside and took the scarf, unfolded it and gazed at the embroidered, crimson 'L'.

It wasn't long before the boy realized that Vizzini wasn't staring at the piece of cloth but rather through it. Being the first time he had actually met Don Vizzini, he respectfully stood silent. After a long while the old man stepped forward, broke into a broad grin and shook his head.

"Salvatore. Salvatore Lucasia."

"What does this tell you Don Vizzini?"

"Something important!" Putting his arm around the young man he started out of the coop and towards the house.

"Such as?" Vizzini stopped in the middle of the yard.

"Some things you should not know."

"But why Don? We fight together. I give my life for you, you know that!"

"I know that mio figlio." He put his paw of a hand on the young man's cheek. "When you become old you will know many things." Vizzini paused at the rear door of the house. "But if you know too many things, you may not live to be old." The Don tucked the scarf in his pocket and opened the door to the house.

"Don, what do I tell the others?" Michael called after him.

"Tell them to meet at Chiesa Madre tonight, at eleven." The teen displayed obvious disappointment. "And tell them that soon we have our country back!"

Michael smiled.

He knew the long awaited day of the invasion was at hand.

✝

03:00, Sunday 10 July, 1943
The Mediterranean Sea
3 Miles Southwest of Gela, Sicily
Onboard *SS Robert Rowen*

D-Day: *Operation Husky*

The fleet had arrived during the night under cover of darkness. The weather was rough but not unbearable, pretty much as it had been since the start of the operation less than an hour ago. Winds out of the West at 35-40 knots, 10 foot chops and just enough rain to make life miserable up on the weather decks. The twenty degree rolls were easily coped with, although they did make life a little less convenient.

The port side, forward look out on the fleet's lead ship had just reported to the Quarter Deck of the Watch on the Flag Ship. The Sicilian coast had been spotted. The information was relayed to the wheelhouse and the C.O. ordered all ahead one third and that the sighting be disseminated to the accompanying fleet.

All two thousand five hundred vessels.

The Wolves of Calabria

So reliant were the Allies on the success of the S.O.E. *Mincemeat* operation and the intelligence provided by their New York Mafia connections that not only were they about to assault the Axis strong hold in the Med with what was the largest armada ever assembled accompanied by 160,000 troops, 14,000 vehicles, 1800 big guns, and 600 tanks all led by their senior Admiral, Sir Andrew Cunningham, but aboard on separate ships were the Allies two most famous, first string, superstar generals, George S. Patton and Sir Bernard Montgomery. The follow on invasion of the Italian mainland through Anzio was already in the advanced stages of planning.

'Old Blood and Guts' George was to lead the U.S. 7th Army in an all out assault along the southern shores while Monty would take the British 8th Army along with the Canadian First onto the eastern shores of the 10,000 year old island country.

The invasion scenario had the Americans, 6th and 12th Army Groups and 45th Infantry Divisions supported by a reinforced battalion of the 82d Airborne, to assault Gela and capture the south-western territories of the island while the Brits and Canadians did the same on the Eastern beaches of Catania. This operation was the first time in the war the Americans and British were to work together on any appreciable scale and it was the first all-out amphib invasion of the war. More importantly, it was the first combat test of the newly formed airborne troops. There was a lot that could go wrong.

There was a lot that did.

As the American Army's target city Gela was a deep water port and the available enemy artillery had been largely neutralized, the fleet's Flag Ship orders were to take her nine inch guns within 2,000 yards of the beach, drop anchor and establish a Command & Control center primarily as a fire base control to support the landings.

Although German Intelligence swallowed the British ruse hook line and sinker, code named "Mincemeat", as to where the invasion would take place, due to traffic control considerations the German High Command were slow to transfer troops to Greece, and so the attacking armies were heading into a significantly bigger fight than anticipated.

At least the weather was with the Allies so although the sporadic winds would be a hazard to the airborne troops, visibility would allow naval gunfire to be brought to bear with more precise accuracy.

Below decks on the 03 level, on board the Liberty Ship *S.S. Robert Rowen*, the chow line stretched back through the hatch to the engineering spaces however, this morning three Marine sentries had head-of-the-line privileges.

With two trays each they pushed in front of a crusty Boatswain's Mate 1st Class who had no sense of humor about being cut off by a gang of Marines and made no secret of his emotions.

"Fuckin' Jarheads!" He cursed aloud.

"Fuck you, Squid!" Corporal Deuth, the Marine detail leader, returned the compliment to the BM1.

A junior Seaman behind the Boatswain peered over his port side shoulder.

"Hey Boats, how come they always call us, 'squids' anyways?" The junior member of the Marine detail leaned over and enlightened him.

"That's because a squid is a small, spineless sea creature which lives off Marine waste."

The cooks behind the line could've cared less who they were serving but hoped a fight might break out, or at least a skirmish, anything to break the monotony. When it didn't they just continued to fill the plates with greasy bacon patties, instant scrambled eggs and cold toast shoving the tin trays back across the stainless steel counter. Once on the trays half the food slid off in the next roll of the ship. The sentries picked the patties up off the deck and plopped them back onto the plates.

"Three second rule." One shrugged.

"What'a ya wanna do about their coffee?" One of the privates asked Corporal Deuth.

"Fuck it! We'll come back for it, or they can get it themselves!" Deuth placed one full tray on top of another.

"They're not allowed out!"

"Then I guess they don't get coffee!" The Corporal led the detail around the galley to the port side and through the forward compartments.

"Who are they anyway?" They talked as they made their way through the narrow passageways.

"Scuttlebutt has it they're here by orders of a special House sub-committee of something or other."

"Yeah? When'd you get that scuttlebutt?"

"Right after we shoved off from Tunisia. Two guys from up in CNC were jabber jawin' and one of 'em said something about spooks being sent out by a Congressional sub-committee."

"If they're so fuckin' important why the hell are they billeted in the chain locker?"

"Must be under a non-fraternization order."

"That's some serious non-frat order!"

"Wake up! They're fuckin' spooks!"

"Thank you Dick fuckin' Tracy!"

"Why do ya think they ain't got no names or ranks on their uniforms?!"

The chain locker of any ship, located in the most forward hold, was never meant to house troops, much less civilians. The overhead is high, the narrow deck is riddled with fixtures and beams, it's usually the narrowest compartment on the ship, and there is no forward bulkhead, only the forward keel. The compartment is half filled with steel anchor chain on both sides, and on a ship the size of the *S.S. Robert Rowan* each link is the size of a man which means there's nowhere to lie down. Except when the ship's at anchor. Of course the problem is it takes about two to three hours after they drop anchor for your ears to stop ringing, even if they're plugged with those tiny, useless little pieces of rubber foam they give you. Oh yeah, there's one additional treat.

The Wolves of Calabria

The two giant, gaping holes in the bulkhead to let the chain out are the same ones which also let the sea, the wind and the cold in.

Although they wore no rank two of the men perched on the huge pile of anchor chain, by their demander and bearing, were obviously military men.

One was a lawyer-turned Lieutenant Commander assigned to Naval Intelligence and temporarily attached to Bill Donovan's Office of Strategic Services.

The other, younger one, was an Intelligence officer nobody could figure out anything about. Except that he always spoke to them in flawless Sicilian. As they were all Sicilian, they didn't mind but figured him to be a lieutenant at least. Probably.

Lieutenant Commander Anthony Marsloe and Lieutenant Paul Alfieri had been assigned this mission for several reasons.

Marsloe, being a long standing fixture in New York D. A. Frank Hogan's office, had been in on *Operation Underworld* almost from its inception last February and therefore rode the wave of transition when it escalated into its present format, known by Naval Intelligence as 'F' Section, which had now become a sub-section of the Office of Strategic Services.

Following Commander Haffenden's orders it was Marsloe who, as former resident 'expert' on Sicilians and the Mafia in the NYC D.A.'s office, organized the offshoot of 'F' Section, an intel office organized specifically to gather intel about southern

Sicily, which they named the 'Linguistics Section'.

Turning in his fountain pen and briefcase for a backpack and .45, he fit right into the early profile of Wild Bill Donovan and the other New York lawyers who made up the early members of the O.S.S. the forerunners of the CIA.

The young, well-built Lieutenant with him was more of a mystery, even to Marsloe. He appeared to be just one of those dozens of kids who kept knocking on the door of Naval Intel trying to get in on the Big Game and who was finally somehow granted admission. Marsloe was the Honcho but in Special Ops that just means you take the blame if things go South.

Of the two Alfieri, looking as if he were going on a woodland hike in his civilian clothes, had the shit mission. It was simple but shit. Get ashore, beg, borrow or steal whatever resources required, locate the Italian Naval HQ outside Gela, as reported by Luciano and his guys, get into the Admiral's office and steal anything you can carry.

"Oh yeah," Commander Haffenden added just before Alfieri shipped out, "We might have some questions. So try to come back in one piece."

They were also there to land four Italians, Sicilians really, tentatively labeled as V.I.P.'s. Their special V.I.P.'s? Gino Giuliani and three others who were lifetime members of the New York Italian American Club on Mott Street.

All were born and reared in Southern Sicily, all except Enrico who was from Brooklyn. The

The Wolves of Calabria

Syndicate members had all volunteered to make the landing and not because they were anxious to once more see their home turf. Two of them could not have cared less if they ever set foot in Sicily again, but someday soon, after the Army, Navy and Marines had fumigated the place of Mussolini's vermin then packed up and gone home, they would act as the forward organizers to re-establish Syndicate operations. Providing the Fascists didn't regroup.

Of course for the time being, as far as the Navy was concerned, they were doing their patriotic duty to aid the landing by acting as forward scouts.

"Why the Feds so interested in Gela any ways?" Gino directed his question at Marsloe.

"According to our sources in New York that's where Mussolini set up headquarters for the navy. We're bankin' on there being some valuable intel if we can get there in time."

"Naval Headquarters in Gela?! You fuckin' kiddin' me? You ever been to Gela?! They roll up the fucking streets at half past eight!"

"Maybe that's the reason he chose Gela!" Marsloe remarked to Alfieri in Italian.

"There you go! See, you ain't as dumb as you look!" Gino quipped.

"Hey Enrico!"

"Yeah?"

"Fuck you!"

Enrico sat isolated from the others. Not by choice but because Gino threatened to knife him if he didn't take his smoked sardine breakfast elsewhere. As it was, Gino had two full sea-sick bags sealed up on the deck across from him and was gradually working on a third.

Suddenly the ten dogs on the single hatch to the chain locker cranked open and the three Marines came in with the breakfast trays. About two minutes after Gino's tray was laid in front of him and he got a whiff of those greasy bacon patties, he was working away filling that third bag.

"Thirty minutes to launch, Sir. Launch officer needs you on deck, starboard side ten minutes prior." Deuth addressed Commander Marsloe.

"Roger that Corporal. Tell him we're in route."

The Commander was the only one who finished his bacon and eggs, and half of Gino's, and the Sicilians were glad when it was time to move out.

Up on the main deck, in the fresh air Gino started to regain himself but became a little concerned when he spotted some flashes of light in the distance, beyond the hills of the town.

"Hey Commander. You sure it's safe to go in there now? I mean we don't gotta worry about bein' shot at or nuthin'?"

"What's'a matter Gino? You gonna tell me you never been shot at?" Marsloe chided.

"Sure! Loads'a times! Just never by nuthin' shootin' fuckin' Buicks!" Gino barked. The Commander laughed.

"Seriously Sir. We got anything to worry about?" Enrico asked. Alfieri jumped in with a pat on the back.

"Look at it this way Enrico. If we pull this off we're heroes!"

"And if we don't?!"

"Then we're dead heroes! Either way, we get a medal."

"Relax Gino. Most of the fightin's died down by now. Besides the beaches are secure. The battle lines are mostly in land now." Marsloe assured.

Although it had been relatively quiet through the boarding and launch of the landing craft as they descended the cargo nets serving as rope ladders, no sooner had they cast off and the cox'wain headed in towards shore when things seemed to pick up.

A stray Italian fighter came out of nowhere and headed straight for their assault boat. The Cox'swain immediately steered into an uneven 'S' pattern, but there was little time. The fighter banked and let go two three second bursts strafing the *Robert Rowen*. The on board crew returned fire, but despite a round pinging around the rear bulkhead of the launch craft, no one was hit.

"Where the hell'd that little son-of-bitch come from?" Enrico asked to no one in particular.

"I don't know, but he's got friends!" Commander Marsloe answered as he pointed off the starboard bow. Three more fighters were bearing down on the convoy.

"A tausend boats in the fuckin' water and he's gotta come at us?!" Enrico cursed.

"JESUS FUCKIN' CHRIST!" Gino suddenly

yelled at the top of his lungs and hunkered down and tried to sink into the wet deck. The wings of the fighters streaked low overhead but didn't fire. Seconds later several of the others noticed Gino staring out off the port side.

There, 100 meters or so out from their boat was the fuselage of an O.D. green, U.S. Army glider minus its wings. However the wreckage was gliding gently towards shore, like a giant, closed-in canoe being paddled by three of the crew on top of it using their rifles as paddles.

"Where's a fucking camera when you need one?!" The coxswain asked out loud.

"GINO! You okay?!" Enrico yelled.

"Do I fucking look o-fucking-kay!? I wanted to come back someday but not like this! TELL THE DRIVER TO TURN THIS FUCKING FERRY AROUND!" Just as Gino was having second thoughts about his loyalty a pair of German bombers appeared out over Gela.

"COX'SWAIN, FULL AHEAD! MAKE FOR THE NEAREST BEACH!" Marsloe yelled. Still three quarters of a mile offshore things weren't looking too good for the O.S.S. group. The bombers came in at danger close altitude and released their loads at about six hundred yards out. The good news was that they released too late and didn't kill anything except some fish. The bad news was they came around for a second pass.

Having saved half their load until they got the windage and elevation, the bombers were luckier this time.

Two bombs from the second bird missed their targets, but the last two hit directly amidships of the *Robert Rowan*.

The force of the explosion lit off the ship's magazine which was enough to lift the entire hull out of the water by three feet. A cylindrical smoke plume rose five hundred feet into the air with searing hot wreckage rocketing out in all directions. Like contrails from a rudderless aircraft burning shrapnel showered the surrounding area and was carried by the wind for over half a mile.

As the shock wave rocked their landing craft several chunks of smoldering shrapnel fell onto the O.S.S. group and two of the crew were burned though not badly. When the dust cleared however, a large smoke pot, part of the ancillary cargo in the boat, was burning away. The Cox'swain was the first to notice.

"GET THAT FIRE OUT!" He yelled at the passengers.

Also on board the landing craft was an Ensign Parle, a 27 year old Naval Reserve officer from Omaha. He was the first to act. He rushed to grab one of several fire buckets onboard but most of the sand had been spilt in the rough seas and what remained was caked thick from the rain of sea water. The smoke clearly marked the vessel for miles around and was noted by the enemy aircraft loitering over the fleet.

What he did next would save the boat and all

aboard, but several days later claim his life.

Realizing attempts at extinguishing the large pot were pointless, he shoved his way through the panic-stricken passengers and blinding smoke and wrestled the device to the deck and away from the large cargo of ammo. Gasping heavily and vomiting from the thick chemical fumes and with his last bit of breath he lifted the 150 pound, smoldering pot over the gunwale and into the sea.

He collapsed to the deck gagging and vomiting more violently before going unconscious.

A squadron of Allied fighters appeared and chased the errant Italian fighters out of the area.

A beach head had been established so there was no enemy gunfire and as soon as the ramp hit the sand several men carried the casualties off the craft and were met by two corpsmen from the landing party who immediately went to work.

The O.S.S. group gathered themselves and made their way up the beach to a command tent to get their bearings.

"Why'd he make such a big deal? It was just a smoke pot!" Gino commented.

"A smoke pot which was sitting on top of 300 pounds of ammo!" Marsloe informed him. Gino turned white. Again.

They looked back out to sea to watch the smoldering wreck of the *Robert Rowen* gradually sink beneath the waves.

"There's a fuckin' close call to tell your grand kids about!"

One hundred yards up the beach they came on a General Purpose Tent, Large and entered. Inside the tent Marsloe took the lead and approached an NCO.

"We're looking for your Skipper."

"That's him over there. Holding court by the map boards." They headed towards the tall Colonel telling a story while surrounded by half a dozen lower ranking officers.

"So Mountbatten grabs the hailer from the BM and yells out to Hewitt, 'How far has General Patton gotten?' And Hewitt clicks his hailer and yells back, 'The General is back on board this ship!' You could hear the laughter all over the decks! I nearly pissed my trousers!"

"Sir, Lieutenant Commander Anthony Marsloe, from F Section. Are you the C.O.?" annoyed by the interruption he looked the group up and down.

"Oh yeah, my Spooks. We got word you were coming in." He turned back to his audience. "Dismissed." The officers dispersed and the Colonel led the O.S.S. group into the rear compartment of the tent. The C.O. took a seat behind a small collapsible table and spread out a map. Marsloe stepped front and center as the others bunched in around him.

"The situation as we speak is that we are engaged in a battle on Biazza Ridge, west of Vittoria, here where it crosses the Gela-Vittoria road." He indicated a point on the map. "It's turning into a regular slug fest with some German tanks and supporting infantry. A little earlier we were able to bring some Naval gunfire to bear thanks to a Navy L.T. who jumped in with the Five-O-Fifth. That was a couple of hours ago but we haven't heard from him or them since." The spooks followed him as he shifted to the larger hanging map. "Everything from this blue line south is secure."

"What's the yellow line?" Marsloe asked.

"What we used to call no-mans-land."

"**I still fuckin' do**!" Gino chimed in. The C.O. pushed on.

"After an unopposed landing the only serious opposition we hit on the whole fucking island was here at Gela! Seems the Krauts didn't get the word to go see the Acropolis. 1st Division was met with a counterattack by German Armor. We were pushed off the grid and by sun-up we were back on the beaches. At one point Mk VI's broke through but were engaged by the cruiser *Savannah* and the destroyer *Shubrick* and are now part of the history books.

Yesterday highways 115 and 117 were filthy with Italian tanks from the Niscemi, and Livorno Infantry who pushed the attack on the city. But again the *Shubrick* with the *Boise* opened up on them and cancelled their dance card. We know the 15th Panzer Division is out there, but we're not sure where. We can't push too hard, at least till they show themselves, or we'll get strung out."

"What's'a all this mean for us, Sir?" Asked Lieutenant Alfieri focused solely on his mission.

"Well, seein' as how I haven't got a god damned

clue what your mission is, I don't know. But why ever the hell you're here, just stay outta the way until the smoke clears, wait till you see the ass end of my jeep headin' north, and then assume the A.O. is yours."

"We're here to assist in the re-organization of the civilian population Colonel." Marsloe Informed.

"Re-organization of the civilian population?" The C.O. wasn't quite sure how to take that.

"Yes Sir."

"Well good-fuckin' luck with that little task, gentlemen."

"Why's that Sir?" Asked Alfieri.

"You ever tried to organize a bunch of Italians? Damn near fuckin' impossible! Like organizin' a Chinese fire drill!"

"We understand sir. That's why they sent Sicilians!" Gino sneered.

"Well, if our Intel is right, in less than 48 hours, Gela is yours, gentlemen. And Sicilians. Questions, comments snide remarks?"

"Just one." It was Enrico. "Where can we get something to eat?"

☦

Dark had begun to fall on the shores of Licata Beach outside Gela when Lieutenant Commander Anthony Marsloe pulled up an empty ammo crate next to Paul Alfieri, who was eating from his tin canteen cup and proffered his assessment of their situation.

"We can't wait until the infantry are finished here. There's no telling what they're going to have to do to push inland. If they have to they'll level everything. If they don't the Germans will. If we wait till that point it will be too late."

"Then we go ask him if'a we can go ahead?"

"I got a better idea." Marsloe motioned for Alfieri to bring his chow over to the large granite doorstep of the concrete beach pavilion where he had a map partially spread out on a sea rations crate. "I think it's a good time to take our little stroll up to try and find the Ministero della Marina. You know where this is?" Marsloe indicated a point just shy of two kilometers due North.

"Si. No-mans'a-land. About two kilometers ahead of the forward columns, which means I used'a to know where it was. But'a those battleships tore'a the ass out of'a that town. Maybe is not so much left to navigate by."

"So what'a ya reckon?" Marsloe asked.

"I think'a the best thing to do is go to the last'a known point left standing and then forget about'a references. After that, pace count and navigate by'a compass. Anything we recognize is'a bonus."

"Sounds like a plan. We leave in ten." Marsloe folded up the map. "Pack light. We're gonna be moving fast. Just your web gear, ass pack, weapons and ammo."

"Si Capo!" Marsloe smirked at Alfieri's quip.

Ten minutes later Alfieri met him just outside the forward Command Post.

"It's light enough?" He held up a web belt, a .45 & holster, several ammo pouches, a carbine and an ass pack.

"What's in the ass pack?" Marsloe enquired.

"Only'a the essentials. Salami, bread, binos and more ammo."

"Bravo! Andiamo." With that they slowly moved out heading roughly north.

As they followed a single lane dirt road the overhead whistle of naval gunfire grew louder and they huddled down attempting to meld with the real estate. A shell suddenly hit a hundred meters ahead and a jeep loaded with gear was replaced with a crater.

"JESUS! You bring a first aid kit too? You know, just in case." Marsloe suggested.

It was around 04:40 when they shoved off and the forward beach command post radioed back to the flag ship that 'Birddog' was away. Fifteen minutes later, without incident they reached the forward most Allied listening post where it started to get more real.

Small arms fire was still reassuringly distant but artillery rounds seemed to be falling at the rate of one every few seconds and worse yet without a discernable pattern. Naval gunfire was still some distance to the North but almost seemed concentrated on the area they were heading for.

A mud stained infantryman popped his head up

out of a fox hole as the two passed an outpost and left the last friendly haven.

"Good luck you guys, you're gonna need it."

"NEVER SAY GOOD LUCK, GOD DAMN IT!" Alfieri chastised. "IT BRING'A BAD LUCK." A second rifleman, recognizing Alfieri's accent, shouted over the battery of explosions on the left. "Allora pisano! In bocca al lupo!"

Alfieri smiled back at him.

"Crepi lupo!" Paul answered.

They made their way up an embankment and around the remnants of what used to be a butcher's shop.

'VIVA USA!' Had been hurriedly splashed across the buildings and shops in thin, red paint. Upon closer inspection Paul turned to Marsloe and commented.

"Commander, I don't think that's'a paint!" Marsloe scurried over to take cover against the wall under the graffiti. A few meters away the decapitated bodies of two German soldiers were crumpled against the wall.

"Guess they didn't really understand who they picked a fight with." Marsloe commented.

About five or six blocks into the what was left of the outer neighborhoods of Gela they froze as a small column of German armored cars escorted by a pair of Panzers crossed through a street in front of them less than 100 yards ahead. Fortunately the column had no infantry escort and so they weren't spotted. They ducked into a burned out schoolhouse.

The Wolves of Calabria

While Marsloe wrestled with the map Alfieri tried not to get too distracted by the children's schoolbooks and toys scattered around the room.

"We'll have to follow the signs for now." Marsloe shook his head as he informed his partner. Alfieri looked out a window and across the cratered road to a former three story, bombed out building. The one where a street sign used to be.

"What signs? The signs from God?" He chuckled as he nodded to where some unknown giant had taken a bite out of the corner of the building.

A hundred and fifty meters away, through the schoolhouse window, a crosshairs was focusing in on the back of Marsloe's head. A hint of a smile pierced dried lips as an index finger calmly slid off the trigger guard and onto the trigger. Through the scope the sniper could see down through the large schoolhouse window to Marsloe's neck line as he was consulting his folded map.

The double report of a weapon echoed through the small bell tower and the German's brains spattered against the South wall a split second before his shot ricocheted off the schoolhouse roof.

Peering up through the trap door in the floor of the bell tower a young Sicilian dressed in the starched white, collarless shirt, black waist coat and braces perched was standing on a ladder behind the German. He calmly broke his double barreled, side-by-side shotgun and emptied the casings onto the floorboards of the church tower then reloaded. A hint of a smile pierced the Sicilian's lips.

"Benvenuti in Sicilia." He whispered before descending the ladder.

The Americans continued on unaware of the bell tower drama.

They pushed on through the surrounding fighting, and although were lucky enough not to encounter any foot traffic, they found themselves only a couple of hundred yards from what seemed to be the crossfire of the German 88's on the high ground to the Northeast picking away at the vital structures behind them and the naval gunfire offshore trying to neutralize the 88 emplacements.

"Why they destroy useless buildings?!" Alfieri questioned as they watched the seemingly wanton destruction.

"Create as much rubble as possible. Slows the ground advancement."

"Fucking bastardi!"

"Might not just be the Gerries. Might be some Italian artillery too."

"Italiani!" The Sicilian noted. "They will be dealt with."

Ten minutes later, maintaining their due North azimuth, they reached Via Leoncavallo just before several rows of railroad tracks and could see a switch house about two hundred yards off to the left.

Alfieri went first to reconnoiter over the tracks and just as he broke from the doorway a scattered squad of Italian troops slowly pushing South through the debris strewn street turned the corner and spotted him. Fortunately he had left his carbine propped against the wall and his web gear open so he was able to drop it before they noticed. Additionally he was wearing civilian clothes so they weren't sure how to take him.

They slowed but didn't stop as he ducked into a second doorway. He lit a cigarette to calm down. A few minutes later he headed back to get Marsloe and they safely crossed the open rail yard and took cover in a bombed out convent. Considering their next move they noted that the artillery had quieted down.

"Thank God for that!" But their relief was short lived. They both froze as a small squadron of aircraft flew low over head. Marsloe peered out the doorway and into the air.

"They're ours. They're starting a bombing run and it's somewhere nearby!"

"How'a you know?" Paul asked as he scurried to the door.

They both stared as they watched the bomb bay doors of the half dozen aircraft slowly open.

"The 88's!" The realization hit them nearly at the same time.

"That's it!" They rushed over to the north window. "Splash one!"

"What?"

"The Naval gunfire stopped just in time and the planes are headed to the exact same location. That means they've got forward spotters in the area." Marsloe ran back inside and spread his map on one of the few intact pieces of furniture, a heavy dining table. "Can't tell exactly where they are but they have to be in this grid square."

"Who the hell in his right mind would be this far into the shit when'a they have got air cover?"

"His name Nunzio." A voice echoed off the walls. Both men turned to see a young boy, barley a teen, standing in the doorway. He adjusted the comically large German helmet wobbling on his head as he spoke.

"Hey Joe! Lei ha perso?" The boy called.

"He ask . . ."

"Are we lost, yeah I got it. Ask him what the hell he's doin' out here!"

"Lei è perso? Perché lei è qui? Chi la sono?"

"Sono la Mafia!" Alfieri laughed out loud. The kid didn't smile.

"He says he'a Mafia."

"Tell him we need to get to the Admiralty H.Q. on the double."

"Diamo trovare Quartier generale di ammiragliato. Pronto." Alfieri explained. Now it was the kid's turn to smile.

"No problem, Joe! Andiamo!" He smirked as he led the way. Less than 200 meters up the hill the kid led them to the converted, sprawling villa of a former Mafioso.

They were told by Luciano before they embarked with the invasion fleet that the Italian Naval Command was hidden in a nearby holiday vista, but took the info with a grain of salt. However, once inside the relatively unscathed villa they quickly realized that they hit pay dirt.

They had been led to the Admiralty Headquarters for the entire Italian Fleet.

Inside they split up and the kid followed Paul. Upstairs in the main offices is where they proved the importance of forward recon. There was a large grey, walk-in safe. Alfieri yelled 'Bingo!'.

"JACK POT!" Marsloe yelled at nearly the same time from down the hall.

"In here!" Alfieri couldn't believe his luck. The triple re-enforced, tempered steel, walk-in safe had been buried in a meter of concrete on five sides backed up by state-of-the-art alarm systems and usually sported an armed guard with orders to shoot to kill or die at his station. However, all the security in the world was useless as in the panic to abandon the headquarters the door to the large vault had been left open. But it got better.

The safe was full.

"Fuck me!" Marsloe mumbled to himself as he stepped into the closet-sized safe.

Five minutes later they met together in the center of a plushly decorated, spacious room.

Together they had just discovered the entire disposition of the Italian and German Naval forces in the Mediterranean. As if that weren't enough, further rummaging through the main office revealed the extent of the minefields located in the Mediterranean area together with overlays of the fields, prepared by the Germans, showing the safe-conduct routes through the dangerous waters.

"References to nautical charts, schedules of ships' movements and – holy shit!" Marsloe declared.

"What?"

"Radio codes!" Marsloe held up a stack of yellow pages.

"What's that?" Alfieiri plucked a half page memo from the handful of papers. "Vizzini-Nevicare?" He read aloud and looked at Marsloe.

"Mean anything to you?" Marsloe asked.

"Vizzini is a name. Nevicare? It means snowfall. But I don't get the connect."

"Snowfall? Must'a be something up in the Alps. Maybe an offensive?" Alfieri guessed.

"Okay, let's pack all this shit up and get outta here!" Suggested Marsloe.

"I got a better idea. Let's break out that salami and bread, hunker down here and wait'a for the cavalry to arrive. We got what we came for. The Germans aren't coming back this late. The rear troops catch up, we can hitch a ride back to Gela and deliver the intell." Alfieri countered.

"A few hours probably isn't going to make any difference. Why not?" Without warning little Nunzio got up and broke into a run.

"Where the hell you going?" Marsloe called over to the kid.

"Sto andando a cercare del vino!" The boy spat back.

"Going to get some wine! Why not? Can't eat

bread and salami without wine!" Marsloe reasoned. Ten minutes later they were feasting on day old bread, cheap salami and del Rosa la Vinyardi, 1892.

✝

CHAPTER II

Operation Husky had achieved its goals. By the end of the first day, the beaches had been secured and supplies were pouring in. More importantly, lessons had been learned for a future invasion. However, the Allies hadn't exactly landed unopposed and there were, as expected, casualties sustained.

Of the 137 gliders launched only 12 made it to shore. Of the 140 C-47 transports which were sent to support the landings 23 were shot down and 37 damaged.

All by friendly fire.

With 2,500 ships, 14,000 vehicles, 600 tanks, the largest landing ever executed, due to Montgomery's inability to reach and take Messina on time, the bulk of the German Army had escaped.

With nearly 25,000 Allied personnel lost and over 67,000 Axis forces killed, wounded or captured, the ultimate irony however, was that no one could have known that at that exact moment Mussolini himself was engaged in secret negotiations with the Allies to broker Italy's surrender.

Meanwhile, back in New York City, Luciano, Costello and the boys lifted a glass of wine to the fact that il Duce had gone a beach too far.

With an ingenious plan devised by a junior Intel officer named Ian Fleming, the invasion of Sicily had actually started three months earlier in a ramshackle, second-hand car lot in Central London . . .

†

Three months prior . . .

**19:20, 17 April, 1943
Honest Henry's Auto Hire
Central London**

The only thing that distinguished the back of the small, under lit car lot was the busy street at the front of it.

The cramped, box-like office sitting dead center of the gravel strewn space stank of coal oil, booze and body odor. "Will you be wantin' insurance with that, Mr. Applegate?"

"No, I don't think . . ." The cloud of gin tainted breath as the fat, little salesman leaned in to speak, pushed the casually dressed client back away from the old restaurant table being passed off as a desk.

"Important point to overlook, Gov'ner!" Applegate's patience was at its thinnest since he and his mate had arrived nearly an hour ago. "Say some drunken fool decides 'e ain't 'ad one too many when everyone else knows full well 'e has? What 'appens then? Or say . . ." The old bentwood chair creaked in protest as an annoyed Applegate turned and glanced at his friend, Smyth, standing off to the side.

The friend nodded.

"Excellent suggestion Mr. Dolittle. We'll take the insurance as well." For the sake of expediency Applegate reluctantly acquiesced.

"Wise choice, Gov'ner, wise choice! Fer an extra one pound five, wise choice!" He congratulated as he scribbled out a second short form.

The salesman finished up the second form, money and documents changed hands and ten minutes later Applegate and Smyth drove their dark green, 1937 Morris Commercial out the gate onto the darkened evening streets of East London and headed West. Save for a few directions, their thirty-five minute drive through the busy city to Mercy Hospital was without conversation.

The well-manicured grounds with clusters of nuns gliding between buildings, blue cape draped nurses and doctors in white lab coats signaled business as usual at the expansive medical complex that evening. Save for the fact that the main gate required a security check and several of the entrances were manned by Bobbies, there was nothing to indicate anything out of the ordinary.

They headed around back of the main structure, across a smaller parking lot to a single story, squat little, granite building and backed up into the covered loading area marked, "Morgue Only". Applegate stayed with the van while Smyth flashed an I. D. card to a tall Bobbie.

"I have an appointment with Dr. Purchase." The Bobbie checked his card and waved him through.

He pushed on through the large, double doors and vanished into the corridors.

Twenty minutes later, leaning against the cab of the vehicle, Applegate thumbed the cherry from the tip of his half smoked cigarette, tucked the butt behind his ear and jumped in the vehicle as the morgue's garage-like double doors were slowly swung open into the building by a pair of men in scrubs. With one of the scrubs directing he backed the Morris in through the doors until it was out of sight and the doors were closed over.

The cargo lift at the other end of the hallway opened and two more men in scrubs, gently supervised by an older doctor, pushed a chrome gurney with a large, steel canister about a yard in diameter and two yards long, stenciled with the prominent label:

"HANDLE WITH CARE – OPTICAL INSTRUMENTS FOR SPECIAL FOS"

Smyth emerged from a stairwell adjacent to the lift accompanied by another man and stood to the side while the medical personnel carefully loaded the cylinder into the vehicle and covered it with a blanket. The stranger climbed into the driver's seat, Smyth thanked the medical men, hopped in the back with their cargo and took a seat on the floor next to the cylinder closing the hatch door behind him.

Dusk was well entrenched by the time the two, now along with their assigned driver were back on the road out of the city and snaking north through the lush English countryside.

"Jack." The driver extended his hand to Applegate who accepted it.

"Ewen Montagu, Lieutenant Commander." He responded over the racket of the poorly paved road.

"Jack Horsfell, chauffer. You can call me Jock." He nodded towards the back. "Who's the stiff?"

"We don't have a name. Just instructions to get the cylinder . . ."

"I mean the stiff lyin' **next** to the cylinder."

Smyth, now reclined on the floor next to the cylinder, sat up in time to catch the glare of the head lamps splash over a small road sign:

HOLY LOCH, 175 Miles

He checked his watch and lie back down.

"Ahh! That would be Flight Lieutenant Charles Cholmondeley."

"Where to once we reach Holy Loch?" Horsfell inquired.

"We'll need to find *H.M.S. Seraph.*"

"The sub?"

"You know her?"

"Only by name. I heard from my father that my mother's uncle's nephew's son had orders to her back in '40."

"Good to have connections, I suppose. I assume that means you have an idea of where we're heading?"

"With connections like that, how could I not?" A rally car-like skid through an 'S' curve was followed by a thud in back which led to frantic banging on the cargo compartment fire wall. "Sub pens are over on the Southwest end of the base." Horsfell informed.

Once back on the straightaway Montagu noticed they had picked up speed again but decided not to comment. However, when they took another corner and nearly went over on two wheels followed by another loud thud which garnered more bangs on the wall garnished with a bit of profanity, he decided to break the silence.

"Just out of curiosity Jock. What did you do before this little shindig broke out?"

"Professional race car driver."

"You don't say?" Back on the straight away they again picked up speed. "I'd have never guessed."

Just before dawn that next morning, in a light but steady drizzle, the three cross country travelers, assigned to Twenty Section, B1 of MI5 had reached their destination, and while three handpicked members of the sub's crew gently loaded the cylinder on board, Montagu signed the mysterious cargo over to *H.M.S. Seraph* and headed off to the Officer's Mess for a hearty English breakfast of milky, watered down tea and rock hard scones.

✝

Paddy Kelly

13:10, 18 April, 1943
Medical Examiner's Lab
St. Vincent's Hospital
Greenwich Village, New York City, N.Y.

If he was black he could have auditioned for a Somalian charity ad. A starving Armenian would have beat him at arm wrestling with one hand while casually making a sandwich with the other.

Leaning on the black, marble lab counter top Doc smirked as he continued to stare at the open white cape of the lab tech's coat as it flared out behind Donnie's rail thin body.

Super Lab Tech! Lab Tech Man. Lab Man! Faster than a speeding centrifuge. Able to leap tall lab benches with two or three bounds! Doc amused himself while he waited.

Like a hungry dog looking to be fed but resigned it wasn't going to happen any time soon McKeowen, tired of trailing the lab tech around the near empty basement forensics lab, had taken a seat on one of the chrome stools at the center table.

Doc was there to find, trick, buy or cajole some lab results from the forensics tech on duty who just happened to be Skinny Donnie.

Just over six foot one tall with dark hair, hazel eyes and a medium build, Mike 'Doc' McKeowen had been a swimmer in his youth, never ate or drank to excess, (well didn't eat to excess anyway), even during the holidays and so was in as reasonable a shape as a forty year old bachelor could be. His idea of good fashion sense was to keep the dark fur collar of his brown, leather bomber jacket clean and to always have his Negro League baseball cap cocked back at the right angle. Except when he was concentrating then it had to be set forward like a big league pitcher at the top of the ninth.

The dungeon of the city forensics lab was dark but spacious with low hanging lights along each of the four long, black marble topped work tables. One of the several centrifuges suddenly exhausted itself and quit humming. Lab Man made his way over to it. Doc's Negro League ball cap suddenly decided it wanted to be cocked back and signaled his arm. He planted both elbows on the table behind him and exhaled a sigh of exasperation.

"Christ Donnie! You practicing to come back as a chicken?!"

"What'a you talkin' about?"

"You been sittin' on this case since May of last year! Why you stallin?" McKeowen prodded.

"These things take time, you know that." Donnie was on the City teat and had no intention of breaking a sweat.

"You said there's been **no** progress!"

"Don't put words in my mouth McKeowen." He crossed the lab and shooed Doc away from the biocular microscope he had been playing with. "I said, there's nothing to incriminate him."

"So why hasn't the case gone to trial already?" The tech turned and made eye contact.

"What'a you care when this case gets heard?! You ain't no homicide detective no more. You don't even work fer the City!"

"Curiosity, that's all." Donnie smirked at Doc's words as he worked.

"Horse shit! You got a stake in this thing! What's the angle? A pay off? A bet maybe? A little under the table cash?" Donnie sniffed around.

"She was found miles from Staten Island, on a hill in Central Park. The police immediately listed the husband as a possible suspect but didn't rule out the possibility that she was killed by an unknown park criminal." Doc challenged.

"So?" Donnie cleverly countered into the microscope.

"So they haven't got a clue who done it, yet they're holding him as the prime suspect without a shred of evidence, and they don't wanna close the case! Being 'suspected' of being a Mob associate is not being guilty of murder. Innocent until proven . . . ring a bell?"

"You'll have to take that up with the D.A. McKeowen."

"What happened, this guy piss somebody off down-town or they just lookin' for another scape goat?" Doc pushed.

"The guy was . . . is known to be one of Frankie Costello's senior torpedoes fer cryin' out loud!" Donnie made his way back across the room. "Besides, word is Chief Sullivan's got a hard-on for this one."

"**Assistant** Chief Sullivan's got a hard-on for everybody, especially when there's a female involved! Thinks he's a knight in shining armor on a white horse!" Doc replied.

"Doc, this guy's got an airtight alibi. I'm not supposed ta be talkin' about this but at the time of his wife's murder he was at a dance hall Uptown. With twenty-two girls who supported his story no less, all sayin' he was there all night." Donnie revealed as he peered back into his microscope and scribbled out a form.

"Twenty-two women?! Seems a bit over the top, don't it?." Doc registered genuine surprise as he surreptitiously spied an updated 8X10 glossy of the suspect husband on Donnie's desk.

"Bingo McKeowen! You should'a been a cop." Doc inched closer to the errant photo. "Every last one of 'em gave statements too." Donnie added.

Over by the desk Doc folded the photo in half and slipped it into the inside pocket of his bomber jacket.

"Son-of-a-bitch! Twenty-two?!" McKeowen declared, watching to make sure Lab Man was glued to the scope.

Donnie worked in rhythm to his own preaching as he started to prep another batch of specimens.

"Sorry Doc. Ya win some, ya lose some and some get rained out but, ya still get dressed ta play for tomorrow!" Doc wandered away from the desk. "You done a spectrographic analysis of his clothes' fibers? Dirt, dust anything in his pants cuffs?"

"Spectrographic analysis? You shittin' me McKeowen?! What'a you think this is, Flash Gordon or something! You got any idea how much those machines cost? We're talkin' years before a police forensics lab gets one'a those tacit, technological toys!"

"Try the universities Einstein! One of those high priced schools ought'a have one! NYU, Columbia. I'm sure one'a them'd run a sample for ya."

"Yeah, okay. I'll get right on that." Donnie sarcastically quipped.

"Just see what you can do will ya? Even if it's just some assurances about a time frame-"

"THAT'S IT!" Donnie cut him off. "Insurance money! You took the insurance case from All Life Premium to investigate a possible fraud! He did it or he didn't, either way you win! But you're on the clock, that's why you're giving me the bum's rush!"

"You should'a been a detective Donnie!" McKeowen readjusted his ball cap and made for the door. "I'll be in touch."

"Ten per cent of nearly fifty grand, I bet you will be in touch!"

As soon as Doc was clear of the lab Donnie crossed to his desk and picked up the in-house phone and dialled. He noticed the black and white photo was missing.

"SON-OF-A-BITCH! McKEOWEN!" He yelled out into the hall.

Hello?! Who is this?! The receiver blurted. Donnie regained himself.

The Wolves of Calabria

"Yeah, hello, Betty, do me a favor love, I got an idea how to solve that old Central Park, wife homicide case. Call NYU, CUNY then try Hunter see if either of their chem, bio or geology labs has a spectrographic analysis machine." There was a short pause. "Spec-tro-graphic analysis. S-P-E-C-T-R-O-M . . ."

Outside the weather was warm and sunny with a mild breeze as Doc exited the ornate, granite doorway of the hospital on the 12th Street side. Just as he headed down the block and came to the corner a middle-aged, balding and bespecled man appeared in front of him and blocked his path. Doc looked down at the intruder. As if his batteries were running low a Bostonian dialect slowly drooled from the little man's mouth.

"I couldn't help but notice yaw just cummin' outta the Coroner's office there Mista McKeowen." The man adjusted the folded suit jacket under his arm.

"I was just heading to my office to call you Oscar!"

"McKeowen, I might'a been bawn during the day but it wasn't yesta-day!" His briefcase switched hands.

"It's looking real good Oscar! Just one last detail to wrap up and the Coroner will sign the paperwork and then it's case closed!"

"Case closed for you maybe! But unless you can prove fraud my company is out $47,000! The deadline for us to claim a case against him is up in three days!"

"You're the guy who bets on people living, dying and getting mutilated Oscar, I just-"

"Mista Tumbolt if you please Mista McKeowen!"

"Mister Tumbolt you engaged my services to find out if this guy was pulling an insurance scam. I promise you we'll know either way in the next 48 hours!" McKeowen resisted the urge to pat the little man on the head and instead patted him on the shoulder and continued up 12th Street towards Seventh Avenue and crossed over.

"Just see if you can beat the Second Coming!" The adjuster yelled as Doc vanished into traffic. "We have deadlines ya know!" Oscar took a threatening step forward for emphasis. "That fraud bonus ain't yaws yet!"

Doc didn't look back.

Buggs Bunny must be thrilled to have the run of the forest now that Elmer Fudd's running around Manhattan!

After a quick lunch at the Woolworth's counter over on 7th Avenue Doc headed back across The Village to his Christopher Street office. To save a few minutes he decided to take the long alleyway which ran the entire length west parallel to Christopher Street which would let him out next to his corner building on Bleaker and Christopher.

This may not have been the wisest of decisions.

The Wolves of Calabria

He was about a couple of hundred yards up the alley, just passed the back of St. John's Church when something didn't seem right.

For the second time in the last hour a man appeared in front of McKeowen blocking his path, but this guy wasn't carrying a briefcase and he wasn't small. Doc had to look up to make eye contact. Also the guy might or might not have been bald. There was no way for Doc to know because this guy had a ladies silk stocking pulled down over his head, was wearing a sailor's, knit, wool cap and had a black handkerchief over the lower part of his face. He reached into his coat pocket and produced a switch blade stiletto and brandished it as he let it flick open at his side. Doc peered around the big man and spied two more thugs down at the end of the alley apparently as back-up. They were dressed the same.

"Any idea who I am, 'Doc'?!" He sarcastically spewed.

"As a matter of fact, I do know who you are. Was in the papers this morning!" The puzzled look in the moron's face was all the pause Doc needed. He faked a lunge at the guy who predictably reacted with his knife hand and as it came up towards Doc's gut he side stepped it while crashing down on the assailant's wrist as hard as possible, with a police issue blackjack. The satisfying sounds of crunching bones and animal like-yelping were the just the hors d'oeuvres. Unfortunately for the used-to-be tough guy this wasn't McKeowen's first rodeo.

As the big man went down he grabbed at Doc just as Doc backhanded his right temple with the blackjack. Tough guy was out cold but McKeowen gave him one more to the back of the head for good measure.

"Yeah, apparently Cecil B. DeMille is in town shootin' a sequel to *The Great Train Robbery*! I can tell by the really keen masks you guys are wearin'!" Doc explained to the near corpse.

On the ground, bent over his prey, footsteps alerted McKeowen that this dance was far from over. Big Man's two mates were Johnny on the spot and Doc looked up in time to catch a poorly placed punch as it glanced off his right cheek. However, as he clung to a leg the kick from the guy on the left caught him square in the gut and took the wind out of him. Fighting to catch his breath he curled into a ball and took the fusillade of kicks and punches as best he could until he looked up and to the side.

The big unconscious guy next to him had a shoulder holster packed with a Smith and Wesson .38 Special.

A second later the guy who had been kicking Doc had a hole on either side of his left knee and Thug #2 froze in his tracks. McKeowen tried to focus as he struggled to his feet while keeping a bead on him.

"What's'a matter Junior, don't wanna play anymore?" The guy raised his hands in surrender.

"Look Mac, we're just the hired help!"

"Turn around, hands behind your head and on your knees!" The man didn't react. Doc aimed a shot between his legs and fired. "On your knees or on your face ass-hole! Makes no difference, they can't trace this gun to me." The guy saw Doc's logic and complied. As soon as he was on his knees Doc took careful aim to the back of his head.

The guy twitched a second before he crumpled to the ground. Doc pocketed the blackjack after hitting him, glanced over at Thug#3 rolling on the ground holding his blood stained knee, shrugged and pocketed the .38.

He searched both of the other two casualties, found no more guns and then commenced on searching the first guy, who was still out, and came up with a wallet stuffed with a couple of hundreds, some fifties, tens and two fivers.

"High Roller, ain't we boss?" He pocketed the cash. The trouser pockets yielded some change and small ring of keys but the big payoff came when Doc ripped the stocking up over his head.

"Fuck me Alice!" Doc declared.

To double check what he suspected McKeowen pulled the folded over 8X10 black and white glossy from his bomber jacket. Except for the rapidly mushrooming bruises, collapsed cheek bone and slowly bleeding abrasions, the face of the big unconscious guy matched the photo. It was the suspected wife murderer. Doc looked over at the wounded mugger.

"If I were you ass-hole I'd run . . . uh, limp for the hills unless you wanna go up the river for accessory to murder one. Big Boy here's got a hot seat reserved for him up in Sing Sing."

☦

Fulton Street Fish Market
Manhattan, NYC

With his red, silk neck tie loosened at the collar and his shirt sleeves rolled up, Joey "Socks" Lanza flung his suit jacket over his shoulder as he made his way down the wooden staircase against the wall leading from his office and out across the expansive floor of the Fulton Street Fish Market in Lower Manhattan. Weaving his way through the hundreds of blood stained, white wooden fish stalls towards the rear exits he stopped just short of the open bay doors on the loading docks and paused in front of a 20 foot long, white marble counter.

Behind the counter a short, middle-aged man with a ball cap and apron which made the Bowery look clean, gutted and filleted fish not only with surgical accuracy and blinding speed but almost as a distraction.

"Hey Vito, how 'bout this fuckin' heat, huh?!" Lanza queried. The fillet knife never stopped as Vito engaged in the conversation.

"It ain't the heat, Mr. Lanza. It's the humility!"

Vito gave a cursory laugh as he threw another cleaned fish into the half full wheelbarrow at his side.

"You seen Frankie?" Socks asked.

"Took off 'bout half an hour ago. Hopped in that red hot rod of his and headed Downtown."

"Fuckin' guy!" Socks cursed. Vito paused mid-fish and made eye contact with the gangster.

"Any word on that other thing yet Socks?" Lanza's answer was generously seasoned with sympathy.

"Not yet Vito. I'll let you know as soon as I hear." Vito gave a quick short nod.

"Thanks boss."

MR. LANZA TO THE OFFICE, PLEASE.

As Lanza was about to step away he heard his name come over the newly installed P.A. system for the fourth time that morning.

MR. LANZA TO THE OFFICE PLEASE.

"God damned thing! Never should'a had it installed." Through the oppressive heat back through the rows of stalls and around the crates of fish he trudged back to the upstairs office of the United Seafood Workers, Local #359. The local he invented, and through intimidation and extortion, had built into a multi-million dollar industry. One of the most successful in the Genovese Crime Family.

"Who is it?" He asked his secretary as he came through the door.

"Your lawyer." Once in his office Lanza glared at the blinking light on the base of the phone and, knowing his phones were still tapped, hesitated before lifting the receiver.

"Who's dis?"

Who's dis? Who the hell ya think it is?! Your guardian angel. What, you don't grill your sexratary before you pick anymore?

"I'm all ears."

A trial date's been set.

"When?!"

Meet me at the other place, we'll talk. Lanza was visibly distraught as he hung up and left the office.

Twenty minutes later Joey was passing under the red canopy of Gallagher's Steak House on West 52nd and handing his hat and coat to the slender, young hat check girl.

"Afternoon Mr. Lanza."

"Hey Dollface. Mr. Polokoff get here yet?"

"No sir, not yet but . . ." She casually nodded out across the street. There, sticking out like a pair of large pimples in the middle of a teenager's forehead, two men in front of the entrance of the *Club Carousel*, were swigging cold Cokes, smoking and taking cover behind the block-long line of parked, navy blue Dodges and black Plymouths.

Lanza ignored her gesture.

"Give us a Dutch Masters Doll, would'ja?" The young girl dutifully removed a cigar box from the glass display case between them and held it open for Lanza who selected one, ran it under his nose and leaned forward. The hat check rummaged through her purse and produced a .22 Derringer, cocked the hammer back and held it under Joey's chin. Across the street the undercover agents perked up, threw down their cigarettes and paid closer attention.

The girl flicked the lighter and held the flame under Joey's cigar and, rotating it, he took a couple of long, pleasurable puffs. As he smoked Socks gave a quick, casual glance out the window and across the street where the young G-men were retreating to the imagined safety of their doorway.

"How long they been there?" She moved to the coat rack to hang his jacket.

"About five minutes before you showed up." She handed him his claim check.

"Little Eddie still giving you a hard time?" He asked. She displayed obvious embarrassment as she answered.

"Sometimes. Not so much now days." Socks put his hand under her chin and stared into her emerald green eyes.

"Afta't'a ta'day he won't be around no more. Okay?" A tear formed in her eye. "He's gonna take a vacation, ya understand?" The girl gave a weak nod as Socks wiped away her cheek.

"Okay Joey." He pressed a fifty into her hand as Moses Polokoff, the longtime Mob lawyer, came through the front door.

"You got a table yet?" The large but aged lawyer asked.

"No. Waitin' on you." Dollface rang a low toned buzzer and the maître 'd suddenly appeared to escort them to their table in the far corner, right under the two neat rows of framed 8X10, black and white, autographed glossies of movie stars.

"So what's the story?" Joey asked. Moses broke a bread stick and took a bite.

"You need to get your affairs in order."

"Meaning?"

"Meaning the fix is in. I got a textbook defense for ya Socks but . . ."

"But?!" Suddenly a waiter appeared. Joey stubbed out his cigar in the ashtray.

"May I take your order gentlemen?" Polokoff didn't hesitate.

"Two T-bones, rare, baked with veg and two whiskies, Glen Levitt, up. Drinks first."

"Scotch. Must be some really good news." Socks made no attempt to hide his sarcasm.

"The Grand Jury has indicted you on all counts and you're gonna be found guilty."

"Guilty?! Just like that?!"

"Guilty. Just like that."

"I don't get ta mount a defense?"

"Sure you do! It's your right as an American citizen! And like I said I got a blockbuster defense fo ya! But you're gonna be found guilty."

"You tellin' me there ain't nuthin' you can do? No strings, favors, nuthin'?" The drinks showed up and Polokoff lifted the heavy rocks glass to his wrinkled lips, took a gentle sip, set his glass aside and leaned into the table.

"Socks, you remember January 31st, 1936?"

The Wolves of Calabria

"You shittin' me? I barely remember January 31st, 1943. What about it?" Socks snatched another of the half dozen bread sticks from the glass in the center of the table.

"It was a bitter cold day, I was in my office taking care of some odds n' ends and New York City's finest were out in force. The phone rang, it was a police friend calling. Dewey had every available cop on the streets, including the gold shields. They had orders to round up every hooker and madam in Manhattan, even the suspected ones. They dragged 'em all in. Jennie the Factory, Sadie the Chink, Frisco Jean, Nigger Ruth, Gashouse Lil. Threw them all together in the Women's House of Detention down in the Village as material witnesses. On $10,000 bond each!"

"I remember reading about that. Costello told me it was about as fuckin' organized as a Chinese fire drill!"

"Organized or not it was under severe and relentless twenty-four hour questioning, no doubt generously sprinkled with all kinds of threats, a handful of 'em were 'persuaded' to mention the name Luciano on the stand, even though none of them had anything to do with him, probably never even met the man. Two days later, bingo! Luciano's indicted for 'organizing a city wide prostitution ring.'"

"Yeah, so what? So they contrived evidence and bullshitted the court. It's their M.O."

Polokoff put the conversation on hold as the

waiter brought the silverware, served more bread sticks and the drinks then left.

"Point is Socks, Dewey hasn't looked at a law book in years. He don't care about the law. All he can see dangling in front of his eyes are the keys to the Governor's mansion where he's gonna plan his assault on the White House! And he's out ta do whatever it takes ta get there."

"Dewey as president?! That'll be the fuckin' day!" Socks threw back his drink.

"Point is Joey, his squeaky clean image is a red flag that he's probably as dirty as anyone which means at the end of the day you're a competitor."

"Lucky should'a let The Dutchman whack that Fuck when he had the chance!"

"Trust me, the heat wouldn'a been worth it. All hell would'a broken lose which is why Lucky stopped him."

"Gangbuster my ass!" Socks signalled for another round. "What's my options?"

"Stay here and do the time, leave the country, turn State's evidence or . . ."

"FUCK YOU!" In the immediate area heads turned. Lanza froze and glared at Polokoff who dropped back in his seat with frustration.

"Just runnin' down the options Socks."

"Or what?"

"I, we, got a pretty good shot at getting you housed Downstate." Lanza glared at the long time Mob lawyer.

"Great Meadows, with Lucky?"

"Exactly."

"How come?"

"No idea. That's between you and him."

Lanza wasn't shocked but he was a bit surprised that Lucky would use up favors to get Socks a relatively cushy gig in minimum security prison with himself.

"What am I lookin' at?"

"With no previous felony convictions, best they can hit you with is seven to ten."

"Seven to ten?! That the **best** you can do!?" The second order of drinks arrived with the food and again they nixed the conversation until the waiter finished serving and disappeared.

"I can't keep you out Joey, but I'm pretty sure I can get you the minimum." Polokoff hacked off a chunk of steak and stuffed it in his mouth. Joey nibbled on a string bean.

"Trial date?"

"Next month."

"What's the fuckin' hurry?"

"Dewey's their Golden Boy." He shrugged. "Since he nailed Lepke, Buchalter and Lucky all he has to do is snap his fingers and they clear the docket. Hell, he could start next week if he wanted to. Besides . . ." Lanza stared up at Polokoff. "Elections are in November, they need time to taut their 'victories'."

"I'm goin' ta take a piss. Get us another round." As Lanza got up to go he glanced at the row of pictures on the wall behind him. He smirked as he noticed he had been seated under a picture of George Raft. "Fuckin' waiter's got a sense of humor!" He mumbled as he vanished around the corner.

Moses sliced off another thick chunk of steak and raised it to his mouth when an unknown voice echoed out from behind.

"Guess that means next time you eat here you gotta sit near a picture of Dewey, hey Moses?" The lawyer jumped and turned around. Although the intruder was in a three piece suit Polokoff immediately recognized Commander Haffenden from their one and only meeting over a year ago at Longchamp's Restaurant when Naval Intelligence first approached the Mob about working for them. "Last time we met was in a Midtown steak house too, wasn't it Moses?"

"What the hell you want?!"

"Just passin' by, looked in the window and saw my two friends so thought I'd say hello."

"Yeah? Well why don't you go find them and annoy them. This is a privileged lawyer-client meeting"

"Mind if I join you?" Haff asked as he pulled up a chair, sat and perused the table. "12 year old scotch, 20 ounce T-bones. Privileged is right! Three shots each, beginning of the meal. Must be some heavy news you brought your client, councilor."

"Come to think of it, Commander, the last time we met was also in a steak house. And it's suddenly comes back to me that we had a very similar conversation." Haffenden smirked as he shrugged and picked a sliver of carrot off Sock's plate. "You remember what I told you then?" Polokoff pushed.

"Not your exact wording, but I remember you weren't very nice."

"Hit the bricks! Mr. Lanza is no longer in your employ. Besides, they're sendin' him up next month, no thanks to you I might add." Moses turned away from Haffenden and returned to his meal.

"Yeah. Seven to ten for racketeering, I heard. Look pretty good on his record when he comes up for parole if he helped out one last time."

"Yeah? What doin'? Chasin' ghost saboteurs?"

"Nope. One shot deal."

"Horse shit!" Moses continued to eat then paused. "Like what?"

"Run a message up to his Capo. That's it. Short and sweet."

Lanza did a double take as he came back around the corner and spotted Haff sitting in the booth adjacent to Polokoff where he had been.

"Ca cazzo fai!?"

"Joey, I swear I didn't set this up!" Moses quickly defended.

"Relax Socks. Your lawyer's clean." The Commander defended. "This time. I had you tailed."

"Really? I hadn't noticed." Socks nodded up the aisle and out to the front window where across the street the conspicuously inconspicuous agents still milled about.

Lanza, who had had no contact with the Commander for nearly a year, was totally taken off guard by the visit as he assumed a false cloak of indifference, took his seat, and resumed his meal.

"Whatever it is you want Commander–" Joey protested.

"Joey, you don't have ta say nuthin'. He's got no juice to leverage you." Polokoff interjected.

"It's okay Moses." Joey said.

"Yeah, it's okay Moses." Haff sarcastically echoed.

"Fuck you!" The lawyer quipped.

"Ya gonna have ta find another pigeon Commander. My dance card's booked for the next few years." Joey informed. Haffenden, who had remained unfazed and expressionless throughout, nicked another sliver of Joey's carrots, then leaned into the table and whispered as he made eye contact with Socks.

"How'd you like to see Mussolini unemployed and get your country back?" Socks stopped his glass halfway to his mouth, glared at Haff and narrowed his eyes. Polokoff gave Socks a 'You gotta be shittin' me look' and gently laid his silverware down next to his half eaten steak.

"I gotta see a man about a horse." Moses excused himself. After his lawyer was out of sight Socks took the bait.

"What I gotta do?"

"Get a message to Luciano."

"And?"

"That's it."

"That's it?"

"Get a message to Luciano without going up to Great Meadows."

"Why without going up to Great Meadows?" Joey asked.

"Lotta people were cut out of the loop on the Underworld Operation. . ." Haff picked a slice of carrot from Polokoff's plate.

"People who ain't got no sense of humor?" Lanza ventured.

"Exactly. And now they're bringin' out the sniffer dogs."

"Youse got somthin' planned for that part of the world. Don't ya?"

"Come on Socks, you know I can't divulge that." Haff smirked. "But I can tell ya that if your boss can get a message to his old pisanos back in the homeland and everything else falls into place . . ." Socks sat back in his chair as the penny dropped.

"That's it? Get Lucky the message, that's all I gotta do?"

"That's all you gotta do."

"Nothing else?"

"Yeah, there is one more thing."

"Imagine my surprise! What?"

"You gonna finish those carrots?"

"Asshole." Lanza pushed his plate away in disgust.

☦

CHAPTER III

**M&M Investigations
1929 Christopher Street
Greenwich Village
New York City, N.Y.**

As Doc was stepping off the open caged elevator he heard the phone in his office ring. He limped to his office door holding a balled up handkerchief to his eyebrow. Through the door he could hear Shirley his receptionist, answer the phone.

McKeowen and Mancino. How may I help you?

Doc came through the door. "Call for you." The pretty twenty-something black girl held out the receiver and smirked as she noticed the state of him.

"Out playing with the big boys again were we?" She quipped.

"Very funny!" He took the phone. "Yeah McKeowen here."

"You okay?" Shirley asked as she noticed his limp. He responded with an upheld hand.

After you left I got an idea. It was Skinny Donnie over at St. Vincent's.

"Yeah?" Doc took the Kleenex tissues Shirley held up to him as he spoke. He took it and daubed his busted lip.

I called a botany professor over at Hunter, a Professor Copeland. He identified some plant spikelet's in the husband's trousers as P.D.M.

"P.D. what?!" Doc wiped his bloody lip.

P.D.M. Pank . . . I mean Pancium dicoth milleflorium, a rare species of plant. It only grows in one area of the city, right here in New York"

"Don't tell me, let me guess. Central Park."

Bingo! They brought it in when they built the park way back in . . . in . . .

"1856, Einstein."

Ahh yeah, I was gonna say 1856. Professor Copeland did a spectrogram and identified the sprinklets as well as some seedlings from the cuff of Mr. Dockland's trousers as P.D.M.

"Hold on." Doc handed the receiver back to Shirley. "I'll take this inside." He headed into one of two fully partitioned office spaces behind the reception desk. The door was lettered with his name while the one to the left read, 'Louis F. Mancino Private Investigator'. He picked up the phone on his desk.

"Interesting. Anything else Dr. Watson?" Doc quipped as he emptied his newly acquired snub nosed .38, opened the middle desk drawer and tossed it in with three or four other revolvers, two Derringers and couple of switch blades.

Fucking neighborhood's really going to the dogs! Doc thought to himself.

Yeah, get this! Donnie continued. *When the police called him back in for questioning and told him what they found, he changed his story!*

"Imagine that."

*So then he changes his story sayin' that he suddenly remembers that he actually **had** been in the park. In September no less!*

"That relevant?"

Professor Copeland then went on to inform me that the spikeletts were at a stage of development that could not have occurred before 10 or 15 October but could certainly have been at that stage of blooming on 1 November, the night of the murder!"

"So basically what you're saying is-"

What I'm sayin' is I ain't no Nostradamus, but I'd say he gets the chair, you get your check and I get my ten per cent commission of our ten per cent!

"Commission?!" Doc snapped.

Finder's fee? Donnie was fishing and he knew it.

"Donnie, let me ask you something."

Sure Doc, anything.

"How much does the Great State of New York pay you to be a forensics technologist?"

A hundred twenty-nine fifty a month. Why?

"Because Donnie, based on your ability to analyze and deduce correlations, I'd guesstimate that's about a hundred and twenty-eight a month too much. Remind me to buy you a coffee and donut sometime. Thanks for the call." Doc hung up.

At the small reception desk outside Shirley gingerly set her phone's receiver back down on the hook.

"Shoot! Kind'a rough on the guy, don't ya think?" She yelled over the partition as she quickly resumed some busy work.

"What'a you talkin' about?" Doc asked as he came through his office door.

"I mean the guy solved the case for you! Least ya could do was say thank you and treat the man civil like!"

"SOLVED THE CASE FOR ME?!" He took a step closer to her desk. "SOLVED THE CASE FOR ME?! I'M THE ONE PUT HIM ONTO THE IDEA OF FORENCIS! I DOUBT HE EVEN KNEW WHAT THE HELL A SPECTROMETER WAS TILL I TIPPED HIM OFF!" He turned and walked back towards his office. "What am I explaining myself to you for?" He was halfway through his office door when Shirley calmly countered.

"How you know it was for sure the husband did it? Maybe it was some freak in the park."

Doc turned and headed back out to the battlegrounds.

"Yeah and maybe, just maybe, she rigged her own death to frame the guy to get back at him because he rolled over and called her by another woman's name one night while they were in bed! Or maybe, maybe she found the wrong colored lipstick on his collar or Macy's didn't have the shoes she liked in the right color that day! I don't really care! All I know is the case is closed and I can collect my check!"

"Uh huh!" Shirley commented as she resumed filing her nails.

"What's that supposed to mean?! 'Uh huh!'"

"It means, I didn't know no better, I'd say that was the cop comin' back out in you!"

"Type something will ya?!" He ducked back into his office and took a seat at his desk.

"SHIRLEY, HOW IS IT I DON'T SEE MANCINO RUNNIN' AROUND THE OFFICE PRETENDING TO BE WORKING?!" He yelled over the partition.

"HOW SHOULD I KNOW?! AIN'T MY DAY TA WATCH HIM!"

She leaned into the brass framed photo on her desk. It was a signed photograph of a handsome, black Army sergeant. After glancing over her shoulder she whispered to it.

"I don't even know why I took this job! At least workin' Downtown fer the Navy I had some kind'a benefits! Only benefits I got here's when he ain't around!" She smiled and blew the photo a kiss. "You keep yo heini safe, you hear me Mista!"

☦

**Off the Coast of Spain
Aboard HMS Seraph
05:47, 20 April, 1943**

"Mr. Halloway, please confirm our position."
"Yes sir."
"We are ¾ of a mile North, Northwest of the mouth of the Tinto River, sir."

"Very well. Please pass the word to convert to blackout mode and rig ship for silent running."

"Silent running, aye Sir!" The orders echoed inside the conning tower and the sub's crew went into action. The white light of the quarter deck immediately vanished to be replaced with an eerie red glow. One minute later the word came down the horn to the Exec.

"All compartments report ship now in blackout mode and rigged for silent running sir."

"Very good Mr. Halloway. Dump forward ballast."

"Dumping forward ballast Sir." A large hand firmly slammed an orange plunger on the bulkhead and a long flushing sound followed. A red needle on a gage sagged anticlockwise to the seven o'clock position.

"Forward ballast away, Sir."

"Hold her steady at 15 degrees. All ahead slow."

"All ahead slow, fifteen degrees, aye." Bathed in the dull crimson glow of the bridge, everyone hung on to pipes and fittings just a little tighter.

"Depth reading please, Mr. Albright."

"I make us 8 fathoms and rising Sir."

"On my mark, mark at three fathoms."

"Mark at three fathoms, aye." Just inside the forward bridge compartment someone dropped a tool. The clang was deafening. Everyone froze.

"God damn it man! What the bloody hell -"

"Mr. Albright. Composure please." The Captain gently reminded.

"Apologies sir." The tension eased only slightly.

"Is there something you should like to tell me, Lieutenant?" Captain Jewell prompted.

The helmsman smirked.

"Four fathoms, sir. Sorry. Stand by for mark."

"Raise periscope. Stand by helm." Jewell ordered.

"Helm standing by Sir." Jewell reversed his combination cap and manned the periscope's view finder.

"Three fathoms!" Came the call.

"MARK!" Jewell ordered and the ship slowly began to level off. "Sonar, report."

"Negative contact three-sixty at one thousand meters Sir." The Captain stayed glued to the periscope as the topside scope broke the surface, the last of the sea water ran down the lens and, in the distance, the surrounding panorama of the wide harbor and connecting river and its banks came into view.

It was about an hour before sunrise as the bow of the *Seraph* gently broke the surface of a calm sea at a point about a 500 meters off the beach near Huelva on the southern coast of Spain.

"Maintain level bubble. Stop all engines."

"Level bubble, stop all engines, aye sir."

At 04:30 hours, Lt., acting Captain Jewell ordered the large silver canister to be brought up on deck of the vessel. The crew had been briefed that a Top Secret meteorological device was being deployed and were ordered to remain below decks in the event of a crash dive. All the senior officers, which Jewell gathered on the fantail were, after a short briefing, given instructions to open the canister and gently deploy its contents over the side.

Excluding the port and starboard watch propped over the rail of the coning tower, who were constantly scanning the horizons with long range binos, the officers were ordered below. Jewell then produced a Royal Navy issue bible, removed his billed cap, tucked it under his left arm and read a short passage.

"Con watch, recover! Pass the order, prepare to dive." The men scurried through the con's deck hatch and scrambled below. Jewell, the last man down, quickly followed down the narrow ladder dogging the hatch behind him.

Twenty minutes later, cruising all ahead slow back out to sea at eight fathoms, Jewel again issued orders to the Exec.

"Mr. Halloway, prepare a signal please."

"Very good sir."

"'Postman to Postmaster: Post delivered.' Get that off immediately."

"Will do sir."

†

4 Miles from Huelva, Southern Coast of Spain

Paddy Kelly

06:10, 30 April, 1943

Well out of sight of land a small, green enameled sardine barco with the name 'Anna' carefully painted on the forward port bow bobbed gently in the calm, turquoise waters of the Atlantic. The dark, aged-before his time, forty-something sailor sporadically mumbled to himself while he worked.

"Perhaps after this day I will take one day off. Monday would be a good day. It would be nice after mass on Sunday to be free for nearly two days. Perhaps Saturday?" He glanced skyward to take a bearing off some gulls who were riding the winds. "No, no day off! That would be slovenly!" He chastised himself.

The world may have been at war, but in the sleepy little village of Punta Umbria on the Playa del Portil, life went on as it had for the last 300 years.

The deep lines in the man's weathered face stood out more when he smiled as they did now when he kissed his fingertips and gently touched the glass enclosed picture of la Virgen de la Cinta nailed to the worn oak mast.

Unlike most of los pescolores, José Antonio Rey Maria had been on a lucky streak. For the fourth day in a row, the hold of his small barco was nearly full to the gun'wals.

He recovered the last of the nets, hoisted and secured the sail and carefully waded aft through the undulating catch of sardines strewn across the deck to man the tiller. Once there he nestled into his seat with the aft bulkhead as a back rest and carefully brought the small craft about. The fact that the shoreline was out of sight was of no consequence. The clouds, the wind and the birds were his compass.

"I don't know why my luck is so much better than the others. But better not to complain, better to be grateful, José." He continued his one way dialogue with the picture of Virgin de la Cinta.

Feeling that the world was once again running on greased grooves, he relaxed and slowly maneuvered the vessel as it waked in a wide arch back to the North East. As the boat glided on the off-shore breeze José basked in the mid-morning tranquility of the warm Atlantic sun and the solitude of the sea. The water was calm that morning, calmer than most mornings, but the off-shore Southerly was just strong enough to allow him to tack leisurely back into shore. He was once again in control of his own destiny.

Then it happened.

Less than one kilometer from shore he squinted his dark eyes to focus more clearly through the blinding reflections of the sun dancing off the surface of the sea. Something dark bobbed in the distance. *A small shark or marlin perhaps?* He glanced over the morning's haul and remembered his mother's watch words.

"Don't be greedy. Be grateful!" He glanced

again to the picture nailed to the mast as he remembered the words of his father. "God helps those who help themselves." He gently leaned into the tiller and steered to port.

"If it's a fish, it's a big fish!" He thought to himself. Drawing closer he muttered, "It doesn't move. Not a good sign." Then his eyes widened and his right hand slowly rose to make the sign of the cross as he realized it was a corpse.

Twenty minutes later, after struggling to hoist the corpse on board and failing, he had the body of Major William Martin, of Her Majesty's Royal Marines secured to the side and was again tacking back into shore.

Back at dock side all work had stopped while the small crowd debated whether or not the body should be moved. Fish had to be unloaded and since unanimous consent determined the Royal Marine couldn't be any more dead, he was unloaded first and respectfully laid off to one side, under the shade of tree.

†

Due to the hour Captain Rodriguez, the town's sole policeman, had not yet reported to the small station just off the town square and so a runner was sent to his home.

It was only a matter of an hour before the son of the German Consul Adolf Clauss, got wind of the

The Wolves of Calabria

discovery of the body of a British Naval officer which had been brought in by a local fisherman.

Upon arrival at the scene he was compelled to push his way through the small crowd on the beach staring down at the decayed officer with the waterlogged briefcase chained to his wrist.

Clauss was delighted.

The Junior consul collected information like some people collected butterflies, coins or stamps. A dyed-n-the-wool wanna-be hero, he quickly realized that the war gods had seen fit to give him his big chance.

Unfortunately for the Germans, Clauss thought in straight lines.

From the time he arrived in Spain nearly a year ago no one bought his cover story. What was a German agricultural expert doing in Huelva, a small sea port? There to teach the ignorant natives how to plant wheat in the sand? Like the dead body rotting in the blazing sun before him, you could smell it a mile away. Clauss was Abwehr to the bone.

He secretly contacted his handlers in the German Consol in Madrid, whom he imagined to be part of a vast, world-wide Abwehr spy ring whose destiny was to collapse the Western economies by undermining their military efforts with himself as a critical lynch pin.

The boys in Madrid immediately sent him a familiar wire which is common to higher-ups when a lower-down has stumbled across something the higher-ups think they can exploit. They told him not to do anything until they arrived, but a small time operator like Adolf Clauss wasn't about to stand by and let his big opportunity slip by. He would open the case, collect the secret intelligence he was sure the case contained, circumvent his handlers and get it to Berlin on his own there-by guaranteeing a promotion, perhaps even a personal audience with Der Fuhrer himself!

Naturally his handlers in Madrid had different ideas. Immediately upon receiving Clauss' message they piled into the single available staff car and were racing south to Huelva. All the dogs smelled the same bone.

Spain was still a neutral country so they all realized the body would eventually have to be returned to the British, but not before Clauss was able to jimmy the locks and take detailed photographs of everything in the briefcase and on the body.

In his haste to heroism he never noticed the single dark strand of hair in the corner, carefully glued across the opening of the case.

The next day the British Vice Consul arranged for Dr. Eduardo Del Torno, a pathologist, to perform a post-mortem. His report stated that the Marine had fallen into the sea while still alive and because the body displayed no bruises, the death was due to drowning. Additionally, he noted, the body had been in the water between three and five days.

A more comprehensive exam was not performed

because the pathologist assumed that, due to the St. Christopher medal in his wallet and the crucifix around his neck, the deceased officer was a Roman Catholic.

Major Karl Erich Kulenthal, Clauss' superior, showed up that evening, stripped Clauss of his valuable booty and booked an overnight train which ensured that the photos of the documents were in Berlin the following day. The documents from the briefcase, including theatre ticket stubs dated April the twenty second, were authenticated, Hitler bought it hook, line and sinker and by supper time that night everybody involved in the windfall was drunk on schnapps and Weiss bier.

Everyone save Field Marshall Erwin Rommel who warned caution.

The coup, as far as the German High Command were concerned, was that the documents revealed that the Allies were planning to invade Sardinia then the Balkans, using Sicily as a feign. The Germans had significant numbers of soldiers on Sicily, troops which had been withdrawn from North Africa and had not yet been reassigned. The result of this find was that much of the German defensive effort currently in Sicily was diverted from Sicily to Greece.

Hitler was so convinced of the authenticity of the bogus documents that he ruled against Mussolini who firmly believed that Sicily was the Allies' real target. Hitler followed up with orders that any activity in the region of Sicily be treated as a feign.

He additionally ordered the reinforcement of Sardinia and Corsica and sent Rommel to Athens to form a new army group. Patrol boats as well as mine sweeps and mine layers earmarked for the defense of Sicily, were diverted.

Perhaps the most critical move of all was diverting two panzer divisions to Greece from the Eastern Front where they were sorely needed, especially as the Germans were preparing to engage the Russians in the Kursk offensive. This significant effect on the Eastern Front was not among the results intended by the British originators of the plan, *Operation Mincemeat*, but no one at the Admiralty seemed to mind.

Forty-eight hours later Spanish authorities returned the body to British Vice-Consul Hazeldene, and three days after the find Lt., Acting Major William Martin, Royal Marines, was buried in Huelva with full military honors.

To further the ruse, a series of urgent messages were made by the admiralty to their Naval Attaché in Madrid demanding the return of the documents found with the body at all costs due to their 'sensitive nature'. Further, to insure this traffic got to the Germans, they were ordered to make the inquiries discreet so as not to alert the Spanish authorities of their importance. The documents were eventually returned on May the thirteenth with the assurance that they were all there.

There was no small amount of tension deep in the dark bowels of Twenty Section, B1 of MI5 in

London when the briefcase arrived and it was discovered that the seal on the briefcase using a human hair had been broken.

A few days later ULTRA intercepted radio traffic containing a German transmission ordering all Mediterranean commanders to prepare for an Allied amphibious invasion.

Somewhere in the Greek islands.

☦

**09:30, 14 May, 1943
Churchill's Residence
Westerham, Sevenoaks**

"Rudd! RUDD!" The tall, late-middle aged butler in black waistcoat and rolled up white shirt sleeves ascended the staircase at his own pace, not too fast not too slow. He dried his hands with a tea towel as he climbed.

"RUDD!" The tall, lanky servant wasn't ignoring the call of his master, it was just that decorum forbade shouting back. "RU–" Rudd entered the white tiled bathroom where Winston Churchill soaked in an oblong, nearly full, soapy bath, a half drained martini glass in his hand. Rudd waved away the fumes of the thick cigar smoke which filled the room.

"Yes Your Lordship?"

"Rudd my bath seems to have gone cold."

Restraining his exasperation Rudd dutifully moved to the side of the tub and checked the long narrow thermometer hanging at the foot of the tub.

"Down by two degrees, Your Lordship." Rudd was running more hot water when the doorbell to the downstairs, rear entrance rang. He closed the tap and rechecked the thermometer. The doorbell rang a second time. "Pardon me, Your Lordship." Rudd descended the long dark stairs at the exact same pace with which he had ascended it. No more no less. The doorbell rang again.

"RUDD! ANSWER THE BLOODY DOOR!" Rudd didn't respond. The doorbell rang for a fourth time. Now at wits' end, Rudd indulged himself in a rare emotional outburst by gently allowing a sigh to escape his pursed lips.

As the bell began to ring yet one more time Rudd opened the black enameled door and peered at the young Royal Marine messenger with his finger on the button. The private looked up to make eye contact with the stone-faced butler then quickly and mechanically withdrew his finger.

A few yards behind the messenger a Royal Marine motorcycle stood leaned over on its kickstand

"Young man, I am fully cognizant of the fact that in your profession shouting, yelling and screaming flood the normal, daily routine, however here at The Residence we are not deaf. How it works is, you ring the bell once, and wait for me to open the door. I then ask, 'How I may help you?', and you state your business. Have I made myself perfectly clear or is it required that I locate a bullhorn to make you feel more at home?"

"No sir! I mean, no sir you won't need a bullhorn, not, no sir you have not . . . you have made myself, ahhh . . . yourself perfectly clear. Sir." There was a short silence and Rudd threw a temper tantrum by sighing more deeply than he had before.

"This is the part where I say; 'How may I help you?', and you respond with . . .?" The lad quickly rummaged through his leather messenger's pouch and produced a sealed manila envelope.

"Message for the P.M., sir! That is the Prime Minister, sir."

"Ahh! I'd been wondering all these years what P.M. stood for!" Rudd reached for the envelope but the messenger quickly withdrew the offering.

"It's for the Prime Minister's eyes only, sir."

"The Prime Minister is indisposed at the moment, I'll take it to him."

"Sorry sir. Orders is orders sir and they say he is to see this message at once, regardless of circumstances. Sir. 'Eyes Only!' if you get my drift, sir."

"See if you get **my** drift. You can give it to **me**. I'll see
that Lord Churchill receives it *post haste*!"

"With all due respect sir, the post would be too slow, what with the war on and all. so-"

"We are just a veritable fountain of colloquialisms today, aren't we? Very well, follow me." The Marine entered to follow Rudd who, without turning around called back. "Wipe your boots!" The young marine scurried back to the doormat, quickly complied and then picked up Rudd's trail, now halfway to the staircase. "Unless you were born in a barn, please be good enough to close the door!" Again he ran back to the door, closed it and resumed following.

On unceremoniously opening the bathroom door at the top of the stairs, to admit the young marine, Rudd made his announcement.

"Message for you Lord Churchill."

"What is it Rudd?" Rudd stared at the dumbfounded messenger standing paralyzed just outside the door and into the bath trying not to gawk at the leader of his country immersed in mostly evaporated soapy water, in the flesh. Lots of flesh.

"Hand the envelope to the Prime Minister, son." The marine again complied and Churchill immediately tore open the cable from his people at ULTRA. Churchill mumbled as he read.

"Shall I wait for a reply sir?" Conspicuously averting his eyes he messenger inquired.

Staring up into the corner Churchill suddenly slammed the water with both hands and yelled.

"MINCEMEAT SWALLOWED ROD, LINE AND SINKER BY THE RIGHT PEOPLE . . . !"

Rudd and the messenger jumped as Churchill sprayed the wall with the remnants of his breakfast cocktail. "In the words of that arrogant, alcoholic Patton, 'THOSE MAGNIFICENT BASTARDS!'

They've done it!"

†

CHAPTER IV

Dominick's Grill
East 87th Street, Manhattan
New York City

A light but constant drizzle fell outside the restaurant as the stubby, sausage-like fingers held the pencil just a little too tight. There was a constant scribble on the pocket, notebook page which continued at a steady flow.

Inside the small burger joint, an increasing rarity on the Upper East Side, the heat from the grill maintained a constant fog on the large paned, picture windows. The short, heavy set guy under the fedora used his shirt sleeve to wipe a clear swath across the glass and through the condensation.

Louie Mancino peered out through the rain spattered glass, across the street yet again to the upscale Empire Hotel. He didn't hear the waitress slip up besides him.

"You been nursin' that coffee fer over an hour. You want I should lend ya fifteen cent so's you can buy a slice a pie?" He looked up at the beefy, middle-aged waitress brandishing the steaming pot of coffee.

"Sorry Doll! Just workin' on something here." Louie replied. She craned her neck to better see the small notebook.

The Wolves of Calabria

"You some kinda' writer or something?"

"Ahh . . . yeah, yeah I am. Workin' on my first novel. Takes place in a hamburger joint. Uptown on the East Side." He slid his chair back from the table. "Features a real hot looking forty . . . eh thirty, ahh . . . late twenty–something waitress." She perused his purple and sun yellow bowling shirt as she refilled his coffee cup for the seventh time.

"Anybody ever tell ya you got a way with the ladies?"

"Funny you should ask! As a matter of fact –"

"They lied." Although he was temporarily stymied he hit her with a snappy comeback.

"Cake. No pie. Ehh . . . peach. Make that apple. Please."

"I like a guy who's decisive." She lethargically mumbled. I'll be right back with your peach apple pie-cake."

As she walked away Mancino glanced out the window across the street and caught sight of a Yellow Sunshine cab pulling up to the entrance of the hotel. A very well dressed and impeccably made up, mid-thirties blond, wrapped in a tight, cobalt blue dress stepped out, paid the driver and scampered under the rain drenched, maroon canopy featuring the gold embroidered logo of the Empire Hilton.

He quietly mumbled as he made an entry in his notebook.

"Subject arrived by cab. lic# 1632. Entered Empire Hotel, Tuesday, 19:45 hrs." He scribbled as he quickly threw on his suit jacket, gathered his small, dark blue gym bag, tossed a bill on the table and made for the door just as his apple pie arrived. The waitress lifted the five dollar note and stared.

"Hey fella, this is a . . . you want I should keep the whole fin?!" Without answering he ducked out the door into the drizzle, dodged and weaved his way across the four lanes of traffic and headed over to the hotel.

Once safely under the canopy, Louie Mancino, P.I. shook the rain off his hat and coat, wiped the toes of his green, white and red bowling shoes on the back of his droopy, tweed trousers and followed the trail through the revolving door and into the lobby.

The saturated sleuth shook the rain from his overcoat looked up to peruse the lobby of a hotel that he and Doris had only seen in moving pictures.

"Empire! No joke!" Mancino mumbled to himself as he surveyed the cavernous, Coco-Baroque lobby.

The alter-sized, Carrera marble reception desk dominated the space off to the right while the lounge area to the left side of this temple to financial prosperity was further adorned with a small forest of square, Corinthian columns. The space along the forest floor was littered with Hepplewhite chairs, tables and plushly upholstered love seats while the wide runway of the central lobby led straight down to a bank of brass plated elevators.

The Wolves of Calabria

Without warning a smartly uniformed bell hop appeared from the sparsely populated lobby.

"Take your bag, sir?" He nodded to Louie's small, blue YMCA gym bag.

"Ehh . . . no, no thanks." Straight ahead in the distance lay the large bank of brass plated elevators and he was just able to catch a glimpse of the tightly wrapped cobalt blue ass entering the lift as the doors slid shut. Louie adjusted his tie and made for reception. As he scurried he kept an eye on the lift's floor indicator over the door. By the time he reached the desk the ornate gold arrow had stopped at '7'.

"May I help you?" Louie set his YMCA gym bag on the highly polished black marble, reached into his left breast pocket and produced his badge and New York State issued private investigator's I.D. card.

"Ah, yeah. Louie Mancino. N.Y.P.D." He quickly restowed the bi-fold wallet. "I'm looking to find out what room that blond in the blue dress is in."

The receptionist suspected this was Mancino's first time in a high class hotel as he voluntarily emitted a condescending sigh.

"Even if I wanted to tell you, which I don't, I couldn't."

"What'a mean?"

"I mean, I would if I could but I shan't since I can't. that's what I mean."

Louie decided to pull out his tough guy routine.

"Ohh! Doctor-patient privacy huh? Hotel policy. No info about the guests. Even to a cop investigatin' a murder case?!" Louie's brain messaged his face to assume a hard assed expression. The clerk turned and didn't notice.

"Nooo, I can't tell you because she's a visitor. I've never seen her before." By way of signalling to Louie his interrogation was over the clerk casually drifted away and resumed his busy work.

Just then the lift opened up and the bell boy who had escorted the blond to her room stepped off. Louie scurried over and cornered him around back in the hallway leading to the dining room.

"HEY Mack!" Louie called. The bell boy stopped and turned around.

"What?" The bell boy challenged in his best Jimmy Cagney, tough guy tone. Louie again flashed his badge and feigned being a cop. The bellboy was unimpressed. "Yeah, so what'a ya want, Louie Mancino, Private Dick?"

"The blond, blue dress. What room ja take her to?"

"Jees, ya know, that was a long time ago. I mean, all the way up in the elevator. All the way down in the elevator. I can't seem to remember, my mind's a little foggy at the moment." Louie reached into his pocket and brandished a five spot. "It's coming ta me now, but not quite clear enough to see. All I'm getting' is . . . is . . . a . . . a seven. Yeah dat's it, a seven." He snatched the fin nte from Louie's hand. "A seven. Dat's all." Mancino held up another fiver. "Wait a minute! I'm getting' somethin' else! That's it, seven, a one and a . . . a nine. 719!" Louie wasn't amused but he gave up the second five dollar bill anyway and turned to walk away. "Hey P. I.!" Louie stopped but didn't turn back to the hop. "First time she's ever here. Upstairs to meet some secret lover or somethin'." Louie turned back to face him. "She was very hush-hush in the elevator. But she's married. Her first time screwin' around."

"How do you know all that?"

"Simple. Wit so many guys overseas fightin' da war we been gettin' them in here fairly regular. Ya can tell 'cause they all got that same look." Louie turned back and took a step towards the bellhop.

"How's that?"

"Shakin' like a dog in a Korean restaurant." Louie shrugged and shook his head. The bellhop elaborated. "Shittin' razor blades!"

"Thanks kid." The kid held up the tenners.

"Pleasure doin' business with ya, Detective Mancino. Come back anytime."

A couple of minutes later Louie was in the hall just off to the left of room 719. He removed a hand-held Kodak from the gym bag, attached a new flash bulb, adjusted the focus and cautiously put his ear to the door. Amongst the muffled giggles and subdued squeals the female voice inside announced she was going to call down for more ice. The guy she was with apparently pulled her back down on the bed and Louie figured it was as good a time as any to go for it.

He cautiously turned the knob, eased the door open and burst in.

The loud, shrill scream that filled the dimly lit room was punctuated with a blinding flash. As Mancino was inserting a new bulb he had to duck a flying lamp which exploded on the wall behind him. The topless blond shot a glance to the tall gangly guy in his socks scrambling out of the bed.

She made no attempt to avoid a second Kodak moment which puzzled Louie, as she casually donned her green, Oriental, silk robe, climbed off the bed and moved away from the guy who was now both hands holding his face and repeatedly cursing.

"Shit! Shit! Shit!"

"What the fuck is this? Who the hell is dis clown?!" The middle-aged blond demanded. "When you said, 'spice things up', you didn't say nuthin' about no God damned three-some!" Louie was completely confused.

Although he recognized the woman, who was brown haired in the photos his client had showed him when he commissioned Mancino to track down the schmuck who was doin' his wife, he couldn't figure out why the guy holding his face next to the bed was his client.

"Linda! Linda, please Baby, I can explain!" The client begged. She vented her anger by screaming back.

"TREE WEEKS, TREE NIGHTS A WEEK I GO TO A SPA, WORK MY ASS OFF TA LOSE A FEW POUNDS TA LOOK GOOD FER YOU, YOU UNGRATEFUL BASTARD! I GET A

COMPLETE MAKE OVER, **WIT MY OWN MONEY**! FER YOU! AND WHAT'A YOU DO? YA HIRE SOME TWO BIT SEAMUS TA SPY ON ME! ME YOUR OWN WIFE!"

It was a firm testament to her multi-tasking ability that not once during her tirade did she stop gathering her things generously strewn around the room, adjusting her robe and occasionally flinging whatever was at hand in the direction of the now repentant husband.

"Gimme a break! I didn't know! We're married twelve years –"

"YEAH TWELVE YEARS BUSTER! AND DON'T YOU FERGET IT!" Like a scolded puppy dog he sheepishly followed behind as she swiftly made her rounds to finish gathering her things. Clothes trailing after her, she headed for the still open door.

"Twelve wonderful, glorious, love filled years Baby Doll! And all of a sudden you start disappearing on me three nights a week! What was I supposed ta think?"

She wasn't finished with him.

"Think what ya want! We're through! And lemme tell ya, this ain't like all the other times! This time I mean it! Do ya hear me?! THROUGH! T-H-R-O-W!" She shoved past Louie and exited.

Out in the hallway doors flew open and heads popped out as she made her way to the elevator at the end of the hall. The car arrived and she got on.

"BASTARD!" She yelled one more time from

halfway inside the car.

"Going down!" The elevator operator announced louder than necessary as the gold Deco doors slid shut. The elevator bell resonated through the hallway leaving the client in his sleeveless undershirt, white boxers, black socks and garters, staring dumbfounded as he stood next to Louie the P.I. with the Kodak dangling from his hand.

There was a long silent pause as the other guests stared back down the hall at the two.

Louie spoke first.

"Well that could'a gone a lot better."

"Nah. You should see her when she's really mad!"

One by one the neighbors receded back into their lives as Louie and his client stood in the hall.

"You know of course, I still have to charge you for my services. Up until tonight of course."

"Yeah, yeah. You want a drink?" His ex-client offered.

"Why not?"

"You want a couple of shaky photographs of a guy and his wife enjoying their last fling?" Louie inquired.

"Nah. You keep 'em. I got the memory."

They made their way back into the room and the door closed over behind them.

✝

The Wolves of Calabria

East Side Docks
Midtown Manhattan, N.Y.C.

A few days after his meeting with Polokoff and Commander Haffenden at Gallagher's Steak House Joey "Socks" Lanza was making his way west across Lower Manhattan on foot where he easily lost his FBI tails and hopped a cab over to the Hudson River side of the island to meet one of his right hand men, Joey Adonis.

A baby-faced, fire plug of a man in a three piece suit, Adonis had not only switched sides to join the Luciano Family during the Castellammarese Wars back in 1931, but assisted in the assassination of Giuseppe 'The Boss' Masseria then cooperated just enough to help blind fold the authorities into believing they had made breakthroughs on the national structure of what they believed was, 'The Mafia' or La Cosa Nostra.

Now, speeding south along the Hudson River in his seventeen foot, mahogany Chris Craft *Runabout* with Joey at the wheel, Socks tried to relax and leave his pending legal troubles on the pier behind him.

"You like takin' this boat out don't ya Socks?" Joey asked.

"Who the fuck wants to sit in a taxi in traffic? And pay for the privilege?" Lanza quipped as he stretched out in the passenger's seat.

"Point taken Boss."

"What'a we hear from Jersey?" Socks asked

"The Camardos are talking a deal with Jimmy The Greek and his people. Sumthin' about the Bayonne yards."

With the Syndicate now largely back in control of the New York City waterfront and in a position to re-establish their old illegal import-export operations, at least along the Manhattan and Brooklyn docks, old rivalries were re-igniting.

Adonis pursued the conversation.

"Word on the street has it Lucky's lookin' at settin' up a new operation importin' sumthin' once the war is over." Socks immediately picked up on the fact that Adonis was sniffing around for some inside info. "Maybe open up some new territories along the way." Joey added. Lanza didn't take the bait.

"Watch ya speed, this is a no wake zone." Socks cautioned. "Last thing I need is a fuckin' ticket!" Joey slowed the boat. Reclined in his seat Lanza looked out over the bow at the City's skyline.

"Fuckin' Frankie Costello and his miserly 10%! You believe that shit? 10% across the board fer everybody!" Socks quipped towards the skyline.

"Dutch Schultz tried pulling that shit back when." Joey suddenly slowed the boat even more as they reached Pier 88 and casually steered closer to the berthing area of what was known as Luxury Liner Row.

Neither man spoke as they cruised past the steel blue hull of the capsized *Normandie*, one huge screw completely out of the water. Harnessed workmen suspended by safety lines were in the process of cutting away her funnels with acetylene torches.

"You think Albert A. really done that? Sunk that big boat like that?" Adonis could have been a child asking about Santa Claus.

"Rumors brother, nuthin' but rumors. Let's go, I got a meet to get to." Joey engaged the throttle again and they were off back down river.

"Drop me at the Warren Street jetty. I'll get a cab over."

Ten minutes later Socks was climbing out of the boat and on to the jetty. As he handed the forward line back to Adonis he made eye contact.

"Joey, don't sweat it. Anything opens up you'll get a piece of the action. Mia garanzia pisano!" Lanza reassured.

"Grazi pisano! Mila grazi! Ciao Socks."

Earlier that day Lanza had sent his young protégé, Frankie The Bellhop, Uptown from Fulton Street in his cherry bomb red, 1932 Ford, hot rod, pick-up truck to get a message to Frankie Costello to set up a meet.

Since Dewey had sent Lucky up the river seven years ago Costello had become much more powerful in The Syndicate now assuming the role of Boss of the Luciano Family. Vito Genovese, as Lucky's Underboss, was next in line, but as he feared prosecution for complicity in the murder of IWW union organizer Carlo Tresca and fled to Nola just outside Naples, Costello got an unexpected promotion. Something Vito wasn't too happy about. Although Lucky still made most of the major decisions from his prison cell, now just a couple of hundred miles North of The City in Great Meadows, it was Frankie Costello who was essentially now Meyer Lansky's right hand man in the overall management of the major New York family of The Syndicate. Not to everyone's satisfaction. Especially Vito Genovese.

Through one of Costello's head bookies, a guy named Eddie Erickson, Frankie The Bellhop was able to set up a meet for that afternoon with Lanza.

It was important there be no flash surrounding the meet, as Lanza hinted it was such a big deal, even the Italian American Club on Mott Street was deemed too high profile, so Costello set the meet in a small café in The Village, just off MacDougal around the corner from Prince Street.

Late that afternoon they met and the old Sicilian woman running the place got them the back room which, to the consternation of a young horny couple, was suddenly closed for cleaning.

Seated at a small round top across from the kitchen, Lanza opened the meet as soon as they took their chairs.

"I got a priority message from the Commander." Lanza opened with.

"I thought you was outta that business?!" Costello challenged.

"So did I." Lanza defended.

"What about the Camardos?"

"Fuck those two retards! Fuckin' messenger boys."

The old woman poked her head through the kitchen door and nodded to Frankie.

"Cappuccino?" Frankie asked Socks.

"Espresso." Frankie indicated two espressos to the woman.

"So what's up?"

"The Commander says ta tell Charlie we gotta get a message to Vizzini's boys."

"I'd havt'a run it by Lucky but I don't see no problem. We can do that. What's the message, what's this about?"

"How big a deal is it? To contact Vizzini I mean?"

"None. Don Vizzini's got a niece over here who calls once or twice a month. The Feds tailed her at the start of the war but gave up after they got nuthin'. We only use her from time to time."

"How you know they ain't got a wiretap on her?"

"She never uses the same phone twice."

"They don't need the phone, the can tap the local junction box." Socks insisted.

"What'a you, a fuckin' Junior G-man now? Relax with the paranoia, will ya?! She's got an older brother's a monk at the cloister of San Giovanni outside Palermo. When it's something important they speak in Catanian, in a code based on old Latin terms the monks use. She loves her old man, hates the Feds and understands the life. She's clean."

"Good, 'cause I got a feelin' about this one." The

woman served the two espressos.

"You got a feelin' Joey, I'm all ears. What's the message?" Socks leaned forward and whispered to Costello.

"Preparare. La cavalleria viene."

It took a few seconds to soak in but when it did it soaked deep. Costello fell back in his seat brandishing a broad smile as he cocked his head to one side. *The cavalry is coming!* He mused to himself. "La cavalleria?" He enquired. "The cavalry is coming."

"Si, la cavalleria." Lanza reiterated. Costello smiled as he stirred his espresso.

"Tell Charlie a communiqué'll go out day after tomorrow."

"Salute!" Socks raised his cup in a toast.

"Ariva derchi Il Duce!" Costello returned the toast.

☦

The Cobalt Club
34th and Sixth Ave.

The ornate soft pink and electric blue Deco décor, highlighted by the occasional black trim, permeated the room on the seats, tables and walls. Haffenden, who had been seated at the horseshoe shaped bar for the better part of half an hour saw his chance as the twenty piece band filed back onto the band stand in the front of the main ball room behind him. He ordered another scotch and soda, waited for the band to strike up their first number and then weaved his way through the crowd shuffling across the dance floor.

Although never having met him, from across the room the Commander recognized Frankie Costello from the N.Y.P.D. mug shots in his Naval Intelligence files. Costello, dressed in a beige three piece, was strategically seated in a curved booth with his left arm around a late twenties-something blond. Two of his torpedoes flanked the pair. Haffenden observed that several other bodyguards were scattered around the perimeter as he approached the corner booth.

"This seat free?" Haffenden asked.

"Depends who's askin'" Costello answered.

"I'm a friend of Joey's. Charlie, Charlie Haffenden."

Costello's frown melted into a smile as he stood and offered a hand. They shook and Frankie dismissed the shapely woman.

"Scuz us fellas!" He half instructed half ordered and the torpedoes faded into the background. "Can I offer you a drink Com-, Mr. Haffenden?" The Commander held up his untouched scotch glass. "It's my understanding we have some coordination to arrange." Costello relayed.

"We do." Haff replied as he took a seat opposite Costello. "Lengthy preparations by both us and the Brits have resulted in a green light for an operation to get under way which will lead to the launch of a major offensive. We have precious little intel on one of the areas concerned. Obviously all this is very sensitive and classed Top Secret."

"The Brits?" Costello was puzzled, but didn't push it. Frankie leaned into the table. "If you're talkin' about invadin' Sicily, me and the boys have already been kickin' around some ideas about where to hit them bastards." Now it was Haffenden's turn to sit back and stare.

"What makes you think we're going into Italy at all much less Sicily?"

"C'mon! You think youse are the only ones who use strategy and planning to take over a territory? Besides, a blind man could see it! How else you gonn'a get into Italy? Over the fuckin' mountains! The Krauts still got the Iberian Peninsula, the Ionian from Greece to Romania is a bastard to get through and we already got North Africa!"

"We?" Haff queried.

"Everybody in this country came from someplace else Commander, but we're all Americans now. Regardless of which side of the fence we're on."

"You're in the wrong line of work! Maybe you should come work for us!" Haffenden quipped. Frankie smirked, slid back in his seat and took a hit of his drink.

"No fuckin' way! Them Gerries ain't like cops! They're trained to hit what they shoot at!"

Haffenden smiled as he continued.

"We need two things. Any and all info you can get us on the south coast and any help you can get us that we can use once we're there."

"I'll do ya one better. There's a small town, Butera. When your boys get ashore get somebody ta get up there and find the Butera Resort, I suspect you'll find something there might be of use to you guys. Meanwhile, I'll see what I can do about arranging a sit down with Charlie."

"Not necessary. We can get you in any time. Let us know the day before and we'll get you an escort."

"Who, you?"

"Yeah, myself and a couple of others. Polokoff has to go Governor's orders, and we'll probably take an intel man. A former D.A.'s assistant, speaks Italian."

"Pauli Alfieri?"

"Like I said, you ever looking for a job . . ."

"Lucky will need to know when your boys intend on startin' the party."

"I can't give you exact dates, they're classified, but tell Eddie Erickson and your bookies not to take any bets on the first or second week of July. We're waitin' on word from our friends across the pond." Haff relayed to him.

"Tell your boys let me know one week prior, I'll set something up. Reception committee or something."

"Will do Mr. Costello."

Just then one of the torpedoes approached and leaned into Frankie's right ear away from the Commander. He whispered quite a long message, pulled back and awaited instructions. Frankie looked over at Haffenden.

"Looks like you got company Commander." The fact that Costello now had no compunction about addressing him by rank alerted Haffenden that it was serious.

"Something you wann'a tell me?" Haffenden asked.

"Two Feds outside, one with a camera. Probably a couple more out back."

"Fucking Hoover! Fuck up a wet dream, the little bastard would!" Haff downed his drink. "Guess it's time for me to go."

"Enrico, show this gentleman the back way out." Haff smiled and shook Frankie's hand. "I'll be in touch. Enrico will escort you through our, 'Press proof' egress Commander."

With *Moonlight Serenade* fading behind them Haffenden followed the strong arm across the dance floor and backstage where they descended a narrow staircase to a formidable looking door.

"Prohibition was good for a few things." The muscular escort quipped as he unlocked and held open the iron door for the commander. They proceeded through a long, dimly lit tunnel, up a similar staircase and out into an alley onto 33rd Street near Sixth Avenue.

Meanwhile, on the street outside the club two bewildered F.B.I. agents were being escorted at gun point into a black limo and away from the premises. Their two colleagues in the adjoining alley, however, were not as lucky. They were being stripped of their mini-Kodak and introduced to two of the Mafia's close acquaintances.

Mr. Black and Mr. Jack.

✝

Great Meadows Prison
Upstate State New York

Three men in expensive suits followed behind two armed guards as they traversed the long, puke green, tiled hallway.

Compared to Clinton State Penitentiary, up in Dannemora only miles from the Canadian border in the desolation of Upstate New York, Great Meadows was a country club. Lucky Luciano's new home, compliments of the U.S. Navy, only less than an hour from New York City, Lucky's life-long stomping grounds and base of operations. Although technically a prisoner of the state his situation at Clinton afforded him most of the amenities he enjoyed on the outside. With his own double cell, which was rarely locked, his own personal chef and people still lining up most days to kiss his ring and petition for favors, he was perhaps the most pampered prisoner New York had ever seen.

Luciano, indisputably the most successful gangster of his era, was a man who if he bumped into you on the street would be the first to apologize and was the exact anti-thesis of what Hoover touted daily to the American public in order to build his own worm-eaten career.

Hoover, who's M.O. as he rose to power, founded on the illegal deportation of thousands of legitimate citizens and included high leveled blackmail, extortion and graft through a quiet participation in the rackets through betting, endured great pains to present himself as the squeaky clean boy scout of the long arm of the law. As most Washington insiders knew, he was one of the most corrupt politicians ever to stain D.C. with his fingerprints.

With the ages old understanding of cementing inter-cultural relations between enemies, Luciano had even donated a large sum of cash to have a chapel built in the prison yard to afford the Christian inmates a place to worship. How he came off so good despite being framed was in large part due to his lawyer.

Moses Polokoff, the master tactician mouthpiece for the New York Mob, was at the top of the food chain of the exclusive NYC legal crowd. He stood clearly on the opposite side of the tracks from D.A. Thomas Dewey, the guy who fried Louie Buchalter, Manny Weiss and Louie Lepke in the electric chair and sent Luciano up six years ago. Luciano, the very man who saved Dewey's life by ordering a hit on Dutch Schultz in a Newark chop house days before Schultz was to assassinate Dewey for prosecuting him.

Polokoff had several times single handedly defeated the 'legal' army led by Dewey to free his mobster clients and was greatly respected on both sides of the law. Only six years apart in age Dewey and Polokoff were considered by the New York legal community to be the cocks of the walk.

And they knew it.

It had been the better part of a year since Haffenden had had direct contact with the Capo di Capi, Boss of Bosses, Charlie Luciano. Having worked closely with him to establish and execute *Operation Underworld*, neither Luciano nor Haffenden believed they'd ever meet again. Both were mistaken.

Along for the trip that morning was Paul Alfieri a twelve year veteran of the New York D.A.'s office. Alfieri wasn't just a suit looking to make a name for himself framing bad guys. One of those clichéd D.A. hacks sucking off the big New York tit with a 'Whatever it takes to get a conviction!' attitude. Alfieri was different. He really did know right from wrong and from the day of FDR's famous radio speech declaring war on Japan Paul Alfieri wanted in on the big show.

Oddly enough his big chance came from someone he had little respect for. One of the hundreds of D.A.'s turned politician who had helped rewrite the book on 'stretching' the rules. The New

York City District Attorney himself, Thomas Dewey.

Now, accompanied by Moses Polokoff and Commander Haffenden, Alfieri was being escorted through the bowels of Great Meadows prison to a meet with the big man himself.

Once in the assigned meeting room Polokoff took his usual seat as he always did on these 'supervised' visits in a corner chair provided for him and dug a stack of newspapers from his briefcase.

As had become unwritten protocol they waited until the guards had cleared the room before beginning the meet.

Luciano sat across the metal table from Haffenden and Alfieri. Introductions were made and the Commander got right to it.

"Mr. Luciano, due to the success of a recent British operation the Allied Command has decided to make a move on Italy." Luciano smiled.

"About fuckin' time! Youse are goin' into Sicily! Ain't ya?" Haff and Alfieri both sat back in their chairs as Haff took over the briefing.

"Charlie, the Brits have no connections with The Mob. Hell some of 'em say you guys don't even exist anymore."

"Dat so? Tell them come on over some time and we'll give 'em an education!" Alfieri fought back a smirk. Lucky leaned into Haff. "Look, if this really is that important, get Dewey to get me out, ship me over through some neutral country, Portugal, Spain wherever, and get me into Sicily. I guarantee you get me there, I'll make my way to Golfo di Castellammare near Palermo. We used it for smuggling all kinds'a shit back in the 20's. It's perfect for sneaking into the North coast areas."

Haffenden and Alfieri exchanged looks. Paul spoke first.

"We appreciate the offer Mr. Luciano, but I seriously doubt our people in D.C. would go for that." He countered. "Wharton, Head of Counter Intel is very politically sensitive. Big plans for office after the war."

"So he just wants us to supply the info, then thank you very much, but fuck off?!"

Haffenden was offended. "Like I told you, on the last deal, no promises –"

"Except my part in this is still classified?!"

"Strictly! But nothing beyond that. I'll go to bat for ya after the war, providing the info you're giving us pans out. But nothing beyond that." Polokoff looked disgusted but kept quiet, just turning a page of his newspaper.

Luciano changed gears.

"I don't know nuthin' about no military stuff, but it seems to me if you was looking to put a bunch of your guys ashore clean and quick like, Licata Beach is where I'd aim for."

"Where the hell is Licata Beach?"

"Down in Gela, in the south." He took Haff's pen from his pocket and on a page of Alfieri's notebook sketched a rough draught of the island of Sicily as he spoke. "We used to ride down there in my uncle's car sometimes, long time ago. There used to be a small resort area set up down there. Hot as hell, but sandy, no rocks, and there's a natural breakwater made by the inlet."

Haff turned to Alfieri who gave his assessment.

"Sounds like it's worth looking into, but we'd still want more detailed info before we commit an entire invasion force."

"Charlie, we'll need more information, you know general stuff." Haffenden explained.

"Like what?"

"Ideally, photos."

"Ain't you got planes and shit for that sort'a thing?"

"Yes, but if we risk reconnaissance flights being seen the Nazi's will know for sure something's up. Maybe one small plane flying low could get through, but . . ."

"I get it."

"We need more subtle methods of obtaining the info."

"You mean like family holiday photos, souvenir pictures and such?"

"Exactly. You got anything like that lying around?"

"Yeah, down in my other cell. The one the Warden let me have for personal storage. The one right next to my private wardrobe cell with all my Armani's hangin' in it." Luciano sarcastically quipped. Paul interrupted to avoid conflict.

"We could requisition the navy do a

hydrographic survey. They've got a UDT unit on stand-by in Algiers." Alfieri suggested to Haffenden.

"No matter what youse do we're gonna' need to get word to the guys over there." Lucky interjected.

"Word of this operation can't leave this room!" Haff demanded.

"Don't sweat it! I'll say nuthin' ta nobody and I'll arrange for the guys over there to get word at the last minute. Twenty-four to forty-eight hours prior to the time you land. Good enough?"

"That could work. What'a ya need from us?" Haff asked.

"Coupla' things. Send Meyer up here next week, alone with Moses and have him bring my yellow scarf."

"Your new cell drafty?"

"No, but trust me, what I got planned will warm your little hearts! Also, when your guys get there, let them know that as long as they're in the neighborhood, they may want to pay a visit to the village of Necemi. I was there once for a vacation. There's an unusual concentration of whore houses, for such a small town I mean. Some of'em on the very expensive side."

Alfieri and Haffenden exchanged puzzled glances. Lucky shook his head and fell back in his chair. "I thought you guys was Naval Intelligence?!" He goaded. Paul shrugged at Lucky. "It's a secret naval headquarters! Ya dolts!" The gangster chastised. "Ergo the high class hookers!"

Haff's eyes shot wide open.

"Anything else we need to know?" Paul asked.

"Anything comes to mind I'll get in touch." The Intel officers rose to leave. Polokoff took the cue. As he stood Lucky took Haff by the arm.

"When this thing's over anything's possible. I may even wind up legit after it's all said and done."

"I'll be the first to write you a letter of reference." Haff assured as he patted Charlie's hand.

"Meyer talks very highly of you. I just want you to know, just like you guys, we never killed nobody that didn't deserve it." Lucky insisted. Haff smirked.

"I'm not a cop." He reassured Lucky. They shook hands and Haff's party left. As they made their way out Haff gave a quick sit-rep to the other two.

"I suspected we were tailed so I stationed a detail out back of the east yard."

He scurried up to the head guard who was assigned to escort them out. "Guard, we need to exit out into the east yard." The guard very briefly looked puzzled, shrugged and at the end of the hall turned right and led them down and out the back. Once the large iron gate was sliding back into place a black Cadillac limo with Navy plates pulled up and they piled in.

As the driver swung around the expansive prison structure and turned left to head back towards the highway, they came to a T junction on the single lane dirt road. Haffenden looked to the left as they turned right and spotted two suites in black shiny shoes and fedoras leaning against an unmarked car.

"Fuckin' Hoover!" He mumbled. The driver glanced in the rear view mirror and smiled.

"You want me to lose them Commander?"

"Yeah, go through the town. We'll lose 'em at the rail junction."

"Fucking cloak and dagger shit!" Polokoff cursed under his breath as he shook his head as he huddled in the back seat.

☨

CHAPTER V

**Office of the Chief
Carabinieri Station House
Villalba, Sicily**

Chief Carabinieri Pino Petrocelli, just starting his evening shift, adjusted the hand embroidered, three legged crest of Sicily above the door of the small, rural station house. Young Petrocelli loved the nation of Italy, but he cherished Sicily. He cherished the people, the language and all that contributed to the rich and ancient culture of his native land.

His mind often wandered through the romantic stories of his grandfather, of the days when Italy matured from a squabbling collection of immature provinces into adulthood and on into a nation fit to take the world stage.

Even in the face of the most threatening invasion Sicily had ever seen, the Nazis, he refused to abandon his post as Villalba's chief law keeper. He could have fled but didn't. He hated the Nazi invaders as much as he loved Sicily and so stayed to fight however he could.

But as bright as his hatred for the now ousted invaders burned, he hated the Mafiosi even more. The Mafiosi and all they stood for.

Five kilometers north of his station house in Vallelunga Pratameno, neither of the two men sitting at the corner of the bar in the hundred and fifty year old Taverna Farini spoke as they waited for dark. There were few other patrons in the bar and the men were on their fourth round since they had arrived an hour ago.

Finally the smaller one determined the light had faded all it was likely to on that moonlit night and quietly signaled to the bar man who wandered over.

"Place the call exactly at eleven o'clock. You understand?" He confirmed. The young man behind the bar nodded in return.

When the other finished his amaretto they donned their jackets and left the small, now deserted taverna. Outside they mounted their horses and disappeared into the dark.

Back at the station house, while sitting at his desk finishing some paperwork, Carabinieri Petrocelli received a late night call. There was a domestic disturbance over on Via Piave on the out skirts of town.

He put on his official winged hat and jacket and, as it was a clear, warm night decided to walk the four or five streets to the reported address. An address he knew well from previous complaints.

He approached the house through the unkempt front garden curious as to why there were no lights on. He stepped up to the front door and raised a hand to knock.

He felt the garrote before he realized it was around his throat. It had come out of nowhere. He struggled and kicked longer than most as he was dragged from behind into the shadows of the narrow lane beside the house. He fought with all he had but it was a lost cause. First his breath, then his arms and finally his mind gave way.

Everything faded to black.

The body was carried by the two thugs around to the back where a stolen horse waited. They draped the corpse over the saddle and the two led the three horses away up into the hills.

Chief Carabinieri Pino Petrocelli was no longer an element in the equation of law and order in Sicily.

In the pathetic after math of the rape of Sicily by the Nazis and their fascist cohorts there were no resources to launch an investigation of the murder of Carabinieri Pino Petrocelli. There was only a small memorial plague along with a flag presented to his grieving mother and sister weeks later when the search for his missing body was finally called off.

Such was the order of things in Sicily in September of 1943.

†

AMGOT HQ
Abandoned Italian Château
Fifty miles Northeast of Gela, Sicily
August 13, 1943 D+43

Following the outcome of Monty and Patton's unauthorized race to Messina, signaling the

The Wolves of Calabria

complete capture of the island of Sicily, allied HQ's on the island was temporarily set up in an 18th Century mansion just north of the American's main landing site at Gela.

The former luxury Italian château now functioned as a forward command post for the Allied Military Government of the Occupied Territories and was in full swing by 08:00 that Thursday morning.

Colonel Charles Polletti, a full bird colonel, the former Governor of New York, (for 29 days), as well as the first Italian-American governor to occupy the seat, was the officially appointed AMGOT coordinator in Sicily.

And, as one might expect, was politician to the bone.

That morning as he burst through the front door and quickly made his way into the headquarters a thousand things ran through his mind. He removed his hat and tossed it at his driver following behind as he scurried across the former ball room which now served as the Allies' main office space of its forward command. He passed the dozen clerks at their desks, typewriters pecking away next to crates of assorted secretarial paraphernalia and made his way up the grand staircase straight for his office on the second floor of the east wing stopping at his office door.

"You seen this?" Polletti asked the Master Sergeant/clerk sitting at the desk just outside his office, a converted master bedroom with a balcony which opened out onto the ball room space he'd just crossed on the ground floor below. The sergeant calmly took the out-thrust, 8X10 leaflet. "G2 brought it over from just outside Agrigento." Polletti informed.

The sergeant took it from him and quickly glanced it over.

SHELTER AND COMFORT FOR DESERTERS!
Shelter, food, clothes and relocation will be afforded all who desert the forces of the invaders of Sicily!

THOSE WHO CONTINUE TO FIGHT WILL BE EXCECUTED UPON CAPTURE!!

"Yes sir. There's hundreds of them all over the western sectors of the island."

"How the hell am I supposed to rebuild Palermo, much less all of Sicily when our PSYOPS people are running amok with their own operations, answer me that?!"

"Actually Colonel it's my understanding these didn't originate with PSYOPS." The Colonel stared.

"Well then where the hell did they come from?"

"The Mafia sir."

The Colonel re-examined the leaflet.

"God damned glad they're on our side!" He mumbled as crumpled the paper and tossed it aside. "We all set for the briefing sergeant?"

"Zero Nine hundred sir. In the 'floral room' as directed sir." The sergeant mockingly responded.

"Fucking floral room!" The colonel grumbled and shook his head as he entered his office to prep for the daily situation briefing.

As Colonel Polletti made his way inside to his desk to prepare for the briefing a messenger was making his way through the back door of the mansion and along a busy hallway of the converted, three hundred year old building until he came to one of the ornate staircases.

"C.A.O's office?" He enquired of a passing officer who relayed directions and pointed up on the run.

"Two up, two over." He blurted out not bothering to stop. About ten feet away the officer looked back over his shoulder. "But if you want the colonel his office is in back of the ball room." The messenger came down the few stairs he had climbed and headed across the big room to the opposite stair, went up two flights and walked until he stopped in front of Polletti's clerk and announced himself.

"Colonel Polletti?"

"Yeah." The sergeant didn't bother to look up.

"Master Sergeant I have a priority message for the Colonel." The NCO made no attempt at hiding his annoyance.

"From who?"

"I believe one of Colonel Donovan's people sergeant." The corporal responded.

Upon hearing the name Donovan the sergeant looked up from his desk.

By the Summer of '43 Wild Bill Donovan, a

former New York lawyer who had set up the U.S. Government's official intelligence agency, the Office of Strategic Services, and his band of OSS secret agents had already reached legendary status.

The sergeant entered, handed his boss the message and waited for a reply. Polletti tore it open and read it. Hundreds of bits of traffic crossed his desk each week but never from the OSS Commander himself. He folded and pocketed it.

"Answer: 'Dinner for two, time TBD.' Send that to Colonel Donovan and send the following to the Admiralty: 'Bullfrog confirms Husky. Awaits dinner reservations.' Have those encoded and out within the hour. Notify me when you receive confirmation from the Brits."

"Yes Sir." The sergeant saluted and turned to leave.

"And get my jeep around front." Polletti called after as he rose to don his pistol belt, holster and hat.

"Colonel, the briefing?"

The colonel's mind shot to Joe Russo, alias Mr. X, Chief of the OSS office in Palermo.

"Contact Russo and let him know we're going to deal with Don Calogero, I intend to get him an appointment. Tell Russo it's to keep it kosher and to help establish a firm foothold here."

Don Calogero Vizzini had no idea but he had just become mayor of the strategically located town of Villalba.

"Sir if you're thinking of setting up a rear guard why not just repatriate the Carabinieri?" The senior

The Wolves of Calabria

sergeant suggested.

"The Carabinieri and Italian Army are satisfactory for local security purposes." Polletti explained to his trusted clerk. "But most of the Fascist army has deserted, and the Carabinieri are powerless. No one listens to them. Besides, the Chief of police in Villalba seems to have vanished." Polletti led them out of the office and down the stairs. "Vizzini's Mafia are far more reliable at guaranteeing public safety. Besides, there's no danger of desertion or traitors. They hate the Fascists worse than we do! And more importantly Joe Russo thinks he can use them later after we've gone, to stave off the communists."

The U.S. Army was not exactly in Sicily to set up affordable vacation homes along the lovely Sicilian coastline. They had their sights set on establishing electronics factories in Berlin after the war and soon they would be out of Sicily and on their way.

Now at D+34 the fight for Sicily was far from over. Although the Germans and Italians were busy evacuating over 100,000 troops across the Strait of Messina, the German's rear guard action was nothing less than textbook. Hastily laid mine fields, snipers and a well-organized and executed rolling rear guard action kept the Allies at bay until the last minute maximizing the petty squabbling in the Allied ranks which in turn bought the Axis troops valuable time to escape.

As Patton rolled into Messina unchallenged on

the 17th of August and Monty struggled to catch up, Polletti was tasked with and went to work on the stabilization of the island to plan the most expeditious way to chase the Germans and Italians across to the boot and push up through the Italian mainland.

Consequently Sicily was a stopover location and the sooner they could get the hell out, the sooner they could be eating bratwurst, drinking Weiss bier on the Rheine and chasing little blond haired frauleins. The last step in the Allies' campaign to free Europe and get back home and eat cheeseburgers. Or fish and chips. Therefore the Allies had to leave somebody behind to cover their rear and who could do the job of policing the people, running the show while they were on the road and who would maintain loyalty to them. Somebody the U.S. government had been dealing with for decades and that they could trust. Somebody who thought along the same business lines as they did. Somebody Polletti had regularly dealt with as a New York politician. The New York Mob.

The only thing that filled the big room as loud as the typing chatter of the clerks was the radio static of the commo point in the corner of the room as Polletti and his clerk crossed the converted ballroom.

"Pass the word to be prepared to relocate to Messina on 48 hours' notice." Polletti smiled as he read the latest message given him by a decoder clerk as they strode across the ball room. "I'd say that qualifies as good news!" He passed the message to the sergeant.

PATTON ON OUTSKIRTS OF MESSINA

Halfway to the door they were intercepted by an elderly, shabbily dressed Italian man accompanied by a Captain from Civil Affairs accompanied by an M.P. Both were escorted up to him. The Colonel returned the M.P.'s salute and dismissed the cop then addressed the Captain.

"What'a you got?" The C.A.O. officer nodded at the old man.

With hat in hand the emaciated man's physical condition displayed doubt as to whether or not he would see the end of the week much less the end of the war.

"Sir I think you need to hear what this gentleman has to say." The captain answered then turned and spoke to the old man in Italian. The man answered with a short 'Si!'

"He says –"

"Yeah, I got it." Polletti then spoke to the man in fluent Sicilian after which he explained to the sergeant who was not bilingual.

"It appears a food convoy of civilian, volunteer vehicles is MIA."

"These things happen in war sir." The sergeant replied.

"Mr. Rorro, colonel, is the only surviving elected council member left in the city." The Captain elaborated. "They executed all the rest when they over ran the town." The Polletti assumed a more respectful air.

"Signor Rorro." He offered his hand to shake and nodded as he spoke. "Mi dispiace davvero!"

Rorro shook the colonel's hand and nodded his acceptance of the Colonel's sympathy. He then began to rapidly spout a more emphatic complaint. The C.O. held his patience, but not the fact that he was slightly annoyed by the delay.

"He claims it wasn't the Germans who stole the rations." The civil affairs officer informed the sergeant.

"Thank you sir." The clerk offered trying to hide his embarrassment at not having learned the language in the time he had been abroad.

"Is he accusing American soldiers of hijacking civilian food?" Polletti asked. The old man spoke again, but only one word.

"Mafiosi."

"Sir," The Captain elaborated. ". . . in addition to the missing food, just three days ago some Italian Red Cross nurses in Gela complained to a Pathfinder medic that a truck load of medical supplies had gone missing."

"Germans?"

"There haven't been any enemy in that area for at least three days, sir." The colonel paid closer attention. "Day before yesterday a deuce and a half we thought captured or destroyed was found abandoned along route 127. It's cargo of dried eggs and meat was gone." The Colonel began to get the picture.

"Sergeant take a message." The sergeant pulled a pad from his breast pocket and wrote as fast as the C.O. dictated.

"It has come to our attention that vital food and medical supplies intended for the help and rejuvenation of the Sicilian civilian population are being pilfered before reaching their rightful destinations." The Captain quietly translated to Mr. Rorro as the Colonel spoke. "This will halt immediately or I will unilaterally reinstitute martial law without further notice. Violators will be shot. End message." The half dozen personnel in the spacious room within earshot quietly pretended to continue work while eavesdropping. "Captain, get that to G2, tell them to use their underground pipeline and get it to whatever Spook contact they're dealing with, what's his name? Make it happen yesterday!"

"Yes Sir!"

"And take this man over to the chow hall and get him something to eat and some provisions to take back to his family."

"Shall I send an escort back to the village with him Colonel?"

"Good idea sergeant. Captain make that so will you?"

"Will do sir." The captain echoed. In his broken Italian the Captain informed the old man that everything would be taken care of. Little could the Captain know the accuracy of his prediction.

A day later the recently U.S. appointed mayor of Gela, Don Calogero Vizzini, got the message about the missing food by special courier. Just after daybreak the following morning a foot patrol found the MIA food trucks, minus half the food and some of the medical supplies. The vehicles had mysteriously re-appeared just outside AMGOT HQ overnight.

At 10:30 hours later that morning G2 received a gift addressed to Colonel Polletti in the form of a small jewelry box. Apparently a token of thanks for the Colonel's good judgment in appointing Vizzini mayor. The gift was couriered over to Polletti's Civil Affairs office in the château straight away.

Polletti arrived late and sat at his slightly damaged, ornate Louis XIV desk waiting for his driver to return from a pick-up when his sergeant entered and handed him the small box. Polletti opened it and stared.

Just then a junior clerk burst through the office door and addressed him without formality.

"Colonel Polletti sir, we're gonna need a pile of civilian clothes and a shit load of spaghetti!"

"What the hell for?!" Polletti closed the jewellery box over and by way of an answer the sergeant led the colonel out onto the oversized veranda of the bedroom.

Down below, parked just outside on the expansive , circular gravel driveway were eight deuce and half trucks loaded with unarmed but still uniformed Italian deserters. The entire company sized element was escorted by only two armed M.P.'s in a jeep.

"Looks like those leaflets did the job!" The sergeant commented.

"Yeah, and I think our pilfering problem has been solved too." The colonel commented as he nodded at the small box then passed it to his clerk just as his jeep pulled up out front.

The clerk opened it and nearly vomited.

It was a freshly severed index finger with a large signet ring, a symbol of authority of a former minor Mafiosi, still attached.

The colonel headed down to his jeep and drove off with his driver/translator, former New York Mafioso hit man Vito Genovese.

☦

To the Allies he was known as Signor Calogero the Mayor of Villalba. To the residents of the village he was known as the Don. In secret Allied communications he was known as "Bullfrog".

Calogero Vizzini knew only one costume, a white tee shirt, white short sleeved shirt with black suspenders and dark, baggy trousers. Like any soldier's uniform he had come to be identified by such attire.

After the North African Campaign concluded in a total Allied victory planners turned their eyes to mainland Europe. A direct assault was still well beyond their capability so a back door had to be found. There was an obvious choice. However, the strategic importance of Lucky Luciano's homeland, Sicily, was not lost on the Germans either.

Prior to the invasion, the ancient island housed several Panzer Groups, an estimated 50,000 troops of various units and served as the base from which the bulk of the Luftwaffe air attacks against the British stronghold of Malta were being choreographed and launched.

However, with those kinds of troop numbers plus air superiority, a frontal assault was deemed extremely risky. In a classic military strategy a two pronged assault was decided upon.

The required back doors to Sicily were Gela in the south and Catania in the east.

The Brits led by Monty had assaulted the East coast while the Americans led by Patton had landed at Gela in the South. Monty's objective was Messina at the very Northeast corner of the island country cutting off the Germans' escape across the straits to the mainland and Patton's was to cut the country in half by pushing north from Gela and taking the city of Palermo.

Monty informed the high command he would need at least two weeks. George S., in his typical humble fashion, reported that he could take Palermo in a week to ten days.

Neither had a clue how wrong they were. Monty would spend the better part of two months reaching Messina, only to discover that George was there to

The Wolves of Calabria

personally greet him when he finally arrived.

With the help of Vizzini's people, sniping Germans, guarding roads, acting as scouts and guiding the Americans through the mountain passes of western Sicily all the way north to Palermo, and against orders from the high command, Patton's army had rolled into the city at around six p.m. on Monday the 22nd of July, just twelve days after the invasion was launched.

Now that the Allied Forces had all but driven the Axis Powers from his country Vizzini intended to make his play as the sole contender to regain control of the island country taken from him and his horde by Mussolini over the last twelve years. He would do this with the Yank's blessing by rallying his forces to the aid of the Americans and jockeying to get himself into a position of authority. The facts that he was anointed mayor and that he was a staunch anti-communist were no coincidence.

Nor was being made an acting Colonel in the U.S. Army.

His reputation was as fierce as the mystery shrouding the details of his life. However, stories abounded.

In a moment of weakness, in the days when Vizzini's men had cornered the market running the farmer's wheat to the faraway coastal mills by eliminating any burgeoning competition, Vizzini had taken in a youth as a favor to the young man's mother. Roberto was fourteen when he fell into this good fortune.

Paddy Kelly

With no children of his own the yet-to-be-Don taught the boy as he grew. Who to trust and why and who not to trust for the same reasons and the relationship blossomed until it was rumored that the young Roberto would one day inherit the throne.

By calling in favors Vizzini sponsored Roberto's wedding to the daughter of a wealthy farmer outside Messina later loaning money to the happy couple to place a down payment on their home.

Then, shortly after their second child, while in the Bay of Gela, tragedy struck. On a weekend outing with his family, the small boat Roberto had purchased suddenly exploded killing him, his wife and children.

It was only by sheer coincidence that Roberto's mother was visiting her sister in Naples when she was warned not to return home and thus lived well into old age.

The week before, Calò's informants had discovered the plot by Roberto and a rival Mafioso to assassinate Calò Vizzini and assume his wealth and territory.

For the rest of his life Vizzini never again took anyone under his wing.

In 1942, looking even further towards his financial future, Vizzini had already put in motion the wheels to set up a legitimate business venture. More or less. A small canning factory on the out skirts of Villalba which in reality was a cover.

From his first meeting with the Allied commanders in 1943 Vizzini came off as nothing more than a simple chicken farmer. Monty refused to believe, even for a minute that he was responsible for the deaths of over two hundred Nazis and their Italian collaborators. These deaths were apart from the dozen individuals he personally sent to meet their maker as a wild and carefree young man before the last war. In light of British high command's false belief there was even an organization known as the Mafia in existence, this is not surprising. Mafia for them, especially in Sicily, was a myth.

Before the war Vizzini became a *cancia*, an intermediary between the peasants who wanted their wheat milled into flour and the mills that were located near the coast. Mafiosi, who controlled the mills and access to them, tolerated no competition.

In the case of Villalba the mills were some 80 kilometers away. To get the grain safely to the mills over roads infested by bandits was no easy task. Unless Vizzini helped. To help the Americans get to Palermo through roads infested with merely Nazis, was a walk in the park.

In the wake of Colonel Polletti's appointment of Vizzini as Mayor of the strategically important Villalba, the rest of Civil Affairs followed his lead and appointed loyal Mafiosi as mayors in many of the towns and villages in western Sicily recaptured by the Allies.

Joe Russo, alias Mr. X, as chief of the Palermo office of the OSS, met with Vizzini and other Mafia bosses monthly all during the Italian occupation as evidenced by classified correspondence revealed after the war.

Now that it was apparent the Allies would invade the Italian mainland before Winter set in, the next step in the control of Sicily, as far as Don Calogero was concerned, was ready to be set in place. The establishment of an organized, operational Black Market to profit from the untold amounts of aid the Americans had promised and in fact had already begun to supply. Vizzini's extensive connections along with the fact that Colonel Polletti, who was once referred to by Charlie Luciano back in New York before the war, as "one of our very good friends", were as Vizzini saw it, the perfect combination to establish that market. Polletti however, would not only be the primary conduit of supply, but a largely unwitting pawn in the overall scheme of things.

Just as the partnership with the U.S. Navy in New York, initiated by the burning of the *T.L.S. Normandie*, once again breathed life into the New York families, the Allied occupation of Sicily and the restoration of democracy slowly reinstated the power of the Onorata Societa in Sicily. Now the two 'friends across the ocean' had only to wait for the inevitable end of the war to consummate their relationship. A relationship which would give birth and blossom into what the world would come to know as The International Drug Cartel.

There was just one missing ingredient. A functioning distribution network for the black market operation envisioned by Vizzini.

A second missing element in the equation was a connection inside AMGOT to ensure the means for distribution of the massive amounts of food, clothes and materials now arriving by the supply ships on a regular basis.

†

Café Capri
Francesco Barraca
Villalba, Sicily

The tiny café lay adjacent to the 17th Century church on the south side of the square and Vito Genovese parked the U.S. Army staff car around back so as not to attract undue notice.

"Lui é sulla sinistra." One of the two lupatra, shotgun totting bodyguards at the door informed Vito as he entered the abandoned café. He made his way through the warren of small tables and bentwood chairs to the open rear garden where Calò Vizzini sat off to the left, in a shaded corner. Two glasses of chilled limoncello SAT on the table in front of him.

"Did your Colonel get our little gift?" Vizzini greeted.

"It's the reason I responded to your request to

come Don Calogero. I like the way you do business. So does the colonel."

"I'm honored Signor Genovese." Don Carlo greeted without standing but offered him a chair and slid one of the aperitif glasses full of limoncello across the table. Regardless of what had been said of Don Calogero's reputation, he was business to the bone. Genovese on the other hand was a different animal.

It's reputed that Vito Genovese was once informed of one of his men cheating him for money. Rather than contract a hit he personally killed the cheater. Then shot the informer for ratting the guy out. Vito was what the New York cops called, 'A real piece of work'.

A standing requirement of membership in La Costa Nostra was to 'make your bones', that is to carry out a hit. Kill someone who it was deemed needed to be killed. You were only required to perform this service once for acceptance into the exclusive club.

Like a middle-aged couple's 20th wedding anniversary Vito seems to have felt compelled to renew his vows. Several times, nearly every year.

During the famous Castellammarese Wars between Joe Masseria and Salvatore Maranzano Vito helped to kill Masseria after which Luciano got his own family in which Vito was made Underboss.

Shortly thereafter, Luciano and Genovese cooked up a plan to snuff Maranzano and take over the entire New York operation, now organized into the

The Wolves of Calabria

five families. This was only fair seeing as how Maranzano had been planning to kill Luciano and Genovese. So when Salvatore sent word for Lucky and Vito to come to his office so his goons could carry out the dirty deed, he was greeted by a four man hit squad posing as tax men who quickly punched his ticket.

A year later Vito fell in love with his cousin Vernotico and wanted to marry her. Problem was she was already married. That would be a problem for any other man. But it wasn't a problem for Vito. By way of divorce her husband was found garroted to death. A short time later, despite being cousins, Vito and Anna were married.

A couple of years later an associate of Vito's, a fella named Ferdinand Boccia, proposed a scam whereby the two would cheat a rich gambler out of a significant amount of cash. The scam worked and when Boccia demanded his cut Vito did what he did best. He gave Boccia a cut. Across his throat.

But Vito was out of the picture by the time Lucky was framed and sent up the river by New York City D.A., Thomas Dewey, as part of a plot by Dewey to establish a bid to get the Presidential nomination, So Frankie Costello became the top dog.

That was in 1936 and by 1937 the NYPD were closing in on Genovese for Boccia's murder so Vito caught the next boat out of The City and sailed home to Naples.

Not one to sit around brooding about bad breaks, in the six years since he had returned to Italy Vito had been an industrious little boy. Shortly after arriving back home the war broke out and Vito, as well as many others, saw a golden opportunity to profit from the inevitable chaos which would soon ensue.

Bribing some Fascist party members Vito was put into the company of Galeazzo Ciano, Mussolini's son-in-law. Ciano had a nose candy problem and Vito was only too happy to supply the young man with all the cocaine he could snort.

It was only a matter of time before Genovese was in the company of Il Duce himself and in typical Mafia fashion became ingratiated to Mussolini by ordering a hit back in New York. The mark was Carlo Tresca, an anti-fascist newspaper man who constantly railed against Benito and his party. Vito arranged for the hit and, after Tresca was gunned down, practically around the corner from his FBI babysitters, Vito was given a medal from Mussolini for patriotic services.

In short, Vito Genovese and Don Carlo Vizzini were a match made in hell.

And so it was on a sunny afternoon, under the shade of an olive tree that Vizzini opened the negotiations.

"It is my understanding that you know the location of the Army storehouses for the grains the Americans have brought." Calò inquired. Vito smiled as he answered.

The Wolves of Calabria

"The storehouses for the grains, the storehouses for the baking supplies and the storehouses for the tons and tons of other dry goods the Americans have graciously brought for our people."

"I wonder how one might go about re-distributing such a large amount of food to the right people. For the right price of course." Don Carlo speculated. Vito smiled.

"The Americans, like the Germans before them are very well organized and have made provision for the transport of such large amounts of goods." Vito elaborated.

Vizzini twirled his half empty cordial glass.

"I wonder than how it might be possible to access such vehicles?" Vizzini pondered out loud.

"I happen to know from experience there is no shortage of U.S. soldiers who are willing to borrow, and even drive such vehicles to anywhere required. For the right price of course."

"Of course! No one can be expected to work for free. That would be unreasonable. And dishonest." Don Carlo sipped his limoncello. "Then too, there is the small matter of paperwork to allow such transport to flow freely to the right places."

Again Vito smiled. He reached into his jacket pocket and produced a large manila envelope and gently slid it across the table. Vizzini slowly picked it up and peaked inside.

"A small token of respect for allowing this meet Don Vizzini." The envelope was stuffed with more than a dozen U.S. Army/AMGOT green A-1 safe passes. Green A-1 signifying they were to be honored anywhere in the country.

Within the week caravans of military vehicles were fanned out over the island with all manner of pasta, grains and bread, canned vegetables, herbs and spices as well as all required official AMGOT papers for travel, all signed, sealed and delivered by the right people.

So that they might reach the right places.

For the right prices.

✝

CHAPTER VI

New York State District Court
Lower Manhattan, N.Y.C.

At about the same time Lord Churchill was launching his day off with his third drink Doc and Louie sat in the back of a New York court room as the jury were escorted back into the expansive, neoclassical room and took their seats in the box. The judge followed to his bench seconds later and as order was called for the room fell silent. Four more armed bailiffs crowded through the two massive oak doors in the rear and into the back of the court.

"Foreman, have the gentlemen of the jury reached a verdict?" The foreman stood to answer.

"We have your honor."

"Bailiff please bring me the verdict." The bailiff took the sealed verdict from the jury foreman and passed it to the judge who opened it and, without visible reaction, read it first to himself before reading to the court.

"The defendant will please rise." Two bailiffs moved in behind Rossini as he slowly rose. "Vincent Joseph Rossini you have been found guilty of murder in the first degree by a jury of your peers." Rossini, with his wrist still in a cast, compliments of Doc's blackjack, feigned a quick, short movement to the right and laughed to himself as the two bailiffs recoiled.

"By special request of the prosecutor and by agreement with the defendant's council, the court shall waive the waiting period before sentencing and proceed at this time. Defense council, does your client still agree to waive and proceed?" Rossini's council looked over at him as he stood next to him. Without flinching or making eye contact with his lawyer Rossini nodded once.

"Defense agrees your honor." The lawyer addressed the judge.

"Vincent Joseph Rossini, by the authority vested in me by the State of New York and for the murder of your wife, Anna May Rossini on or about September of last year, I sentence you to be remanded in custody and transported to Sing Sing State Penitentiary where you will be incarcerated until such time as a date can be fixed for your execution in the electric chair." A few gallery spectators, apparently relatives of Mrs. Rossini, applauded.

"Order in the court!" The double clap of the judge's gavel silenced them. "There being no further business I declare this case closed!"

"All rise!" The judge vacated the bench as the crowd stood. The two bailiffs cuffed Rossini's good hand to his waist chain.

In the rear of the room the bailiffs there held back the press who clambered to get photos as condemned man was led away. The crowd, including Doc and Louie, had to wait until the press were allowed out first before heading for the door. As they passed by the insurance adjuster who had harassed Doc throughout the case was seated in the row behind them, Doc stopped and made eye contact then smiled.

"Don't gloat McKeowen, you got lucky." Tumbolt quipped as Doc stopped and looked down on him.

"Always nice to know you care Oscar but never forget, my 'luck' saved your company exactly $42,300 in fraud money." Doc patted the cantankerous little man on the back and smiled more broadly. "I'll have my secretary get you that invoice first thing in the morning."

"Contract stipulates thirty days to pay McKeowen!" Tumbolt grumbled.

"We'll wait." Mancino added as he and Doc exited out into the hall where Doc turned to Louie.

"Insurance adjusters, they're like lawyers! One step above child molesters!"

"Beats divorce cases Doc though don't it? Pays a helluv'a lot better too!" Louie said. "Four thousand seven hundred somolians! Now them's the cases we need more often!" Louie declared as they made their way down the hall.

"As much as I agree Louie, these cases are only a fluke. We can't be counting on 'em."

"Yeah but, we're doin' alright now! We got a back log of three or four cases, we got a possible shot at another, albeit smaller, insurance case -"

"Whoa! Did you just use the word, 'albeit'?" Louie was worried and slightly embarrassed.

"What?! Ain't that right? Al-be-it?"

"No, it's right alright! You been readin' the dictionary again?"

"Everybody's got a right to improve themselves Doc!"

"I know, I know! I'm just sayin' –"

"Then don't be so condensating!"

"And he's back." They reached the elevators and Louie rang for the lift. "Louie, I been thinkin'-"

"Did it hurt?"

"Very funny. I been thinkin' about goin' away for a while."

"WHAT!? Why? Where?" Louie fired back in panic.

"Things between me and Nicky have been a bit shaky and with Dewey on the rampage all the crooks are keeping their heads down or relocating."

"Somethin' big'll break Doc!" Mancino pleaded.

"You kiddin' me? This town's as quiet as a mute rabbi in a synagogue on a Sunday afternoon! Besides, I'm getting' a little gun shy about have'n to come into court all the time and testify."

"Why for God's sake?"

"Ever since sitting through my father's case I began to realize, if a couple of cops could plot and successfully murder another cop, especially a senior cop, and get away clean, somethin's wrong. I mean, anybody with half a brain has to ask themselves, is this the best we can do for a system?"

"Maybe you're over thinkin' it Doc!"

"Maybe, but with five or six thousand executions so far in this country, ya gotta figure a percentage of those guys had to be innocent! That's not even taking into account the people who are doing life!"

"You growin' a conscience Doc?"

"Could be Louie."

"I still say you're over thinkin' it. You're just stressed from the work. But I know what ya mean. Imagine if Rossini didn't do it! That would be a real bitch!" Louie conjectured. Doc didn't answer. He pressed the button for the ground floor as they boarded the lift.

"Wouldn't exactly be a first for these courts." McKeowen snarked.

"Let's get some breakfast Doc. Never met any solution couldn't be found over a good plate of food!"

†

CHAPTER VII

Times Square
Midtown Manhattan
19:45, May 8th, 1945

Pepsi Cola, Chevrolet, Bond's Men's tailored clothing, Florsheim shoes and Dewar's Blended Scotch Whisky.

As if part of a strategically planned frontal assault of unabashed capitalism the extravaganza of garishly imposing neon signage flashed without pause as dusk settled over the world's most famous intersection presently flooded with a million or more revelers.

In the streets below the human tidal wave continued to undulate without ever actually changing location.

Moses Polokoff and Lieutenant Commander Charles Radcliff Haffenden, both in dark suits and ties, were primary players as well as the brains behind the anti-saboteur effort *Operation Underworld*, initiated three years earlier both now sat at a window seat in Sardi's on W44th two blocks north of Times Square.

Polokoff stared out the window at the melee the streets had become. Haffenden stared up at the running message on #1 Times Square which had first flashed across the time and temperature sign last night at 07:18 sharp. Being a Tuesday evening, combined with the ongoing gas rationing rush hour traffic was non-existent as the perpetually running sign flashed the most important war news the world had heard since 1939.

WAR IN EUROPE IS OVER! GERMANY QUITS!
KEITEL SIGNS DECLARATION OF PEACE!
WAR IS OVER!

Amid the drunken celebrations inside the swank restaurant a radio blasted away into the crowd as a small army of tenders worked insistently from behind the bar to quench the thirst of hundreds.

. . . 23:10, 7 May, 1945 we are told is the official time of
signing of the unconditional surrender of the Nazi forces!
Speaking from the White House President Truman claims this is his most memorable birthday and went on to say he dedicates this victory to his predecessor, FDR, who died less than a month ago! Truman is quoted as saying: "I only wished that Roosevelt had lived to witness this day."
Flags will remain at half-mast for the remainder of the official thirty day mourning period
From London it is reported that Churchill appeared on the Palace balcony to cheering . . .

The 8th of May would forever after be known as

V. E. Day, Victory in Europe.

By next morning not only had the world-wide celebrations not abated, they had gained momentum and would continue well into the next night.

Of course World War II wasn't completely over, there was still a minor skirmish in the South Pacific with those pesky Imperial Japanese forces, but now with the full might of the Allied Powers able to be focused on defeating the Japanese it was only a matter of time.

That and the Yanks were about to unleash the most devastating weapon in history, one which would simultaneously wipe out approximately 300,000 civilians and usher mankind into what would come to be called The Atomic Age.

"Maybe now we'll be able to get rid of these goddamn B ration cards!" Polokoff looked over at the commander.

More bodies pushed to the bar as the crowd in the room seemed to be expanding like a dry sponge in a slightly filled water pail.

"Look, I'm in a real bind here." Polokoff, cutting to the chase, pled. "The Parole Board refuses to even consider the fact Luciano helped you guys out unless they hear something from you or the Navy. Dewey won't even show up at the court hearing and, to tell you the truth I'm having a little bit of a struggle fending off the reporters. The rumors are flying and despite the fact we have an agreement, I don't know how much longer I can sit on this!" Haff's only response was to look down and flick a crumb from the table. "If it breaks in the papers that Naval Intelligence went to The Mob for help the shit's really gonna-"

"Kind'a ironic ain't it?" Haffenden smirked.

"Ain't what?"

"The fact that Dewey's the one that put him away and now, as Governor, he's the one's gotta sign the parole order."

"Put him away? Framed him to be more precise! And don't get too snarky Commander, the parole board can still approve his release over and above Dewey's rubber stamp."

"Well, he's had his eye on the White House for the last ten years, he's failed twice and this is probably his last shot at the whole enchilada. Ya can't really blame him for dragging his feet now can ya, Moses?"

"Let's don't forget the fact that Mr. Dewey has twice lost by a narrow margin and there's no reason to expect that won't happen again especially if this little episode comes to light. With the right spin on the right story released to the public at the right time, that little margin could split wide open." Polokoff threatened. "And don't think Dewey's not gonna use everything in his arsenal to see squash the whole story!" Haff twisted around, sat both arms on the table and faced the seasoned lawyer.

"What story would that be Moses?"

"The story that a certain presidential candidate while in the employ as NYC's Cracker Jack D.A., appearing to be stomping on crime was in actuality working hand-in-glove with a certain naval commander to cooperate with said organized crime figures. Including Public Enemy Number One."

"Are you trying to blackmail me Moses?" Haff casually asked.

"Technically that would be extortion."

"And who do you think's going to believe you?"

"Commander Haffenden, please, this is America! You just fought a world war to preserve our way of doing things. It doesn't matter who believes it, once the story is out there the investigations will begin. And that means that every snot-nosed politician with diaper rash will be lookin' to climb up your ass with a microscope in order to make it look like he gives a shit in order to boost his poll numbers."

Haffenden sat back and sized Polokoff up before standing and throwing back his drink.

"Well?" Polokoff pushed.

"Well what?"

"You said you'd help him out!"

"I said I'd go to bat for him! He's payin' **you** to get him out." Haffenden called over his shoulder as he headed for the door.

"I got the petition papers typed up and ready to file right here!" Moses pointed under the table to his briefcase. "You gonna keep your word?" Polokoff called after Haff who didn't respond.

Moses turned to stare out the window at the middle aged couple tightly hugging each other. More revelers squeezed in through the door as Haff pushed his way out.

The Wolves of Calabria

Moses stared out the picture window at the people staring up at the time and temp sign which continued announcing the news.

THE WAR IS OVER! GERMANY QUITS!
KEITEL SIGNS . . .

✝

The new corner office of M&M Investigations fronted the street on two sides on the fourth floor. It had two rooms and its own toilet. The outer space had been converted into a reception area complete with a secretary, desk, filing cabinet and new phone and intercom. The new girl Shirley, Nikki's former workmate from the Woolworth Building, even brought a couple of plants from home.

"Hey doll. What's shaking?" Doc greeted Shirley as he entered.

"One call this mornin' Mr. McKeowen . . ."

"Shirley, I thought the sign painter was scheduled to come in yesterday to letter the door?" He asked as he sifted through the mail.

"He was Mr. McKeowen, but Mr. Mancino told him come back next week."

"And do we have any clue as to my erratic partner's motivations for said action?" Doc was greeted with a shrug and a face as blank as a politician's promise.

"I'm not sure, sir. I think he said somethin' about

a new name for the firm."

"The Firm?"

"Uh huh."

"Now we're a firm?" Doc repeated to himself as he shuffled through the mail and made for his office. He stopped just short of the door. "Shirley, call me Doc will ya? Ya make me feel like I'm a hundred years old with that 'mister McKeowen' shit."

"I know. I just like sayin' it. **'Mista'.** McKeowen!' Sounds so official! **'Mista'**."

"Okay, I get it! You said there was a call?"

"Yeah, one. A Mrs. Worthington up on 64th and Third. She thinks a man is following her and wants us to send someone over ta check it out."

"Edna Worthington?"

'Uh huh."

"Wait till tomorrow morning, call her back. Tell her we caught the guy and turned him into the police and that she shouldn't have any more trouble. Bill her for one hour."

"Jees that was fast! How'd ya know where to find the guy? Who is he?"

"Me." Her pretty face scrunched up.

"I don't get it." Doc stepped back through his office door into the reception area.

"She hired us last year. Thought somebody was trying to break into her penthouse on the fortieth floor because the window was open when she came home one night. After hours of intensive investigation we determined that she left it open when she went out. Then, because we solved the case of the phantom burglar so quickly, just before Christmas she dropped by to see if we could trace her husband who apparently disappeared."

"Did you find him?!"

"Yeah, yeah we did. He's in Forrest Lawn."

"THE CEMETARY?! Oh my god! Was it murder?"

"No, it wasn't murder. He died thirty years ago. He was a passenger on the Titanic."

"Oh pa-lese! So the old broad's Looney Tunes?"

"Bats in the belfry. Elevator doesn't go all the way to the top, know-what-I-mean? Speakin' of which, call the Weinstein's office again about that damn elevator!" Doc entered his office, closed the door and took a seat behind his desk. Shirley yelled in after him.

"DOC, WHAT'S THE STATUS ON THE CHASE MANHATTAN FRAUD CASE?"

"SHIRL?" Doc yelled back from his office.

"YEAH?"

"WE PAID $59.95 FOR AN INTERCOM."

"SORRY!" She reached across her desk and flicked the toggle on her intercom box. "Mr. McKeowen, are you in?"

"Yes Miss Beckinworth. I'm in. What is it?"

"Mr. McKeowen, what's the status on The Chase Manhattan fraud case?"

"It's finished. Nearly"

"I'm gonna need the details to send the invoice and client report to the bank."

"Okay, grab your pad and come on in." He

directed.

"And Mr. McKeowen . . ."

"Yes Miss Beckinworth?"

"It's Mrs. Butler now." She corrected.

"Mrs. Butler?" Doc clicked her again.

"Yes Mr. McKeowen?"

"Grab your pad and come into my office please."

"Yes Doc. Also your ten o'clock is here, out in the hall. A Mrs. Dunlevy."

"What's she doing out in the hall?"

"Afraid somebody's gonna see here. So she says."

"Alright. Oh, and Mrs. Butler?"

"Yes Mr. McKeowen?"

"Find Mancino for me will ya?"

"Sure thing . . . Doc!" Just then Mancino came through the door. Shirley once again manned the intercom.

"Doc, I mean Mr. McKeowen, I located Mr. Mancino. Will I send him in?"

"Give me a minute Shirl. Send Mrs. Dunlevy in first. Tell Louie I'll be right with him." Doc returned his attention to the report he held in front of him, the preliminary report on the client, Mrs. Dunlevy from Staten Island.

A middle-aged housewife type draped in a plain beige kerchief, entered. She was short, stocky and clutching her purse as if it were about to be snatched at any moment. The nervous looking woman took the chair in front of Doc's desk. She suddenly popped back up and scurried to the office door, locked it and returned to her chair, clearly uncomfortable as she twitched in the seat.

"Mrs. Dunlevy, what is it we can do for you today?"

She bent forward leaning on the desk as she whispered over to him.

"My husbant! He vants I should be dead!"

"Exactly what makes you think your husband is trying to kill you?" Doc fought to keep a straight face.

"Who else would do this?!" She reached into her knapsack-sized purse and produced a can of chopped Italian tomatoes. Only the can had been opened, was wrapped in tin foil and was only a little over half full. The lid was still partially attached and the tomatoes were mixed with a fine whitish-grey powder which had partially coagulated. "Who else would put this poison in my food?" She insisted. Doc reached across the desk for the can and examined it.

"Well Mrs. Dunlevy, we don't know if those few little white flakes were actually poison and it's not strictly speaking, 'your food'. Have you eaten any of this?"

"You think I vould still be here if I ate?! Why you are asking?"

"In the report here you said you picked it off the shelf in the A&P. How could your husband possibly know that you would pick that exact can of tomatoes? I mean he's not likely to have poisoned all the tomatoes in the supermarket and he wasn't with you when you were shopping, was he?" She shied away like a guilty child and displayed obvious shame as she looked down and shrugged.

"No but . . . he could do it when I vasn't home sometime, you know! He could svitch da cans mit some other cans!"

"You did say here in your interview you thought he had no chance to get into the kitchen cabinet and switch cans, is that right?"

"I swear he don't even know where is the kitchen! We eat in the parlor all the time, so's he can listen to the ball games on the radio while we eat!" Doc further peeled back a flap of the foil tightly wrapped around the can. Doc examined the contents more closely.

"Tell ya what." Doc signaled her time was up as he stood, shook her hand and came around from behind his desk to walk her to the door.

"How about you let me send this to a lab and who knows? Maybe it will turn out to be talcum powder accidently spilled in at the factory's processing plant?" She hesitated in response. "At the very least you should have a good shot at a handsome lawsuit against the tomato company!"

"You think it's possible to have for me some money?"

"Depending on what we find, yes I think so."

"Okay, I guess." She inched towards the door as Doc unlocked and held it open. She stopped, looked around and drew in closer to him, whispering. "Whatever you do, say to him nothing! If he find

The Wolves of Calabria

out I think he try to kill me, he will murder me!"

"I promise, not a word. I'll call you next Tuesday, as soon as I hear from the lab."

"Thank you Mr. McKeowen." She glanced over at his Negro League baseball cap hanging on the King Edward coat rack near the door. "You play baseball Mr. McKeowen?"

"No ma'am, I'm a watcher. Mostly the Negro League."

"Oh my god that Satchel Raige!"

"Paige, Mrs. Dunlevy It's Satchel Paige."

"Yes, and I believe that it's purely a matter of time before they sign that nice black boy from Pasadena, what's his name?"

"Jackie Robinson Mrs. Dunlevy."

"Jackie? I was always thinking this is a name for a girl!"

"It's a nickname, his name is Jack Roosevelt. Meanwhile, try and relax. Act normal when you get back home. I'll be in touch."

Mrs. Dunlevy left. Doc put the can of tomatoes aside on the bookshelf and resumed his paperwork.

"Shirl, send Louie in."

"Yes Mr. McKeowen."

✝

Great Meadows Prison Yard
Sunday, February 10, 1946

By nine months after the war, angered by the

Navy's continued evasion and outright non-cooperation of their investigation as to whether or not Lucky Luciano had made a contribution to the war effort as his lawyer had claimed, the New York State Parole Board had unilaterally awarded Charlie Lucky parole. However, to avoid public scorn there was a hitch: immediate deportation to Italy.

"Hey Al! Get a load'a this!" The gate guard perched in his tower high above the prison walls called over to his partner as a black, chrome-plated, Chrysler limousine pulled up outside the steel gates of the prison.

"Three guesses who that's for, and the first two don't count." The second guard replied.

From their vantage point the guards continued to watch as the limo pulled up next to the granite wall beside the gate, as Meyer Lansky got out followed by Frankie Costello.

Both were dressed in dark silk suites and Costello carried a clothes bag and a pair of brown wingtips in a heavy zip locked bag. The two made their way through the gates with no resistance from the sentries, who knew why they were there. In fact, by way of every newspaper in the country the entire New York penal system knew why they were there. Lucky Luciano had made parole.

Due to his notoriety as a top hood it had been a bit of a fight for Polokoff but the mounting frustration of the N.Y. State Parole Board due to the fact that the Navy brass refused to cooperate with them and divulge just how much Luciano had contributed to the war effort, led them to convert his remaining years to parole.

Once officially granted parole the now Governor of New York, Thomas E. Dewey, the very man that took credit for his conviction so as to advance his own career, was compelled to sign Luciano's release papers.

An hour later, dressed in his new, charcoal grey suit and brown shoes, Lucky escorted by Meyer Lansky, walked through the prison gates a free man. Sort of.

Even though the board granted him parole, they were ever mindful of their own political careers ergo the board, the circuit court judge and the Governor attached severe restrictions aside from the one big restriction they had already made clear, to get the hell out of the country now! Among the potpourri of conditions set was to get out, go straight to the boat under state supervision, stay on board until it sails, also under state supervision, never come back and if you are caught coming back or trying to come back, serve the last fifty years of your sentence.

Ironically it was New York D.A. Hogan, the Third Naval District Commander and Prison Commissioner Lyons who were directly responsible for Lucky's favorable parole decision. Despite the fact he had up to fifty years remaining on his greatly inflated sentence, he was walking through the prison gates to freedom due largely to the aforementioned bureaucrats' refusal to cooperate with the State Parole Board.

Despite his wartime rhetoric of how vital it was for the Mafia to work with the Navy Hogan, as most D.A.'s do, had political ambitions and to appear to have associated with a gangster of Luciano's magnitude, particularly after his very own office touting the gangster as Public Enemy No.1 for so many years, would stop Hogan's political ambitions dead in their tracks.

Hogan, who in 1942 went hat-in-hand to Luciano, now tried to distance himself from any association with The Mob.

So instead of being told that Lucky had or had not made a significant contribution to his adopted land, the parole board investigators were essentially told it was highly classified.

So, by way of showing their authority, and the fact that they had no sense of humor about being snubbed, they set Lucky free. This of course brought into serious question why he was given thirty to fifty years without chance of parole, on circumstantial evidence for pandering a crime that the statute books mandated a maximum of ten.

Not for the first, nor the last, time the U.S. political-legal system had been made a joke of.

"Do you, Charles Luciano, understand and concur with all the conditions of your parole as set forth by the New York State Parole Commission?" The tall, lanky parole administrator, one of the two who would accompany Lucky down to New York City and keep him under close eye until Monday morning, spoke mechanically as he filled out yet another document for Lucky to sign. Lucky smiled at him. "Mr. Luciano, do you understand all the conditions of your parole?"

"Sure, I understand. You want me to take my boys and go home."

"Sign here please." Lucky signed and without waiting for his copy of the papers, walked out of the office and out into the hall where Lansky and Frankie Costello rose from the bench to escort him to his limo. The two administrators followed the new four door, black limousine in their grey, government issued, 1934 Ford.

"So how long you got?" Lansky asked Lucky in the limo as they made their way down the mountain road and onto the four lane black top which led into The City.

"Forty-eight hours. Then they get'a watch me leave."

"These rat bastards gonna be with us until Monday morning?" Costello asked.

"They might hang around but sometime tomorrow they'll take a powder and some INS guys'll show up. They're the one's got'a put me on the boat."

"The boat? Why don't you fly Boss? You could go first class! We could'a brought you a ticket!" Frankie asked.

"They're the ones kicking me out. Let them pay for the ticket!" Lucky looked out the window at the world he hadn't seen for six years. Smirking he added, "I'll take a plane when I come back." An hour later they were approaching the Brooklyn shipyards.

Across the Hudson from where the last of *Normandie's* charred hull was still being cut apart to be sold as scrap, the eloquent but ageing luxury liner, *Laura Keene* was moored in a berth on the Brooklyn side and scheduled to depart for Rome the next morning.

Lucky's limo pulled up in the sprawling dock-side lot adjacent to the amidships gangplank.

From stem to stern the Keene was surrounded by longshoremen brandishing various tools of the trade such as bailing hooks, "J" bars and skiff hooks. They stood shoulder to shoulder behind a rank of U.S. Coast Guard sailors armed with white Billy clubs. As an added precaution, Mayor LaGuardia had ordered the pier canvassed with city cops. That day Lucky would have more protection than any American president before or since.

The only people, without exception, who were permitted to board the beautiful vessel via her single gang plank, were those who the Chief Stevedore decided were legitimate ticket holders. For fear of trouble, the crew members had been ordered to report aboard the night before.

"Fuckin' Sicily! What a shit hole! I'll be back here before the end of the year. Have everything ready." Lucky directed his comments to Meyer, sitting directly across from him in the back of the black Chrysler as they pulled off Bank Street and onto the pier.

"Whatever happened with that treasury agent, wanted to get in on the ground floor with us?" He asked.

"He was gonna come up from D.C. so we could see what he had. Never showed for the meet." Meyer shrugged.

"Fuck him. There's plenty'a others where he came from. Keep things ready, you'll hear from me in a coupl'a months."

"Okay."

"I got an idea in the back'a my mind. Something I dreamt up while I was in stir."

As the limousine turned off Bank Street and drove onto the dock, past the "No Vehicles Beyond This Point" sign, the longshoremen forcibly parted the mob of reporters and rubberneckers.

Lansky was compelled to yell over the din of the crowd as they got out of the car.

"Hey Charlie!"

"Yeah?"

"How does it feel to be a star?"

With his topcoat draped over his shoulders he made his way to the gang plank escorted by six of Lanza's union men while ten federal officials, representatives of various agencies, rushed to meet him but were not allowed to come in contact. As soon as his foot touched the deck of the *Laura Keene*, the Feds considered their duty done, and disappeared back into the crowd.

Despite the fact his deportation was ordered by

the U.S. government, Lucky was determined to disallow them to play a part in the actual execution of the order.

Although he had no idea what he would have done had trouble broken out, the Captain of the liner considered it his duty to be there when his famous guest came aboard and so symbolically stood by at the top of the gang plank.

The reporters were unable to accept the fact that they were not going to get to grill Lucky and so pushed forward and shouted questions at him, even after he was out of sight. When this tactic failed, they turned back on the government bureaucrat standing to the side of the ramp, on the inside of the human cordon.

"We were told by Immigration there was gonna be a press conference with Lucky!" One reporter yelled out, receiving jeers of support from his colleagues crowded around the entrance, unable to cross the triple picket line. Formal notices had been sent to the press by the Immigration and Naturalization Service that Lucky would give a press conference. Unfortunately, no one at INS told Lucky.

The lanky INS officer now stood erect on the gang plank, behind the army of longshoremen, and adjusted his glasses as he responded to the agitated demands of the press corps.

"I'll see what I can do." He said, in an attempt to placate the angry mob. He made his way up the ramp and vanished into the passageways of the ship only to return a few minutes later, physically escorted by two of Lucky's torpedoes back to the top of the gang plank.

"Ahh . . . Mr. Luciano has changed his mind and declines to speak to the press at this time."

"Give us a break! Your office released an official memo yesterday saying he would talk to us if we showed up!"

"This wouldn't be a political ploy to show us what a good job you're doin' after we criticised you for lack of criminal deportations during the war, would it, Francis?" One reporter shouted out.

"Well? How 'bout it, ya schmuck!" Another yelled. The government official made a lame attempt at self-defence.

"Mr. Luciano just wants to relax in his modest accommodations and is looking forward to seeing his homeland."

Finally the reporters had little alternative but to mill around the dock and speculate.

"What the hell is all the mystery? It ain't like his deportation wasn't in the papers for the last two weeks!" One of the frustrated pressmen said to a colleague. Being pushed aside to make way for a second, third and fourth limousine, the second reporter responded as they watched a New York District Court judge, a well-known former police official and several prominent businessmen get out of the cars.

"There's your answer!" Impeccably dressed and bearing fruit baskets, boxes of expensive clothes and other gifts, the newly arrived entourage approached the gang plank brandishing Longshoreman's Union identity cards.

"Dock workers must'a gotten raise!" The second reporter commented as the officials were permitted to board the ship.

"Yeah, looks like they're payin' damn good these days!"

The first reporter, determined not to accept the chain of events, made his way to the gang plank entrance, only to be stopped with a hand to the chest by a pugnacious stevedore.

"Sorry, dock woirkers and union members only! Dis here's a dangerous place. You could axsa'dentaly trip over a deck fixcha' or something. Next ding ya know, dar's lawsuits and what not!"

The reporter looked to the two NYPD uniforms who were standing a short distance away, watching the scene.

"Well? How 'bout it?!" He approached and addressed them in a frustrated tone. The two cops smiled at each other, and shrugged to the reporter before resuming their conversation about the Yankee's victory over the Dodgers.

Lucky's deportation was in reality a *bon voyage* party in the grandest sense. Anyone entering the first class cabin was greeted with visions of elaborate, oversized fruit baskets, a room full of dignitaries, canapés and a glass of Dom Perignon served by a ship's steward standing behind the four foot long, chocolate layer cake in the shape of a luxury liner.

No one showed up without an envelope, a small package, or in Frankie Costello's case, a valise full of cash to pay homage to the god of organised crime who, in 1907 arrived at this very same port, riding in steerage on a freighter which was one step above a garbage scow. Now, with his abject poverty and squalor a distant memory, Lucky Luciano was being sent off with the honors of a prince.

A prince of thieves.

☨

Lower Manhattan
14th Street West of McDougal

It was just before noon and Doc was heading back to his office above Harry's Front Page News on Christopher Street. As he rounded the corner on McDougal he came on a small crowd staring up at the rooftop of a Brownstone walk-up. There was a black Plymouth police unit from the 1st Precinct pulled halfway up on the sidewalk with both doors flung open and two uniforms in between the small crowd and the eight story building. Doc recognized one of the cops from his old beat.

"Hey Speedy."

"Hey McKeowen! How's tricks?" They both looked up at the roof as they spoke.

"Same old same old. What's the buzz, ya got a

jumper?" Doc asked.

"We just got here but near as we can figure from some of the witnesses some young guy's gone out, got himself on a good drunk and now's threating to do a Clark Kent." They looked back up together and could see a pair of legs dangling over the roof ledge where somebody was sitting but there was no discernable movement.

"Any demands?"

"Not so far."

"Did ja call anybody?"

"Somebody recommended a local shrink, lives two doors over on the ground floor. He came out, took one look at the situation and passed. Said he's a doctor not a high wire artist."

"Huh, real humanitarian ain't he?!" Doc smirked.

"We're waitin' on another one from Uptown." Doc looked up again and the guy seemed to be moving.

As they spoke Speedy's partner, a hard looking son-of-a-bitch type drifted over, shrugged and added his two cents.

"Probably just looking for sympathy." Doc glanced over at the clichéd tough-guy cop who continued spewing. "If he was serious he'd done it by now. Personally I think all that dream analyzing stuff they been writing about in the papers is a bunch of horseshit." He babbled.

"Sure it is. That's why people pay twenty-five bucks an hour to pour their hearts out to those guys." Doc informed. Speedy was gob smacked.

"You serious McKeowen?! Twenty-five bucks an hour?!"

"Serious as a double dose of the clap, Speedy. How about him? He look serious to you?" Doc nodded up to the roof.

Speedy's partner continued his professional analysis.

"Would you be serious if you came home from the late shift one morning and found your old lady with her bags packed givin' a blowjob to the grocery store delivery boy?"

"My ex-wife? Wouldn't even be surprised." Doc looked up again. "Speedy, you still smoking Camels?"

"Yeah, why?"

"Gimme me your butts."

"Since when you smoke?"

"Since just now. Gimme me your butts." Doc held out his hand and Speedy handed over an open pack of Camels. Tough Guy Cop spouted some more background information.

"Got the story from one'a the bystanders. Says half hour ago the guy was sittin' here on the curb spillin' his guts out."

Just then a second black Plymouth, also from the 1st Precinct, came around the corner.

"Better keep a low profile Doc, I think that's Sully's unit!" Speedy warned.

Assistant Chief Sullivan was a longtime nemesis of Doc's and his father's old precinct house boss.

He got himself demoted to Assistant Chief after getting caught with another cop's wife at a sleazy motel over in Jersey one Saturday night after a PBA function. Sully was one of the cops McKeowen suspected had something to do with his father's murder.

"Still pissed off about that counterfeiting case is he?" Doc probed.

"Yeah, claims ya broke the law by not bringing it to the attention of the proper authorities."

"Meaning him."

"Meaning him."

"Tell ya the truth Speedy, I would have gone to him except . . ." McKeowen walked over to the steps of the double wide, red brick porch leading up into the Brownstone. "I didn't want the bad guys to get away."

"Hey Mac, where the hell you going?!"

"My girl's away. I'm horny. Gonna have a chat with this guy see if his old lady's still at home."

"You're a sick bastard McKeowen!"

"So I been told."

The pugnacious Sullivan barged through the now swelling crowd and made his way up to Speedy and Tough Guy.

"Kaminski, who the hell was that just went in that building?!"

"I-dun-know Chief." He shrugged. "Some guy lives up on four. Says he left the coffee pot on. Afraid it was gonna start a fire."

"Oh, okay. I guess that's alright. Get these

rubberneckers back! That asshole decides to do a Peter Pan off that roof we'll have several D.O.A.'s to write up instead'a one!"

"Already on it Chief."

As the cops cordoned off the area around the façade of the tenement Doc rounded the landing on the seventh floor and was compelled to take a breather.

"Christ, I don't remember being this outta shape!" He panted as he caught his breath and pushed on. "Good thing I was a cop. I'd been a shitty fire fighter!"

Out on the roof it was cold with a slight wind but tolerable and Doc was moved to put the fur collar of his bomber jacket up as he made his way around some vent pipes and across the frozen tar. The sun was bright behind the jumper and McKeowen had to shield his eyes as he approached the figure who was now standing upright on the granite ledge. He could make out a tall, strapping figure of a man as he drew to within fifteen feet or so.

Having no clue who or what he was dealing with he thought it better to keep some distance.

The jumper heard his footsteps but hardly flinched, he just balanced on the ledge and stared out across the residential panorama of the city in front of him.

"Nice day if it don't rain, huh?" McKeowen called over. No reaction. "You got a name?" He probed.

"What the fuck's it matter to you asshole?!" The

jumper barked back without turning.

Huh! Definitely a New Yorker. Doc thought as he noted by the back of the man's head he was black and his dialect was distinctly New York.

"It don't matter to me one way or the other but, I was just wonderin'. Must be a bitch signin' checks with that name!"

"Never knew no cop was a comedian!"

"I ain't no comedian brother and I damn sure ain't no cop! You can take that to the bank!"

A siren sounded in the distance and the jumper turned his head. Doc caught his first good glimpse of the jumper.

It was Leon, Redbone's nephew who had helped Doc spy on a Meyer Lansky meeting with the D.A. about a year ago at an Uptown restaurant, near Woolworth's where Leon was a bus boy. Strangely, Leon didn't seem to recognize Doc.

"Leon, it's me McKeowen." He slowly turned, and with glassed over eyes Leon stared back at Doc. Still no recognition registered. He slowly turned back away.

"Sorry, all you white people look the same to me."

"I paid you to eavesdrop on some guys last year."

"That make us war buddies or somethin'? Fuck off."

This guy's in a bad way! Doc thought.

"You want a cigarette?" He brandished the pack towards Leon. There was still no reaction. "You owe it to Redbone to keep your shit together man!"

The Wolves of Calabria

At the mention of the name 'Redbone' there seemed to be some recognition. "He's good people and you know it! He wants to see you succeed, make something of yourself!" Do pleaded.

Leon turned almost all the way around, a crazed look across his face.

"I'm doing this for him." Just as Doc began to slowly approach, Leon closed his eyes and went limp. His listless body crumpled over the concrete ledge and vanished.

In the blink of an eye young Leon became a statistic.

Out of reflex Doc dashed to the ledge and looked over. The cops looked up to see McKeowen peering down at them.

It seemed forever before the sound of the dull whack reached back up to the roof, followed by an interminable pause before the inevitable barrage of screams and wails. Doc saw the mangled Leon sprawled across the walk, one deformed leg on the granite steps, a pool of blood slowly forming around his skull.

Doc pushed up off the ledge, walked back across the roof into the stairwell and lowered the collar of his jacket. Once back inside he sank against the landing wall at the top of the stairs, plopped down and stared.

It took Doc nearly half an hour to get back downstairs and when he did he was in no humor to put up with Sullivan who, upon seeing him come out of the doorway, immediately shuffled over to him and attacked.

"I ought'a run your ass in McKeowen!" Doc brushed past him without a word and headed down the block. Sully, in a lame effort to assert what little authority he didn't have, scurried around in front of McKeowen. "I'm talkin' to you McKeowen!" Doc had had it. Using his body as a plow he backed Sullivan's pudgy frame up against a parked van.

"Fuck you! What'a ya gonna arrest me for Sullivan?! Doin' **your** job, ya limp dick!"

He let Sullivan fumble for his service revolver and as the cop raised it Doc slapped it out of his hand and Sully watched it skate across the sidewalk to rest under the parked ambulance which had just arrived. Sullivan turned white and stared. Doc glanced back at the mangled black athlete's body in the pool of blood and brains spattered across the sidewalk.

"Quit gawkin' at me and get a fucking blanket and cover him up will ya!?" Doc said before casually walking away. Sullivan dashed to retrieve his weapon then back over towards the scene and the other two uniforms.

"You two saw that! Both of youse are eyewitnesses! He assaulted an officer of the law!!" Kaminski, who had turned away as soon as he saw Sully coming towards him, feigned looking in the Chief's direction for the first time.

"What's that Chief?" Speedy innocently asked.

"I SAID, YOUSE ARE BOTH WITNESSES! YOU SEEN HIM ATTACK ME!"

"Sorry Chief! I was helpin' keep the people back. I didn't see nuthin! Hey Jonsey, you see what happened over there wit that guy and the Chief?"

"Sorry Kaminski, I was taking a statement." He returned to the attractive thirty-something blond he was chatting up.

"Tits on a fuckin' bull!" Doc mumbled as he walked off.

By the time he reached the corner Doc decided it was time for a Baptism.

✝

Paddy Kelly

CHAPTER VIII

**Harry's Front Page News
1929 Christopher Street
Greenwich Village**

Guarding the southern edge of The West Village, Christopher Street runs nearly eight blocks perpendicular to the Hudson. 'Nearly' perpendicular because, like most things in New York City, nothing is straight forward.

Number 1929 is a late 19th Century, six storey office building boasting all the period blandishments of a time when architectural craftsmanship in the City was at its height and the word 'craftsman' meant 'skilled artisan'.

The front third of the formally spacious lobby had been taken over and rented out as commercial shop space during the Great Depression and was now occupied by *Harry's Front Page News*.

Inside, straddling the single door entrance of the corner news agent a pair of tall, black wire twirly racks stood sentry, each sparsely stocked with postcards. Mostly pre-war scenes of the Empire State Building, the Brooklyn Bridge and for some reason the Lincoln and Holland Tunnels.

Two gondola shelving units ran the length of the place leaving a mere few feet to the counter in the rear of the place which sat perpendicular to the shelving.

The Wolves of Calabria

Stocked with an odd selection of merchandise, the slightly dusty, lazily arranged tins of beans, powdered eggs and toiletries were not the usual fare expected to be found in what New Yorkers commonly called a 'candy store'.

On either side the walls were adorned with an array of magazines, out-of-town newspapers, a selection of paperback books and a handful of left over cellophane bags of cheap, children's toys, mostly cast lead soldiers and mini-replicas of cars and trucks from the First War era.

In the back a second glassed door exit sat off to the right of the counter which led out into the hallway of what was now the lobby with a single caged elevator, the stairs and one apartment reserved for the superintendent of the building.

Harry, a former art student at Parsons, was old by some standards, not so old by others but the fact that he fought in the Great War as a young man where he lost a leg while serving as an artillery man when the Germans over ran his position attested to the fact that he was at least past his prime.

Following military service Harry again went to work for the federal government establishing a successful career as a federal convict when he was busted in a counterfeiting ring. Harry's artistic talents in the years before his arrest enabled him to gather an appreciable little nest egg before moving into Sing Sing and following his release this secret nest egg was used to purchase the abandoned Christopher Street shop which he then transformed into *The Front Page*.

The six foot long counter at the back of the store was tightly stacked with a collection of a dozen or more brands of chewing gum, various chocolate bars, pastilles, lozenges and gum drops. Shelves below the counter were laden with all the latest dailies and with rationing now lifted, cigarettes and tobacco were plentiful compelling the chocolate bars and chewing gum to fight for space.

Harry had owned the small news and magazine shop since the year after Prohibition was declared and thanks to consecutive administrations, first Wilson then Harding, refusing to pay the money they promised the men of the Bonus Expeditionary Force for fighting for their country in the First War, most other vets of the time were unemployed and starving.

Not Harry who, in the Fall of '21 when released from prison, mysteriously came up with a wad of cash to buy the store outright. It was only a few years ago during the crooked Treasury Agent case that his expertise in the field of funny money came to light and eventually it was Harry's expertise that allowed Doc to nail the crooked Treasury agents.

From somewhere on the small, crowded premises, a radio softly but constantly wafted orchestra music into the air.

Well hidden in the dense foliage of sweets, cigarettes and cigars was a space just narrow enough to transact trade through.

From 06:30 each morning until closing,

whenever that happened to be, it was behind this chink in the wall that Harry The Leg could be found, his wooden prosthetic propped up in the corner behind him.

This evening as Doc banged through the front door, Harry sat on his usual high backed stool behind the shelves of cigarettes and boxes of budget cigars, his leg in his lap, a can of *3-In-1 Oil* in hand.

"Hey Doc."

"Hey Harry."

"Doc, you thought about making that girl of yours legitimate yet?" Harry quipped tapping his one good foot to Benny Goodman. Doc stormed to the back and took a paper from below the counter. He tossed a nickel on the well-worn, rubber mat stuck to the counter by years of grime before snapping back.

"Ain't it about time you thought about retirement, Harry?" Doc shot back as he moved through the store without pause. "What'a you, 90 pushin' 100 by now?"

"That's hilarious Doc! You should write for Jack Benny. Only problem is he's funny." The grey haired, thin Harry returned volley without looking up as he tended to the mechanical knee joint on his leg.

"You seen Redbone Harry?"

"Not since this mornin' Doc." Harry failed to pick up on Doc's sour mood until he yelled back over his shoulder as he pushed through the rear door into the lobby.

"BAPTISM TONIGHT AT SIX. BE THERE!"

"Aye aye, sir!" Harry gaily mocked a sharp salute, but Doc was gone.

Baptisms were for special occasions. Special occasions being when Doc was in a bad mood.

The side door off to the right of the counter connected *Harry's Front Page* with the office building's small lobby and as he moved into the hallway and over towards Redbone's door, the building's super and maintenance man, Doc zeroed in on the lead story from the front page of the *Daily News.*

MACARTHUR TO IMPOSE DEMOCRACY
ON JAPS!

With Nikki and Doris's consultation, Doc and Louie had spent their windfall from the Treasury case wisely.

Due to the spectacular ending of the case and the fact that the government was in no hurry to garner the negative publicity the Press would no doubt have assigned the story, the authorities never looked close enough to find out that the money lost on the Staten Island Ferry that night a few years back was in fact the phony money and therefore had never discovered that Ira Birnbaum, the loyal Treasury employee, had left Doc and his cohorts all the actual cash following his murder.

Sitting on it for several months so as not to raise eyebrows, the four principles sat around playing

The Wolves of Calabria

Gin Rummy for the better part of 24 hours one Saturday night formulating a business plan as to what to do with the $167,000 bequeathed them by the little old Jewish man, Birnbaum, a guy they never really knew but later figured out had a pretty good sense of irony.

Especially after he left them the rough equivalent of four to five year's salary each.

After the first four or five hours of cards and casual brainstorming, Irish whiskey was seen as a necessary adjunct. At least by Doc and Louie. Twenty-five minutes later Doris and Nikki vanished and reappeared with a bottle of *Cordon Negro*.

Open a bar with the money? Although a tavern was a good pipeline to filter cash through Doc didn't want to be around that much booze all the time so no, a drinking establishment was quickly ruled out.

A restaurant? Italian naturally. Maybe Downtown off a side street somewhere, complete with red & white checkered tablecloths, half melted candles in wine bottles and a black mimeographed picture of George Raft on the wall behind the cash register?

Tempting, but Louie reckoned he'd weigh 400 pounds inside of a month and Doc was never that much of a gourmet.

Scratch 'Mancino's Cucino Italiano'.

By about 14 hours into the card game, Doris and Nikki figured they'd both be able to think a lot more clearly and make more of a contribution to the mission if another bottle of *Cordon Negro* could somehow be located. It was and they did.

A beauty salon maybe? Something the two girls could run while the guys kept up the agency?

However about halfway through that bottle, both women realized that, short of what they had read in women's magazines, applying moisturizer or putting cucumber slices on their eyes, neither knew anything about beauty treatments. Plus neither had any interest in dealing with busy bodies all day.

So beauty salon? Probably not.

Eventually the most logical conclusion was arrived at: sink the cash back into the existing business. The theory that the P.I. game couldn't help but pick up on the heels of all the P.R. the papers afforded the Treasury story, was a sound one. By its second year business was good and now, a few years later, the guys were turning cases away.

Harry's few short years of experience on the other side of the fence in prison were of no small contribution in imagining ways to launder the considerable sum of cash.

In spite of the post-war economy showing signs of slowing, work coming into the agency had been very steady for the last year. The downside, despite a variety of clients, was the spike in infidelity cases, which Doc hated. With the sudden increase of men signing up and being shipped out during the war came a corresponding increase in the non-availability of male companionship for the ladies left behind. This was the period when the myth that mostly men cheat was put to rest.

Although Doc wasn't thrilled with these cases,

The Wolves of Calabria

Louie, having developed an instinct for behavioral patterns in such cases, was in his glory with all the work and had, in the last year become something of an expert.

Also the cases were short, court appearances were rare and the money was good.

Additionally, Doc and Louie both kicked in a couple of hundred each, Doris, Nikki and Kate volunteered a couple of weekends and a month later Redbone, the ageing, black janitor/handyman for the building, was able to move out of his ratty one room place up on 127th Street and move into his near-brand new, two bedroom apartment on the ground floor, behind *Harry's Front Page* just off the lobby. Now 79 years old Redbone didn't have to slog through cold winter days and nights to catch a bus to get to work. He just had to step through his front door.

Another part of the new business plan called for the guys to negotiate a new lease, better rental terms and move upstairs to the vacant double office on the fourth floor. The plan also called for Weinstein & Weinstein, the landlords, to fix the elevator.

After popping his head into the refurbished, ground floor apartment to check in on Redbone, who wasn't home, and with the *Late Edition* tucked under his arm Doc rang for the elevator. Several minutes passed and no elevator. Doc pushed the button several more times and heard the car door close up on four then begin to descend. He heard a bang, looked up through the open elevator cage and could see the car stuck between two and three.

Apparently Weinstein & Weinstein didn't get the last memo.

Resignedly he climbed the recently painted, ornate metal staircase to the fourth floor and headed to the last door on the left off the landing which was now where he and Louie called home.

Despite the fact that they had moved in months ago, there still had been no decision on a title for the partnership. Discussions had been ongoing but it was only last week at a Yankees' game they agreed on 'M&M Investigations'.

Doc had asked Louie to handle the signage for the door and windows and his aggravation was again stirred when he pushed through the front door and noted there was still no name painted on the frosted glass panel.

It had been a while since Doc, Louie, Redbone and Harry had held a Baptism, Doc's code word for an all-night drinking session.

Over the years the arrangements had fallen into a routine. Doc would set a time, usually around six p.m., send Louie around the corner for a couple of bottles of Jameson Whiskey and, meeting up in the office, the four of them would launch off around half six.

In spite of this being the third or fourth Baptism in the last year, they had yet to solve any of the world's problems.

Although it had only been several hours since Leon's suicide Doc hadn't seen Redbone around the

The Wolves of Calabria

Christopher Street building all day.

As Doc arrived at Harry's that evening Leon's body was being held in the morgue under a John Doe pending notification of next of kin. Redbone was Leon's next of kin.

Louie was on his way over from home where he had secured permission from his wife Doris to participate in the evening's ritual.

Since he had met Nikki, McKeowen had all but stopped the whiskey benders he had become prone to after his wife bailed on him six years ago with a well-to-do lawyer. But the general consensus between Louie and Doc was that this dark event, Leon's untimely death, called for a time out. Besides, Doc figured it was a good idea to get a few drinks into Redbone before he broke the news about his only living relative.

After Redbone, now looking at the upside of eighty, lost his wife to cancer almost two years ago, the old man had no other living relatives. Leon was not only Redbone's ward, but also his future hope and reason for living.

It was half past six when Harry made it upstairs and entered the office.

"Doc!" Harry yelled as he let himself into the office.

"In here old man. Grab a chair be right out." Doc answered through the reception intercom.

Harry froze in his tracks and perused the room.

"Doc?!" Harry said to the ceiling.

"What!?" This time the answer seemed to come

from Shirley's desk. Harry slowly backed away from the possessed piece of furniture then jumped as Doc came through the door of his office.

"Harry, you goin' deaf or what?"

"How in Tarnation you do that?!"

"Do what?!"

"Be in there and . . . ferget it!" Harry walked clear of the desk as he grabbed a chair from the few against the wall intended for clients and dragged it to the middle of the room and sat.

"Where's Mancino?" He asked.

"On his way." Doc did likewise and then sat a bottle and four glasses on the reception desk.

Thirty minutes later Louie, Doc and Harry, who was two shots ahead, were well dug into the first bottle, through their third round and starting on their fourth.

Conversation had been minimal to non-existent as the three patiently waited to reach the right altitude and log onto the right radio frequency.

"Ja see where they're debatin' about havin'a a woman judge in city hall?" Louie kick started the conversation waiting to evolve into a debate.

"Won't make no difference. Women, men . . . they're all politicians. Sell their mother for a vote." Doc threw in his two cents.

"You think men and women are all the same?" Harry asked with just enough sincerity to matter..

"As lawyers, politicians and judges, yeah."

"Women can't never be men and men can't never be women!" Louie firmly reaffirmed.

"Maybe not, but there's a coupl'a guys over on MacDougal Street that come pretty close to bein' women, and it ain't from lack of tryin'!" Harry laughed.

"I'll tell ya why they can't ever be the same." Mancino challenged. "Women got no idea what it's like walkin' around with a 458 cubic inch, eight cylinder, Ferrari engine between ya legs 24-7, ya know what I mean?"

"I used ta, but not no more brother, not no more!" Harry solemnly replied.

"Louie, you ever worry about your relationship with Doris?" Doc asked. "They say a man's not a complete person until he's married."

"I don't know about complete Doc. Finished maybe!"

"No, seriously."

"Doc, I married Doris for her looks. Not the ones she's been giving me lately . . . but-"

"I'm serious. You tell Doris everything? I mean, you ever tell her half-truths?"

"Nope. No point."

"Why not?"

"Once the trust goes out of the relationship, it's no fun lying to 'em anymore." Mancino explained. Doc having unsuccessfully broached this ground before with Louie, surrendered his efforts.

"That's what I admire about you two." Doc added. "Open, honest relationship."

"It is what it is Doc and getting' stressed about ain't gonn'a change nuthin'!"

"Amen to that." Harry added downing his shot. In the ever spiraling encroachment of a drunken stupor, Doc tenaciously clung to his train of thought.

"How can you be so sure all the time that Doris' eyes never go wanderin?" He asked.

"I can't! But I don't know for sure the little light goes out when I close the fridge door either. Some things ya got'a take on faith, ya know?"

"Amen to that." Harry announced with another shot. Everybody joined in.

They once again fell into the downward slope of the drinking rhythm by sitting silent while the latest dose of booze permeated their livers. Finally it was Louie who again broke the silence.

"Read in the papers today where Dewey hit a triple header!" Louie offered.

"Yeah, how's that?" Doc queried.

"Mendy Weiss, Louie Capone, and Louie Lepke all got the chair. Within minutes of each other!"

"Huh! How about that. Strange thing ain't it, Louie?" Doc taunted.

"What's that Doc?"

"Louie Lepke. Louie Capone, Louie Mancino . . ."

"Fuck you Doc! You know I'm only Italian in name! I'm as American as the rest'a you guys!"

Harry shifted in his seat before he cut in.

"Mancino! What'a you got against being Eye-talian anyways? Yer always bitchin' about it. I don't get it. Eye-talians is great people. Great wine, food. Women that'd give dead man a hard on!"

"Hard enough to crack walnuts!" Doc added.

"Harder than Chinese arithmetic!" Harry returned.

"Hard enough to –"

"Hey! Abbot and Costello, we get the freakin' idea!" Louie cut them off.

"It's the image Harry." Doc explained. "Louie comes from an honest hard working family, it's all the gangster stuff puts him off." Louie sat silently as Doc defended his partner. "Private Detective Mancino doesn't like being associated with all those criminal types in the newspapers." Doc reached into the large ice bucket, popped a bottle of beer and passed it to Mancino. But it was only partially out of kindness. He was also in the habit of keeping an eye on Louie's whiskey intake.

Mancino had demonstrated, more than once in the past, that while under the influence of three or four shots of John Barleycorn he became bullet proof and irresistible to women and ergo needed a babysitter. Doc gently moved the whiskey bottle to one side.

Louie downed his fifth shot, chased it with some beer and got quiet. Harry and Doc, afraid they had struck a nerve, quieted down also. A moment later Louie begun to quietly speak to no one in particular.

"His name was Giovanni."

"Who?" Harry asked.

"An uncle on my mother's side, back in Reisi in Sicily. Giovanni was a 'made man'."

Mancino, although not a quiet guy, wasn't

exactly known for sharing. At this rare window of insight Doc and Harry were prompted to pay attention.

"One time the local boss wanted to prove he could do anything. That his men were blindly loyal to him. So he ordered my uncle to whack a small time local politician the boss had a beef with, you know, to prove his power in the district. My father, who knew the politician to be a good man, got wind of it and set out to try and stop Giovanni. He didn't make it in time."

"What happened?!" Harry slid forward on the edge of his seat.

"I'm tryin' ta tell ya!" Louie snapped without looking at Harry who inched his ass back up the seat. Louie shot another whiskey and Doc refilled his glass but only halfway. "Like I said, my father was too late. The councilman and his family were dead." Harry started to speak again but, with a raised hand Doc stayed him. "The next day they argued and Giovanni shot my father." Louie relayed the death of his father completely devoid of expression. Both Doc and Harry sat back as Mancino finally raised his head and made eye contact.

"That's when my mother decided to leave Sicily for America. She wound up in Brooklyn. Figured nobody'd find us in a big city."

"Anybody ever catch your uncle?" Harry enquired.

"Didn't have to." Now Harry and Doc hung on

every word. "About a week later, in total secrecy she had us, her, me and my kid sister, all packed and the night before we were to leave she asked my uncle Giovanni over for dinner. Said she wanted to forgive him for what he did, tell him that it was a brotherly fight. Nothing personal."

"You mean like a farewell dinner?"

"Yeah Harry, kind'a. Only he didn't know it was a farewell dinner. She poisoned his soup."

"Her own brother?" Harry blurted in astonishment. Louie took a long pull on his beer.

"When the poison started to take effect she ushered him outside to puke up in the outhouse. And, as she held his head over the toilet . . . she slit his throat with my father's straight razor." Mancino looked around and shrugged. "She was a good housewife though."

"How's that?" Doc asked.

"As small as she was she managed to hold his neck over the toilet to minimize the mess."

"Jesus Christ Louie!" Harry blurted out. Louie locked eyes with him and without blinking, maintained his detached demeanor.

"You know that saying about blood being thicker than water?" Louie postulated. The other two nodded. "Not always! The second he pulled that trigger and killed my father, he wasn't her brother anymore. She loved that man more than life itself."

"Apparently!" A shocked Harry added.

"Jesus Louie, that's some dark shit." Doc consoled.

"No Doc. The thing that's dark is, she never saw me that night . . . watching the whole thing from the back door of the kitchen." He lifted the beer. "And I never told her before she died."

Louie picked up his whiskey glass but didn't drink and like cavemen huddled around a fire, he along with the other two stared into the middle of the room. No one spoke for the better part of twenty minutes.

Mancino finally drained his glass then spoke. "I always wondered-"

"You did the right thing!" Doc reached over and patted Mancino's shoulder. Again there was silence.

"Well I can sense the zebra in the room! So I'll just say it!" Louie declared. Harry glanced over at Mancino.

"It's 'elephant in the room', Louie." Doc smiled.

"I know that. I was just seeing how drunk youse were."

"We're not drunk Louie." Doc assured. Harry leaned in and refilled Louie's glass. "Maybe you should have another one."

"Well, god-damn-it! I'm still gonna talk about it! What the hell was Leon thinking?!" Louie demanded.

"Son-of-a-bitch had everything going for him! Young, good looking guy, athletic!" Doc added.

"Real good looking kid from what I heard." Harry threw in.

"Intelligent and astute." Doc lamented.

"Yeah, and sharp too!" Louie added.

"Hey speaking of which, either you guys seen Redbone at all today? I left him a note to come up but-" Doc asked.

"I seen him this morning when he was mopping the hallway." Harry volunteered. "Maybe he was too tired to come up and just hit the sack early, called it a day."

"Yeah, could be. Shit!"

"What's a matter Doc?" Harry probed.

"Doc's pissed off Harry because this Baptism wasn't exactly combustible!"

"Jesus H. Christ Mancino! Go into my office will ya?!"

"HOW COME?!"

"Because there's A FUCKING DICTIONARY ON THE BOOKSHELF THAT'S HOW COME!"

Harry leaned over to enlighten Louie. "I think you mean 'spontaneous' there Sparky."

"OKAY, SPONTANEOUS GOD-DAMN-IT!" Louie reaffirmed.

"That's better." Doc said as he took another hit of the second bottle of Jameson's which had mysteriously emerged from Doc's office about a half hour ago. "God-damn-it." Doc sighed.

"What's the matter?" Harry quietly asked.

"Doc's got a burr under his saddle because he was plannin' on getting' a few drinks into Redbone before he sprung the news on him about Leon." Louie informed.

"Can't say that's the worst idea I ever heard." Harry agreed. "If'n it's a real bitch Doc, I could do it fer ya." Harry was a genuine altruist at heart.

"Nah, thanks anyway Harry. I'll do it first thing in the morning. I usually bump into him when I come in."

"Doc?!" Louie was struck with a thought.

"Louie?" Doc shot back.

"That Puerto Rican waitress Leon was seeing, they were close?"

"Any closer they'd'a been behind each other." Doc answered.

"She still-" Louie cut himself off as Doc, with some effort, readjusted his position and stared across intently at Louie. Louie stared back. "What now?!" Mancino challenged.

"Nuthin'." Doc answered.

"Bullshit! You were gonna say something sarcastic again, wasn't ya?!" Louie challenged.

"Not necessarily. Could be condescending, rude or derogatory." Doc poured himself another drink. "But in point of fact my trusty partner, I was about to compliment you."

"On what?!" Louie's suspicion grew.

"On the application of your ever developing P.I. skills."

"How do you know what-"

"And on the suggestion you were about to make of cruising Uptown tomorrow and having a friendly chat with that waitress Leon was schtuping. To see if . . .?" He let it hang for Louie to pick up on. "To see if . . .?" Doc hinted again. The penny finally dropped on Louie.

"To see if she knows anything about . . .?" Louie wasn't imitating Doc, he had just hit a dead end. Doc bailed him out.

"To see if there was any possibility it was because of her that Leon off'd himself."

"Yeah! I was gonna say that!" Mancino unconvincingly bluffed.

"Good. You leave at nine in the morning. I'll call, make sure you're up."

Harry still sitting roughly between the two had been watching the verbal ping pong.

"You two assholes ought'a get married." Harry quipped. "Doc, you reckon the kid had something else on the side?" Harry asked. Doc was approaching 30,000 feet and staring into the distance. Louie answered for him.

"Leon?! Probably not he was head-over-heels over that waitress."

"I meant playin' around with drugs." Harry queried.

"We'll know in a day or so." Louie informed.

"How's that?"

"New York State regs. Toxicology report-on-all-suicides. Required by law."

"Phil-os-o-physin'!" Doc blurted out staring at the floor. Harry jumped.

"What the hell's he babblin' about?"

"Philosophysin'!" Doc repeated. Again, Mancino filled Harry in.

"He gets this way sometimes. Gets pissed off about the political situation . . . the state of the country. The lawyers, the judges . . .the political situation. I think he gets frustrated on account'a he couldn't serve I the war. He was 4F–"

"On account'a his ear, yeah, I know." Harry finished Louie's explanation.

"Oh. Didn't know you knew, ya know? Ya know how some people get belig . . . belogent . . . bellierent when they drink?"

"Belligerent. I know what you mean."

"Yeah that's what I said. Some get sappy or real quiet? Doc gets sociably and politically philosophical. Listen, sometimes it gets interesting." Louie tapped Harry on the arm and crossed his legs, sat back and made himself comfortable. "Pass me a beer." They both kicked back to enjoy McKeowen's impending monologue as he stared into the distance.

"Then . . . The War came along." Doc addressed the empty chairs along the wall as if they were a classroom full of students. "All the potential catastrophic battles and imagined enemies of the United States the politicians had been hittin' us over the head with all these years vanished in the night. Slammed into perspective, became real." Doc downed his shot.

"After Pearl Harbor even the badest of the bad guys, politicians, gangsters . . . hell even the Republicans were seen as 'swell guys', seen to be pitching in and 'doing their bit'. Abruptly and without prejudice, all slates were wiped clean.

However this presented a problem to the Boys on the Hill! Domestically speaking that is. No more domestic enemies to pit against each other!"

With only a slight wobble Doc groaned to his feet, stood and shuffled around to the back of his chair.

"Until the perfect solution to the age old technique of creating an enemy that only that politician can vanquish ambled down the path. Only that poitician can vanquish providing he's re-elected to office of course!"

"What enemy Doc?" Louie egged on as he refueled Doc's glass.

"Communism!" Doc dramatically exclaimed. 'The perfect cocktail of champagne dreams and cyanide kisses' is how they touted it. The collapse of Western Civilization as we know it! They touted it until every last American believed that the Russian people were born with horns on their heads and forked tails coming out their hind ends!" With one hand on the back of the chair he established a controlled sway and assumed a mock haunting voice. "Then . . . up through the floorboards it rose-"

"Communism?"

"NO! The smell of fear. Panic politics permeating Wall Street, the House and the Senate alike until the toxic fumes of hate and discontent waived once again through every metropolis, town and village in the land. The unmistakable, putrid stench of blind, craven fear." Doc took his drink, poured another and shifted back to his chair.

"To say the Boys on the Hill were able to exploit

the blind fear they had created in America with the Commie paranoia they have carefully crafted before the war is to say the Pope is an okay guy." He winked and gave the thumbs up then threw back his shot but held onto the empty glass as a reinforcement prop.

Neither Harry nor Louie gave much credence to the current commie scare being peddled by the American Press but listened intently anyway as McKeowen continued.

"In their defense though, they probably imagined themselves to be as ancient kings and princes in a long-forgotten land fighting over . . . imagined, inherited territories and rights to titles. The brave, stalwart D.C. politicians doing battle wherever and whenever needed and fighting the good fight to leave their mark for prosperity . . . oh sorry, posterity.

They are not Senators and Congressmen only, but lawmakers of the kingdom, rulers of an imaginary, autonomous world like the elves and dwarfs of Tolkien. Ancient kings and princes in an ancient land fighting over territories like Medieval Celtic chieftains to protect the little people like us. You and me. To protect us from a danger that will never come." He sighed. "That probably doesn't even exist."

He sat back in his chair and got quiet again as he stared off to some distant place this time beyond the wall.

"You okay Doc?" Louie asked with genuine

concern.

"In reality, they are the Lilliputians the Lilliputians read about." Doc responded.

"Champagne dreams & cyanide kisses eh Doc?" Louie broke the silence. Doc seemed to snap out of it, if only partially.

"Looks like it Louie. Looks like."

"I was just thinkin'" Louie jumped back in. Doc slowly turned to him.

"Did it hurt?" Doc laughed. Ignoring the insult Louie presented his thesis.

"Ya ever contemplate the really important questions of the universe?" Mancino asked to no one in particular. Doc attempted to lift his head and look at Louie but, after several attempts gave up.

"Such as?" Harry asked.

"Do crowded elevators smell different to midgets?" Louie seriously posed. Doc finally managed to turn his head towards Mancino and stared at him for a long minute before he spoke.

"You need help Mancino, ya know that?"

"Well . . . I sure as hell . . . don't need no more whiskey." Louie confessed.

"You two make some pair, ya know that?" Harry sarcastically threw out.

"Don't we though?" Mancino encouraged. "Wonder who'll play me in the movie?"

"Well . . . Warner Brothers will probably do the picture." Doc slowly conjectured.

"Yeah?! Ya think so?"

"Sure! They got . . . the only . . . actor under

contract capable of capturing your . . . depth of character, your level of charisma." Doc passed Mancino the second half empty bottle. "Your good looks and charm."

Louie pushed himself upright in his chair.

"Yeah? Who is it Doc?! Who do think'll play me?!"

"Elmer Fudd."

"You're an asshole ya know that Doc?"

The discussion was interrupted by Harry suddenly snoring in his seat. Then they both watched as, the old man, his prosthetic leg now in his dangling hand, slowly slide off his chair and onto the floor. They stared, for nearly ten minutes then both looked back over at Harry curled up on the small reception couch with both arms hugging his wooden leg, his face now sporting a huge smile.

"Hey Doc."

"Yeah Louie?!"

"Maybe it ain't so bad bein' Italian."

"You ain't Italian. You're Sicilian. Be proud of it!"

"Maybe it ain't so bad bein' Sicilian."

"Maybe it ain't Louie. You gonna be alright?" From his chair Doc patted him on the back.

"Yeah, yeah! I'll grab a cab. See ya at nine." Mancino headed for the door as Doc shuffled into his office then collapsed onto his office couch.

"Louie!" Doc called out from behind the partially closed over office door. "Good job on rememberin' Leon's waitress friend."

"Hey Doc!"
"Yeah Louie?"
"Guess the little light only goes out sometimes."
"Guess it does Louie. I guess it does."

✝

Onboard the *Luara Keene*
Atlantic Ocean

A scattered colony of gulls flocking overhead signaled the ship was nearing the Italian coastline while, basking in the cool, clear morning air Charlie Luciano, leaning on the rail of the fantail, stared out across the broad Atlantic and pictured himself sailing back the way he'd come. Back over the distant horizon and back into the glitz and glamor of Manhattan social life. The plan to evade his temporary deportation, temporary as he saw it, had already been put into motion even before his release from prison in New York.

Following the all-night party back in New York Lucky didn't have much to do for his ten days at sea on the return trip to Italy. He was however grateful for the fresh air, down time, good food and beautiful women but was mindful of the fact that after docking in Rome all that would change.

At no time during his nine year stint in Federal prison did Luciano sit idle. Surreptitiously using Polokoff's special arrangement with the office of Naval Intelligence fresh contacts had been made, plans had been set and things were ready to be done. There would be no shortage of work to be done to get Luciano back in the game. There was an unending list of tasks to do in order to get re-established on this side of the world and the fifty year old Don had no intentions of dragging his feet. He already missed his celebrity lifestyle in the midst of the New York high life and knew full well the fastest road back was through that most American of mantra: money, money, money!

As the aged *Laura Keene* approached what would be Charlie's, new home former prisoner #92168 focused more on his future than the misfortune of his past. It was no coincidence that Salvatore Lucania had been re-christened 'Lucky' Luciano.

A short time later, as the mid-ships gangway was manhandled into place, down on the dock a special police escort fell into place to cordon off the mob of press dispatched to cover Luciano's return to Italy.

Notoriety, earned for good or for bad, was treated the same everywhere.

"Hey Lucky, what are your plans now that you're back home?" Up on the rail at the head of the gang plank, a couple of the small cadre of New York reporters who had followed him across the ocean asked as the other passengers began squeezing out onto the pier.

"I ain't home yet boys! New York is my home!" He called back as he pushed towards the gate. "But I'll be back soon enough, you can bank on that!"

"Rumor has it you're gonna open a restaurant, or a chain of night clubs?" Another inquired.

"Whatever I do fellas take my word for it, it's gonna be strictly legit. Strictly legit!"

"What'a you think about the federal authorities talking about brining you back for another trial?"

"They just got rid'a me! You think the American taxpayer's gonn'a wanna pay for a return trip plus another trial?" Lucky stopped in his tracks. "That guy in the Narcotics Bureau, Asslicker, claims I set up the whole world-wide drug ring! Nice trick considerin' I been in the joint for the last ten years!"

Under the watchful eyes of a plain clothed detective and several uniformed Carabinieri Lucky was met by two local Italian strong arms and escorted out of the terminal and into a waiting sedan.

They say a man's importance can be measured by the strength of his enemies. Although fully aware he had no shortage of enemies, what Lucky had no way of knowing was the number and strength of those still plotting openly against him as well as the several others lurking in the shadows waiting for an opportunity to take him out. Or fill his shoes.

He was, however, well aware that the longer he was away the less his chances of regaining the American throne back in New York

Although Charlie maintained a strong say so in the rackets, would receive regular 'tributes' and was still well respected, Frankie Costello had already been named Tutti di Cappo. This with Lucky's blessing, but only as temporary holder of the crown, to babysit things so-to-speak, until Luciano could engineer a way back into what he now considered his true country, the U.S.A.

As the black sedan rode away from the steamship terminal in Rome, Charlie 'Lucky' Luciano had no idea how much more important he was about to become.

In the back of the sedan, as it drove off, the curtains were dawn across the windows and Lucky was greeted by Don Vizzini.

☦

Louie remembered the place Uptown where the Puerto Rican waitress worked, Kitty's Koffee Kafe on 58th near the Queensboro Bridge. He remembered it from a few years back when Doc first called him from a pay phone across the street where he spotted a D.A. having lunch with Socks Lanza and Charlie Luciano's long-time partner Meyer Lansky.

Smelling a rat, Doc enlisted Leon, who was working as a bus boy just up the block at Bloomingdale's in the downstairs cafeteria. He paid Leon twenty bucks to pretend being an employee at Kitty's to get into the restaurant and ease drop on the D.A. and the mobsters.

Leon, not trusting Doc but working for less than minimum wage, jumped at the twenty bucks.

The Wolves of Calabria

In the process young Leon met young Rosie Rosario, who was hopping tables in the place.

As he made his way Uptown that morning Louie had no great expectations of gleaning any useful information from the attractive waitress who until his ill-fated drug trip, Leon was seeing on a very regular basis.

It was mid-morning so, with the exception of an old fella sitting in the corner drinking coffee and working the race sheets, the place was dead.

Mancino came in through the front door and glanced over at the female cashier mounted on a stool behind the register, her face buried in a copy of *Hollywood Glamor Magazine* and probably wouldn't have heard a grenade go off.

Rosie was at the far end of the counter on salt and pepper refill duty. Weaving between the tightly packed round tops and bentwood chairs Mancino made his way over to her. She didn't bother to look up as he approached.

"Hi ya." Louie greeted. She responded by looking him up and down then returning to her chore. "My name's Louie Mancino." He instinctively reached for his badge and I.D. but remembered what Doc taught him about easing the witness into the initial Q&A and not producing I.D. unless asked.

"And?"

"Mind if we talk for a little while?"

"You a cop? You dun look like no cop."

"I ain't a cop."

"You're a cop you gotta tell me."

"No cop, no Fed, no wire. Scout's honor." Louie raised his right hand in the Boy Scout's salute and pulled the flap of his coat aside.

"Ya wann'a coffee?" She asked.

"Sure." Louie took a seat at the counter.

"You here to ask me about Leon?"

"More to talk about him really."

She served Louie his coffee and went back to condiment duty as she willingly opened up to Mancino.

"He was a good man, a real gentleman. Not a bull shitter. Kind'a guy ya trusted, ya know?" She spoke with obvious sincerity.

"We all felt that way sister, trust me. He had a future, not like some guys of his . . ."

"Color?!"

"I was gonna say age." She eyed Louie with suspicion.

"Nice save!"

"Leon had and uncle-" Louie prompted.

"Yeah, Redbone. He loved that old guy. I met him once when he had us over for Sunday dinner." She smirked as she recalled. "I wound up doing most'a the cooking, neither of them was worth a shit in the kitchen. But I remember coming away thinking, 'these are good people'."

"Ever run into any problems with, you know, his habit?"

"I suspected he was into the junk about four months in, but it never really came up. He kept it to himself. We had an unspoken understanding. He don't play with that shit around my house, and I don't put his ass out on the street. He kept to his end of the deal."

She started cleaning up around the end of the counter wiping down the now full salt and pepper shakers and placing them on a large black serving tray.

"Miss Rosario-"

"Rosie."

"Rosie, he ever truck around with ropey characters?"

"Not really. Well, one time, the only time I ever came across anybody suspicious. Was a guy came around asking for him."

"Do you happen to remember when that was, more or less?"

"Sorry I don't but I clearly remember it was gloomy afternoon the day that creep came looking for him." At that Louie unobtrusively reached for his note pad and began jotting down notes. "It was the same day he didn't show for our lunch date." She added.

"What can you remember about him, the creepy guy?"

She slid the tray of salt and pepper shakers off the counter and moved out onto the floor. Mancino followed giving her a hand setting the condiments on the tables next to the ketchup bottles and chrome napkin dispensers.

"Kind'a well-dressed, like a pimp. Alligator shoes, fancy suit, tie, starched shirt. Must'a thought he was Don Juan or sumthin'. Hit on me three times in as many minutes."

"Didj'a happen to get his name?"

"I asked him, 'Who should I say is callin'?', but he just shrugged it off and sad he'd catch up to Leon later."

"Was he colored?" Louie asked. Rosie shook her head no.

"Na uh, white boy. Must'a thought he was black or somethin'. First gringo I ever seen with corn rolls!"

"Any particular accent that you can recall?"

"Spoke in what he must'a thought was street English. Sounded like a moron to me. Manhattan, Uptown, South Brooklyn maybe, but definitely from The City. 'Course allot'a Jersey-wanna-be's move over here lookin' for fame and fortune and change their accents."

"Any other physical characteristics?"

"Five six, five seven maybe."

"You think he might have had something to do with Leon's death?"

"I doubt it. Struck me as the kind'a guy would get somebody else to do his dirty work. He wouldn't want to get his hands dirty. Smelled a bit like a fed to me."

"Anything else come to mind? Anything different or peculiar about this guy?"

"I remember one thing stands out. He smelled like . . . like the circus." Mancino looked up from his pad.

"You mean like elephants or something?"

"Elephant shit maybe, he was so full of it." She emphasized.

"Ya remember what month it was?"

"It was rainy. September maybe."

"Okay if I call ya if anything crops up?"

"Not like you don't know where to find me." She quipped.

Louie pocketed his pad and pencil, tipped his hat and turned to leave.

"Rosie, we're all real sorry about Leon. Really."

"Ya win some, ya lose some and some get rained out, ya know what I mean?!" She smiled and shrugged.

"Yeah I do."

Louie left. Rosie faded back into her world.

✝

Paddy Kelly

CHAPTER IX

**Kandahar City,
Kandahar Province
Southern Afghanistan**

The monochromatic hills and arid plains of Kandahar province give the impression that some prehistoric beast might at any minute flap its wings and come soaring over the mountains.

The towering, rugged ranges of the province, with its tiny, compact villages and tightly packed farms lining the long narrow valleys is reminiscent of the Arizona landscape minus the bright red hues and plethora of green cacti.

Stagnated in the Seventh Century the city of Iskandar, the local transliteration of Kandahar, the regional version of Alexandria, is also one of the most culturally significant regions of the Pashtun people. Founded by Alexander The Great in 330 B.C. Kandahar has been the traditional seat of power for over two centuries. One of the oldest human settlements excavated to date sits just outside the city itself.

Oddly enough, it was an Italian trader who six centuries earlier inadvertently helped the earliest drug trade routes to establish themselves.

The farming techniques as well as the way the harvested narcotic is hauled across these territories for trade in the western parts of the world remains essentially unchanged since the days of Marco Polo in the 13th Century.

Although many of the traditional routes out of the Middle East were now blocked as a result of the war, new routes were established while new farms entered the international market in Burma, Laos and Viet Nam.

From 1932, the first year in which opium production was recorded, Afghanistan alone produced 75 metric tons of the lethal poison.

It was here, just outside the city that the process of supplying the world's junkies would begin.

Northwest of the city, in one of the few open fields nestled between the mountains, a dozen women and children tended to the business of working their way through the crop, knives in hand, lightly scoring the poppy bulbs with half a dozen, equally spaced slices. This in order to 'bleed' the sap from the mature bulb to later be collected and dried in the sun to allow the reduction process which would yield the dry powder to be shipped to and sold on the open market.

From its origins in Kandahar in south western Afghanistan, to the borders of Iran and Pakistan south, the dried sap of the poppy bulbs would be packed onto a pair of mules to embark on the first leg of its long journey.

At one end of the field a collection of dried mud houses and a small barn served as the settlement for a farmer and his extended family.

As two workers finished wrapping and packing

the opium a nineteen year old boy, a Mauser rifle which had seen better days draped across his lap, squatted next to a forty-something man who sat on a low stool just inside the faint light of morning sun.

Behind them two children carefully laid small dollops of sap on swaths of linen while two older children carefully carried them over to make-shift drying racks positioned to catch the first rays of sunlight as it crept over the mountain side.

With controlled intensity garnered by experience Mazin al-Bakawi spoke to the attentive teen, Ibrahim.

"Last week word arrived from other couriers that fierce fighting has broken out along the Turkish border so it will be necessary to take a new route, the one to the south."

"I am prepared for danger!" He proudly bragged as he patted the WWI era Gewehr 98 resting in his lap.

Mazin leaned forward and lifted the weapon from the puzzled Ibrahim gently laying it on the ground next to his own seat.

"No weapons my brother."

"But–"

"If you are stopped there will be more of them than you and if you are unarmed you will not be considered a threat. With a military weapon they will kill you and take our cargo. Better to come back alive with nothing then draped over your donkey." The deflated Ibrahim nonetheless understood his brother's logic.

The Wolves of Calabria

"Always remember, keep a true south bearing. By Allah's blessing this will guide you straight into the small port of Pasni. About five days journey. You have enough food for six and you will cross many rivers, drink and water the pack animals often."

"Yes brother." The teen assured.

"At Pasni you will wait until the next day when you will meet a motorized ferry called the *Markeb*. This boat will take you up the straights to a port called al Faw. You will be met by military supply vehicles and driven north to Khvoy west of Tabriz. Here you will deliver the harvest and be paid."

"Mazin . . ." Ibrahim averted his eyes as he spoke. ". . . you attended the university in Bristol. You understand these people. How these men make a profit with such long distance to travel and so many mouths to feed along the way?"

"Western economics is a wondrous thing my brother. We have been toiling for hundreds of years to eke out a living growing our plants, processing our paste and drying it for hashish only. But now, the westerners wish to help us open new markets. 'Expand our horizons as they say. Who are we to stand in the way of progress?"

"It doesn't seem like . . . like good business."

"Ibrahim, we gave them astronomy, navigational techniques and the magic of zero. Now they pay us back with hard currency. Think of it as royalties."

"But . . . the Qa'ran . . . it is wrong to kill."

"It is they who poison their own bodies. Again,

keep south and you will pass the towns of Quetta and Balochistan . . ."

Following Ibrahim's delivery the small shipment would, along with several other shipments, travel north by truck along the Persian border and on into Turkey crossing the border at a small, inconspicuous village named Umurlu and, under military escort, provided once a month by elements in the Turkish Ministry of Transport, make its way around Lake Van to Agri.

From Agri the small convoy would be met by planes from the German businessmen who had vested interests in getting this powder to the west to be flown to Ankara then on to Bursa to refuel and finally to the port of Pozzallo on the island of Sicily.

The Germans no longer controlled the air space over the Adriatic and the Middle Sea so to avoid the 1200 plus kilometer sea journey around Greece and the never ending tribal wars of the Iran and Iraq territories, the skies were the answer.

†

West Side Docks
Lower Manhattan

The cold, drizzle which continuously fell saturating the timber planks of Pier 17 didn't make life any more pleasant for those hustling to make up for lost time. Lost time and lost wages of the war

The Wolves of Calabria

years.

The cold wind ripping across the open harbor was intermittent but seemed relentless to the dozens of stevedores scurrying around the pier unloading huge, hemp slings of cargo and reloading them onto trolleys, dollies and hand trucks to be registered, routed, signed for and finally reloaded onto trailer trucks, flatbeds and the smaller, box trucks known as 'straight jobs'.

With his hands crammed in the side pockets of his bright yellow slicker, shoulders hunched up and his hood pulled over his head it was with a particular sense of purpose that the dock foreman made his way through the drizzly morning along the pier south of Luxury Liner Row on the west bank of the Hudson. He found the young stevedore he sought huddled against the side of the small radio shack.

"You yelled fer me Kid?!"

"Yeah Nick, I did. Over here." Butchie handed the weathered boss a wet manifest and led him down off the pier and back onto the main dock. They talked as they walked. "I got what you might call a conundrum."

"You takin' night classes Butchie?"

"Beats readin' the *Daily News*."

"What exactly is your conundrum?"

"Why would somebody ship 1200 cans of imported Italian tomatoes up from Florida to a distributor in New York to the docks before shipping them to a warehouse over in Jersey?!"

Butchie explained. The foreman studied the damp manifest.

"That don't make no sense!" He verified.

"Right? Why wouldn't they just ship them from Italy to Jersey, save all the extra time and expense? Jersey got docks same as us, plus they got half the tariffs!"

They stopped a hundred yards down the dock near one of the bay doors of the terminal. The Foreman stared at the stacked crates of tinned tomatoes.

"Hence, my conundrum." Butchie added.

"What the hell you talkin' about?" The foreman perused the freight, a tall pallet of crates of canned tomatoes which sat off to the side.

"I got a six tier pallet over here come in from Sicily through Florida. Now it's supposed ta go over ta a warehouse in Bayonne!"

"So what's the problem?!"

"The import docket's gotta be wrong!" The kid indicated the document the foreman had in his hand.

"Guess everybody's gotta get their cut Butchie." Nick shrugged. "Or some jamoke's got more money than sense!"

"Yeah but-"

"So what'a you Dick Tracey? What'a want me ta tell ya?! Just load 'em up, send 'em over to Jersey and quit bitchin' will ya?! Ya startin' to sound like my wife."

"I seen your wife. I look a helluva lot better!"

"I'm in stitches! Now c'mon help me out here,

will ya?! We got another freighter comin' in at six!"

Nick gave him back the manifest docket and made his way back out into the drizzle.

"Hey, when you see The Big Man, remind him the war's over, time for that raise we were promised!"

"Trust me, he knows!"

Butchie proceeded to break down the pallet into individual crates and load them onto his hand truck.

"Must be some pretty fuckin' special Eye-talian tomatoes!"

☦

It was Saturday morning, two days after the baptism and Doc was feeling a little regretful about his rant, but getting it out in the open was a major part of having office baptisms. Besides, it wasn't exactly Harry and Louie's first rodeo.

With his feet up on the desk and his door open, McKeowen held an official typed report and contemplated the implications. He glanced at the clock. Ten thirty-five.

Doc and Mancino agreed to meet at ten and kick around ideas about setting plans for alternate Summer vacations so as not to have to close down the office altogether and avoid some cases going cold. Louie, as usual was late.

Characteristically and sans an apology, Mancino showed up as if on time and breezed into Doc's office.

"What's ya got Doc?" He off-handedly inquired. Doc lowered the lab report below eye level and stared as Mancino pulled up a chair on the opposite side of the desk.

"Morning Doc, sorry I'm late Doc. How are you this morning Doc? I'm fine Louie, how are you?" McKeowen mocked.

"I'm doing good, thanks fer asking." An unfazed Mancino replied. "So . . . what's up Doc?"

"Never gets old Louie." Reaching over the desk he handed the report to Mancino. "Leon's blood toxicology report."

Louie scanned it over.

"Jesus Christ on a cross Doc! Is that right? 92% pure?"

"Give or take 5%. The sample was fresh but the heroin was ingested over twelve hours prior so was mostly absorbed."

Just then Redbone entered the office.

"Hey." The old man greeted as if nothing out of the ordinary had happened.

"Hey!" Louie greeted. Doc put his feet down and sat up, picking up on Redbone's efforts at normalcy.

"Redbone, glad you're here Brother. Grab a seat. There's something –" Doc started to explain but was cut off. The elderly Cajun smiled and nodded.

"I hoid, was on da news. Went down ta the morgue, identified him last night." Doc moved to Redbone and put a hand on his shoulder.

"Anything we can do for ya brother?" Doc

asked. Redbone put his hand on Doc's and squeezed.

"I 'preciate ya wantin' ta be the one ta break it ta me Doc. Harry told me. Means a lot. But I got it covered." He dragged a chair in to the office from the waiting room.

"Can I throw something at ya?" Doc probed.

"Shoot!"

"Redbone, just before he jumped Leon said, 'I'm doing this for him'. That mean anything to you?" Doc inquired. Louie scrunched his face up in puzzlement. Redbone eased himself down into the chair and sighed a pause before he spoke.

"He was givin' me money every couple'a weeks. More
than he was makin' uptown to the Woolworth's. Not sure where he was gettin' it, but I has my suspicions. I think he might'a been suspectin' that I was gonna confront him about it."

"Any idea who he was hanging out with? Seeing or meeting with on a regular basis?"

"There was that waitress-"

"We know about her." Doc assured. "Anyone else?" Redbone broke eye contact, thought deeply and sighed out a lazy response.

"To tell the truth, he was kind'a' keepin' to himself these last few weeks. But I wouldn't know nuthin' 'bout his friends and all."

"You wanna drink?" Louie offered.

"Naw, I be alright. Sorry I missed ya'll's baptism. I hoid you got a little wordy Doc." Both smiled.

"It was the booze talkin' Redbone, just the booze." Doc defended.

"If'n it's awright wit you fellas, I'm gonna take a day or so off. I gots some arrangements ta make. But I be back by Tuesday, Wednesday fer sure."

"Take all the time you need brother!" Doc reassured. "Louie will be glad to take up your slack if anything needs to done. Won't you Louie?" Doc smiled at Mancino who was shocked.

The old man pushed himself back to his feet and shuffled to the door.

"You need anything be sure and let us know." Louie added. Redbone stopped in the doorway.

"Well, next time ya'll has a baptism, ya'll be sure to save my old ass a seat! Long time since I hoid Doc runnin' off at the mouth."

Doc and Louie stood silent until he was gone. Both family oriented men couldn't help but wonder how it would be to be that old and lose your last known living relative.

Louie took another quick perusal of the lab report and then laid it back on Doc's desk.

"Doc, you remember when you told me to take them tomatoes from that Jewish lady over to the precinct house and give them to Chief Sullivan?" Louie finally broke the silence.

"You mean two or three whole days ago? Yeah, what about it?"

"Well what would'a happened if I . . . you know, accidently speakin', I forgot to do that?" Doc looked up at him starting to get pissed off.

"Now why on earth would you do that Mr. Mancino? Except by accident of course."

"I don't know . . . maybe ya might . . . you might need them. You know, fer if you finally decide to take the case."

"And what case would that be, Sherlock?" Doc prodded.

"The one where we find out where this white shit is coming from, who's sellin' it and do what we can to shut 'em down." Louie was treading water and he knew it. "That case."

"I was crystal clear that we were gonna start steering clear of any more oddball cases which wandered in here, no matter how much money they offer to throw at us! Besides, what makes you think I might wanna take that case?"

"Nothin' in particular! I was just applyin' speculation. But if you wasn't gonna take it . . . I was . . . you know, kinda -"

If McKeowen was surprised by this revelation he hid it well.

"And how exactly were you gonna explain your time away from the office? Not to mention the eventual paperwork you were gonna have to generate? Not to mention the headlines you would'a garnered after you got your ass killed?!" Louie just stared. "It means amassed–"

"I KNOW WHAT IT MEANS!" Louie's dejection peeked. "I ain't as dumb as I look God damn it!" He fell back into the chair. Doc continued to stare at him. "Guess I didn't think it through."

Mancino finally admitted.

"You never do!" Doc snapped forward in his chair. "That's why I get pissed off at you! You got a wife and probably at some point in the future, a kid. Then probably another one somewhere down the line. Whose gonna feed all them little Mancinetts if you get snuffed?" Louie just gazed out across the room.

Despite the time and resources required to pursue the case as well as the potential scope of an investigation which could easily balloon out of control, Doc's apathy was transitioning into reluctance to get involved in the case of the 'weird' canned tomatoes. Then he was hit with Leon's suicide which he now knew was drug influenced.

In reality, his interest began to pique.

What Doc was not ready to reveal was that he heavily suspected the drugs were probably tied into a Mob operation, or at least some small-time wanna-be, hood who was kickin' back to one of the five families somewhere.

They sat in silence for a couple of minutes when Doc spoke up.

"Maybe if we had more to go on." Doc spontaneously prompted, half to himself and half to Louie while being careful to avoid eye contact with Mancino.

Louie lit up like a Christmas tree, sat up in his chair and dashed next door to his office returning seconds later with Mrs. Dunlevy's open tin of tomatoes now wrapped in aluminum foil, along with a sheet of paper. He sat the can on Doc's desk and handed the paper to McKeowen. Doc was taken completely off guard.

The paper was a lab report with a quantitative analysis of the can's contents.

With the score tied, bases loaded, bottom of the ninth and a two and two count, Louie wound up for his game winning pitch.

"Okay, you told me to take these tomatoes to Chief Sullivan." Louie blurted out.

"Make it good Mancino!"

"Lemme ask you this: what'a the odds of two samples from two separate batches bein' the same exact percentage?"

"Percentage of what?"

"I had that shit in the can analyzed. It's 92% pure heroin." Louie's hands found his hips as his green and orange bowling shirt struggled not to pop several chest buttons as Doc perused the report, smiled and shook his head. Louie felt it necessary to drive the point home.

"92% pure scag. Horse. H, Mr. Midnight, the White Wonder Dust. A one way ticket to La La Land –"

"Louie! I got it!" Doc blurted out. Louie quieted and took a seat.

"So? What'a ya think Doc?" He cajoled. There was a long pause.

"I think ya did good Louie."

"I know that! I mean about the case!" Louie begged like a kid just been promised there might be a trip to Disney Land in his near future. Doc peeled back the foil, lifted the open can, stared at it and sighed.

"I think it's one of the weirdest things I've ever seen in a can."

"What'a we do? How do we go about this?"

"Where'd she buy these tomatoes?" Doc grabbed a pencil and found the contents difficult to stir. They were viscous and off color.

"Said in her preliminary screen she normally shops at Carrelli's on 6th Avenue, but she's been talking about trying that new whatch'ya call it down on 9th? The super -"

"Supermarket, the A&P?"

"Yeah, the Supermarket!" Doc scrutinized the inner lip where Dunlevy had applied the can opener then took a closer look inside the can.

"Judging by the inner lip it looks like it was filled and sealed before shipping. Not after."

"Yeah, that's what I thought too!"

Doc shot Louie a 'sure you did!' look.

"On Monday have Shirl give Dunlevy a call, or better yet, you get over to Dunlevy's house today. Tell her we need more details and then get over to the A&P and shag some contact details from the store manager as to where they get their canned tomatoes, frequency of deliveries and so on and so forth."

"Okay sounds Jake!" Louie sprang to his feet. "What'a you gonna do?"

"I'm gonna snoop around, try to find some

people who are versed in illegal narcotics. See what they can tell me."

"You mean like doctors, scientists, feds from the Bureau of Narcotics. Good thinkin' Doc!"

"Actually I was thinking more like actual experts in the fields. You know, farmers."

"FARMERS?!"

"I'll explain later. How's Doris?"

"Good, why?"

"Glad to hear it. When you get home tonight, work out a Summer vacation plan and let me know on Monday what ya wanna do."

†

West Side Docks
Lower Manhattan

It was just before five that afternoon when the truck driver took the stairs two at a time as he adjusted his Brooklyn Dodger's ball cap then entered the offices of United Freight and Shipping just off the West Side docks in the center of Hell's Kitchen. Stepping up to the counter he produced a claim docket for 100 flats of imported Neapolitan tomatoes. The printed letter head on the docket read Tose Trucking and Shipping, Jersey City, New Jersey.

The clerk at the counter perused the docket and asked the driver to wait. He disappeared into the back of the office only to return a few minutes later.

"Well I found your shipment alright Mac and found the merchandise but it looks like only seventy-five cases made the trip. We ain't got a hundred cases on the dock." The driver was visibly not happy with the news.

"Look fella, my company paid for a hundred cases and we want all one hundred, you savvy?!"

"I would be more than happy to oblige you, my perturbed colleague in transport, however I ain't able to give to you somethin' of which I ain't got. You savvy?!"

"You got any idea . . ." The driver started to allude but thought better of it. The two workers emphasised their argument by engaging in a short Mexican standoff of a staring contest until they realized nothing was to be gained.

The clerk gave an exaggerated smile and the driver cracked first.

"You got a phone?!"

"Local call?" The clerk firmly inquired.

"Yes!" The driver firmly responded.

Without speaking or shifting his relaxed position leaning on one arm the counter clerk produced a black, Bell telephone from under the service counter and gently placed it on the counter top in front of the slowly fuming driver then, with one finger, delicately pushed it forward. The clerk then returned to the business of stamping and filing while the driver placed a quick local call.

Twenty minutes later it was apparent the driver

had pulled out the big guns.

A very well dressed, very large man sporting a goatee. Fedora and white silk scarf appeared at the doorway of the office and quietly but briefly aside, spoke to the driver. With his black trench coat unbuttoned to reveal his impeccably tailored pin striped suit and his scarf draped around his neck the big man gestured with his gloves in his hand as he asked to see the manager, a request the clerk politely obliged.

"Good afternoon sir, how may I help you?"

"My name is Paolini, Alfonse Paolini."

"Pleased to meet you Mr. Paolini. I'm Frank Burns, Shipping & Receiving Manager. What can I do for you?"

"Your company was contracted to bring some tomatoes from my friend in Italy to New York."

"So my clerk has informed me."

"Then he has also informed you that it appears you have misplaced some of said tomatoes, yes?"

"Actually no."

"No?!"

"No! We ship what we receive Mr. Paolini. We received seventy-five cases and so we shipped seventy-five cases."

"Lemme see that!" Paolini demanded of the driver as he grabbed for the driver's copy of the docket. Behind the counter the office clerk feigned busy work as he awaited the outcome of the current office mini-drama. Paolini reopened the contentious negotiations allowing all airs of cordiality to evaporate.

"I ain't real educated but I can read numbers! This here docket says one hundred flats. One hundred, not seventy-five!"

"With all due respect Mr. Paolini, you're correct the original docket shows one hundred crates shipped from Cavallo Canning in Palermo, Italy. However, if you'll look at the lower left hand corner of the docket you'll see that the 'OS&D' box, Over, Short or Damaged, is ticked and, as required, has been counter signed by someone from your company accepting partial delivery, to wit twenty-five flats." He reinforced his argument by pointing to the box on the form. "As you can see there's a signature and a date. I can't read the sig but the date is from two days ago." Paolini gave the universal Sicilian sign for displeasure at being proved wrong. He grunted.

"Sorry about the inconvenience, Mr. Paolini. If you'd like to fill out a claim form I'd be happy to–"

Paolini grunted at the manager then at the driver again and barged out the door, the driver in tow behind him. As he did the clerk, still behind the counter, eased over to the second story window and peered down through the Venetian blinds in time to see the driver apparently receiving orders from Paolini before mounting his straight-job truck and pulling away.

Paolini climbed into the back of his black, Lincoln limo with tinted windows and followed suit.

The Wolves of Calabria

CHAPTER X

**Chanze Chinese Chippy
Lower West Side, Manhattan**

Tony Joaquin Hernandez walked and talked like a New York City homicide detective. He always asked questions like a New York City homicide cop conducting a murder investigation and just like an NYPD cop, regardless of what anyone told him, he never believed them.

In essence Hernandez was the antithesis to his partner Jack Benson whose entire life was predicated on the preservation of his youth, even though he was only a few months shy of his in his forty-sixth birthday.

To Benson's credit he was always upbeat, annoyingly so to some, adhered to a religious physical fitness regime and was always there to help out a friend. The fact that he had not had a serious romantic relationship since high school led some to speculate that maybe Benson played for the other team. Being perpetually well groomed and physically fit reinforced the rumor mill. Neither Hernandez nor Benson were cops.

Both were now assigned to the New York Office of the Department of Foreign Affairs which meant one of two things: They royally screwed up somewhere or kissed some major royal ass back in D.C. to get posted in New York.

Hernandez crossed the street just south of Peck and the FDR Drive and into the small restaurant frequented by local workers.

The Italians had their pick of restaurants, the Jewish dock workers usually brought their meals with them, but the Irish and the British workers were blessed with The Chinaman. The Chinaman, no one could pronounce his real name, owned and ran Chanze Chinese Chippy, which served the most authentic fish and chips in Ireland's western most county, New York.

He shook his head and wondered as he glanced at the six stove pipes Chan had installed at different points on the roof and exterior walls.

The pipes served no structural purpose, but instead vented the smell of the fried fish dishes in various directions, and could be opened or shut individually so as to allow the aromas to waft in any given direction.

The strategy of course, to this venting conspiracy, was to entice patrons who might otherwise waste their time eating more healthy lunches and suppers

"What the hell's with all the vent pipes?"

The tall, thirty-something Puerto Rican entered the eatery and out of habit, took one of the red and black enameled booths against the back wall. It was a basic tenant of his that when in a public place always sit facing the front door. A habit which had twice saved his life.

The place was empty at that hour and as he slid into the booth he adjusted the green, alligator skin strap on his wristwatch and checked the time. It was 10:30 a. m.

An attractive Chinese waitress in her late teens, one of Chan's sixteen offspring, came up to the table and spoke through the large wad of gum in her mouth.

"You want I should bring you a menu or sumthin' Mac?" Despite being Chinese the girl had been born and raised in Brooklyn or so spoke perfect English.

"You got a house phone here, Chica?" She eyed him from the face down not concealing her disappointment at the barrier of the table.

"Yeah." She spat. A minute later she returned with a house phone, cleared the long wire over the adjoining chairs and set it on the table.

"Chicken Chow Mein, steamed rice and . . . you got jalapenos?"

"Hal-a-what's?" She asked.

"Never mind." She left, he dialed and the line on the other end rang.

Over in Brooklyn Heights, behind the desk of the reception area of the Jack Lalanne Health Club, a female receptionist laid the phone receiver on the desk, checked that her stocking seams were straight, smoothed her grey flared skirt and slid from around the desk and crossed the gym floor to where a dozen men pumped weights, did calisthenics and posed in front of wall length mirrors to check their imagined progress. She moved directly to her mark approaching the well-built, dark haired club member who was doing bench presses. Spying her approach, he paused until she stood just alongside the bench, then slowly grunted out an extra two or three reps.

As he sat up and methodically wiped his neck with a towel he focused his crystal blue eyes on hers. The gesture had the intended effect. After sopping herself up from the hormone puddle she had become the leggy brunette delivered the message that he had a phone call at reception.

The former O.S.S. officer smiled, continued to slowly towel himself down and walked to the desk.

"Yeah?" He answered into the transceiver.

We need to meet up. I might have a lead over on the East Side docks. Fella named Nick the Bull. Might'a seen something last week.

"That's a lotta might'a's there Inspector Hernandez."

Well – Hernandez answered

"Deep subject my taco eating friend."

Yeah, first time I ever heard that one, Gringo. Now if you're finished trying to cock bait whatever, naïve, young female, or in your case young male you wann'a fuck tonight, can we get together and run down this wafer thin lead so's I can scratch it off the list?

"Where are you now?"

Some Chink joint on the Lower East Side.

"Chanze?"

Yeah! How'd you know?

"'Cause you used the word 'Chink' and you hate

Chinatown."

I didn't use the name of the place!

"Yeah, but most of you Spick pendejos are racist bastards. See you in about half an hour. Get me an order of egg rolls, will ya?"

Go fuck yourself! Hernandez hung up.

In their two years working together Benson and Hernandez had developed a loving relationship.

†

Forty-five minutes later, dressed in a dark, three piece Armani and biting his last egg roll in half as he passed through the gate of Pier 18, Special Agent Benson walked out onto the dock and mounted a bollard on the edge of the creosote soaked pier and looked out over the harbor. His breath formed into condensation as he exhaled and with perhaps more affection then a man should, perused the two mile expanse of the New York harbor. Hernandez trailed behind.

The post war economic boom which fueled the controlled chaos Benson now marveled at across the harbor transformed him back to his childhood in Bayonne, New Jersey.

Ships, sea going tugs and various sized craft of every description traversed the massive river in both directions.

"I ask you! Is this the most magnificent city in the greatest country on the planet or what?!"

"You smoke some hooch on the way over here?" Hernandez grumbled.

"Nah! That shit's for losers!" Hernandez made no attempt to hide his impatience as Benson communed with nature.

"Hey, Ansel Adams, can we get this fuckin' show on the road?"

"What, you got a date? Don't worry, hookers in this town work 24-7!" Hernandez didn't respond. Benson knew his limits with his partner and succumbed. "Alright, let's go find this schmuck."

He hoped down off the bollard and followed behind as Hernandez led them back up the pier and towards the terminal.

A burley, middle-aged guy dragging a 'J' bar behind him crossed their path. Hernandez went to flash his badge but Benson put a hand up and stepped in front of him then approached the dock worker.

"Hey, how's it hangin?"

"Low and to the left. How's about yerself?" The dock worker shot back.

"Hell, I can't even remember last time I had the damn thing out!" Benson extended the banter. "Hey, we're lookin' for the foreman." The stevedore sized him up and down and smiled.

"Yeah, no problem. You want Big Nick, he works outta the Tose trucking office." Benson gestured to his partner as if to say, 'See how it's done?'

"I thought he was called The Bull?" Hernandez

challenged.

"You ever been to Pamplona?" Benson threw out. His partner stared in puzzlement. "You know, bulls chasing assholes in white suites, red scarves, running for their lives?"

"Can't say as I've had the pleasure." Hernandez sarcastically replied.

"Well if you go, be careful. Some'a them fuckin' bulls are pretty big." The dock hand pointed back towards the terminal as he walked away.

"That's him over there." He indicated a tall husky, forty-something parking and dismounting a yellow, Hyster forklift.

"You Nick?" Hernandez asked as they approached.

"Depends." The foreman shifted the unlit cigar between his cheek and teeth.

About a hundred feet down the dock a young stevedore stacking fifty pound sacks of potatoes on a pallet glanced over and spotted the agent flashing his badge to the Foreman. Benson picked up on Nick glancing over his right shoulder and turned in time to see the young stevedore drop a sack and sprint down the pier in the opposite direction.

"God damn it!" He cursed as he nudged Hernandez and lit out after the pale skinned suspect.

"WAIT RIGHT HERE! DON'T MOVE!" Hernandez ordered the foreman as he took off after his partner.

"Sure thing, Pal." The Foreman replied. As soon as they were about ten feet away he remounted the forklift and went back to work. "Fuck you, jerk-off!"

Now approaching Pier 20 the dock worker was swiftly putting as much real estate between himself and the agents as possible.

Vaulting freight, equipment and weaving in and around workers like a champion running back both agents were impressed. The suspect suddenly cut right and veered into the terminal building on Pier 20.

With the entire center span of floor space piled high with all manner of freight, he had no choice but to turn right or left. With a pair of forklifts on the left he dodged right and took the next left. Past crates, barrels, workers and long lengths of iron pipe he paced himself and glanced back over his shoulder to see the hounds just turning the corner.

"Little bastard's fast!" Hernandez quipped.

"Probably half Spic." Benson spoke with hardly a breath as he picked up the pace.

"Fuck . . . you!" Hernandez panted.

By this time the worker was running out of dock and had another choice to make. Ahead, the entire far end of the long terminal was occupied by a walled office area the upper half of which was windowed. Through the large window he could see that inside the office the staff milled about.

Quickly glancing back he noted Benson gaining on him and made his choice.

Grabbing a fire axe from a pillar without breaking stride he flung it ahead of himself and sent it crashing through the plate glass.

Screams emanated from the office area as, without hesitation he vaulted the three foot high base frame and combat rolled into the office and back up on his feet.

With workers still shrieking as they scurried to the sides he barged his way through a pair of staff, burst through the front doors and made his way out onto the street.

By this time Benson was about fifty yards behind him while Hernandez, now completely out of gas, was propped up against a post back in the warehouse panting heavily.

Outside the terminal under the six lane, elevated highway of the West Side Drive, due to a fender bender on the south-bound lane the two lanes of traffic at street level had slowed almost to a halt.

Benson vaulted the office wall, dashed across the office and burst through the front door and out into the bright winter's sun where he scanned up and down the traffic and spotted his man about ten car lengths to the north sprinting up and over the roof of a Yellow Sunshine Taxi.

"Fuck this noise!" He ripped off his over coat, peeled off his suit jacket, letting it also drop to the pavement and dashed into the morning shadows of the West Side Drive weaving a path through the slow moving vehicles.

For better than five city blocks the two man parade of the stevedore and Benson dodged and wove their way through the morning Manhattan traffic under the WSD until they reached the Christopher Street Pier where Benson was quickly gaining on him. Hernandez was nowhere to be seen.

The runner suddenly cut left towards the river and headed towards the pier which housed a ferry point. As Benson made his follow-on maneuver he was nearly nailed by a black Pontiac and was forced to mount the fender and roll over the hood falling off the other side at which point he narrowly dodged being squashed by a delivery van which only just managed to brake and swerve into the Pontiac. Both drivers sprang from their vehicles and engaged in that most favorite of New York past times, arguing in traffic.

Back on his feet and in the race the D.O.F.A. agent sprinted out onto the dead end pier and knew he had his prey cornered. Or so he thought. Looking down the dock he stopped and watched as the runner showed no signs of slowing down.

"No, no, no!. Don't even think about-" Benson stopped and stood halfway down the pier and watched in horror as the stevedore didn't hesitate for a moment but ran straight off the edge of the pier and into the freezing water of the Hudson.

"SON-OF-A-BITCH!" Benson swore as he peeled off his silk tie and kicked off his $100 alligator Florsheims, jogged to the end of the pier and followed the suspect into the Hudson with a near perfect swan dive.

Not banking on the unknown guy following him into the water and exhausted from the short marathon of a chase, the suspect was hard pressed to swim very far in the freezing water. Benson casually free styled over to the dock worker where he tread water near a piling and slapped him in back of the head.

"ASSHOLE! What the fuck were you thinking?!"

Back up on the pier a small crowd had gathered along with some ferry workers and ten minutes later Benson and the handcuffed suspect were sitting next to each other, propped up against a collection of wooden kegs of butter gathered around a bollard. The runner shivered uncontrollably as Benson knelt and searched his pockets for I.D.

A Yellow cab pulled up outside the dock and Hernandez, followed by an irate taxi driver jumped out and raced out onto the pier.

"HEY ASSHOLE, YOU OWE ME A BUCK FIFTY!" The driver yelled after Hernandez.

Along with some I.D. Benson pulled a handful of crunched up one dollar bills from the suspect's pocket, fished through them and handed two to his partner.

"This ain't Tijuana, pay the cabby!" He ordered Hernandez. Turning his anger to the suspect Benson slapped him again across the head.

"That god damned coat was cashmere! You know what cashmere is you stupid fuck?!" Benson slapped him in the head another one. He rifled through the few I.D. cards.

"Son-of-a-bitch!" Benson declared as he read a

driver's license.

"What?!" Hernandez asked as he thrust the dripping dollar bills at the cab driver.

"He's a fuckin' Canadian! You believe that shit?! Canadian! Couldn't even be a real illegal!"

"What's that supposed ta mean?!" Hernandez asked.

"I keep forgettin' you got your badge through mail order. It means he's not our man Sherlock!"

Hernandez figured it was time to get in on the hard cop-dumb cop routine and gave the seated suspect a swift kick and joined in on the chastisement.

"Why you come all this way? No jobs in Canada?! Should 'a come in through Mexico. They got road signs to the border, rest stops with taco stands along the way and free tequila at the border." He administered another half-hearted kick. "There ain't even no fence!"

"Encoulé les flics!" The shivering stevedore spat on the ground in front of the two.

"What the fuck is la Flick? He think I'm a cigarette lighter?" Hernandez asked Benson.

"It's French-Canadian. I think he told you to fuck off."

"You fuckin' Kanuck bastard!" The burly Puerto Rican broke into a fusillade of uncontrolled kicks on the handcuffed suspect.

"WHOA, WHOA WHOA!" Benson jumped between them pushing his partner back. "Easy man! Not like he's a fuckin' murder suspect or somethin'!" He pulled Hernandez aside and gathered up his shoes. "Baby sit this asshole till the uniforms show up will ya?! I'm goin' back to the shipping office and see if I can shake another lead."

With the freezing cold, shivering Canuck sitting handcuffed against the stack of kegs and Hernandez, glaring down with an unsympathetic eye, Benson grabbed his shoes and caught up with the Yellow taxi.

Ten minutes later, and still dripping wet he entered the doorway with the white sign and blue logo of Tose Trucking & Shipping with the hand pointing upstairs.

Up in the office he questioned the guy at the counter who knew nothing but remembered an incident a few days ago.

"Carmine?" The office clerk called out to the back. There was no answer so he took half a step backwards and gave it a second shot. "CARMINE!"

"WHAT?! I'M RIGHT FUCKIN' RIGHT HERE!" Carmine counter attacked with a mouth half full of salami and cheese on rye as he came out from the back office and moved up to the counter.

"What'a ya want?!"

Carmine's co-worker nodded over the counter at Benson.

"Here's your big chance at glory."

Five minutes later Benson left with the plate number of the delivery truck and the limo which had come to collect the canned tomatoes nearly a week ago.

Paddy Kelly

†

State Route 9
Springfield, New Jersey

It was one of those late winter days you don't mind, clear and crisp but not too cold. It was around ten in the morning when Doc and Louie caught the 10:10 for Trenton out of Grand Central Terminal. An hour later they were heading south on State Route 9 in a taxi. Three miles from the train station the cab pulled off the two lane blacktop and took the single lane, dirt road past a lone, bread loaf mailbox on a pole and headed towards the large farmhouse in the distance. They were only thirty five miles outside Manhattan but they might as well have been in rural midlands of Nebraska.

The old four lane, cross state highway, Route 9, while providing work to Depression Era jobless just fifteen years ago as well as providing a faster safer route for an increasing commuter driven population, had also left all the ancillary businesses and farms cut off from easy access to the urban areas and so too their century old revenue stream.

The cab driver steered the car past the acres of marijuana crop straddling the road and up in front of the house alongside the huge porch.

Doc gave the driver a tenner and, as he dropped the meter arm and rummaged through his pocket for change McKeowen stopped him.

"Keep it."

"Thanks pal."

"Just pick us up in about an hour."

"Sure thing." Doc and Louie both noted that the four foot high crops extended around and well beyond the back of the house as the taxi drove off.

"Why'd you tell him to come back? We could'a just called from the house?"

"You see any telephone lines to the house coming off the main road feed?" Louie glanced back down the dirt drive to the road. There were no poles or lines.

"Oh, you just know everything, don't ya?!"

Up on the porch two poorly dressed but clean young kids played with toy farming vehicles made of stamped metal.

"Think we'll get anywhere with this guy?" Louie asked on the way up to the door.

"No tellin' but one thing's for sure."

"What's that?" Mancino asked as Doc pulled back the screen door and knocked.

"We'll know as soon as he opens his mouth." On the third attempt a tall, middle-aged and grizzled farmer type came through the front door with a 16 gauge, long barreled side-by-side, leveled at them.

Louie raised his hands. Doc made eye contact and held it.

"You two assholes from the F.B.N.?"

"No, nothing to do with the Bureau of Narcotics. And we're not cops either." He quickly informed the farmer. "You Mr. Kerns?"

"Depends. Who's askin' and why!"

"Nice to meet you Mr. Kerns. We're in the way of researching the local agriculture. Mind if we pick your brain a little?"

"Sheeet! You blind boy?!" He lowered the blunderbuss and smirked. "You see my situation!" He nodded around to his scrap filled yard, dilapidated house and shoeless kids. "Ain't gonna be much for ya ta pick. But you can go at it if'n you've a mind to." He went inside not bothering to hold the door open for Doc.

Meanwhile Louie was attempting to make friends.

"Hi ya! How you guys doing?" Louie greeted as he squatted down next to the eight year old pigtailed girl.

"You a stranger?!" She confronted.

"Well, yeah I guess so." Louie answered. She folded her arms and turned her back on him. The boy, about five, called over.

"We ain't allowed ta talk ta strangers. You should'a said you was a visitor or a revenuer."

"What would you'a said if I was a revenuer?"

"Nothn', my dad would'a shot ya." He then approached the now standing Louie and immediately started tugging on his trouser leg.

"Hey Mista, ya wanna hear a joke? Ya wanna hear a joke? Ya wanna hear a joke? Do ya, do ya? Ya wanna hear a joke?"

"Kid! Not the trousers, Okay?!" Louie pulled

away and stepped back but was doggedly pursued.

"Ya wanna hear a joke? Do ya? Huh? Ya wanna hear a joke?"

"Yeah, can you tell the one 'Far, far away'?"

"Say knock knock! Go on say knock knock! Say knock knock!" The kid directed.

"AWRIGHT ALREADY! Knock knock!"

"WHOSE DARE?" The boy asked. Both kids laughed hysterically.

Inside the kitchen Kerns poured Doc a half full coffee cup of clear liquid from a clay jug and passed it to him.

"Here's to the end of the war. Bottom's up!" He threw back his drink like a pro. Doc followed suit and nearly choked to death. The farmer laughed.

"So what part'a the city you from boy?"

"Greenwich Village. It's in Manhattan." Doc coughed out.

"A village inside a city! Ain't that sumthin?!" He mused as he poured himself and Doc another. Doc's was smaller.

"What exactly is it you're after, Mr. . . . ?"

"McKeowen, Mike McKeowen."

"And why me?" Doc set the drink aside.

"You because you're the largest farm within driving distance. But mainly because there's been a lot of activity in the government lately centered around closing down the hemp farms around the country, even the licensed ones. And a lot'a talk about how hemp leads to heroin addiction."

"I don't deal in that shit. That's for suckers and

the big boys with big money backing them up."

"And guns?"

"And guns." The farmer affirmed. "Besides it ain't like the days of Prohibition, nobody brings that shit in through Jersey."

"Yu know something about the hard stuff?"

"Rumors mostly. People around here talk."

"What do people around here say about off load points for heroin?"

"Detroit in from Canada, Philly to some extent but mostly Florida from what I hear on the street."

"That being the case the Feds are gonna be lookin' to be clamping down on everybody wouldn't ya think?" Doc asked.

"You're a little late with that news partner. I was served this 'bout two weeks ago." He pulled an official government manila envelope from the cupboard behind him and passed it to Doc who opened it.

It was a Cease & Desist order to stop planting and to destroy all his hemp crops.

"This order legit?"

"My family lawyer says it is."

"You plan on obeying this?"

"Sure, just as soon as them pricks down in Washington get me another way to support my kids.

"What'a you plan on doing when they come to close your farm?"

"Why you think I carry this?!" He tapped his shotgun. "My daddy was crippled in the last war. Part of the Bonus Expeditionary Force. They promised he would be paid enough money to buy him and his family a house if he went over and fought the Kaiser." He handed Doc his empty glass. "You see what's in that glass?" Doc knew the history but glanced down anyway. "That's what he got when he came back all busted up and couldn't work no more." Doc thought about setting the glass aside but didn't. "No house, no money no nothin'!"

He retrieved the glass from Doc and poured himself another. "Then comes a new war. Against the same people! Government says, 'You farmers can help win the war if you grow hemp. Country needs hemp.' So we convert our lands, convert our machinery and replant. We grow hemp. Nearly 500,000 acres of it. Pay an extra tax to Uncle Sam for the privilege on top of it. What do we get now the war's over? 'Hemp is bad! Causes crime, makes niggers crazy and white men insane. You keep growin' hemp, we gonna put you in jail!'"

"What about the tax you paid?!"

"Tax cert's been revoked, commensurate with the Cease & Desist order. No refunds on the monies paid either!"

"Compensation?"

"Sheeet! That corn liquor must'a hit you harder than I thought."

Doc, having been blindsided by this latest American Dream travesty was at a loss as to what to say.

"Guns on the table Mr. Kerns, honest opinion. Any idea how this happened?" Doc probed.

"You see who's John Hancock is on the bottom of that order don't ya?" Doc re-examined the document.

> By order of Harry J. Anslinger, Commissioner
> Federal Bureau of Narcotics

"You know what they say about birds of a feather . . ."

"How'd ya mean?" Doc asked.

"Anslinger was the Assistant Commissioner of Prohibition under Hoover. He's a fucking Hoover wanna-be! Now he's playin' the oldest trick in the book. Ya wanna be a big shot politician with all kinds'a power? Create an enemy, secure financial backing, and convince anybody who'll listen you're the only one can slay the dragon. Asslinger learned that under the master himself, J. Edgar Hoover." Doc sipped his moonshine as Kerns continued. "To reinforce his place in the Ivory tower of justice Asslinger even married into the family."

"Who'd that be?"

"Martha Kind Denniston."

"Who is?"

"You ain't exactly Mr. Current Affairs are ya boy?" He sipped his drink. "The niece of the Secretary of the Treasury."

"Andrew W. Mellon, the guy financing Anslinger's anti-drug campaign!?" Doc realized out loud.

"You ain't as dumb as you look, Doc. Have

another drink."

A half an hour later Louie and a semi-sober Doc were walking down the dirt drive out towards the main road.

"So the Senate passes the mandatory hemp bill in 1942 to supplement the loss of the Philippines to the Japs. Then what?" Louie pushed.

"The country needs the hemp to make rope for the Navy, miles of it! So thanks to the superiority of U.S. farming and manufacturing, soon what's left of the Free World market is booming. Now they research for other uses for hemp. Lo and behold, they find a way to produce fast cheap paper. Bad news for newspaper magnet Hearst who owns millions in acres of forestry." Doc explained.

"Despite the fact those acres were obtained illegally when the Taft Administration sold public lands off to him and the other industrialists for pennies an acre." Louie added.

"Impressive Mancino! You been reading?"

"Not really. You told me that last year during one of your rants while we was having a baptism."

"Fair enough. So that leaves millions of dollars for those acres, millions which he didn't pay! He gets two bites of the cherry, unless . . ."

"Unless the trees are devaluated by cheap paper made from hemp!"

"Bingo!"

"Scary as it may sound Doc, I'm following ya so far but, what's all this got to do with heroin?!"

"Nothing, except that right in the middle of all

their problems Hearst, Mellon and DuPont get themselves handed a get-out-of jail free card by Lucky Luciano and the New York Mob when they find an excuse to back track on all that brew-ha-ha they made ten years ago about how much the country needed hemp! The Mob sets up an industrial sized, heroin export-import operation. So, with Anslinger as the puppet-front man, they build the whole thing into a campaign! An anti-drug campaign."

"Not just heroin, all drugs!" Louie realized aloud.

"Posters, so-called public service announcements, school visits even short films in the cinema!"

The taxi met them right on time and they were at the train station on schedule to catch the 1:15 back into The City.

By the time Doc and Louie were halfway back to Manhattan, to forage for a restaurant and plan their next move, the unspoken realization was not only had they learned something, but they both realized that the rabbit hole was a helluva lot deeper than then either had imagined.

✝

New State Department Building
Virginia Avenue
Washington D.C.

Three days after their New York City

The Wolves of Calabria

misadventure Benson and Hernandez were back in their D.C. office for some housekeeping duties. Along with the entire rest of the U.S. Department of State they found that the building was in complete chaos.

Earlier in the year President Truman had given the final okay to move and consolidate the Department, now significantly more expansive in size and function then it had been before the war. Now in the process of being relocated into a new headquarters building the great move was underway.

With a pre-war roster of less than one thousand employees the department had ballooned during the war years and was now topping the five thousand employee mark. Additional need for the more space was inarguable.

Additionally with the department spread all over the greater Washington area, located in as many as fifty separate buildings, a simple errand could take up to half a day to complete.

The new spacious fifth floor, open plan office was to be mutually occupied by the entire nine person staff of the Investigations Branch comprised of two secretaries, six investigators and the Branch Head, known to the staff as, (and not always affectionately), the 'Chief', presently made up the roster.

With furniture, filing cabinets and myriad personal belongings strewn about, the office itself was essentially in a shambles.

Suspended a yard above the floor by a thick

forefinger a large coffee mug bearing the U.S. Navy logo floated across the room. Clenched in the tall, not-so-overweight branch head's ham-of-a-fist the mug led its bearer through the front door and straight up to Hernandez who was stuffing files into the top drawer of a four drawer filing cabinet.

"Where's Benson?" The body growled.

"Right behind you." Hernandez casually replied over his shoulder. The Chief turned to his left in time to see Benson over in the far corner charming one of the secretaries.

"BENSON!" Benson read his tone and disengaged from the woman. "You two get anywhere on the smuggling operation?"

"Looks like a freakin' Block Buster went off in this place!" Benson casually threw out as he weaved his way around some furniture and approached his boss. "Morning Chief, how's tricks?"

"I reiterate, you two get anywhere on the smuggling operation?"

"I thought you were supposed to cut back on the caffeine!" Benson nodded at the large coffee mug.

"I am A-hole, it's Coca-Cola and if I have to ask you a third time -"

"Well Chief –"

"I'll take that as a no. You do understand that Anslinger has given us thirty days to come up with something he can use or he's gonna give it to the Farged-ups Beyond Imaginations?! That was ten days, sixteen hours, twenty-minutes and about thirty-seven seconds ago. But who's counting?"

"Chief, I promise we'll have an update report written up by the end of the day, but right now we really got to get all this stuff stowed and filed so we can set up our desk and get back at it!" Hernandez coaxed. Benson then jumped in on their well-rehearsed, tag team routine.

"Chief, we have a hot lead we picked up in New York at that trucking company. As a matter of fact I'm due to make a call right about -" Benson glanced at his gold Rolex with the green, alligator wrist strap. "Now."

"Don't bullshit me Benson! If you two haven't unearthed something by the end of the month, I'm gonna tell Anslinger we got nothin'!"

"Chief, don't lose confidence!"

"Jack I gave this to you two because of your record. You've got nearly as many collars as the other two teams combined. That Kansas City bust was inspired!"

"Thanks Chief, we appreciate the way you wrote it up and -"

"However, my two little snowflakes! That was last year, which means its old news, which means nobody gives a shucks! Ergo, if you can't tell the U.S. government who is attempting to flood our streets with that white sheit, I shall be compelled to help Mr. Anslinger's Narcotics Bureau locate someone who can."

He turned to go and stumbled over a wooden crate of files left on the floor.

"Why the hell didn't they put us in the Pentagon

like the rest of the War Department?!" He kicked the packing crate. "I seen better organized riots! Farging bastones!" He stepped around the wooden box. "Three million dollars you'd think they would have had an organized plan for moving!" He stormed off back towards his office. "WHERE'S MY G-DAMN INVENTORY FOLDER?!" He yelled from inside the office.

Benson looked at Hernandez who immediately gave commentary.

"Why the fuck can't he fucking curse like a god damn normal person?!" Hernandez blurted as he turned to Benson who was heading towards the door. "HEY! Where the hell you goin'?" He gestured to the chaos of files which smothered their desks.

"I gotta make a farging phone call." He yelled back to Hernandez knee-high in packing crates.

Downstairs Benson made his way through the lobby and out onto 21st Street where he turned onto Virginia Avenue walked a bit then stopped at a news stand to get some change and made his way to a bank of phone booths about a hundred yards further down the avenue. Feeding a nickel into the box he dialed and waited. It rang twice and a receptionist answered.

"It's me. Lemme talk to him." Benson tersely directed. A male voice came on the line.

Yeah?

"It's Benson."

You got some news?

"The dock lead in New York was a dead end."

The Wolves of Calabria

So what'a you all intend on doin' now?

"I need more information. There's defiantly somebody else out there trying to set up an operation but no idea how big. If I'm gonna locate him and put him outta business I'm gonna need more info. I can't run leads on thin air."

You are the investigator Mr. Benson. If you want your part of the prize, you'll gonna do your part as agreed!"

There was an uncomfortable silence before the other party, in his slow, articulate drawl, spoke again.

Snoop around the files of an Agent White. He works directly for Anslinger and is lookin' ta make a name for himself. From what I hear he's a sneaky little shit that'll do whatever he has to do ta score points. Maybe he's onto somethin' you can use.

"I'll get on it today."

Do whatever ya have ta do agent! I don't want no competin' inter-ests getting' in our way once this thing is set up!

"I understand." Benson quietly acquiesced.

*Ain't nobody getting' any younger son, and when it comes time for the gold watch ceremony where they put yo' ass out ta pasture, only thing you gonna be able ta do ta sustain the lifestyle in which you have become accustomed to is with what **you** gots stashed away! Not that piddlie-ass, little pension they gonna give you. We on the same sheet of music young man?*

"I understand Senator. I'll be in touch." The line

went dead.

✝

CHAPTER XI

The Majestic Arms
115 Central Park West
New York City

There are any number of places on the planet where heat and humidity can be suffered, but a hot humid day in Manhattan has a debilitating character all its own. At only half past ten on that May morning it was already ninety-two degrees with 90% humidity and climbing in Midtown Manhattan as Joey Adonis turned off 71st Street and cruised into the lobby of the palatial Art Deco Majestic Arms.

Glad to be in the shade of the lobby Joey took a minute to compose himself.

The Majestic was well known throughout New York society not only for its innovative architectural design and decorative opulence but for the notoriety of some of its residents.

Meyer Lansky took up residence in 'The Arms' a few years back until he relocated to keep a lower profile, Charlie Luciano until his arrest and subsequent deportation and Louie 'Lepke' Buchalter, owner operator of Murder Inc., until he relocated to his reserved seat in the electric chair, compliments of the New York City D.A. Thomas Dewey.

There was also a collection of entertainment personalities such as the famous cigar chomping comic Milton Berle who became the world's first T.V. star when he moved from radio after he was contracted to host the ill-fated CBS radio show *Kiss and Make Up*.

Walter Winchell, the influential broadcaster who, after a run-in with Luciano while passing through the lobby one afternoon, took great pains to avoid bumping into him in or around the building ever again, was also resident.

As Joey Socks Lanza had promised his aid Adonis, before 'going away', if things expanded Adonis would be cut in on the deal. Lanza, now also convicted and serving time, had from prison sent Adonis to today's meet as his chief rep.

How he handled himself in front of the senior Mafiosi at the meeting, due to start at eleven, would determine his future in the organization.

Anxious to one day man his own crew and possibly work his way up to having his own family, Adonis quietly rehearsed in the elevator on the way upstairs.

He stepped off the lift on the twentieth floor, made his way down the hall to apartment number 206 and pressed the bell in the center of the polished mahogany door. An eye appeared in the peep hole and he heard the door being unlocked. It opened and Joey waltzed into the room.

The plush, three bedroom apartment featured a sprawling suite with a large couch, two love seats and a half dozen Louie the XVI chairs which lined the perimeter of the sunken parlor. Original oil

The Wolves of Calabria

paintings complemented a small collection of pedestal mounted marble statuary and the rear wall, dominated by a floor to ceiling picture window framed by red and gold velvet curtains festooned with black corded ties, overlooked Central Park and out across the splendid panorama of the Manhattan landscape.

Comfortably seated around the perimeter was Frankie Costello, as it was his apartment, Jimmy and Frankie Camardo, Johnny 'Cockeyed' Dunn, the recently returned to America Vito Genovese and finally the man who was respected above even the dons themselves, Meyer Lansky.

Adonis took a chair near the window.

Sometimes respectfully known as 'The Accountant', Meyer Lansky, born in Grodno, Poland came to The States in 1911 where he and his family settled on the Lower West Side. While in school he met Charlie Luciano who tried to shake him down for his lunch money. Meyer told him in no uncertain terms where he could stick it. They beat the hell out of each other and became best friends ever since.

By 1936, the year Lucky was sent up by D.A. Dewey, Meyer had massive gambling operations already set up in New Orleans and across Florida. Having the foresight to see that the Caribbean was exempt from U.S. gambling laws and therefore wide open and ripe for the picking, he had cracked the Cuban market. Gambling was the perfect vehicle for the massive laundering operations required to cleanse the piles of dirty money generated weekly by the busy little bees of the New York Families and their loosely connected associates who, by virtue of this meeting, were about to became a little less loosely associated.

Lansky maintained a Swiss bank account to protect himself and was currently in negotiations to buy his own offshore bank.

A young well-dressed, black yarmulke wearing type with both hands on his briefcase sat quietly in the opposite corner. A couple of the guests had drinks and there were two large trays of finger sandwiches, untouched, on the glass topped table in the center of the room. Perusing the room Adonis shifted nervously in his seat.

The dark haired, round chinned Lansky stood and stepped to the center of the room.

"Shall we get this thing started?" There were nods of agreement all round. "Before we start I just wanna say that Lucky's behind this thing all the way, he is in fact the man who gave birth to this idea even before the war broke out. He worked on it while he was on the inside and ran the rough plan by me the night before he set sail to go back to Italy. As most of you know I took the limo ride with him down from Great Meadows the afternoon before he was deported. We'd already discussed the plan and the bulk of our conversation was about ideas on how to work out the details. Which we did. In that light, I speak for the both of us in regards to all issues concerning whatever it is that we agree on here today. Once we agree on a path of action the other families will be notified and a grand council will be convened at an appropriate time and place. Frankie I believe you have some particulars for the group."

Frankie Costello, as de facto head of the Luciano Family had been working with Meyer Lansky for the last two years to plan out a workable solution to maximize profits and keep the peace not only in the five New York families but all the associated mob families which had evolved following the end of the Castellammarese War in 1932.

"Gentlemen, the general layout is straight forward. We pool our resources, work more closely with certain already established overseas interests, who will act as suppliers and now that we have the juice, establish a national distribution network, along the lines of the gambling rackets using the old bootleg routes where applicable."

There was the usual shifting in seats at being asked to consider another large scale investment particularly in light of the fact that Bugsy Siegel's Flamingo adventure out in Las Vegas wasn't going so well. One of the group spoke up.

"Frankie, with all due respect, there's a good chunk of our money already tied up out the Vegas operation, I mean, it's over two years now and-"

Costello glanced over at Lansky who instantly spoke up.

"Gentlemen, as we speak a delegation is currently preparing to travel to Las Vegas to negotiate with Mr. Seigal. They are empowered to offer a deal that will rectify the situation to everyone's satisfaction." Meyer made eye contact with the group as he spoke. "You have my word we will keep you appraised as things develop." Any apprehension in the group was quickly quashed by Lansky's assurance.

Costello pushed on.

"You are the most important players in the greater New York area, at least the ones we are interested in inviting. For a more detailed layout I brought someone along I think can do it better justice as well as answer any questions you might pose at the present."

The black yarmulke, a Magna cum Laude Harvard Business School graduate in investment accountancy, never broke a sweat as he spoke for nearly thirty minutes giving a detailed financial plan to the most dangerous killers and racketeers in the world.

His briefing included projected profits for the next year, suggested tax avoidance techniques and outlined legitimate investments to ease the increased money laundering requirements which would result from the proposed expansion of the operation. The guys were impressed.

There were a few basic questions which he deftly addressed, then was thanked for his services as he was handed an envelope and escorted to the door.

Lansky retook the floor but Jimmy Camardo immediately posed a question.

"What'a we do about the Chinks?"

"What about 'em?" Meyer responded.

"They're movin' a significant amount of junk through Chink Town bringin' it in from Frisco. Been doin' it since the twenties, now it looks like they got their slanty little eyes on spreadin' up to the Village."

"They gotta cross Mott Street first!" Eddie Erickson added. Meyer turned to Erickson.

"Eddie, get Sammy to contact Socks then give me a call in the next day or so. Let's see what we need to do about that situation."

"Will do Mr. Lansky, I'm meeting up with him tonight at the Samoan for a drink."

"Good. Bring him up to speed on what we talked about here today."

"Will do."

"Anybody got any other questions?"

"Yeah, how's we gonna handle shipping, in country I mean? Them new inter-state laws they set up during the war where they allow stop and search?"

"We got somebody on it, it's under control." Costello answered.

"Pending unanimous agreement here today Lucky has asked me to contact him and work out the final details. Gentlemen, any other questions?" Meyer asked.

"Yeah Mr. Lansky, one more question." It was Jimmy Camardo again. "What's this all so valuable commodity you asking us to invest in, both financially and career wise?"

Lansky maintained an expressionless face as he answered.

"A commodity which is, as we speak, is being set up for mass manufacture, on an industrial scale. The crop of the future gentlemen." From the table in front of him he retrieved a small, carved oak box, set it on the table in front of Camardo to his left and opened it. It contained a large quantity of fine white powder.

"Dis' heroin?!" Camardo asked.

"Yes, heroin."

As the box was passed around Joey Adonis sat forward in his seat and smiled.

The future looked b right.

†

Pursuant to the questions raised at the Majestic meeting a few days ago concerning how to handle the Chinese drug ring in New York, it was decided to approach the Tong and attempt a negotiation with the Asians.

This would prove to be delicate on two counts.

Essentially aside from chop suey, egg rolls and fortune cookies, the Italians knew literally nothing about them and had never had to deal with the Chinese. The two more or less had simply ignored each other for the sixty to seventy years they had been neighbors in lower Manhattan. Ignored each

The Wolves of Calabria

other until expansion by both communities caused their paths to converge along Mott Street north of Canal back in the Twenties.

Additionally, at any prospective sit down, Lansky's boys had to not let slip their plans for national expansion of the drug trade, a planned expansion which would go ahead with or without the Oriental's cooperation.

New York City's Chinatown contains the largest concentration of Chinese in the United States as well as the home of the largest concentration of Chinese in the Western Hemisphere.

Arriving years before the Italians, largely as a result of the Great Gold Rush and the Transcontinental Railway to work as cheap labor, the New York Chinese considered themselves more indigenous than the 'gwai lo'. Gwai-lo, frequently used as a racial slur by the Chinese, means 'ghost man' and not 'white, uncivilized, hairy-faced, heathen, barbarian devil' as is commonly believed.

Early on in America racial tensions in the west gave way to violence and so pushed many of the Chinese east and the small, formerly Irish slum of The Five Points eventually became a Chinese enclave.

Formed in the second half of the 1800's, The Tong gangs, led largely by the Hip Song Tong, were modeled after, though not related to the famous Triad and were comprised primarily of marginalized immigrants to the U.S.

As a way of protecting themselves against

'nativists', that is people who didn't want them, or any other immigrants in America and the racially/economically motivated *Exclusion Act* drafted specifically against the Chinese, people would turn to the Tong.

Unbeknownst to either side the Tong bore remarkable resemblances to the Sicilian la Cosa Nostra both in structure and methods of operation.

None of these historical tidbits however altered the fact that the New York Italians being white saw themselves as more American than the Chinese.

It was a clear case of who came first: the chicken parmesan or the egg roll?

A few days later, after the Majestic meet, to the surprise of Costello and the others, the Tong leaders agreed to a pow wow but with a couple of conditions.

The meet would be on their side of the fence at a time and place they would designate. A set number of men would be allowed, five, and firearms were strictly forbidden.

The untrusting Sicilians discussed it and argued for ten men but the superstitious Cantonese, with heavy roots in Numerology, finally agreed on seven.

Consisting of Eddie Erickson and two torpedoes along with two of Frankie Costello's men the contingent would be headed by Joey Adonis. Finally back in circulation after disappearing a few days after setting the *Normandie* fire, back in '42, but having recently returned, Albert Anastasia was put in charge of security.

The Wolves of Calabria

The next day, a Saturday, word was sent that the meet would take place in an eatery called the Dim Sum on the north side of Pell Street on Sunday.

"Fucking Chinks don't wanna give us a lot'a time to prepare do they?!" Adonis commented as he read the message just brought into his office in the Fulton Street Fish Market by a runner. Sharing a large fish lunch at his desk that Saturday was an old friend.

"Just because they don't speak no English don't mean they're stupid." Anastasia in a rare moment of insight preached.

"Maybe you could give them some English lessons?" Adonis suggested.

It was twelve noon that Sunday when the Italians found their way to Pell Street and appeared at the restaurant.

They were greeted at the heavily ornamented, wooden door by an attractive twenty-something girl who escorted the seven to a back room obviously used for small parties and banquets.

"Wouldn't mind crackin' open that fortune cookie" One of the torpedoes commented as they followed the young, long-haired beauty to the back.

"Get yer fuckin' head in the game!" Anastasia slapped him on the back of his head.

The room they entered was clearly prepped and preserved for the meeting. Tea pots, cups and small plates adorned the long mahogany table.

Before they were admitted into the back room however, they were met by a pair of tall, pugnacious dragon tattooed strong arms in white tee shirts no doubt designed to intimidate the largely overweight Italians dressed in Armani suits, Campenelli shoes and silk ties. As was to be expected the men were given the customary pat down as they entered the room.

As he entered Anastasia removed his dark grey trench coat and black fedora then unbuttoned his suit jacket. He compliantly shuffled in behind Erickson holding his arms out at his sides to allow the Chinese bodyguards to pat him down. While this occurred he let the trench coat dangle by two fingers at the end of his outstretched arm and held his hat in the other.

The Chinaman on his right felt something in Anastasia's suit jacket pocket, reached in and pulled it out. It was a ten inch long switch blade stiletto. Albert made eye contact with the Chinaman and smiled.

"Belonged to my grandfather, gave it to me on his death bed." The only Chinaman grunted at him. "Go on, keep it." Anastasia smiled at the strong-arm, who kept the knife as Albert re-donned his fedora.

They entered and were directed to take seats around the red, rectangular mahogany table. Adonis admired the elaborately carved legs before taking his seat.

The two Chinese bodyguards chose not to take seats but remained standing along the back wall. The Italian security contingent, basically Frankie Costello's two men, followed suit but behind the

The Wolves of Calabria

Italian contingent. Anastasia readjusted his seat to sit nearer the door.

Once all were settled Eddie Erickson was at one end of the table and a middle-aged, scar faced, dark complexioned, bald Chinaman who introduced himself as Hong, sat at the other end. Eddie did likewise before opening the meet.

Reasons for the meet were spelled out, questions were posed, translated for Hong and answers offered.

As an appeasement to the Orientals Lansky had authorised the contingent to offer the Tong a chance to sell whatever heroin they could bring in through the West Coast to the Italians. Hong appeared to be considering the offer with one of his lieutenants. Then, as if a bad omen from the drug gods, negotiations were prematurely terminated before they even really got off the ground.

Suddenly and without warning Chinese tough guy #1, closest to the door decided it would be a good idea to stick the knife he had confiscated into someone. This turned out to be a bad idea for several reasons not least of which it really pissed off the big man he stabbed. The big man was Albert Anastasia.

The veteran of Murder Inc. grabbed the Chink by the neck as he stood and slammed him against the wall while he looked over at the weapon sticking out of his right shoulder.

The muscular Oriental struck half a dozen blows to the Italian's chest while attempting several, poorly placed side snap kicks which only enraged Albert even more. Pulling the knife from his shoulder as he kept the struggling Chinaman pinned to the wall by his neck as he slowly slit his throat from ear to ear as everyone stared. He let the convulsing body slump to the floor, grabbed one of the cloth napkins from the table and wiped his blood soaked hands.

By now all were on their feet and every Chinaman, Hong included, brandished some sort of weapon. Knives, several axes and half a dozen Tong-weapon-of-choice, the meat cleaver, mysteriously appeared.

After all the invite was clear; 'No firearms'.

"So much for working with the fucking Chinks!" Anastasia shrugged as he used the knife to slit open the lining of his trench coat and drew out a military issue .45 automatic. He immediately retired the two Tong members closest to him hitting a third in the leg as the Chinaman tried to scurry through a hidden wall panel in the back of the room.

He reflexively scanned the room and spotted Hong going after Erickson who had his back turned struggling with another Tong member.

Albert wasn't the only one with foresight and three other Italians had smuggled pistols into the meeting. The room was instantly transformed into a carnival shooting gallery with live Chinese Tong members in place of metal ducks on a wheel.

Outnumbered as several more Asians came in through the hidden door Erickson's men fought their way out of the room through the restaurant and over the top of the handful of wait staff setting up for the Sunday dinner rush.

As they scrambled out through the front door carrying two wounded torpedoes with them, three black Chryslers pulled up and blocked off Pell Street from both ends. Several bystanders ran for cover when two Thompson totting men jumped out of the lead vehicle and faced west while another two sprang from the rear car and took up positions facing east effectively cordoning the entire two lane street to allow escape of the Mafia contingent.

By the time all of the members of the Luciano Family had vacated the restaurant into the street none of the Tong were following them. This primarily because they were all dead or dying.

One of the machine gun over watch crew stepped through the broken glass and rubble littering the sidewalk, produced a one foot square, hand painted sign from inside his jacket and hung it on the damaged door.

Once all were safely inside the cars and fleeing the scene cross-town Erickson attempted to issue orders to head over to the East Side Drive, but was cut off by the passenger up front.

"Relax Eddie. We're headin' Upstate until this blows over." The driver informed.

"Who the fuck are you?" The passenger laughed and turned to face him. It was Jimmy Camardo.

"You got any extra holes in ya?" Camardo smirked.

"Nah! I'm alright. Two of Frankie's guys took a hit though. What the fuck'a you doin' here?"

"Mr. Lansky wasn't too sure about them Tong assholes. He thought it a good idea to send back-up."

"I'm gonna haft'a apologize to him for this not working out so well."

"You ain't gonna haft'a apologize. It worked out just fine."

"What'a you talking about? You see the state of that place?"

"Mr. Lansky talked to me yesterday after the Chinks sent word about the meet. He figured they wouldn't take the offer to sell what they import, they'd want more. Even if they did take the offer, they'd get greedy sooner or later. Now they know they ain't invited to the party."

They drove across town until they hit Broadway where the three cars split up.

"Too bad we didn't get ta eat." Jimmy commented. "I love Chink food!"

Back at the scene on Pell Street, highlighted by a continually screaming waitress, the interior of what used to be an upscale Chinese restaurant was riddled with bullet holes along with dead and wounded Chinese.

A bystander ventured over to the storefront of the devastated restaurant and noticed a sign amongst the wreckage.

Closed until further notice.

The Wolves of Calabria

Due to death in family.

✝

**Via Toledo
Montecalvario District
Naples, Italy
June 30th, 1946**

Shortly after the end of the war, coincidentally right around the time Luciano was paroled and deported, Don Calò Vizzini established residency north of Sicily in Naples. The move wasn't to enjoy the beauty of the sprawling port and scenic hills and the aging man had little interest in working on his tan by frequenting the sandy beaches of the local resorts.

Now flush with cash from his and Genovese's wartime exploits in the Black Market, the 'simple old' chicken farmer had gone corporate.

That afternoon Luciano stepped over the raised threshold of the narrow, rear security door and followed Vizzini into the sun-splashed, alley and through the back door of a 100 year old warehouse. They were located just off the Via Polvica in the foot of the hill country where access could be controlled but was still within easy reach of the docks in downtown Naples.

The noise level rose appreciably as they approached the compact but fully operational assembly line set about 50 yards inside the place.

A dozen workers clothed in white lab coats, green rubber gloves and hospital hair nets were evenly distributed along the convoluted conveyer. The belt crept at a snail's pace to allow each of the stations to complete their tasks.

The assembly line started at the furthest end from where they entered and was manned by a young teen. It was his job to cut open the cardboard boxes of newly delivered tin cans which were stacked twelve high behind him, remove the cans, which he did eight at a time then set them single file on the conveyor to shimmy down the belt to be corralled into the filling area.

The next station, about five yards up, was manned by a pair of middle aged women, one each side of the line but off set from each other. Behind each was a metal table holding a pair of vats, one twice the size of the other. The larger one, about the size of a kitchen sink and about as deep, held a fine white powder. The adjacent bin, half as large as the first, held a dirty brown powder similar to brown sugar in texture and appearance.

The two substances were carefully measured then mixed thoroughly together in a third tub in front of each worker. When the two powders came to an even light brow mix they then filled the lidless cans with two ladles full of the finished product. This would fill the tin nearly to the top.

"What's the white shit?" Luciano asked.

"Amphetamine."

The Wolves of Calabria

"Amphetamine? Ups the price, no?"

"If we don't spike it they just fall asleep when they inject it. Then word gets out our product doesn't deliver."

"Huh." Lucky grunted.

"But don't worry, we cut the speed down to just enough so they feel it. About ten percent. The rest is castor sugar, flour, talcum powder, whatever's handy."

At the next station sat a 'counter' whose job it was to hold the row of cans after every count of twelve. When the incoming cans backed up enough to allow the next dozen to flow forward, he would let the next batch through.

Next sat another youngster, barley in her teens, who carefully dropped one disc shaped lid onto each of the cans.

A few yards up the line two delicate little, overhead welding wands on spring loaded extension arms were manned by a pair of skilled laborers who maneuvered the arms down over the cans and were welding the lids on at the rate of nearly one per minute.

When the cans reached the end of the line they were carefully wiped clean, went through a hand operated labeling devise, weighted, and stacked into cardboard boxes in two layers of twelve each.

"These cans look a little funny. Not the right color." Lucky commented.

"That's because they're not regular cans. You can't make skag as heavy as tomatoes unless ya wet it. Then it's no good to ya. So to make up the difference in weight we get special cans made. The tin is mixed with a coupl'a ounces of lead ta give it the extra weight." Vizzini explained. Lucky plucked a can off the line and hefted it in his hand. "Each can comes in at exactly twelve ounces." Lucky nodded his approval. "The Customs guys'll never know the difference." Calò assured.

The filled cardboard boxes were then carefully stacked into wooden crates and packed with straw. The sealed crates were in turn being carried away by two older men to be stacked in the back of the warehouse on wooden pallets.

Pleased that the packaging operation was running smoothly Lucky lifted one of the labeled cans from the conveyer.

"Huh!" Luciano scarfed. "Napoli Brand Tomatoes. Packaged in Naples, Product of Italy!" He read aloud.

"We got the conveyer, lid welder and label application machines up in Rome. Harder to trace." Vizzini informed him.

"Smart. I notice half'a dozen boxes of labels in the corner. What's our source?" He dropped the can back onto the conveyor.

"Don't worry, it's secure. My brother-in-law in Rome. Good price too."

Having graduated from Mayor of a small, essentially valueless village, save for its strategic location during the war, to an international importer-exporter, Don Calò, who had met

Luciano's relatives in Sicily, was more than happy to have finally met the master criminal face-to-face. Thereafter it took little persuasion to maneuver him into a partnership.

"You did good with the money I sent Don Calò. My hats off to you!"

"Hey you!" Lucky pulled one of the packers off the end of the line, a guy who appeared to managing the line.

"Yes?"

"You know who I am?"

"Everybody knows who you are, Don Luciano. You are famous."

Lucky produced a wad of notes from his hip pocket and peeled off a dozen or so.

"You like workin' here?"

"With the whole country leveled by those bastards, 80% of the population out of work and the rest dead? I like it just fine, sir." Lucky handed him the folded over wad.

"You make sure nobody else here knows me." The foreman took it. It was more money than he had seen in the last six months.

"I'm sorry sir, what was your name?" The worker asked. They both smiled.

"Any problems, you let me know! Capish?"

"There is one problem sir." The worker said to Lucky.

"What's zat?"

"Not enough cans!"

"I'll see what I can do." Lucky smiled.

"Finalmente, siamo di ritorno sulla pista!" Lucky happily stated.

"Yes, finally, we are back on track!" Calò confirmed.

Once back outside Don Calò bade him goodbye and instructed his guards to see that Lucky got back to his hotel.

As Vizzini walked away and climbed into his limo, Lucky glanced across the busy six lane avenue and noticed a paparazzi focusing in on him and taking pictures. He nodded at two of the goons standing nearby who carefully weaved their way through the slow moving traffic and crossed the street to where the little guy was snapping away no doubt fantasizing about his upcoming big bonus check.

He never knew what hit hm.

After he was pummeled nearly unconscious, the goons went to work separately one smashing his camera while the other squatted down, rummaged through the hapless shutterbug's pockets, fished out his I.D. and confiscated it.

Once they were back across the avenue Lucky pulled a wad of bills out of his pocket and handed them to the head bodyguard.

"Give 'em a couple bucks. Buy him a new camera and send it to him. He'll get the message."

✝

The Wolves of Calabria

125th Street and Seventh Avenue
Harlem, NYC

It was about an hour or so after dark when Manny the Pusher turned the corner into the alley off 125th Street and found himself behind St. Mark's church. It was getting chilly and the wind had started picking up. He pulled his shin length fur coat tight around his waist and buckled the belt as he tip toed his red alligator Florsheims around a puddle and some potholes strewn across the back alley.

Manny was there for a meet, his fifth of the day.

As one of the half dozen or so black heroin pushers in Harlem, Manny was quickly getting rich off the Negro ex-GI's. As the last hired, first fired their contribution to the war effort, now that U.S. capitalism was back in full swing, was minimized even more so than was that of the white GI's.

Manny perused the shadows as he patiently waited when suddenly he heard a voice mumble through the encroaching night.

"Yo!"

"Who's dare?" He froze and called back.

"You the one they calls 'Manny'?" The pusher looked down and to his right, between the church and the adjoining tenement. Tucked in a nook, there was a huddled figure wrapped in a worn Army blanket.

The old black man curled up and dressed in tatters appeared to be suffering from withdrawals.

This warmed the cold cockles of black Manny's

black little heart. Dollar signs always did. Manny launched into his routine.

"You got it old man! I'm the cat what's gonna hook you up so's you don't feel no mo' pain!" Manny reached into his jacket pocket and produced a cellophane wrapped nickels' worth ball of heroin. The old man struggled to look up.

"I'm on'a need some woiks too." The old man shivered occasionally as he spoke. "My old lady flushed my shit when she split, you dig?" Manny smiled and reached into the opposite jacket pocket and produced a dirty, white cloth napkin, unrolled it and showed it to the man. It contained a small spoon, a needle and a makeshift tourniquet. "How I'm a poss'ta cook that shit?"

"Dig, I got you covered Pops! It's all in on the deal, know what I'm sayin'?" Manny showed the man a one inch tall, half consumed tallow candle and some matches.

The old man struggled up the wall to his feet and stood erect. He didn't speak and for a second Manny was afraid the old man was about to pass out depriving him of a sale.

"Yo Pops, I gots shit ta do! Can we close this deal and . . ." The old man let the blanket fall away and suddenly produced a sawed off shot gun from behind his back and held it at hip height. Manny reflexibly dropped the works and threw his hands up.

"Pops! What's with the heat?! I thought . . . c'mon brother, I'm sure we can work out whatever this out!" The pusher slowly took a step towards the old man. Maintaining eye contact with his intended mark. With his right hand Manny reached into his pocket and produced a thick roll of bills held together with a wide, red, rubber band. With his left he slyly slid a stiletto out of the other pocket. "Take my bread man! Here!" He tossed the wad at his assailant's feet and stepped closer, now nearly in reach of the side-by-side, 12 gauge.

The old man kicked the money aside and took two steps back.

"I ain't come for yo money, Punk!" He spit at the bewildered pusher. "Put yo hands a 'hind yo head!"

"Yo, dig old man . . ."

"Hands a'hind yo head or the first one goes in yo balls!"

"You wouldn't do another black cat now, would you brother?"

"Black? Is you color blind or sumthin"? I ain't gonna shoot you. I'm on'a edjucate your ass, Young Buck!"

Manny, fully aware he was bargaining for the last few moments of his life, struggled but obeyed.

"Toirn around!" Doing as he was told the next command came in the way of a hard blow to the back of the head with the butt of the shotgun followed by a second with a blackjack.

Manny crumpled to his knees, wobbled a bit then fell forward face first into the cracked black top. The old man wasted no time in dragging the dealer's semi-conscious body further into the narrow alley between the church and the tenement.

After tying his wrists tightly behind his back, the old man then went to work rummaging through Manny's coat pocket and produced a cellophane bag. He then wasted no time pouring the entire contents of the bag of brown scag into a table spoon he produced from his own hip pocket. Flicking a lighter and melting the deadly powder he kept one eye on his prey who occasionally moaned and attempted to move his injured head.

After drawing the entire contents, three or four times the 'normal' dose, up into Manny's syringe, he sat on top of Manny, wrenched his arm further behind his back, pulled up his sleeve to expose the forearm and tied the tourniquet off below his coat sleeve. Under the dim glow of the alley light the old man could see the arm veins on the back of the forearm as they immediately stood out.

"This goin'a hoirt you a lot more than it's gonn'a hoirt me!" He preached as the located a vein in Manny's lower arm.

And with that Redbone quickly injected the entire syringe full of scag directly into the distended vessel. As he did he leaned into the helpless heroin pusher and whispered into his ear.

"You should know a-fore you meet yo maker, I used to be a Christian." He stood up and straddled the soon to be deceased drug pusher and looked down with no trace of remorse as Manny's listless body slowly graduated into convulsions. He leaned down and cut the wrist bonds which allowed the pusher to make a pathetic attempt to raise himself up but instead collapse back down and began to flop around like a freshly hooked fish.

"Not no more!" The man calmly whispered.

The church bells chimed to signal the beginning of the late evening mass. The old man looked up at the belfry and grunted.

The morning tabloids would carry a twenty-five word blurt on page seventeen, ten pages behind where Leon's death notice had appeared in the same newspaper a week ago to the day, of how another negro was found dead of an apparent overdose while shooting up behind St. Mark's Church.

"Catch you later. Brother!" Redbone stowed the shotgun, threw the works on the ground and with the needle still dangling from Manny's arm, walked away.

"White boy with corn curls! What's this world comin' too?"

†

CHAPTER XII

**Congressional Chambers
Washington, D.C.**

Just as J. Edgar Hoover did, Harry J. Anslinger had strong religious convictions. And just as Hoover did Anslinger used those convictions to paint himself a moral pillar of the community. The wider community. The entire nation as a matter of fact.

The Federal Bureau of Narcotics, Harry J. Anslinger Commissioner, was the former Bureau of Prohibition, which fell under the Department of the Treasury whose head was, not-so-coincidently, Anslinger's uncle-in-law.

Of course being married to your boss's niece didn't hurt, but being married to the niece of the boss of the entire Department of the U.S. Treasury pretty much assured you'd have to be a fuck-up of immeasurable magnitude to not be set for the rest of your life.

Anslinger was set for the rest of his life. And he knew it.

As scores of American politicians had discovered before Anslinger the American public responds well to alarmist claims, factual or not, so when he finally got his greatest wish, to speak before a Congressional hearing to sound the panic alarm, argue for more money, raise his profile and further strengthen his political influence on The Hill, the door was open to him.

So it was, well prepared script in hand, without fear of contradiction or interference that the Commissioner of the Bureau of Narcotics, in his role as self-appointed Guardian of the American Public, launched into his Evangelistic-like, fire and brimstone tainted tirade.

Seated before the raised, crescent shaped committee desk which dominated the front of the chambers, Harry proceeded to make his pitch.

"Colored students at the University of Minnesota partying with white female students and smoking marijuana ply their sympathy with stories of racial discrimination and persecution. The result? Pregnancy!" Just as taught him in high school speech class he was sure to make eye contact with the Chairman of the committee,

"A youthful addict who goes to school, gets good grades and has an active social life, comes home one day and suddenly, without provocation, attacks his mother, his father, his two brothers and his younger sister hacking them to bits with a hatchet. When the police arrive he is wondering around in a daze in a human slaughterhouse."

Cue dramatic pause.

"When the police finally arrive he states he has no recollection of committing the multiple crimes. Later it is discovered he had taken marijuana!" Anslinger paused to peruse the room and gauge the reaction of his audience. "Several young negroes ply a girl with drink. Entice her to a dark room and brutally assault her. They later admit to taking marijuana. In another state two negroes took a girl fourteen years old and kept her for two days under the influence of marijuana. Upon recovery two days later she was found to be suffering from syphilis."

Unobserved by Harry an attractive, smartly-dressed, thirty-something brunette sat quietly off to the side observing.

"Commissioner Anslinger, are you telling us that these 'dangerous narcotics', hemp, hashish, marijuana, have a particularly devastating effect in that they actually induce people to commit murder?"

"Yes I am Congressman. That's exactly what I'm saying!"

"And are you telling us that according to your research there is a more pronounced and evil effect on the Negro population? More so than on whites?"

"I'm not necessarily saying that Senator, but the truth speaks for itself."

Congressman Thomas seated to the left of the Chairman, spoke up next.

"Commissioner Anslinger, this Congress already has legislation in place regarding these narcotics. We asked you here today to justify considering additional, even more expensive legislation. Why, coming out of a protracted, devastatingly expensive world war are you asking that we increase your already considerable budget? A budget I might add which was granted to you on little or no evidence of . . ." The Senator glanced down and quoted from a report on the large, desk in front of him. '. . . dangerous narcotics flooding the streets of America?'"

With a bolstered sense of the dramatic Harry was Johnny-on-the-spot with his rebuttal.

"The *Uniform State Narcotic Act* and the *Marijuana Tax Act* to which you refer Senator may just be a start or it may in fact be too little too late! I propose that it is far too little!" He leaned forward into his table for emphasis. "By the **TON** this poison is coming into this country, the deadly, dreadful poison that racks and tears not only at the body but the very heart and soul of every human being who at once becomes a slave to it in any of its cruel and devastating forms." He strained to gauge their reactions. "Marijuana, quite simply gentlemen is nothing less than a short cut to the insane asylum!" Harry took a deep breath and reclined in his chair.

Like a Holy Roller canvasing the Bible Belt Harry J. knew how to work the crowd. Especially one that could fatten his purse. He sat back upright and pushed for the big finale.

"Hashish, marijuana or hemp! Smoke it for one month, and what was your brain will be nothing more than a storehouse of horrid specters!"

"Thank you Commissioner. You may step down. Master at Arms, I am given to understand we have a representative from the LaGuardia Commission here today? Is that right?"

"Yes Senator."

"May we hear from him please?"

As the Senator spoke into the microphone the well-dressed, pin striped suited brunette off to the side stood and moved to take the stand. She removed a thick file folder from her designer leather briefcase and sat both on the table in front of her.

"I apologize Mrs. . ."

"It's Doctor Goldberg, Senator." She replied as she moved to the place at the table Anslinger had just vacated in front of the committee. "But I'm sure the Chairman meant no offense." Goldberg barbed.

"Doctor Goldberg, what can you tell us based on your study?"

"Mr. Chairman, members of the committee, both the former Mayor of New York City, the Honorable Fiorello LaGuardia and myself as well as all the members of the LaGuardia Commission wish to thank the members of Congress for allowing us some of your valuable time." Anslinger, seated a few yards to her left at an adjoining table, rolled his eyes.

"Please proceed Doctor."

"Gentlemen, I believe you have all been provided with edited, final copies of the *LaGuardia Committee Report*."

Several opened the blue booklet in front of them, a few didn't. "Our five year study was in cooperation with the New York Academy of Medicine and involved over ten thousand interviews to include doctors, police and an array of citizens across the country. Some 80 actual test subjects under constant supervision, were observed, documented and continually interviewed." There was a notable rise in the attention level of the committee.

"In the interest of time Doctor, please tell the committee, what did you find?"

"Our team of twenty-five medically and academically qualified experts has concluded there is no evidence to support the theory that marijuana leads to addiction, either in the medical sense of the word as Mr. Anslinger has claimed, or in any other definition of the word. In other words gentlemen, there is no empirical evidence that any of the cannabis herbs act as 'gateway' drugs as Commissioner Anslinger's office has so often claimed."

"I see." The Chairman commented.

"Additionally gentlemen we believe it is far too premature to assume that, although we did find the center for marijuana sales in the greater New York City area is Harlem, the supposition that Negroes have a greater propensity for the use of hemp or crime than do their white or Hispanic counterparts is completely without foundation."

Doctor Goldberg removed a sheath of papers from the folder in front of her and thumbed through them. She selected one sheet and read from it.

"Despite the Commissioner's claims, upon contacting the University of Minnesota the President of the university related to us that no record of sexual assault, rape or illegitimate pregnancy of any co-ed in the last two years, interracial or otherwise, had been reported."

Another of the senators took up the questioning.

"Dr. Goldberg, what has your team found regarding the effectiveness of our present laws? That is effects to date regarding the *Uniform State Narcotic Act* and the *Marijuana Tax Act*?"

"Senator Vandenberg we interpreted our brief from Mayor LaGuardia's office to be restricted to the sociological and medical effects of the plant however, opinions of the many board certified physicians were offered by every one of the more than 100 doctors to whom we spoke. They felt that the laws were inadequate in some areas while being quite adequate in others."

"And their overall consensus was?"

"Although the *Uniform State Narcotic Act* was thought needed at the time, the *Marijuana Tax Act* of 1937, as written, is all but ineffective in controlling the growth and distribution of cannabis and contributes nothing to the control of such."

"Anything else?"

"Yes sir. It is generally viewed as burdensome, unnecessary and harmful to the point that due to the fact that physicians and pharmacists who would otherwise prescribe the drug for known therapeutic reasons, avoid doing so as to avoid having to pay the burdensome tax which they alone are solely responsible for. In effect they feel they are being penalized by Mr. Anslinger's Bureau, particularly in light of the fact that cannabis is the only narcotic they are required to pay tax on. Morphine and other opiates do not carry the same regulation."

"I object!" Like a Harry-in-the box Anslinger sprang to his feet.

"This is not a trial nor is it a court of law Commissioner. You have been given your time by the committee. If you have something to add you may do so in writing!" The annoyed senator spat back.

"As Commissioner of the Bureau of Narcotics I demand the N.Y.M.A. cease all further experimentation under the guise of research without my expressed written permission. And then only after I have been completely informed of everything they are doing!" He hysterically demanded.

Dr. Goldberg was now Johnny-on-the-spot.

"Mr. Chairman, along with a request or any verifiable information his office might like to add Mr. Anslinger's office was sent a copy of the report the committee now have in front of it. If he has misplaced his copy, I happen to have a spare on hand."

"Commissioner Anslinger, have you any credible evidence or third party testimony to back your claim that 'tons' of marijuana is being smuggled into the country?" Vandenberg pressed.

"Plenty Mr. Chairman, however, those reports are at present classified as they may compromise our ability to identify and apprehend several suspects we currently suspect of associated illegal activities."

"Doctor Goldberg, is there anything else you'd like to contribute?" The Chairman inquired.

"Yes Mr. Chairman. If Mr. Anslinger has any verifiable police reports form the Florida police force, or the Minnesota authorities to which he earlier alluded, we would be most appreciative of his attempts to help us get to the truth of such cases, as we had found not one violent incident solely attributed to the intake of cannabis, either in Minnesota, Florida or the State of New York."

At Goldberg's last words Harry stepped from around his table.

"All I can guarantee this committee is that, as we speak, my people are diligently tracking, confiscating and destroying all contraband drugs with the sole purpose of putting these thugs behind bars and out of business for good!"

As Anslinger turned and left the chambers, Goldberg shrugged and placed the folder back in her briefcase as she fought back a smirk.

✝

Across the ocean in Naples, right about the time Anslinger was speaking in front of the committee assuring them that his agents were on the job, a large squad of Carabinieri in two Fiats accompanied by a small panel van rounded the corner off the avenue adjoining Luciano's canning operation and skidded onto the side road screeching to a halt outside the back entrance to the warehouse.

Simultaneously there were another three vehicles pulling up outside the double-sized roll down door of the front entrance.

With them, by special arrangement with Anslinger, was Agent White of the U.S. Bureau of Narcotics who had flown in the day before to coordinate the raid.

Unseen and unnoticed on the other side of the busy avenue the reporter who had been beaten up by Vizzini's torpedoes less than a week ago watched and smiled from a café across the road.

The cops broke down the rear door and rushed the warehouse, spreading out with weapons drawn and on high alert.

They were shocked to find the place abandoned. Completely cleaned out.

One of them looked down to spot a single tin disc, the top of a tin can, on the floor near the back wall.

Waiting until the cops had cleared the area twenty minutes later so as not to raise any eyebrows, the reporter finished his cappuccino, dropped some coins on the table and left the café with his newspaper folded under his arm.

He made his way back to his office at the *il Denaro* press offices. Unobtrusively taking a seat at his desk in the back corner of the massive open office, he slowly slid open the center drawer.

Under a file and some loose papers there was a

manila envelope. He scanned the room to be sure no one was watching and, keeping the envelope inside the drawer, peeled it partially open. Inside was 30,000 lire in small bills accompanied by a note.

'Grazi. Your friend. L'

He set the envelope back on the desk. Next to his new Audax camera with the telephoto lens.

†

Late that same night, 20 miles offshore in the dark Mediterranean a schooner named *Dame Rapide* slowly swayed in the gentle swells. Balanced next to the helm on the rolling quarter deck of the two masted vessel, a weather beaten, old sailor glanced down through the mist at the fluorescent dials of his hand held time piece. It was 02:17.

"Merede!" He quietly declared.

Even though the war was over the Italian Coast Guard had yet to come back to strength in any appreciable form so the night runs were relatively safe. But, with laneways limited by currents and occasional winds, a chance encounter could not be ruled out any more than a hijacking by rivals could be discounted.

Hijackings were profitable because not only had the product been manufactured and packaged, but this far out the victims, if you could call them victims, had gone through the trouble to bring the cargo out past the patrol limits for you.

The dark green hull and dirty white cabin of the first fishing trawler slowly broke through the dark mist of the Sicilian Mediterranean.

The Frenchman on the quarter deck signaled the First Mate who was standing back amidships. The portly Mate waddled over to the deckhouse and rang the brass bell with three double rings in succession.

The stocky trawler captain squinted through the pilot house window, spotted the outline of the *Rapide* two points off the starboard bow and then returned acknowledgement with the same signal.

"Se dépêcher, dépêcher! Rapidment!" The schooner captain called over to the First Mate standing across from him. The Mate scurried down the short ladder to the cabin, banged on the door and yelled.

"VENEZ, VEET, VEET!"

From inside three strong, young men appeared on deck and fell into a well-rehearsed routine.

Schooners had quickly become the vessel of choice for running illicit cargo through the Med, an adaptation learned from the Yanks and their rum-running days all along the Eastern Seaboard. With a custom fitted, twelve cylinder, Briggs and Stratton engine to supplement their spar rigged sails they could easily outrun and out maneuver a battleship.

One of the deck hands manned a forward

mooring line and stood by while the trawler cut engines, heaved her rubber fenders over the rail and slowly drifted alongside. The other two schooner sailors lifted the gang door from its slides on the rail and set it aside on the deck. The Italian crew of the trawler moved a little slower.

Fifteen minutes later the trawler cast off to start its morning fishing run. Minus twenty crates of canned, Italian tomatoes.

A half dozen trawlers would follow before the sun broke over the horizon and the schooner would set sail west for Marseilles.

†

There's some dispute regarding who exactly first developed the 'Mozambique', the Nazis or the Mafia, the OSS or the SOE. Point is that it has evolved as the best way to be sure the individual or individuals you set out to kill are well and truly dead when you've fished the chore. Short of God himself there isn't a being in the universe who can save anybody with that much lead in those particular locations.

The idea is to put one bullet through the brain and two in the heart, preferably at close range. This also leaves a message that the shooter was a pro.

Under increased pressure to track down the rival gang he had been searching, Agent Benson had let it be known on the street that some particularly valuable freight had mysteriously vanished somewhere along the West Side docks.

A mere twenty-three hours later he got a message from an informer, a two time loser, junkie called Benny Hoskins. The caller said he thought he had a line on the items Benson was looking for.

A half hour after the call Benson and Hernandez were lingering across the street from Sal's bakery on MacDougal in the Village when a shadowy figure peered out from the doorway of an abandoned, six story tenement across the street and waved them over.

They crossed the near empty street and squeezed through the barely hanging door to get out of sight.

"I told you come alone!" Benny's panicked voice loudly whispered.

"It's alright, he's from the Health Department." Benson wisecracked. "We got a call there might be some rats." The increasingly nervous Benny led the way into the abandoned tenement and up stairs to the second floor.

Two doors, one each side of the top of the staircase, faced into the hall. The informant went to the one on the right and produced a key which he used to unlock a heavy reinforced Master lock shackled through a hinged hasp. A second, skeleton key unlocked the door's jamb lock.

Inside, the box car styled apartment was sparsely furnished with a couple of broken chairs and a table improvised from some sheet material thrown on top of several crates. The walls hadn't seen fresh paint since before the First War and the torn linoleum revealed blotches of the original wood flooring below it, now starting to rot.

Fresh evidence of recent squatters was everywhere.

"Jesus Benny, what'a ya got dead animals in here or what?!" Hernandez declared as the stench became more pungent.

Benny led them back to the middle of the place and to what used to be a bedroom.

"Toilet's been busted for a coupla' years." Benny explained.

"I'd write a strongly worded letter to the landlord Benny." Hernandez quipped.

Benny pulled back the unhinged closet door to reveal a tarp covered box about the size of a standard fruit crate.

"Do us a favor, keep an eye on the front door." Benson asked Hernandez.

"Okay, just make it snappy, I'm getting' hungry."

"You're preoccupied with your belly!"

"What can I say? It's my second favorite organ." Hernandez headed out of the room and back to the front door.

"Remind me to get you a discount at my gym!" Benson called after him.

Benny pulled back the tarp to expose almost two dozen, flats of tinned tomatoes. Each flat held twenty-four cans.

Benson moved in to examine the booty. He reached in, grabbed a can and hefted it in his hand to estimate the weight. Then he stood, dropped the can on the floor and stomped on the middle of it several times until it burst open. The magic brownish-white powder spit all over the floor and up his trouser leg. Benson smiled.

"Ya did good Benny. Real good!" He brushed the dust from his leg.

"So what should we do? I mean, if that's what I think it is, there ought'a be some kind'a reward or somethin'. Yeah?"

THWACK, THWACK, THWACK! Benson rewarded Benny with a Mozambique.

Hernandez, hearing the muffled shots, dashed back into the room, pistol drawn. He stared down at the startled face of Benny's corpse.

"You think that was necessary?"

"He was a junkie." Benson shrugged.

"Well in that case, fuck 'em." Hernandez casually replied as he re-holstered his weapon.

"Exactly. Gimme a hand with this shit will ya?"

He picked up two of the flats and headed to the kitchen. Hernandez dragged the used-to-be Benny aside and followed suit with a couple of more flats. After all the flats were neatly stacked in, on or near the kitchen stove, Benson grubbed a cigarette from his partner, produced a packet of paper matches from his hip pocket and lit the unfiltered cigarette. Next he tucked the lit cig into the match packet and folded over the flap to hold it in place leaving the cig to stick out about two inches. He opened the oven and set the improvised fuse on top of the four flats and reached behind the appliance. Feeling behind the stove for the metal flexi-hose from the gas feed he yanked it free. Gas quickly flooded into the room.

"Let's go." Benson grunted.

Being sure no one saw them come directly out of the place, they left the tenement pulling the front door shut tightly behind them.

Once back down on the street they crossed over MacDougal and headed towards the park.

"What'a ya say to a slice of pizza?" Benson proposed.

"Yeah, why not? I know a place close by."

The two agents were nearly two blocks away when the Greenwich Village skyline behind them exploded into deep orange and red tinted with green.

†

Christos Diner
Jersey City, N.J.

It was in a back booth of Christos Greek Diner on Hudson Boulevard where Doc and Louie sat after they stopped for lunch on their way back into the City. The diner near the Jersey City Port Authority-Trans Hudson station was just off Journal Square.

"What'a ya say to a couple'a nice field, green salads?" Doc asked from behind his menu with a straight face. He enjoyed knockin' a rise out of Louie on occasion. It was still so easy.

"To hell with that! I didn't work my way to the top of the food chain to be a vegetarian!" Louie snapped back. The waitress came up to the booth and Mancino wasted no time. "Two orders of the beef lasagna, side of spaghetti with meatballs, basket of bread, Coke and a coffee, black." He handed the waitress back the menu and nodded across the table to Doc. "What'a you havin'?"

After the waitress figured out Louie wasn't joking, she took Doc's usual order of a cheeseburger, fries and a Pepsi and left. Doc returned to his newspaper.

McKeowen had summed up Anslinger's best agent from the moment he first read about him in the *New York Daily News*.

"This guy White is a mis-guided Bozo!" Doc declared as he perused the afternoon edition. "Kind of asshole that goes out and picks a fight with the Indians then runs home and hides under the porch while others have to do the fighting!"

"Sure, that's all well good Doc but, how do you really feel?"

Ten minutes later the food arrived and Mancino wasted no time in dumping one plate of lasagna onto the other and digging in. As they ate, a pudgy waitress stopped by and refilled Louie's coffee cup as he attacked his double plate of lasagna.

"Can I get another Coke too, Sweetheart?" He asked.

"Sure thing Big Boy!" She shot back with a huge smile. Doc's half eaten burger sat idly on the plate as he continued reading the paper.

"Eleven thousand known heroin addicts in this country and these Keystone Cops are busting marijuana farmers! Guys who pay taxes no less. Guys who they gave licenses to a couple'a years ago!" Doc sipped his Pepsi.

Louie polished off the lasagna and attacked the side of spaghetti.

"That lasagna sucked!" He declared as he ate. Doc glanced around his newspaper at the empty plates.

"That why you ate it all?"

"My mother taught us to clean our plate! Don't mean it didn't suck!"

"Louie, it's a Jersey City diner! What'a ya expect? Luigi's? This ain't Brooklyn. It's Jersey! It's for people too poor to live in New York."

Mancino polished off his Coke, wiped his mouth, sat back and pushed his stack of plates away in disgust.

"Yeah, I guess. So what'a we do? About this dope stuff. I mean you seemed pretty occupied with it, so . . . ?" He asked.

"I am! Seems like everywhere you turn there's stories about more dope in the City, more heroin addicts more dope coming into the country!"

Doc brandished the folded over newspaper and indicated a story about a drug bust in the Bronx the cops pulled off that morning. Louie was dismissive of the article.

"Ahh don't get your panties in a bunch! That's just the Press trying to dig up stories now that the war's over! They gotta sell papers. That's what they do!" Mancino argued.

"I know that! I just don't wanna see that shit on the streets across the river in our neighborhoods."

Doc put the paper aside and dug back into his cold burger.

"What'ja get outta Leon's waitress?" He quizzed Louie.

"Leon had a dope problem. We talked for a good fifteen, twenty minutes, she seemed sincere. I believed her."

"Well I figure there's two chances of us finding the guy who sold that shit to Leon, slim and none. And Slim just left town!"

"I agree. Probably some scumbag, muli dealer over in Harlem." Louie offered as he picked at Doc's fries. Doc pushed the half empty plate across to Mancino.

"Possibly. With any luck he'll get his, but we need to decide how deep to get into this thing. I mean we ain't gonna stop the whole heroin trade, that's a given. But-"

"Shit!" Louie declared.

"What?!"

"Whenever you're reluctant to get involved in something and there's a 'but', insurance companies start shittin' themselves and people get hurt."

"As I was sayin', by now anybody with half a

brain knows my father was dead right. This town needs a dedicated anti-drug squad. But as long as people like Sullivan are calling the plays, it ain't gonna happen. I get murder, I get robbery and I get B&E but I don't get why somebody would commit slow suicide with that junk! And I have less use for the scumbags who push that shit then balls on a priest!"

"Says the guy who can down a whole bottle of Jameson's whiskey in one session."

"Okay asshole, point taken. That don't nullify the fact that whiskey's legal and heroin ain't! What I'm really sayin' is I can't stand seein' that brown shit creeping into the Village like some cancer from another planet."

"Well, what'aya think we should do?"

"I think we gotta look further south."

"You mean like Staten Island?"

"A little further south."

"Doc we're already in Jersey!"

"Florida Louie, Florida! That farmer told us Miami is the primary point of entry for the bulk of that shit."

"So what'a we gonna do? Go down there and single-handed stop all the Cubans from sendin' that shit over here?"

"I'm not so sure it's all Cubans. I think Anslinger and White are just using them as scapegoats. Guys like that are pretty adept at playing up racial stereotypes. I don't think any of those assholes in D.C. have a clue where the shit is coming from. Or who's moving it for that matter."

"So what would we go all the way down there for?"

"You know, fill in some blanks, get some answers. Get closer to the source." Mancino looked reluctant. Doc picked up on his reticence. "Unless of course, instead of an all-expense paid trip to Sunny Miami Beach and a pitcher full of margaritas served by a beautiful, well-tanned waitress you'd rather hang around here and do divorce cases?"

"Whoa, whoa, whoa! Before you get too carried away Doc, I got a coupl'a questions."

"Shoot."

"When do we leave and how long do I pack for?"

"That's what I figured. Let's go."

Louie flagged the waitress as she passed by. "Can I get a piece of that cheesecake ta go?" Louie asked. Doc threw him a look.

"WHAT?!" Louie defended. "I need something to wash the taste of that lasagna outta my mouth!"

While they were paying the bill up at the register the chubby waitress brought the cake in a mini-box to go wrapped in a ribbon and topped it off with a broad smile.

"Stop by next time you're in the neighborhood!" She smiled at Louie in no uncertain terms as she nodded down at the pretty, pink cake box Louie saw it had a phone number scribbled across the top.

Without response the guys made their way to the door and out into the parking lot.

"I think you're onto something there Mancino!

Ya want me to go back to the City alone? You can hang around here for a while."

"Be serious! If I did anything like that Doris would kill me, divorce me then take me for half of everything she made me buy! Besides that waitress was married."

"You saw a wedding ring?" Doc was impressed.

"Yeah, her left hand briefly passed in front of her right breast." Mancino informed.

They made their way across the narrow lot and onto the boulevard.

"I just thought of something else." Mancino said. Doc was pleased to see Louie was, for some reason, more focused on his detective work recently.

"You're a regular thinking machine Louie! Talk to me."

"You suppose they got good restaurants in Miami?"

"How should I know?"

They crossed the boulevard and made their way towards the train station three blocks away.

"I figured since you been there before and –"

"Don't start!" Doc warned.

"I mean you went there to try and kiss and make up with your ex -"

"You know Mancino, there'll be a shit load of crappy cases coming down the pyke and somebody's gonna need to do all that tedious, boring leg work."

McKeowen still had no sense of humor about his ex-wife screwing around and moving to Florida with a rich Jewish lawyer.

"No, no! I'm curious. Really, did you have time to eat out down in Miami in-between sending her telegrams, flowers-"

"I never sent flowers when we **were** married!"

"Just curious Doc."

"Something else occurs to me Louie, now that the war's over, there's a dozen other guys more qualified then you who'd jump at this job. Probably for half the pay, and give me half the shit." Doc quipped. Louie clammed up.

✝

CHAPTER XIII

52 Miles Northeast of Barnes Sound
Southern Tip of Florida
17:30, Tuesday

Jimmy 'Cat Man' Dugan was an ex-hot shot scout pilot from the Eighth Army Air Force.

He earned the moniker 'Cat Man' after he was shot down for the third time and evaded capture. The third time may have been a charm, but the fourth time was nothing short of a miracle.

When he crash landed behind his own lines they counted 96 holes in what wasn't left of his Curtiss Seagull, single engine aircraft. Ninety-nine if you counted the holes in him.

He was recommended for the highest honor the Army Air Corps could offer for chucking hand grenades out the window onto German FLAK positions while dodging the Allied bombs that were being dropped from 20,000 feet above. It was along the northern Sicilian coast and the fighters couldn't get low enough to hit the positions and in doing so it was deemed that Jimmy helped to save a squadron of very expensive aircraft. Oh yeah, and some lives too.

He also got his picture plastered all over the papers back home but his mom, dad and future ex-fiancée would never know his notoriety wasn't due to his reported mad-cap heroics.

The Wolves of Calabria

The morning of said mission, Jimmy was about to be nailed for running contraband out of Messina. Not just trinkets and tinned beef either. Class A drugs. Narcotics. Lots of 'em.

Thanks to a tip-off he ducked out of the officer's barracks and on to the airfield two steps ahead of the Military Police and since his flight plan had already been filed, he was able to put about ten thousand feet between himself and the Mickey Mouse Patrol in a matter of minutes.

He joined up with an in-flight bomber squadron a half hour later and since the order for him to return to base was conveniently 'garbled in transmission' and he wasn't sure what the hell else to do, he joined the bombers and ran the mission. He did this half hoping to get shot down rather than have to go back and face the Judge Advocate's pit bull prosecutors.

While he was airborne it occurred to the slightly over ambitious young man that returning alive meant one of two things. Life in a military stockade at the mercy of merciless goons or a bullet in the head from a bunch of pissed off Sicilians who wouldn't believe the truth. Namely that, without Jimmy's knowledge, Army Intel was tipped off by a third party about the narcotics shipment plain and simple.

In the end, low on fuel and seriously wounded, he decided to return to base.

So after spreading his aircraft over half a mile of airfield while being observed by Curtis J. LeMay's personal Aide de Camp, who always made it a point to be in the tower to "Welcum da boys home.", and who hadn't yet been briefed on Lt. Dugan's illegal improprieties, Jimmy got heself an Air Medal, a way out of the Army, some major headlines and a ticket home.

Mysteriously the three cases of morphine, two cases of pharmaceutical grade coke and four cases of chloral hydrate, even after the M.P.'s reached the wreckage, were never found.

Now out of the Army and back in Civ Land, like so many other ex-G.I.'s Jimmy couldn't quite seem to make it on the $27.50 a month for disability Uncle Sam was rewarding him with for risking his life to rid the world of Fascism and so was putting his U.S. Government acquired skills to work in other fields of endeavor.

Namely working for the Mob.

It was during his third hour sitting on a hard wooden bench in the Philadelphia V.A.'s clinic that the guy with one arm sitting next to him struck up a conversation.

Turns out the guy, who lost his arm in a tank barrage at the Battle of the Bulge, was there to collect his monthly benefit which he always gave to his parish church.

Through further inquiry Dugan discovered that the guy's real living, as he patiently explained to Jimmy, was working as a 'drop man' for a small branch of the Mob right there in Philly who were actually headquartered down in Hot Springs, Arkansas.

The Wolves of Calabria

"They give me a package, letter, envelope whatever, along wit' an address and 'ABRA-KA-DABRA!' coupl'a times a week I'm a mailman."

When old One Arm further elaborated on the amount of financial compensation offered for such services, Dugan gave it a full two seconds before he decided to commit and apply for a position. Two days later Jimmy was being introduced to the right people in Hot Springs, Arkansas and a week later he was down in Cuba picking up his first load of 85% pure heroin.

Legal-wise it was risky as well as physically dangerous but no more so than flying over German anti-aircraft positions chucking hand grenades out the window and, at 2% of face value a load it beat the hell out of $27.50 a month.

Jimmy's first run netted him six and a half grand, tax free. The rough equivalent of a year's salary for someone twice his former rank.

Aerial drug running routes into the States had been planned, mostly by the Luciano and the Luchese Family, before the war and by 1944-45 had been well established.

Although for hundreds of years the poppy crops had been grown and harvested in regions of Afghanistan, Iran and Iraq, due to gangs of bandits spurred on by the flood of weapons into these areas during the war it was now safer to buy from Turkey, ship through Greece then to Sicily for processing and on into Marseilles and finally into the big money market, the U.S. through Florida,

Philadelphia, New York and Detroit.

The massive Texas Gulf Coast was a new area currently being explored by the drug runners.

Narcotics had grown from a trickle in the 1930's to a steady flow during the war and, with Lucky and Calò Vizzini's new enterprise expansion, were fast on their way to flooding the Americas.

As the first island off the Florida Keys crept over the horizon Jimmy downed the last of his flask in relief. Although not his first flight up from the Caribbean, it had been a long one and even though available government manpower for coastal surveillance had been weakened by the ongoing recession, military reserve installations could be quickly alerted.

His destination was a small private airstrip just outside Manatee Bay on the southern tip of the state and by dusk he reached the area and was taxing his Piper Cub off the one lane tarmac and over to the trailer home serving as a terminal.

A husky man approached the plane as Dugan shut down the engine and climbed out.

"You da guy they call Catman?" The pugnacious Cuban-American with the neck tattoos grunted.

"That's me brother! Jimmy Dugan." Jimmy extended his hand but instead of a hand shake the Cuban snatched the phoney paperwork from Jimmy's top pocket and signalled back to the trailer for a couple of Hispanic coolies to bring a hand truck. An unperturbed Jimmy went around and opened the small side hatch of the fuselage to expose a dozen crates of canned tomatoes.

"They told me thirteen cases!" The Cuban challenged.

"Really?!" Dugan bent forward and peered into the cargo hatch as he peeled his aviator goggles off his head. "That don't seem right! I was told twelve. It's always been twelve the last few times, and as you can dig man, ain't no roooom in there for much more than twelve! What I'm tryin' to say my brother . . ." He took one step towards the hostile Cuban. ". . . is, twelve's all the dude with the funny grey threads in Havana gave me."

"I ain't yo fucking brother gringo and eet's thirteen or no deal!" Tattoo insisted.

"Aww, c'mon, don't be a drag man! I got to buy juice for my bird. I need bread to buy my old lady a new dress, I mean, what do I say when she wants some weed and I can't cough up the green to set her right? Then we don't do the horizontal boogie, I don't get my tires rotated, I'm outta tune . . . well you dig Daddy-o, right?!"

"What the fuck you talkin' about gringo?! I ain't your brother and I sure as hell ain't your daddy! I been speakin' dis language all my life I never heard no fucked up accent like that! Where the fuck you from?! Mars!"

Jimmy maintained his friendly demeanor.

"Originally form Anaheim, California but, my dad was Army so . . . we moved around a lot. But know what I learned in the Army, Pedro?

"FUCK YOU PENDEJO! My name ain't Pedro!"

The Cuban cursed as he stepped in closer to Dugan while producing a ground down machete from behind his back.

From the shoulder holster underneath his leather bomber jacket Jimmy produced a Colt .45 and without hesitation performed a knee-ectomy on the stocky Cuban's right leg.

The big man hit the dirt like a 200 pound sack of fertilizer, dropping the machete and grabbing the bloody spot where his kneecap used to be while rolling around like a dog in a grassy field yelping loudly. The approaching two coolies froze in their tracks and raised their hands. Jimmy looked down at the casualty.

"Deny everything, admit nothing and make counter-accusations. That's what I learned in the Army." Jimmy casually lectured as he holstered his weapon and approached the howling thug. "But that's probably too many big English words for you, ain't it? **Pedro**."

Carefully straddling the ever widening pool of blood Jimmy retrieved the machete and stuck in his belt. He then proceeded to empty the guy's pockets and still counting the large wad of cash he had appropriated approached the two frozen coolies.

"Habla Ingles?"

"Si, si!" They blurted in unison.

"Good. Get that shit off my plane, and get it to whoever's waiting for it, comprendo muchachos?" They vigorously shook their heads in the affirmative. He stuffed a couple of twenties into each of their half opened, sweat stained shirts, pocketed the rest and went over to a nearby palmetto bush to take a piss.

Thirty-five minutes later Jimmy Dugan was airborne again with his tanks, his pockets as well as his tequila flask refilled as he piloted out over the ocean and off north to Philadelphia to party with his latest sweetheart until he got word on the next run.

"Just like a Spic, bring a machete to a Colt .45 fight!" He mumbled as he tossed the machete out the window into the ocean and rechecked his bearings.

†

Paddy Kelly

CHAPTER XIV

**The Lamar Bath House
Bath House Row
Hot Springs, Arkansas**

About fifty-five miles from the Arkansas capital of Little Rock lies Hot Springs a town which, from the end of the Civil War in 1865 until the turn of the 20th Century was essentially a war zone for the two rival factions fighting for control of the gambling rackets, the Flynns and the Dorans.

Both the Garland County Sheriff's office and the Hot Springs P.D. were employed as torpedoes and strong arms by the two factions breaking bones and driving out potential third party competitors as required.

Along with such noted landmarks and events such as Bathhouse Row and the Arlington Hotel, The 1913 fire and Al Capone's retreat, all of which are still talked about, the 1899 Hot Springs Gunfight is legendary.

In true American style, in a firefight which made the O.K. Corral look like a school yard brawl, about a dozen police and deputes shot hell out of each other in a day long gunfight which included one of the wives behind the trigger.

Owney Madden of Max Baer, Primo Carnera boxing fame, re-established the place as a gambling haven featuring horse race betting on any track in

The Wolves of Calabria

America via telegraph and telephone complete with prostitutes and drugs over twenty years before William Wilkerson conceived of Las Vegas.

A retired Civil War Major, a hardcore war vet handy with a gun who eventually killed ten of the politicians' cronies in fair gunfights, was brought in by the city fathers to clean the place up. Which he did. Right before he was ambushed and murdered.

A retired sheriff followed.

He pushed to have the existing anti-gambling laws enforced and to establish honest elections by stopping the practice of politicians using the names of deceased patrons to cast votes to sway the elections. He was murdered.

Again no one was ever charged.

During the war years the U.S. Army took over Hot Springs and transformed it into a rehabilitation and redistribution center for wounded soldiers and sailors.

Things calmed down. Temporarily.

Following the war, with the soldiers and sailors gone, again replaced by hookers and casinos, Hot Springs reverted to a wide open town status and things were back in full swing.

An additional attraction was the one hundred year old, nationally famous bath houses less than one hour away from the capital.

It was in these Hot Springs baths that the honorable, large-of-girth gentleman from Texas, Senator F. L. Woods, now waited while the colored attendant opened the door to the polished, chrome steam cabinet and handed him a fresh terrycloth towel. The Senator waddled out and made his way across the elaborately tiled room liberally decorated with Areca palms, rich Art Deco motifs and poorly paid Negroes.

He made his way over to the mineral bath to have a leisurely one hour soak which usually stretched into two.

It was twenty minutes later that, without use of a crane, he eased himself into the steaming pool and resting from his great work with his ample aspidistra firmly planted on a step, arms and hands awkwardly clamped to the sides of the pool, Senator Woods was approached by a different attendant escorting a visitor carrying a message.

"Courier for you Senator." The attendant respectfully informed.

"Thank you." Woods responded as the attendant escorted the casually dressed, thirty-something into the tiled and humid bath area. The courier stood dutifully by as Woods read the message.

The sealed note indicated that Woods was to meet Mr. C in the lobby of his hotel later that afternoon.

"Tell him half past eight. We'll have dinner."

"I'll do that Senator." The messenger left.

The messenger was Eddie Erickson, Costello's right hand man and the guy entrusted to run the names of the winning ponies, that is the ones which would win each week, at the Belmont and Aqueduct race tracks up in New York to J. Edgar Hoover and

The Wolves of Calabria

a small handful of other favored clients.

In return for the winning tips J. Edgar would consistently deny the existence of organized crime in the major dailies in the U.S. whenever questioned by the Press.

The Lamar Bath House in Bath Row on Central Avenue where Woods now rendered his impression of a New York Harbor buoy was just up the road from the most luxurious hotel in town, the Arlington.

Situated in the middle of the Hot Springs National Park at the intersection of Fountain Street and Central Avenue, the Arlington was the place that anybody who was anybody stayed when in town.

By half past eight that evening Woods was already on his third Jack and Coke as he now sat in the lobby of the hotel.

Costello came through the front door with his overcoat draped over his arm and shook hands with Woods.

"Evening Senator. Would you like to get a drink first?"

"Woods smiled and pointed to the two empty rocks glasses on the table in front of his easy chair and then at the near empty glass in his hand.

"Then shall we proceed to the restaurant?" Costello suggested.

Minutes later the two were discreetly seated in a back booth of the four star eatery.

"Things going well on The Hill?" Frankie opened the business meeting.

"Better than in this town."

"Yeah I heard. They indicted Mayor McLaughlin on racketeering charges."

"Hell that old fool gettin' too big for his breeches anyway. They was bound to get him sooner or later." Woods grumbled.

"He might have been indicted but he'll be acquitted." Frankie confidently conjectured.

"You got a crystal ball under your coat Mr. Costella'?" Woods challenged.

"Just bettin' the odds Senator. Just bettin' the odds. Word on the street is that cocky D.A.-"

"McMath?"

'Yeah. Word is he's organizin' a bunch of the local ex-G.I.'s to march on the Governor's office. The state'll be paying more attention to that fiasco then to a rinky dink little mayor of a small town."

"How's things in the crime bidness?"

"You mean the other side of your business? Two sides of the same coin, ya know?"

"Yeah, but at least my side'a the tracks is legal."

"You think?" Frankie became more serious as he elevated the conversation beyond the casual. "Let me ask you something Senator, guns on the table." The mob man leaned forward and smirked.

"Well, I ain't carryin' no guns Frankie." He mockingly opened his jacket to show he was unarmed.

"How is it of all the potential candidates for the Construction Union representative in the Congress you were the least known, the best financed, entered

The Wolves of Calabria

at the last minute and yet got elected by a 'landslide'?"

Woods shifted his Cubana between his teeth.

"As you have so astutely pointed out in the press Mr. Costella, the construction game is a lot like the political game."

"Refresh my memory."

"In both games there are basically three kinds of people; whores, hookers and prostitutes."

"I guess I did say that, didn't I?" Frankie signaled for a waiter. "Word has it that FDR did a good bit of business down here himself." Costello prodded, fully aware that it was a well-known fact the entire senate knew FDR had had several face-to-face meetings in the past in Hot Springs with major players in the Mob to include Capone and Luciano himself.

"I wouldn't know nothin' 'bout that Mista Castella!" Woods quickly disavowed in his hallmark drawl.

Frankie discreetly slid the mustard yellow, cloth napkin from his side of the table over to Woods'. Wrapped inside was a manila envelope. The Senator's regular monthly envelope to be exact. Woods carefully lowered it beneath the table, peeled it open and flipped through the stash of crisp hundred dollar bills.

"It would appear they's a little more than usual in this an-velope." He remarked as he tucked the swollen envelope into his left breast pocket then casually refolded the napkin.

"Yes, there is." Frankie folded his hands in front of his face.

An attractive, young waitress came up to the table.

"Can I get you gentlemen something? Appetizers, cocktails perhaps?"

"Yes Darlin'. I would like another one of these and my friend will have a Manhattan, extra bitters, two cherries." He glanced over at Costello who nodded. She left to fill the order.

"Okay Mr. Costello, it ain't no where's near Christmas so why the bonus?" Frankie smiled and leaned into the table.

"We understand you've been re-elected to the Inter-state Transport Committee for another four years."

Woods had been in this position more than once with Costello. Although he gratefully grabbed at the 'retainer' the Mob's Commission had voted to keep on doling out to him, he was still skittish when it came time for them to collect on their investment.

"Impressive Mr. Costello, you read the papers."

"We ain't all from the wrong side of the tracks Senator."

Hot Springs was and had been a wide open town for more than half a century so there was little danger of Woods being tagged by The Press for meeting there with a top hood. Even if he was recognized there was little danger. But if word got out back to D.C that he had been seen, the heat he would receive from his colleagues in the Senate could be his downfall. Not from the scandal of collusion with the criminal element, but the flak he would receive because half the Senate was on the take one way or the other and nobody wanted the apple cart upset.

Woods braced for the punch line.

"As you are well aware my people have a vested interest in the trucking industry." Costello continued. "An industry that, like every other industry in the country is on the verge of undergoing an explosive growth now that we won the war and things are almost back to normal."

The waitress dropped off the drinks. Frankie ignored her and kept talking.

"You gentlemen ready to order?"

"We call ya when we ready Darlin'." Woods said and she left.

"We are specifically concerned with the proposed new bill to not only keep the upgraded security on the highway system they established during the war but to possibly tighten it."

"I see." Woods sat back in his chair and twirled his drink on the table.

"Of particular concern is the announced plan to lengthen and expand the Lincoln Highway. We understand there's talk of adding check points, scales and tolls."

"Tolls I can't do nuthin' about. Ya'll's just gonna havt'a pay your fair share fer usin' that road just like anybody else. Check points I might be able to help ya'll with."

"In what way?" Costello needed specifics to take back to The Commission in New York so a consensus on future strategy could be agreed upon.

"I could do something with the new I.T.C. bill which lies well within my purview."

"I don't know what a 'purview' is but as long as you have the authority I think we can come to an agreement." Costello reaffirmed.

"I have the authority." Woods indignantly confirmed. "I could propose a rider. Somethin' like, special priority plates or stickers like we used during the war for gas rationin'. I'd reckin' your people would have no problem getting' yo' hands on as many of them puppies as you need. For the right price of course."

"Of course. Should present no obstacle." Costello shrugged.

"'Course to get such a rider to pass I'd have ta grease a few palms, especially Senator James head of the committee. He's key."

"We'll be happy to supply all the lubricant you need Senator." The waitress reappeared.

"Are you gentlemen ready to order now?"

"As a matter of fact we are young lady! Let us have two large sirloins, medium rare, extra garlic mash, what's the veg tonight?"

"Baby LeSeure peas sir."

"Sounds good."

"And two more drinks, please." Frankie added.

"Careful now, careful." The Senator quickly interrupted. "My doctor says I'm to cut down on my caloric intake, on account'a my weight." Costello nodded.

"What would you like to do, sir?" She asked Woods.

"Hold the peas Darlin'. Bring the drink." Woods added.

"Yes sir, no peas." She noted.

†

By half past three in the morning the lights were still on in the plushly decorated house in the immaculately groomed shruburb of Belvedere, Maryland just outside D.C.

The rhythmic scratching of the needle on the end grove of the 78 rpm was an indication the party had pretty much run out of steam and the carnage, attested to by the body count strewn across floors and furniture, bore testament to those who had once again done battle with the bottle.

Once again the bottle won the battle.

An evening gown draped 30-something stumbled over to the Victrola, reset the needle and for the fifth time in succession *Moonlight Serenade* again wafted through the downstairs rooms.

She refocused, moved back across the floor then flopped back into the Queen Anne, wing backed chair and returned to her old friend, semi-consciousness.

Still dressed in his light grey, pin-striped suit and

red silk tie, Michael Cerani, a tall, well-built Neapolitan, was feeling pretty good himself and not just from the coke and booze. He had been brought down from The Big Apple specifically to arrange a couple of such get-togethers over the next few weeks to show key players in D.C. a good time and more importantly, get a gauge on where Frankie Costello and the New York Mob stood with Senator Woods and the cronies from the Inter-State Transport Commission. Of particular interest was the upcoming vote to ease inter-state transport regulations.

Coincidently, something else came up.

Somewhere in a back room a phone rang and Michael disappeared from where he was leaning on the open double doorway between the hallway and front room surveying the night's casualties.

"Hallo!" There was a stunned silence as Cerani tried to clear his head.

"Cappo?! Sei tu?!"

Si, sono io. It was Frankie Costello.

"Che cosa Cappo?" They continued in a southern dialect of Sicilian.

Is our man from the sub-committee there? Cerani glanced back into the room at the overstuffed leather couch where a tall, lanky 50-something man was currently occupied trying to coax the professional blond actress/model/dime store clerk/soon-to-be professional prostitute into a bedroom. The 'Onable Gentleman fum Lou-see-ana' didn't appear to be having much luck.

"Yeah he's here." Michael relayed back into the phone.

Is he still conscious?

"He's still up and movin', if that's what you mean."

Here's what we need. Word's out the Interstate Transport Bill proposal is gonna be piggy-backed onto the trades proposal. Capish?

"Si, si Cappo."

"Bene! Michael, we need his vote. See what you can do. Let me know. Ciao."

"Trust me Mr. C."

Although D.C. wasn't his playground, there was a reason Cerani was picked for this important mission. Even before he had the receiver back on the hook he knew how to handle it.

Remembering the girl who dropped her purse on the large hall table when she first showed up, Michael made his way back over a couple of the unconscious bodies to the hall and retrieved it. He slipped an over-sized, white gold cigarette case into the beaded clutch and then headed for the couch.

"Jen?" The blond gazed up as the Senator romantically slobbered all over her neck. "This your purse?"

"Geez, Mikey thanks! I forgot all about that!"

"Better have a look inside, make sure nuthin's missin'."

"Oh, that's okay! Wasn't nuthin' much in there anyways."

"I'd feel better if ya took look." He insisted.

She gave him a heartwarming grin and drooled out in slow motion, "I like you Mikey! You always look out fer us."

"That's what I get paid for Doll!"

Peering inside the clutch she smiled at the cigarette case. Opening it she was pleasantly surprised at the folded over hundred dollar bill considerately keeping the small field of white powder on the bottom of the case from escaping. It didn't take a Western Union for her to get the message.

Suddenly the sound stage was a hive of activity and she could hear the director giving orders.

"Okay, Kid. Here's your big chance!"

"Yes Mister DiMille!"

"You know what to do, you nailed it in rehearsals, now nail it here!"

"Yes Mister DiMille!"

"QUIET ON THE SET! LIGHTS!"

"Tenners up!"

"SOUND!"

"Speed!"

"CAMERAS!"

"Rolling!"

"Aaannnddd . . . ACTION!"

She looked over at the Senator and smiled up at Mikey as he walked away.

"Hey." She pried the Senator's enormous head off her neck. "Hey, Lover? What say we charge the engines one last time and head into the hanger?" She brandished the open cigarette case of coke minus the cash and nodded towards the bedroom.

"Ohhh . . . I be awright without none'a that shit up my nose, Darlin'. Less go." He stumbled to get up off the couch but she pulled him back down.

"You don't always have to put it up your nose, silly!" She licked her fingertips, touched them to the magic dust and slid her hand over and under his pot belly then down the front of his trousers. The bleary eyes of the entrusted public servant suddenly shown a little more brightly. "I read where this is how Errol Flynn does it." She informed him.

"Well call me Robin Hood and let's go to Sheerwood Darlin'!"

He scooped her up like a teen-aged bride and broke the land speed record for the Congressional free sex-booze-and-drugs-gravy train-getting-to-the-bedroom which turned out to be just over twice as long as it took the 'Onable Gentleman fum Lou-see-ana' to close the deal.

✝

That morning in the plushy decorated house in the immaculately groomed shruburb of Belvedere, Maryland Senator Jesse J. James of Louisiana sat propped up in bed. Still slightly disoriented from something other than the bottle of 25 year old scotch floating around in his system he spoke through the bathroom door.

"Sorry if I fired the cannon a little too soon

darlin'! Maybe next time I'll try more'a that there little cocaine trick you mentioned to me."

The movie star wanna-be he had spent the night with was currently in the imitation Roman bathroom and stood wrapped in a white, terry cloth towel in front of the mirror making herself presentable.

"You did fine lover. You did just fine." She cajoled devoid of emotion as she brushed the knots out of her hair.

"Hey beautiful, you need cab fare?" He asked as he pushed himself upright and leaned against the ornate headboard.

"Nah, they arrange limos for us." She called back through the partially closed over toilet door.

"I want ya'll ta know I thoroughly enjoyed myself."

"Me too lover. Me too." She mechanically responded.

"You need anything?" He asked as she sashayed back over to the bed and let the towel fall away completely exposing herself.

"Well, we ain't supposed to take tips, but if you wann'a make a contribution to my three favorite charities . . ." She mounted the bed on her knees and let her left hand slide under the covers and up his thigh to fondle his penis which quickly rose to the occasion.

"And what charities would they be, Darlin'?" He inquired as she ducked under the covers while she answered.

"Me, Myself and I." He slid back down on the

bed and moaned as he pulled a wad of cash from his pants pockets which had been draped on the bed's nightstand. He peeled off two fifties and tossed them on the nightstand.

"Some might say . . . what you're doin' is . . . amoral." He moaned. "Personally, I admire a girl with goals!"

✝

Congressional Chambers
Washington D.C.

"OY-YEA, OY-YEA, OY-YEA! THE EIGHTYITH CONGRESS OF THE UNITED STATES, SPECIAL SESSION IS NOW CALLED TO ORDER!"

Outside the chamber along the immaculately polished marble hallway a searing sun blasted through the tall windows lining the façade of the Capital building where just outside of the main chamber entrance, Senator James of Louisiana quickly said good-bye to a small cluster of lobbyists and dashed inside and down to his desk.

The clamber gradually died down to the shuffling of feet, a few sporadic desk tops closing and the obligatory short cacophony of coughs as the portly Master-At-Arms entered the chamber at the head of the small entourage and took his place in front of the Speaker's dais.

The Speaker of the House, his secretary and the MAA all took their seats followed by the rest in attendance.

Roll call was a mere preliminary and even to a first time visitor a quick glance around the room would reveal that this wasn't a very important session. Three quarters of the seats were empty. The notes of the old business were read and new business was called for. Senator James from New Orleans was the first one to stand and in his heavy dialect request recognition.

"Mr. Speaker I request, in light of the criticality of the matter at hand we delay the routine of scheduled new business and proceed to the report to the House of the Special sub-Committee on Inter-State Transportation appointed herein last session."

"You have some matter related to the I.S.T. report Senator James?" The Speaker inquired. James cleared his throat before answering.

"A recommendation that may well expedite the impasse we seem to have run into last week regarding revocation or re-enforcement of the policing measures presently in place on our burgeoning inter-state road system."

A single bang of the gavel resonated through a silent chamber.

"Motion has been made to forego then proceed. Is there a second?" From somewhere in the ovoid chamber came a response.

"I second Mr. Speaker." Senator Leary of Georgia called back.

The Wolves of Calabria

"Let the record show motion has been made and seconded. Senator James, you have the floor."

"Thank you Mr. Speaker." He referenced some blank papers on his desk and remained standing as he spoke. "Mr. Speaker, Honorable Gentlemen of the Chamber. According to a report on a study I have here in front of me the proposed legislation before the House, to wit the mandating of a Federal regulation code over the existing, more than adequate, State systems of codes is not only unnecessary but, as written, completely redundant!"

James knew, as did everyone else in the House, the bill was going to pass and that the upcoming vote was a mere formality. However, he had to dress his impending proposal in the guise of genuine public interest for the record and in order to achieve his real goal.

"Rather than burden the proceedings with picayune objections and inane arguments that may delay this bill for an indefinite length of time, may I cite the ruling in U.S. v Delaware & Hudson Co., 213 U.S. 366, 1909. 'The hauling of commodities in which the carrier has at the time of the haul a proprietary interest is strictly forbidden.' Gentlemen, if the learned lawmakers of the Supreme Court of the United States have ruled this then as a humble Senator of the people, the rider I am about to propose -"

"Senator James, we are not in a court. There is no need to cite case law!" The Speaker, by now well used to James' tactics, sought to keep him on track.

"Of course Mr. Speaker, I merely wish to present the whole picture as it were."

"Mr. Speaker," It was Senator Feinstein of New York who spoke up. ". . . the ruling in question, and so eloquently sited by my learned colleague, also clearly states that if any ruling, law or incident effects commerce then the Federal Government, specifically the United States Senate, has a proprietary interest in such affairs. Ergo, the Bill, with a projected cost of $37.66 billion to be paid over the next 20 years, has no doubt been thoroughly researched by the committee's framers, should have its integrity preserved and therefore should be taken as is."

"Thank you Senator." James shot back. "It is exactly in that light that my proposal to lift the war time restrictions on interstate travel, particularly if we are seriously considering moving forward under the provisions of The Federal-Aid Highway Act of 1938 and begin apportioning funds to the various states, some form of tracking of large amounts of goods crossing inter-state lines should be included in the Bill."

Feinstein again interrupted.

"The Honorable Gentleman from Louisiana is fully aware that, as cited in paragraph six, page nine of the proposal before the House that, 'haulers, trains and trucks alike', are currently required to be prepared to be stopped and inspected at all major artery crossing points of all these 48 Continental United States."

The Wolves of Calabria

"And I ask, how much time will this take? How long will the hard working truckers of these United States, many if not most of whom have recently arrived back on these shores after fightin' a ferocious war for liberty against a determined enemy mind you, be compelled to delay their journeys? How long?!" James persisted.

Feinstein suddenly realized that James had already bought or traded the necessary number of votes for his rider, whatever it was, so all that he had to do now was get the Speaker to agree to a hand vote. Feinstein had no choice but to accept the reality that further banter was pointless.

"I have taken the liberty to undertake, in my own time and at no expense to the taxpayer, just such a study! A detailed study to be precise." James rummaged through his brief case and produced then held up the sheaf of blank papers bound together which convincingly looked like some kind of 'study'.

"Seein' as how we have already acted on these recommendations I should think we owe it to the people of this fair country to expedite matters and proceed with our paid duties. Mr. Speaker I call for a hand vote on the said rider for the roads bill before the House." As Senator James continued Feinstein reluctantly came to terms that the last nail in the coffin had been driven. "May I also remind the Honorable Gentleman from California that our problems over in Europe are far from over and the imposition of yet more transport regulations, while possibly having the effect of impeding criminal movement within our borders, would certainly have a negative effect on the free movement of much needed food, machinery, weapons and medical equipment to defeat our tenacious enemies abroad."

The Speaker conceded and a hand vote was called for.

"All in favor?" Hands were raised.

"All opposed?" The majority wasn't overwhelming but a win was clear by the minimum number of holdouts.

Once the vote was concluded the secondary items of business were completed by lunch time and the Speaker called the session to a close and dismissed the chambers.

Out in the hall James once again met with a pair of gentlemen who represented 'an interested party'.

As there were only so many miles of designated federally financed highway allocated and the new bill was based on each State receiving a share of the annual Interstate Construction fund, every Tom, Dick and Harry wanted the new national highway system to go through their stretch of turf from Bumfuck to Hootersville.

These gentlemen, coincidently of Italian extraction and representing Senator Woods' district, were there to convince James to make the right decision regarding dispersion of funding. But, in the overall picture, these were small potatoes by comparison.

The Wolves of Calabria

Minutes after leaving James these gentlemen phoned Frankie Costello who phoned Meyer Lansky as soon as he got the good news. Meyer smiled as he hung up.

James's rider, now approved, would be tacked onto the new Interstate Transportation Bill.

The New York Mob wa very nearly fully back in business.

✝

New York State Executive Mansion
Eagle Street, Albany, New York

A hundred and forty five miles north of Downtown Manhattan, about three hours by car, lies the official residence of the governor, Thomas E. Dewey.

With its exaggeratedly tall chimneys and medieval like towers the red brick, Italianate Classical mansion features a drive through portico at the front door and a generous distribution of white columns, lattice work and trim. Surrounded by immaculately trimmed shrubbery and handsomely groomed lawns the mansion, in reality, is a museum posing as a residence.

The interior is no less plush with a mix of Hepplewhite, neo-Classical and Colonial furniture and with woodwork topped by crystal chandeliers.

That day the interior was as busy as a beehive.

With the mansion as a campaign headquarters former New York District Attorney Thomas Dewey, now Governor Dewey was, for the third time, plotting his attack on another mansion, the one located at 1600 Pennsylvania Avenue, in Washington D.C.

By all accounts he was a shoe-in.

Being the first presidential candidate born in the 20th Century, the youngest Republican candidate ever and the generally perceived malaise towards the Democratic nominees all combined to give the Dewey camp an all too dangerous false sense of security.

Gathered around a giant mahogany dining table, scattered with 'Dewey for President' posters, placards and lapel buttons, a gaggle of twelve men, his management team, was discussing the attack strategy for his presidential bid. Dewey spewed the words of wisdom luxuriously afforded someone in charge.

"One thing ya gotta remember boys, the keys to the White House ain't under the door mat! They're on the front pages of America's newspapers! Never forget that! Control the Press and you control the people!"

"Long as we can down play the Luciano fiasco and focus on all the guys we put away!" One of the faithful chirped up.

"We put away?" Dewey clipped.

"**You** put away T. D.!" Flunky #1 corrected.

"Yeah! Put away alright, **for good**!" Flunky #2 echoed.

However, even after Dewey's self-declared Public Enemy #1 had been convicted, imprisoned and deported, Lucky Luciano remained a thorn in Dewey's side.

The fact that Dewey, as well as any other politician who could, got so much mileage out of Luciano's blown-out-of-all-proportion evilness backfired was because Dewey had to sign Charlie's pardon which left a stink cloud that wouldn't go away.

To exasperate matters the fact that Anslinger was now basking in the 'Luciano' headlines and squeezing them for all they were worth for his own benefit, didn't help Dewey's cause at all.

"Even with that two bit bum still in the news, you're looking at the next president of the United States!" Flunky #3 chimed in.

A pair of Negro butlers moved through the room refreshing drinks and tending to ashtrays.

"Governor Dewey, we need to work on a couple of good sound bites for the radio shows. Something we can work up into a slogan or two." Someone informed.

"Okay Orville."

"Something like, Dewey. The Way Forward!" Flunky #2 suggested.

"Or Dewey - the Law and Order President!" Flunky #3 jumped in. Dewey cut them all of with his own favourite.

"No, no, no! It's gotta have drive. Gotta have punch! something like, 'Never forget! Your Future is Still Ahead of You!'"

After losing out on the election for the third time, Dewey would always be remembered as a master of the obvious

✝

CHAPTER XV

Although *Operation Mincemeat*, a British S.O.E. operation, came after and was unrelated to *Operation Underworld*, an American O.S.S. operation, they did cross paths through *Operation Husky*, the official name for the invasion of Sicily which resulted in the unofficially named *Operation Snowfall*, a joint Sicilian Cosa Nostra/New York Mafia operation which now seemed well on the way to fruition.

As most times it would take a gun to the head for the O.S.S. and the S.O.E. to share information during the war, it also took a gun to the head for the various mob bosses not to collaborate on Intelligence sharing. So by the time the Brits and the Yanks ticked onto the ins and outs of the Intel game, the people erroneously known by The Press as the 'Mafia' had been at it for 80 years and by 1946 the Mob's info network would start in Rome and spread from Messina through the New York City waterfront across the country and was slowly but surely working its way out to the West Coast of the United States.

By way of example there was the time, after the war, when a gang of U.S. senators along with a gaggle of aides and a small army of reporters in tow showed up in Messina on an anti-commie fact finding mission, (alias taxpayer funded junket/holiday).

When they found half the population starving and three quarters of them in rags, they didn't attribute it to the Mafia extorting the aid being sent to Italy, but nearly killed each other in the stampede tripping over themselves to exploit the cold, hard facts of 'life under a Communist government'.

This of course played well with audiences in Des Moines, Iowa and their God-fearin' cun-stit-u-ents in the Bible Belt. However, the fact was that the current Italian government was in fact a coalition with less than a 14% Communist minority, half of whom were in reality hard core Socialists with no thoughts, dreams or desires to engage the U.S. in debate much less overthrow its government as taught by the communists.

This had of course no effect on the politicians like Anslinger, Hoover and Agent White who not only pushed for but aggressively facilitated violent action against any Italian politician who may have one time even uttered the word 'communism' in a sentence.

Anslinger, Hoover et al had no official authority to destroy a suspected Italian politician in Italy but they had enough financial influence on the people who did.

Specifically, Calò Vizzini's La Cosa Nostra.

✝

The Wolves of Calabria

M&M Private Investigations
Greenwich Village, N.Y.C., N.Y.

The sign painter was putting the finishing touches on the door window as Louie paced the office inside and Doc argued, begged and persuaded.

"Aw come on Louie! Nice two day trip south across the country! Jersey farmlands, the Delaware Water Gap, the rolling hills of Pennsylvania. D.C. the nation's capital! How many Mancino's been across the Potomac? You'll be the first!" Doc cajoled.

"Doc! It's a giant river! I been across the Hudson, ta Jersey, twice. Which is why I always come back! But I don't commencerate it every year with a drink and a party! All I'm sayin' is . . . two days on a train?! TWO FREACKIN' DAYS? I could walk halfway to Florida in two days! What the hell we gonna do on a frickin' train for two God damn days?!"

"I'm sensing some resistance here Louie." Doc came out from behind his desk. "Look, beautiful scenery, good food, drinks, beautiful stews! And we don't have to do anything! We can relax, maybe get some work done if we feel like it. If not, we take it easy, pretend we're a coupl'a big shots for once. Stare out the window, take in the sights." Doc stepped a bit closer to where Louie sat. "It'll be just like we're on vacation."

Louie was unimpressed and so offered a solution to their conundrum.

"What about if you take the train, I'll stay here for a day, get some work done, and fly down on Thursday? I land ahead of you, organize the hotel and stuff, and I meet you at the station with a Hertz rental? It'll be like you had your own private chauffeur!"

"You're not a chauffeur, you're a P.I! Come on Louie! We're a team now, ain't we?"

As Louie mentally formed his arguments he was very careful to remind himself to avoid reference to Doc's fear of flying. Having only been in an airplane once before, McKeowen swore a personal oath; *Never again!*

Louie crossed the room through the open door to his own office space and plopped down behind his double wide desk, reclined in his new brown leather, overstuffed swivel chair and pouted. Trying not to look like a kid who didn't get his way, he sat silently.

Mancino might have been slowly coming to terms with his ethnicity as an Italian, but one thing Louie Mancino would hate for the rest of his life is sitting around for long stretches doing nothing for prolonged periods of time. In essence, waiting. On the rare occasions they came up, he still dodged routine stakeouts.

"Shit Doc!" Mancino plopped his feet up on his desk. From the front reception area Doc heard the feet hit the floor, heard Louie's swearing and read the resignation.

"That's the Louie we've all come to know and love!" Doc called back over to Mancino's space as he sprang up and moved next door. McKeowen's elation did nothing to cheer him up. "We'll shove off on Tuesday so we get there early Thursday. That'll give us the weekend to goof off and sight see! I'll tell Shirley to pick up the tickets for us."

"Nah, leave it. I'll do it. The weather's nice, the walk Uptown'll do me good."

"Way to take one for the team Buddy!" Doc grabbed his bomber jacket hanging next to his double breasted suit jacket which was coated in a fine layer of dust. "I'm heading home after I go to the archives so I'll see ya in the morning."

"Yeah Doc. Hi to Nikki and Kate."

†

Mid-Town Manhattan
West 34th Street

Doc and Louie stepped out of the cab at a not so busy Penn Station that Tuesday afternoon around half past ten. Louie had the tickets and assured Doc there was plenty of time before they shoved off. He wasn't lying. At least about having plenty of time.

Doc looked him up and down.

"Louie, why the hell you always wear bowling clothes? You look like you're on your way to the lanes when you got sidetracked by your job!"

"What'a you want? I should drop fifty to seventy-five bucks on a new suit every year?! And you seen the price of men's shoes lately?! Florsheims, on sale mind you, are starting at twenty, twenty-five smackaroos! Here's a shopping tip: any bowling alley, perfectly good shoes, fifteen cents!" He brandished a foot to emphasize his point.

"You can take the boy off the garbage truck . . ." Doc shook his head.

The tickets were actually for a four o'clock departure time, but Mancino told Doc they were for ten forty-five.

"Which track for *The Blue Zephyr*?" Doc asked a porter.

"Track 17 sir." The grip noticed Louie's oversized bag. "Would you like a luggage cart, Sir?"

"No thanks, we'll manage." Doc signaled yes as he held up his small, blue, YMCA gym bag.

If Mancino was still depressed about the nearly two day, arduous journey ahead he hid it well, especially while they were getting settled into the plush seats in the rear of the dinning & bar car.

The large maroon and gold crushed velvet arm seats with the thick gold strips running down the middle of the back rests were complimented by the green Connemara marble topped tables which had been polished to a high sheen. The dark green and gold curtains had been drawn so as to hide the dismal dark of the underground lower platforms of the station thus affording the azure tinted fluorescent lights to have maximum effect. The mood was relaxing. Doc relaxed and submitted to the ambiance. Even Louie, to an extent, let it envelope him as orchestra music softly played in the background.

Mancino immediately noted that the bar staff, exclusively female, were all exceptionally attractive.

"Jesus Doc! These girls are right out of the pages of Vogue, only with arms and legs that move!"

He was basking in the highest level of luxury he had ever been exposed to when he caught Doc holding back a fold of curtain and staring out the curved picture window on the rear of the car and out across the busy platform.

"Ya miss her already, don't ya?" Louie asked. Doc forced a smile.

"You taking night courses? Cause if you are they're payin' off!" Doc replied. "She's got my heart in her hands, Louie." Louie smiled to himself.

"Be right back Doc." Mancino made his way down the aisle to the bar at the other end of the car and approached the six foot, good looking, 30-something, not-so-natural, red head behind the counter.

Perusing her short, green, flared, velvet skirt and matching short sleeved blouse with the flared shoulders, she was accented with black hose and green heels.

He adjusted his collar, smoothed back his jet black hair, turned on the charm and casually took an elbow at the bar.

"How ya doin' gorgeous?" The battle hardened barmaid didn't even look up from the fashion magazine splayed across the marble bar top she was propped up on.

"Hit the bricks Lover Boy! I don't date guys under four foot nuthin'."

Mancino's hull was damaged.

"Huh! And here I was gonna invite you out to my 5,000 acre ranch at Lake Tahoe." Louie shot back.

"And I'd'a probably gone. Except my husband, Alan Ladd, is waitin' at home for me in our 10 room, Beverly Hills mansion." There was a not so pregnant pause before she reloaded. "Oh yeah! I just remembered something else." She added as her steely blue eyes made direct contact with Mancino's.

"Yeah? What's that, Doll?" Louie asked as he leaned into her.

"I don't date Guidos."

"Who said I'm Italian?!"

"Who the hell else would show up with a first class ticket on the *Zephyr* wearing a blue and orange silk bowling shirt, badly tailored pants and two toned bowling shoes? What'd ya think we had a bowling alley on board?"

"So I heard wrong! So sue me! Look, foreplay aside, I goot a problem."

"I'd'a never guessed!"

"Serious,ly Sister! My buddy down there just got back from overseas and . . ."

She craned her neck but continued to lean on one elbow as she glanced down the lounge aisle at Doc who was just sat back from staring out the window. She nodded her approval.

"Not bad. Was he wounded?"

"Ah, yeah. Yeah, yeah. He got hit pretty bad. Grenade, to the head."

"Geez! That sounds like the pits!"

"Yeah it was. He's okay now, but he had anesthesia for nearly six months and can't remember too good you see and the thing is . . ."

"You mean amnesia Sparky?" She casually corrected.

"Yeah, yeah. Anastasia, amnesia whatever, you know what I mean. Like I was sayin', he has to cope, ya know?"

"I know what ya mean. Me, I always take life with a grain of salt. Plus a slice of lime and a shot of tequila."

"A shot a day keeps the doctor way!"

"It's a girl ain't it? I mean your buddy. Girl trouble?"

"You taking night courses? Cause if you are they're payin' off!"

"HEY! Can the sarcasm Bob Hope!"

"Sorry! It's his high school sweetheart! He's head over heels about her, and . . . Well, when I think how beautiful what they got is I . . . I can only describe it as . . . well let's just say she's got his heart in her hands!" Big Red fought back a wave of sentimentality as she glanced over at Louie.

On cue Mancino tagged his story.

"Only he's scared see?"

"Scared 'a what? He ain't gonna remember what to do when the lights go out?!"

"Yeah! Exactly! He needs a bit of courage."

"Is she a looker?"

"Right out of a film magazine."

"Then don't worry, he'll remember what to do!"

"I was just wonderin' . . . I mean, I know it ain't exactly policy, but . . ." Louie said as he pulled a small wad of cash from his hip pocket.

"Hey, what'a you think ths is, a - ?"

"No, NO, NO! Nuthin' like that! I'm talkin' about drinks! I was wondein' if you'd get us some drinks!" She looked him up and down, again.

"What'a you think I got this skimpy green outfit on for Sherlock?! A sequel to the *Wizard Of Oz*?! Sit down and I'll bring ya some drinks!" Louie covertly slid the small wad of bills across the bar.

"I'm not just talkin' about drinks, Sister. I'm talkin' a whole bottle! And he can't know it's from me! Tell him it's on the house, for services above and beyond, something like that." She took the wad and counted it out.

"What kind'a courage your friend like?"

"Irish. Jameson."

"Classy! A bottle'll run ya 10.50." She untangled and counted out the wad. "This is 11 bucks!" She reminded him.

"I know, but that's okay! Keep the change." Louie sincerely said as he headed back down the aisle.

"Oh gee! You sure?! I mean **Mrs**. Rockefeller ain't gonna get sore or nuthin', is she?"

Ten minutes later heads were turning as the

The Wolves of Calabria

statuesque redhead sashayed down the aisle with a silver tray stacked with a small jug of water, two rocks glasses and a bottle of Jameson's and made her way to the rear of the car. Doc was surprised when she set the tray on their table but the two business suits in the center seats nearly fell out into the aisle when she bent over, unnecessarily far, to pour the water.

"Here ya go G.I. It's on the house, for services rendered. Enjoy!"

Doc dug in his pocket and came up with a twenty spot but Louie stayed his hand.

"It's okay Doc. I already tipped her."

She might have let it pass but the wink Louie threw her put it over the top which is why, as she poured the water for Louie's drink most of it mysteriously missed the glass.

Followed by profuse, animated apologies, Mancino would spend the rest of the morning looking like he wet his pants.

Although he had no idea why, McKeowen deduced Louie had somehow earned it the assault.

Handing Doc his drink she made eye contact and smiled. As Louie dealt with his wet trousers Doc slipped her the twenty bucks under the table.

"Lemme ask you sumthin'." Louie insisted to her. "What'a you got against Italian guys anyway?" She didn't miss a beat as she retrieved the empty tray.

"Coupl'a things. My father Lorenzo. My brother Alfonso, my brother Mateo, my brother Joey. My father's brothers Enzo and Frankie. My mother's brother's . . ." Her voice trailed off as she wiggled it down the aisle back to the bar. Even Doc found it hard to avoid any reckless eyeballing as she made her way back up to the other end of the car.

"That Treasury case must've made more of an impact than I thought!" Doc commented. Louie was already filling the crystal rocks glasses with the whiskey.

"Never underestimate the power of the Press, Doc!" Doc held his glass to the light.

"Didn't really plan on getting' drunk. Been a while." Doc commented.

"The last baptism wasn't it?"

"Seems like a while ago."

"I didn't know any better, I'd think you really were in love with Nikki." Doc stared out the window again then threw back his drink.

Louie was unusually vigilant about being sure that Doc's glass was never empty and a little more than an hour later he was compelled to enlist the help of a couple of porters to help carry Doc off the train and back out to the platform.

It took some effort but once off the train he scrounged a luggage trolley and got Doc across the concourse to a cargo lift. After tipping the elevator operator he pushed McKeowen and their luggage across the main promenade to the 45th Street side of the station and over to the taxi rank. People stared the whole way.

A burly, dock worker type stepped out of the cab

and came around to Louie. He shifted the stogie in his mouth as he perused the load, Doc's arms and legs dangling from the side of the trolley cart.

"You wanna put him in the trunk?" The hackie joked.

"Why would I wanna put him in the trunk?!"

"I take him as a passenger its regular rates. Put him in the trunk, he's luggage." Louie thought for a moment, looked at the trunk and said, "Nah. I'll pay the extra."

"Where to?"

"LaGuardia, terminal one, gate three."

It was about ten minutes before last call for boarding the flight, as Louie checked them in at the desk.

The only viable way to get Doc out to the aircraft and across tarmac was strapped upright onto a baggage trolley with the help of a porter. Once again people stared.

With Doc over his shoulder Louie climbed the portable boarding stairs to where the smartly dressed, humorless stewardess stood at the door holding her hips. Mancino popped a smile at her.

"Shot down over Malta. Afraid of flying. Family Doctor gave him a few sleeping pills." He tilted McKeowen forward so the stew could see Doc's brown leather bomber jacket and handed her the tickets. She leaned in and sniffed Doc's face.

"Huh! Whiskey flavored sleeping pills! Had a few of those myself once. Go on, get goin'. And no trouble!"

"Do you serve in-flight drinks?"

"I'll bring you a rocks glass and a twist. You can wring your friend out."

Thirty minutes later they were 20,000 feet over The Delaware Water Gap heading south.

☦

A little over two and a half hours into the three and a half hour flight McKeowen started coming around. At the first signs of Doc's stirrings Louie strategically decided to check out the little boy's room at the back of the cabin and so made himself scarce.

McKeowen tried rolling over but found he couldn't and so cursed out loud when the small of his back hit the aisle arm rest. The old couple in front of him harrumphed a couple of times then turned away and the attractive business type across from him shook her head and reconsidered her earlier impulse to strike up a conversation with him.

As he peeled his eyes open and the cabin's interior slowly came into focus and he realized where he was a wave of panic washed over him. He grabbed the seat handles either side of him and sat bolt upright. Still a little drunk, he focused on controlling his breathing, stared straight ahead then looked around to get his bearings.

One of the two stewardesses noticed and brought him a tall glass of water and two Bayer aspirin.

As she offered him the pills he instead grabbed

the bottle and poured a small hand full of the tablets.

"It's on the house." He didn't take the water as she cast a look of genuine concern. "You okay?" As if autistic Doc stared, looked around then cleared his head and spoke.

"Whiskey. Neat."

"I think you should –"

"Lady, PLEASE! I know what I need for a hangover. Trust me." She stared still holding the water. "Whiskey. Thank you." He quietly repeated. She was back in a minute with a double.

"Hey mister, we got a doctor flying with us up front, you sure you're okay?" She inquired.

"Yeah, yeah I'm okay. My friend's got a sick sense of humor. Where're we heading?"

"We had a short stopover in Raleigh but we're about twenty, twenty-five minutes out from our final approach into Miami." Doc looked up and set the empty drinks aside.

"Thanks. Was there a guy with me. Short, chubby-"

"Lou Costello's brother?"

"Yeah!"

As if on cue Mancino popped his head out of the toilet door. Doc leaned over in his seat and peered down the aisle at him.

"You want me to find him?"

"Thanks, no. I found him." Doc waved him back to the seats. Louie came up the aisle a little over halfway but was hesitant to close the distance to Doc. "It's alright." He reassured Mancino as he threw back his drink.

"Ya sure?" Louie asked still maintaining more than an arm's distance.

"Yeah, yeah. Sit down." Mancino complied. "What the hell? Time I confronted this thing anyway. Not like air travel is gonna go away. Besides, you're doing pretty good dealing with your Italian thing, so . . . Remind me to thank you." Doc stared out the window, tightened his seat belt and gripped both arm rests as they started their decent into Miami.

Once they both stepped off the portable stairway a half hour later and were out into the warm breezy air of Miami International and onto the runway, Doc signaled Louie aside.

"Come here."

"What?!" Louie took a step backwards.

"No seriously, come here." Louie inched forward. "I really feel like I need to thank you. This fear of flying thing's really stupid." Doc said. Louie smiled. "I don't know if I'm completely over it but . . ." Mancino extended his hand. Doc took it, pulled him forward and clocked him across the jaw with a left cross.

As a member of the ground crew stood there wide-eyed Louie's knees wobbled, shook and just before he collapsed onto the tarmac he looked up at Doc cross-eyed.

The fur draped, elderly woman coming down the stairs ahead of the old man screamed, the stew at the top of the rolling stairs shook her head and held the people back while Doc wrestled Louie up onto a luggage cart, helped the negro grip strap him down and with a woozy Mancino stuffed down into the trolley, pointed the cart towards the terminal.

They headed across the tarmac and through the bright white Art Deco terminal to a taxi stand outside.

People stared as Doc and the driver loaded him into the back seat.

Doc felt bad about hitting Louie.

But not that bad.

✝

CHAPTER XVI

Hotel Flagler
637 W Flagler St.
Miami Beach

Being mid-morning on a weekday there was little traffic on the way to the hotel so the trip was steady but the cabbie felt compelled to strike up a conversation. When he discovered that Doc and Louie were from New York, he was bursting to tell them he was born in Brooklyn. On finding it was their first trip to Miami, he asked if three dollars for the five and half mile ride to the hotel would do, the guys agreed and so he shut off the meter and gave them the fifty cent tour enroute.

Unfortunately for Doc's head, the tour was about eight miles long.

They pulled over off the four lane boulevard long enough for Doc to run into a pharmacy and get some aspirins and then were off again. He popped four or five as the driver wanna-be tour guide returned to his spiel.

"Few people realize that St. Augustine, right here in Florida is the oldest European settlement in North America! Additionally few people know that greater Miami is the only city whose boarders encompass not one but two national parks!"

"I did not know that, Herb." Doc slurred back,

nursing his hangover, trying not to get car sick.

"Clearwater, Florida holds the world's record for, guess what?! Go on take a guess!"

"Hookers per square block Herb?" Doc half moaned.

"NO! Lightning strikes per capita! Most in the world a given year! Right over in Clearwater!"

"Herb is our hotel anywhere near Clearwater?" Doc sarcastically ventured.

"No! Not at all!"

"Good, then we're okay yeah?"

"Yeah, yeah sure!"

Herb's seemingly never-ending verbal torture ended twenty-five long minutes later as they pulled onto Flagler Street near Bayfront Park about three blocks north east of Little Havana. They gave Herb a fin note and got out. As they did Louie stared up at the street sign. McKeowen could see they were only a block and a half from the Miami River.

"Nice. But it ain't the Hudson." Doc volunteered.

"Hey Doc look, Flagler Street." Louie pointed at the sign then to the hotel. "Hotel Flagler!"

"How 'bout that Louie!"

"Where ya suppose they got the name?" Louie jibed as Doc, gym bag in hand, trudged around to the side entrance of the hotel.

"Beats me."

Sitting in the middle of the block between NW 6th Avenue and SW 5th The Flagler was a whitewashed, three story, imitation adobe with a row of souvenir shops across the entire front of the ground floor. The black, wrought iron main entrance was around the side down a gravel alley way which opened into an expansive front garden and both P.I.'s were pleasantly surprised upon entering the lobby.

It was unexpectedly spacious in comparison to the exterior of the structure and, as expected, heavily accented in Spanish Colonial décor.

Their room was on the second floor and the bags no sooner hit the floor when Doc, still fully dressed, hit the bed.

"Okay then, guess I'll just go out and wander around." Mancino shrugged.

He was answered with heavy snoring.

✝

Two and a half hours later Doc started to stir as he heard the jingle of keys in the door when Mancino returned to the room.

"Hey Doc, you done sleeping? What say we get somethin' ta eat then take in the races, you ever been?"

"Went out to Belmont Park once with Nicky." Doc rubbed his eyes, went into the bathroom and splashed his face with cold water. "It was a simple trip. We showed up, we bet, we lost, we left. Besides, the track's a good five miles away and its ninety degrees outside!"

"That's okay, I seen one of them Hertz Drive-Ur-

Self offices around the corner on 7th Avenue when we came in."

"You know I don't have a licence!"

"And you know I do!" Mancino countered.

"What'a we gonna rent a garbage truck?!"

"Nice to see you're back to your old sarcastic self. Licence is a licence ain't it?"

"I guess so. When's the last time you drove?"

"Ahh, it's like riding a bike, once you learn ya never forget! Come on, my treat."

"You feeling alright?" Unless it was to set it on the nightstand to go to sleep, Louie rarely removed his wallet from his trousers.

A half hour later, like two New York corporate big shots, McKeowen and Mancino were cruising up State Route 7 chrome glistening in the bright Miami sun, in a 1945 dark maroon Packard heading towards the world famous Hialeah Race Track.

†

Hialeah Race Track
Hialeah, Florida

The bell sounded, the retainer gate lifted and ten thoroughbreds ripped out of the stalls. The fans in the seats and stands in the lower bleachers were on their feet while in the upper tier's more expensive seats patrons sat quietly, maintaining their composure as horses and riders rounded the first turn.

Inside the pavilion hundreds milled about or made their way to their seats via the twenty-five betting windows.

Race five finished and the majority of betters tore up tickets and cursed.

It was just after four in the afternoon when the P.A. again blared to life.

And welcome ladies and gentlemen to the sixth race this afternoon at Hialeah on a sunny, dry afternoon. This race will be run minus the two year old My Lady Can due to a last minute withdrawal. Refunds will be paid at windows 12, 14 and 15.

We are approaching gate time for the sixth race of the day so please make your way to the window and place your bets.

Back in the twenties the world famous track was the seed that blossomed into the city of Miami. Nestled between East 4th and West 1st, the significance to the economic lifeline of the entirety of southern Florida was evidenced by the fact that it was the track itself that determined which side of the city you lived on and ergo your perceived social status.

Department of Foreign Affairs agents Benson and Hernandez, under the guise of taking a vacation and under increased pressure to find a lead, had flown down to Miami in the hopes of tracking the unknown new source of heroin which had been slowly permeating New York City.

On their second day in town they had confiscated a back room in a federal mail storage facility to serve as a temporary office and it was about three hours after they got tucked in there that one of their reliable informants up in Hoboken, New Jersey took the abnormal step of making an unscheduled contact by sending a wire to their D.C. office, a Western Union that had reached them through the Miami federal mail storage facility.

Now, sitting in a private box, high up in the back tier of the track Benson, Hernandez next to him in the aisle seat, glanced at the telegram one more time.

```
Stranger   in   on   Tuesday   last
asking questions STOP Fighter pilot
type   STOP   Request   instructions?
STOP
```

"Who's that?" Benson asked when he noticed Hernandez nod at a couple of suspicious looking guys a few rows over and down to their right.

"After Rossini got tagged I was curious about who nailed him for us. Apparently the insurance company hired some gumshoe to see if it was a fraud case. Turns out the little son-of-a-bitch got lucky when Rossini jumped him in an alley way with two torpedoes. Some schmuck named McKeowen. Figured I'd check him out, see if he's clean or dirty." Hernandez explained. Benson sat back and nodded.

"Very impressive. And they say beaners have small brains!"

"Could be worse. I could be a small-dicked gringo."

"So who are the trench coats?" Benson asked as he nodded down and towards the right at a pair awkwardly pretending to watch the next line up as the horses were being set in the shoots.

"After I I.D.'d McKeowen I put a Narcotics Bureau guy on it. Fella named White. He's working out of the Tampa office at the moment but he's lookin' to move up to D.C." Hernandez reported. "I figured it was better not to use someone outta state. Too many questions when it comes to paperwork otherwise." Benson grunted his approval as his partner elaborated. "Turns out he worked with the Treasury Department before switching over to the Bureau. I told him this McKeowen clown is posing as a P.I. and working with the Mob to help set up drug routes to the north."

"Is he?" Benson pushed.

"How the fuck should I know?! I just threw it in as bait for White. He's a real gung-ho asshole type, always gotta be fightin' for a cause, or a flag or some shit."

"So he's a moron?"

"Precisely."

"Bring him up here." One of the two in the lower seats glanced up and Hernandez waved the two up to the box. The short, chubby guy in the trench coat and fedora rose from his seat and made his way up to them. The other stayed put and out of ear shot but turned slightly to afford himself a better view of the meet.

"Agent Benson, Foreign Affairs. Glad to meet you."

"George White, Bureau of Narcotics, D.C, office." They shook hands while both Benson and Hernandez ignored the fact White introduced himself as being out of the D.C office to increase his own prestige just before he shifted the toothpick protruding from his lips.

"How long you on the job Agent White? Have a seat."

"No thanks. Twelve years next month." He stood to the right of Hernandez on the stairs.

"No plans to retire and migrate back north?" Hernandez probed.

"I got a few irons in the fire. Working on an investment deal through my brother-in-law. Soon as it comes through, I'm history. Maybe open up my own detective agency."

"Sounds like you know what you're doing. What's ya got on our boy?"

White pulled out a standard issue police pad but hardly referred to it.

"Looks like we got ourselves something of a minor celebrity here. Ex-cop, now a P.I. Made the headlines a few years back when he murdered a Treasury case officer and apparently engineered a pretty good frame up on two others. Got away with it clean plus got himself a medal from Mayor

LaGuardia. Has his own agency down in the Village, nothing big just him and a partner. Still carries on with some cockamamie theory that his father was assassinated by a bunch of crooked cops on a drug raid back in the Thirties."

"That's a bit far-fetched. No crooked cops in New York, are there Tony?" Benson elbowed Hernandez and looked over at him.

"Not that I ever seen, Frank."

"Now he's sunk to the level of a two bit gumshoe whose wife dumped him. Has a girl who looks like she's getting ready to bail. Bums around with a half-witted partner who used to be a garbage man. Now he's down here snoopin' around. Probably tryin' to figure out who's on to him. Bottom line is . . . he's not a threat."

"This the clown killed a Treasury Agent named Johnston by pushing him off the back of the Staten Island Ferry?" Benson asked.

"Think so, yeah. Maybe. Prob'ly." He hedged.

"And he's down here now?" Benson sought to confirm.

"Yeah. Him and his sidekick are stayin' over on Flagler Street. One question though." White pushed.

"What?"

"Why don't we just pop this guy and put him behind bars. Ya do it down here and I can make sure any judge'll give him twenty to thirty years on your testimony alone, probably won't even need a trial."

"That's a fair question Agent White. We thought about it but decided we want to send a message to the criminal community at large that Florida's not an open state and the governor intends to keep it that way."

"It's your show Mr. Benson. How ya want me ta play it?" White asked.

"Take him out. Make the body disappear. You need a disposal crew?"

"Nah! This is my neck of the woods. I got it covered. There's not a contractor in Dade County don't owe me. With the amount of building going on now, I can have his body spread over a dozen construction sites inside of a day. Don't worry, I'll erase him clean."

"Don't use anybody they can trace back to us. Use a couple'a local goons, reliant but experienced. Ya got it?"

"Yeah. What about the dumpy one?"

"Rough him up and put him on a plane back to New York. He can spread the message this isn't an open town. Benson directed.

"Let us know when it's done." Hernandez added.

"I'll be in touch." White turned to leave and signaled for his buddy to catch up and halfway down the steps towards the exit Benson called down to him.

"George! This will reflect on your next fitness report."

White smiled and with his partner headed for the exits.

After he was gone Hernandez spoke first.

"You think this McKeowen clown is after the

same thing we are?"

"Well, with a profile like that it's a pretty safe bet he ain't down here to start muleing his own dope up to the City."

"Maybe he's on the junk? Took to the needle after his old lady bailed and his career on the force fizzled out? "

"Nah, not plausible." Benson confidently declared.

"Enlighten me oh wise one in the ways of the world. Why not?"

"Simple. He's Irish. None'a those guys are junkies. They're all alkies."

The bell sounded, the retainer gate lifted and nine thoroughbreds ripped out of the stalls about five minutes before a couple of hundred fans ripped up their ticket studs and cursed.

†

Coincidentally while Benson and Hernandez sent their pawns White and partner out the south exit, Doc and Louie had just parked their rental out in the expansive lot and were leisurely strolling in through the North Gate of Section C of the track.

Their day at the track turned into two and half races, three over-priced drinks at the Tiki Lounge bar in the pavilion along with two lousy imitation, authentic New York hot dogs before the decision was made to go back to the hotel and prepare for a night on the town pretending to be drug dealers from the Big Apple looking to make 'the big score'.

As the city council had outlawed live entertainment in the hotels back during the pre-war boom, they would have to play their charade while working the night club circuit.

Later that afternoon Louie was at the wheel of the maroon Packard and Doc was slouched down in the passenger's seat resting, his ball cap pulled down over his face.

It was shortly after leaving the track, as they were driving south on Palm Avenue heading back to the hotel, that they noticed it. Louie called it first as he once again glanced in the rear view mirror.

"Hey Doc?" Doc was already sneaking a peak through the passenger side mirror.

"Yeah, the dark blue Plymouth sedan three cars back. The one with the three inconspicuous assholes sticking out like a triplet of hemorrhoids."

"They picked us up on the other side of East 17th."

"Yeah they did. But I think the driver was scoping us out back at the parking lot." Doc added.

"What'a we do?"

"Well, we could pull over and offer to buy 'em a cup of coffee, but I doubt they'd take it in the spirit in which it was intended. Think you can shake them?" Doc asked. Mancino froze at the wheel. "Louie! This is the part where you say, 'Yeah Doc, I think I can shake these gavones!' Capish?"

Louie looked over at Doc, smiled and nodded.

"Si piso, capito." Mancino finally said as he hit the gas and left an inch of rubber on the road.

Still three car lengths behind in the same lane, the Plymouth was cut off by a taxi as it tried to cut left and overtake the cars in front of it.

A block later their presence known, White and the guys in the Plymouth made no pretence other than that they were gunning for Doc and Louie. They had regained lost ground and stayed in the outside lane still heading south on Palm.

Two blocks further south Mancino began to slow the car as they approached an intersection.

"What'a ya doin'?!" Doc calmly inquired. Louie didn't answer he just leaned as far forward as he could into the steering wheel and peered around the corner and up the intersecting avenue as they approached the traffic light. Doc glanced in the rear view mirror and saw the Plymouth coming up on them.

By the time they reached the intersection Manccino had slowed to a coast and all but stopped.

"I think they just upped the stakes!" Doc informed. Through his side mirror Louie could see one of the three thugs hanging out of the rear passenger's window brandishing a long barrelled .45. "What is this Cowboys and Indians?" Doc asked.

"Who the hell are those guys?!" Louie wondered out loud.

"No idea, but . . ." Doc was cut off as Louie floored the gas and cut in front of a slow moving tour train towing three, open air passenger cars which were trailed by half a dozen other cars and a taxicab backed up behind them.

Once on the other side of the street he swerved around through the intersection, gunned it and lost the tail. Unable to get by the train of vehicles, the Plymouth almost smacked into the Mr. Gator Happy Tours tractor.

"Amateurs!"

"Nice move." Doc congratulated Louie.

"I know." As they drove Doc sat up straight.

"Turn right here." Doc instructed.

"Why? What for?!"

"Just turn here!" Louie obeyed and put them on West 29th heading west.

"The hotel's the other way!"

"You know that, I know that. That means they know that."

"You think they know where we were going?"

"Whoever's in that car they ain't Cuban gangbangers! They know what they're doing which means they scoped us out before making their move."

"Why didn't they just jump us at the hotel?"

"Not sure but the fact that they felt safe jumpin' us in the middle of town in the middle of the road also means they ain't afraid of the law. Not in this town anyway."

As they passed a parked police car outside a drive up burger stand Doc didn't notice the fact that one of the two cops waiting to be served his burgers

Paddy Kelly

and fries spotted them and manned the radio telephone from the dashboard.

"Central this is Alpha 5-1."

Alpha 5-1, go ahead.

"I do believe we just sighted that there suspect maroon Packard containin' two white, males of Caucasian persuasion inside. Request instructions. Over."

Alpha 5-1 this is central. What is ya'lls twenty?

"Central, we are at the White Castle hamburger stand on West 23rd. Over."

There was a pause.

Alpha 5-1, maintain feedin' ya'lls face. Central will relay the information to a more professional unit.

"Central, we was gonna bring you back a coupl'a burgers Darlene. Guess you just gonna havt'a fend for yerself for lunch now! Not that you need to feed that fat ass of yours anymore!" Both cops had a good laugh.

Billy Bob, you know full well that's baby fat from my last delivery, 'en it takes time ta lose that fat!

"But Darlene, little Rufus is goin' on near two years old now! How much time you reckin' it's goinna take?"

Go ta hell Billy Bob! You go straight to hell! They's a unit already in pursuit. Central out!

Wrestling with the question of who the mysterious marauders were while settling into the relief of having lost them, Doc had temporarily drifted out of the zone. He immediately chastised himself as he again gazed into the side view mirror and spotted the dark blue Plymouth again gaining on them.

"Louie."

"Yeah Doc?"

"Our friends are back."

"Ba fangulo!" Louie swore as he looked into the mirror.

It was as they made a sharp left turn that Doc noticed the white star painted on the side door of the sedan as it too made the turn.

"SHIT!" Doc swore.

"What?!"

"Looks like they're cops!"

"SHIT! If they're cops how come they ain't using their lights and siren?" Mancino questioned.

"Probably because they're not cops. At least not local law." Doc thought for a moment. "Head back around 180. If they were at the hotel earlier and didn't try something there might be a reason. We'll head back there. See what happens."

Louie took a left south then took the next left and headed back east.

White and his crew wasted no time, sped up and, coming alongside the Packard while drifting into the on-coming lane, made two attempts to fire a shot into the tires. The first shot missed and the second went wild when they drifted into the oncoming lane and a bus nearly took them out and forcing them to swerve across three lanes of traffic to avoid a head-on.

It was in Little Havana that Doc and Louie pulled in behind a large, Gothic cathedral and made the decision to abandon the car. Around back there was a large parking lot out of sight of the main road so they parked between two other cars, shut down and locked up.

"Louie!" Doc pointed to the far corner of the church where there was an access ladder going up. "Let's take the high ground!" They scurried up the ladder to the roof of the choir and peered out over the edge to watch for the bad guys. They didn't have long to wait.

The Plymouth pulled into the driveway in the front of the church and Doc and Louie had a ringside seat as the car slowly cruised around into the parking lot. A minute later White's men found the Packard and were swarming all around it.

"Who the hell are those guys?!" Louie demanded as they crouched behind the peak of the roof.

"No idea but we're sure as hell gonna find out! One way or the other."

From the ground one of the thugs looked up and spotted them and the made for the ladder. Two of them climbed up while White ran around front and entered the church.

Continuing to crawl on all fours Doc and Louie slowly traversed the roof's peak towards the belfry, struggling to maintain balance. As they crawled, Doc in front was pausing to take time to yank the single roofing nail which held each slate tile in place across the top course of the large shingles. But he only pulled the nails from every other one and let the weight of the curved crown cap they were wedged under hold each tile in place. At least until the most acrobatic of their pursuers crested the top of the ladder.

Being the daring little devil he was, he decided to cross the roof tight rope style, upright on both feet as he drew his .45 and took aim. Wide open with no cover Doc and Louie looked back and froze.

As he stopped to aim the Wallenda-wanna-be became a flying Wallenda as he stepped on one of Doc's sabotaged tiles and lost his footing when the tile ripped loose.

The guy fought to balance but only managed to drop his weapon which bounced down the roof and lodged in the rain gutter. Squatting down while fighting desperately to find a grip, the tiles yielded nothing as he slowly slid, face down to the edge, found a brief reprieve as his feet hit the rain gutter which then gave way spitting him over the eaves.

"One-thousand one, one-thousand two-" Doc counted. There was a loud thud accompanied by the muffled crunch of a car roof. "Huh! Two hundred, two hundred and fifty feet. How about that?"

"Hey Doc, I thought most people were supposed to scream when they fall to their deaths?" Louie quipped as they clung closer to the roof.

"Maybe he forgot. At least he had the car to break his fall."

Across the church roof at the steeple Doc reasoned there would be an access hatch down into the church and directed Louie to follow him as they headed the rest of the way across. Louie's hand hit one of the loose tiles which dislodged and slid off the roof.

"Jesus Doc! Did ja havet'a loosen so many tiles?!"

"You got a .45 bullet in ya?"

"Not yet!"

"You're welcome ass-hole! Let's go!" Doc noticed Louie was sweating pretty good and starting to shake. "Louie! Just keep looking ahead, don't look down and you'll be okay! You won't fall!" Doc coached.

"It's not the fall that I'm worried about Doc. It's the sudden stop!"

"Just don't look down!" Across the narrow ledge, on hands and knees they inched their way to the steeple. Across the peak past one flying buttress after another they crawled until they reached the belfry.

Doc, balanced precariously on the peak of the roof where it joined the six inch ledge of the belfry then glanced back at Louie who had stopped and was gawking at the top of the steeple above Doc's head.

"What the hell you lookin' at? It's a lightning rod!"

"I know! And this is a church!"

"So?!"

"Talk about lack of faith!"

"Good point!" Doc shrugged. "Now can we go?"

The Wolves of Calabria

Once on the south side of the belfry and peering through the windowless openings Doc watched as the other crony, who had doubled back, popped up through the one-man floor hatch inside the bell tower. Doc signalled Louie to be silent as they carefully inched to the other side of the tower and around to the north side of the steeple. White's crony came out of the roof access hatch and gun drawn, inched his way around to the North side of the tower where Doc and Louie had reached the end of the ledge they stood on but were crouched below the window opening.

The guy's gun peeked around the corner first and Doc took the risk and grabbed it, twisted it outwards and jammed the guy's thumb and forefinger until he broke them at the first joint. The thug screamed as McKeowen ripped the gun from the mangled digits and pressed himself flat against the tower, focusing to maintain his tenuous footing.

As he did he watched the guy grab at the wooden frame lining the opening with his good left hand but the short screws holding the sill were never intended to take the full weight of a man struggling to save his own life. He tightly held onto the narrow plank as he fell backwards, screaming and fell out of sight until there was no loud thud as expected.

Doc carefully peeked over the roof's edge and saw that the now banana–shaped man was impaled through his back on the six foot high, wrought iron fencing bordering the narrow alley below.

"Two down . . ." He looked over at Louie who

was working on a shade of green Doc couldn't recall having seen before.

"Sal?! Sal, d'ja get the bastard?!" White, called up through the trap door from part way up the ladder inside the bell tower.

"Yeah!" Doc yelled back in a muffled voce.

"Alright, good job! Let's get the hell outta here! It's quittn' time!"

"Right!" Doc listened carefully until he heard White's footsteps descending the wooden ladder before reaching over and helping Mancino to hold onto the belfry window frame.

"Hey stud, you gonna make it?" Doc asked as Mancino stared, glassy-eyed, through his partner. "C'mon, let's get down and go get a pizza." Doc joked. Mancino fought back a retch.

"No pizza, no pizza! Just . . . get down." He eased Louie into the big bell tower and towards the access door.

"You're doing okay. We'll be down in a minute." McKeowen peered down the hole and saw the empty ladder. Louie reached over and tapped him on the shoulder.

"What?"

"We gotta . . . get that . . . scumbag!" Louie eked out seconds before he projectile vomited out over the edge of the window.

It took another minute or so for Louie to struggle to the ladder but seemed steady on the way down as he continually mumbled. "Get . . . scumbag!" Doc checked the magazine then pocketed the .45, smiled

The Wolves of Calabria

and followed Louie down.

They made it down to the parking lot in time to see White's car screeching around the corner and out onto the street heading East. Reflexibly they dashed after the speeding car and out into the street with no prayer of catching him.

"SHIT, SHIT, SHIT!" Doc cursed as he watched the chrome laden rear of the auto grow smaller. His mind raced as he stood amongst a small cluster of kids sitting on the sidewalk playing. A small boy looked up at Doc then over to Louie who was closer to the kids.

"That man said a bad word!" He declared to Mancino pointing at Doc.

"No he didn't kid, it sounded like shit, but he said 'shat'. It means 'good-bye' in his language. He's from France."

As Doc and Louie scrambled back to their Packard and squealed out after Agent White a mom popped her head out the window of the nearby tenement.

"Jimmy, time to eat! Come inside Honey!" Jimmy packed up his toys to go.

"Shit you guys! See ya later!" Little Jimmy called back.

"SHIT JIMMY!"

"SHIT JIMMY! SEE YA!" His little friends yelled back.

Racing back to the Packard Doc and Louie held out little hope of catching White as they chased him south, south East across the city and through the streets heading towards the ocean, a few minutes later reaching the residential waterfront.

By the time White had reached the edge of Bay Front Park, jumped out of the car and dashed across the lawn towards the recreational area of the sea Doc and Louie had just pulled the Packard up besides the curb and were some three hundred yards behind.

Once out of the car Louie began to recover from his queasiness. He looked around and seemed to recognise the place.

"Hey! I seen this place in the Newsreels! This is where that guy tried to shoot Roosevelt!"

"Yeah. An Italian wasn't he?"

"Don't start that shit Doc!" They argued as they ran into the open park area.

"No no, I'm just sayin', was a good thing he was a Guinea!"

"Why?!"

"Cause he couldn't shoot for shit, otherwise he'd hit the President instead of just the mayor."

"Doc?"

"Yeah Louie?"

"Fuck you!"

"And he's back!"

A string of small boat docks bordered the entire eastern perimeter of the small but scenic park and it was clear where White was heading.

"Why ain't he shootin'? He's gotta realize by now we ain't shootin' at him?!" Louie called over to Doc as they maneuverered through the pedestrians on the paths and lounging in the grass.

"A little louder, I don't think he heard ya!" Doc made for a small narrow craft tied up on the right. "This one!" He directed to Louie. Mancino ran over and jumped in. "Grab that bow line!"

Louie complied.

"Doc, this boat's one'a the smallest one's in the harbor! Why'd ya pick this one?" Doc perused the dashboard, found the red ignition button and pressed it. The motor kicked over immediately. He blurted out his answer as he backed away from the dock.

"Performance factors are determined by weight to measured speed ratio. The less displacement, the more speed the boat is capable of." Doc slammed the throttle forward and launched Louie into the back seat and onto his ass. "Of course we are starting off with a weight disadvantage." Doc said as he nodded towards Louie.

"Maybe Doc, but you'd like to have the money it cost to put this on!" He countered as he tapped his belly then climbed back into the front.

"This is a Chris Craft Runabout with an Evinrude 4.2 horsepower engine. Chris Craft was the first company to take advantage of hydroplaning design. And do you know why?" Louie was once again annoyed by Doc's unexplainable breath of knowledge of seemingly trivial matters.

"Pray tell, why?!" Louie bit as he kept both eyes on White's speeding craft 100 yards ahead of them.

Doc pointed to a brass engraved plaque on the

dashboard of the boat. Louie leaned over and read it.

"Huh! Designed by Carlo Riva. Italian!" He said with no small amount of pride.

"That's right, Italian! That prick ain't got a chance of out running us! Capish?" Doc asked. Louie smiled.

"Capish!" Louie smiled back.

"Doc, you ever drove a boat before?"

"How hard can it be?"

Doc hard throttled to starboard spraying a rooster tail ten yards high and fifteen yards long behind them. Louie maintained eye contact with their prey.

White had a pretty good start on them so rather than try to run him down McKeowen decided to try and intercept him. He guest-timated an azimuth to a couple of points off the starboard side and headed into it.

It was two and a half miles east across the south bay to Fisher Island and it appeared that's where White was heading. He deftly dodged several boaters while avoiding coming too close to shore. Seeing that he wasn't going to lose Doc any time soon White tried heading straight for a large channel buoy only to swerve at the last minute in the hope Doc would follow and not turn in time. It didn't work.

"Guy's pretty good!" Louie said.

"Maybe when this is all over he'll take you out for a boat ride and a picnic!" Doc responded.

That's when White got serious. With one hand on

the wheel he faced 180 degrees to the rear and popped three rounds in rapid succession at them as he sped by.

Louie ducked but what little sense of humor Doc had was rapidly evaporating as he slammed the throttle forward and ripped across the calm water.

Out of nowhere a 48 foot fishing skiff suddenly came into view on their starboard side. Louie's eyes went wide as saucers and he grabbed onto the dashboard.

"HONK THE HORN!" Louie yelled.

"THIS AIN'T A GODDAMN TAXI! THERE AIN'T NO HORN!"

Although the skiff attempted to swerve to starboard it was just too cumbersome and so slowly veered only a couple of degrees at a time. Doc had no choice but to cut hard to his port but as he did he immediately realized there was less than fifty yards of water between his bow and the beach. A beach packed with sunbathers, kids and sight seers.

"GET READY TO JUMP!" He yelled.

"What?"

Doc aimed the boat to the one clear spot on the beach he could see, locked the wheel with the retainer line on the dashboard and yelled at Louie.

"JUMP!"

Louie watched Doc jump, then looked at the swiftly encroaching beach and followed suit.

The boat ran harmlessly up onto the beach about ten or fifteen feet and sputtered to a halt.

As they treaded water they could just make out a

smile on White's face as he waved and sped off down the channel between Fisher and Dodge Islands through Government Cut and towards South Beach where he would commandeer a car and get away up Collins Avenue.

Doc and Louie waded into shore and took a seat in the hard pack just above the waterline.

Sitting on the beach soaking wet, in dripping clothes Louie leaned over to Doc.

"Look at it this way Doc, things could be worse."

"Louie, we're in Miami less than a day, been in a high speed chase, produced two dead bodies haven't done an ounce of work, stole a boat, are sitting on a beach fully clothed and soaking fucking wet with fifty people staring at us. How exactly could things be any worse?" Doc snapped.

"They could'a been Treasury Agents."

"Anybody ever tell you, you got a knack for making a guy feel better?"

"As a matter-of-fact Doris –"

"She lied!"

"Shit!" Louie spat as he stared up river.

"What?!"

"I think things just got worse." Louie nodded back towards the far shore as a Dade county police patrol boat drifted up onto the beach alongside them prompting an even larger crowd to now gather.

A tall, very tall, very large park ranger climbed out of his boat, donned his official ranger hat and ambled up to the two drenched and defeated detectives.

"Afternoon officer." Doc looked up and greeted.

"Welcome to Miami boys. Looks like ya'll made quite a splash today."

"Hey1 That's pretty good!" Louie snickered.

"Course, it's not a regulation or nothin' but ya'll do realize that most folks around here swim in bathin' suits as opposed to their everyday clothes?" The cop came back in a slow drawl.

"Left our bathing suits back at the hotel." Doc answered in his natural New York dialect.

"Also most folks around these parts park their boats over at the docks. Keeps 'em outta the way of the swimmers."

"No change for the meter, officer." Doc shrugged.

"Uh huh. I don't suppose either one of you city slickers has a valid, Florida state boating license?" Louie fished out his wallet, drained the water from it and handed the cop his dripping NYC Department of Sanitation license. The cop took it, read it and handed it back. "It's expired. Ya'll got anything else?"

Doc reached up to the officer and handed him his private investigator's license.

"A P.I. licence! Ya'll P.I's?"

"Yeah, yeah we are." Doc not so proudly affirmed as he stood up brushing wet sand from his trousers.

"I'm afraid you boys are gonna halft'a come with me."

"Okay if we drive our boat back and tie her up?

It's my uncle's and he doesn't exactly know I took her out." Doc bullshitted.

The cop sized them up and agreed to let them drive the boat back in before escorting them to the patrol car which had just driven across the open park.

At the station house Doc explained that they were just down there on vacation and about how the ambush must have been a case of mistaken identity, the cross town chase and that there were two dead bodies at the church but couldn't explain why when two patrol cars sped over there no bodies were found.

Later, after some quick double talking where-by McKeowen convinced the desk Sergeant that they didn't hear any shots fired and the reports by the few eyewitnesses must have been a mistake, they were released on their own recognisance.

Turns out the Chief was former NYPD and so let them off with a $25 citation for reckless boating and a warning however, despite having New York licenses to carry firearms, he confiscated the .45.

Late that evening they recovered the Packard and made their way back to the hotel.

†

Doc was bent over the hotel bathroom sink washing his face and hands in the hotel room. Louie sat at the small writing desk sandwiched between

The Wolves of Calabria

the beds when Doc called out to him.

"HEY!"

"Yeah?"

Doc came out drying his face.

"Let's talk about what's going on Louie."

"I got a better idea! Let's talk about what's going in Louie! I need a beer."

"Okay but first I wanna track down Jimmy Moscawitz, we can talk on the way."

"He exists?! I thought you were bullshitting that cop."

"I more or less was but then I remembered for his last three years on the force Jimmy moved to Jersey so his wife could be closer to her specialist out in Bayonne. After she died he relocated down here."

Moscawitz was listed in the phone book and an hour later they were hopping out of a cab in the north side neighbourhood of Miami Springs. They left the Packard at the hotel to avoid detection and hopefully trick whoever was after them that they were either still at the Flagler or were just out on foot somewhere close by.

Jimmy remembered Doc and as they sat in the kitchen sharing a pot of coffee Jimmy answered Doc's inquiry about his wife.

"She had a hard time of it there near the end. But wasn't nothin' anybody could do. They kept givin' her morphine but a fuckin' quarter grain at time! What the fuck good's that gonna do anyone when your body's riddled with cancer?!"

"Sorry we weren't around to lend a hand Jimmy."

"Aww, wasn't nothin' ya could'a done anyways Mike. Besides, I took care of her. When those fuckin' quake doctors weren't around I'd slip her a micky or two. It was the only time I seen her smile."

"My pop spoke highly of you two." McKeowen complimented. "Sorry I didn't know you guys better back in the day."

"Fuck it! What'a-ya-gonna-do?" Jimmy rose, poured more coffee then limped to the cupboard. He returned to the table with a half empty bottle of Johnny Walker Blue label and poured a bit in each of their cups. They gave a half-hearted toast.

"So what'a you two jamokes doin' down here in the land of sun, surf and illegals?"

"Funny you should mention drugs Jimmy." Jimmy's ears perked up.

"Yeah, why's that?"

"There's an old black fella takes care of the building were we rent space for our office. His nephew did a Peter Pan off the roof of a tenement in the Village about a week ago. His blood tox came back 92% pure for heroin. We're down here snoopin' around for the supplier. We figure with the amount that's been coming into the City lately, must be somebody down here. It's the most likely place anyway."

"Any leads or ideas?" Moscawitz asked.

"No but we must'a rattled somebody's cage because this afternoon coming back from the track three hoods in a Plymouth started playin' tag with us. Two of them took a dive off a roof and the other one escaped across the south bay."

"During the chase one of the guys called another one 'White' while that guy called one of the others 'Sal'. Names mean anything to you?" Louie asked.

"White from the Bureau of Narcotics?! Sounds like Anslinger's getting a bit liberal with his interpretation of the law ain't he?" Jimmy prophesized.

"If Anslinger sent them." Louie threw in.

"Good point. Lot'a cowboys in that office." Jimmy glanced at Louie then narrowed his eyes at Doc.

"Thought you quit the cop business Mr. P.I.?"

"This is personal Jimmy."

"What'a I look stupid?! I know that." He poured more scotch into his empty coffee cup. "Guy I use'ta buy my shit off bounces in and out of radio. Contract player for NBC. I never needed much, just a few grams or so for the wife until she checked out. But I understand his people were all over in Hoboken."

"Any leads on where abouts in Hoboken?" Doc asked.

"No, all I can remember is it's a dodgy neighbourhood but, as far as the Narco guys at the precinct house could figure, whoever runs that operation supplies most of Jersey, Manhattan, The Bronx and Staten Island. Probably has half a dozen other places sprinkled around the City. No doubt in my mind who ever dealt to your buddy's nephew is outta there or connected to 'em." Doc and Louie sat back in their seats. Jimmy continued.

"I wouldn't just go snoopin' around over there either. Go see Eddie Maloney, he's the Assistant Station Manager over at NBC at Rockefeller Plaza. Handles all the big name talent. Holds their hands when they start whingin' about movie and radio studios screwin' them out'a work all the time. He's got a guy supply's him. He's got a nose candy problem from way back. Graduated to the hard stuff just before the wife and I moved out of the City. Dealer's name is John Billinghouse. A little light on his feet but he ought'a be able to give you an update on all the connects."

"So you're telling me we could'a saved a bunch of time and money with a simple phone call to you before we came down?" Doc declared.

"Hey, hindsight's always twenty-twenty, ain't it Mike?" Jimmy quipped as he poured another drink.

✝

CHAPTER XVII

Federal Bureau of Narcotics
Treasury Building, Washington D.C.

Harry A. wasn't a particularly happy camper that morning when he got to the office late. He hadn't slept well, his wife was angry about him keeping her up half the night and so accidently on purpose burned his bacon. Also his scrambled eggs were too watery. Sometimes life's a bitch in the big leagues.

Harry leaned across his expansive desk and depressed the 'open' switch on the dark oak Dictaphone.

"Come in here please." A minute later his middle-aged, very conservatively dressed secretary entered his office and took a seat in front of his desk.

"Take a memo. To: Agent White, regarding yesterday's hearings." Anslinger dictated to his secretary.

"Efforts must be intensified so as to increase the number of arrests of drug users and known associates of the hemp suppliers in this country. I believe this to be the most expedient path to the increased funding we urgently require to expand the agency. Hemp is the number one gateway drug to heroin and must be dealt with through the control of such gateway drugs. This must be achieved through any means required. Underline 'any'. Signed H.

Anslinger, Commissioner."

"That all Mr. A.?"

"Do we know when Agent White's back?"

"I believe he's in New York at present sir, due back this weekend, but I can double check."

"Not necessary. Get that out by special inter-government post today."

Harry's top dog at the agency was a one Agent George H. White. Ever since serving with the OSS during the war as an instructor due to his narcotics connections, the fat balding maverick saw himself as a super-secret agent.

Although with a reputation for bravery during the war he was now careful to avoid any situation where he might accidently stumble into harm's way, he was a J. Edgar Hoover wanna-be not quite sharp enough to make the FBI roster and so figured the fledgling Bureau of Narcotics was the next best thing. Any office where he could hang a gun and badge.

Habitually trumping up his minor triumphs touting them with as much religious zeal as Hoover and Anslinger did their own, he fit right into that not-so-exclusive, D.C. good 'ol boys club who lived by the motto, 'Never let a good crises go to waste. Even if you have to fabricate one'.

In essence Agent White was a self-serving buffoon whose mantra was whatever it took to make himself look good while harbouring no compunction to wet his beak whenever possible.

There were a lot of honest men walking the

streets with guns and badges; cops, D.A.'s, FBI, OSS. George just didn't happen to be one of them.

But that's not what made him dangerous.

White was a born sociopath and so had evolved into a notoriety junkie constantly in search of his next vein full of the junk he constantly craved – fame and recognition.

Eager beaver that he was the same afternoon he received the memo from his boss White concocted a plan to win brownie points with Big Harry A. So, the following morning around mid-day he was ascending the granite stairway outside 260 Madison Avenue. The building he arrived at sat between East 38th and 39th Streets overlooking the upscale Murray Hill district smack in the heart of Manhattan, five minutes from everywhere. Once upstairs, a moment later he was outside the office of the President of the most powerful medical body in the western hemisphere, the American Medical Association.

"Agent White, Federal Bureau of Narcotics here to see Dr. Puppet." He flashed his badge. The secretary wasn't impressed.

"It's pronounced Pu-pay Agent White." She corrected as she continued to type.

"You'll have to forgive me, my French ain't none too good."

She rang through on the intercom.

"Doctor, an agent White is here to see you."

Yes Janice, I'm expecting him. Show him in.

She led him in holding the office door open as he entered the plush room.

"Janice see that we're not disturbed."

"Yes Doctor." She left.

White was impressed by the wall-to-wall bookshelves, mahogany judge's paneling and art collection adorning nearly every square inch of the walls. All except the four foot wide space which was occupied by a massive trophy and awards case.

The doctor extended a hand as he came around from behind his Brobdingnagian desk to greet White.

"Agent White, pleasure to meet you."

"Likewise Doc." Dr. Puppé directed him to the far corner of the gentleman's private club-like room where a pair of leather upholstered Queen Ann chairs sat in front of an unlit hearth. Ignoring the early hour the doctor stepped to the small bar on the side and began to prepare some drinks.

"What can I help you with Agent White?"

"Doc I'll level with ya, we got a problem."

"So I'm given to understand."

"Somebody talk to you already?!"

"No, no need. I follow the papers quite closely. Particularly when it has to do with the health of New Yorkers and the entire United States."

"Oh yeah, yeah. Makes sense."

"Your boss had quite a hard time of it up on The Hill a few days ago didn't he?" Puppé commented as he poured two brandy snifters of bourbon.

"I guess you could say that."

"Agent White, do you read the *Bible*?" White was taken off guard.

"How do mean?"

"I mean, do you read *The Holy Book*? Scriptures, the Written Word?"

"I'll be honest with Doc, I'm waitin' on the movie."

Having entered the meeting with the full intention of dominating it, White was derailed at being swept aside so effortlessly.

Puppé crossed back over to the chairs and handed a drink to White but didn't sit.

"Well millions upon millions of people believe that the words in that book are the absolute truth. The facts. The Gospel truth if you'll forgive the pun." White didn't have to forgive the pun, he didn't quite get the pun. "And just like Mayor LaGuardia and the New York Medical Academy's alleged 'report', truth is in the eye of the beholder."

"I thought it was beauty, beauty is in the -"

"As you may have guessed we here at the Association, well most of us particularly this office, are vehemently opposed to Truman and his ridiculous health plan! Free health insurance for everyone?! Followers of the Moscow Communist Party line, that's all that is!" Puppé's made no attempt to mask his aggravation.

"Doc what I came for is-"

"What you came here for Agent White was to persuade me, convince me to undertake a study to refute LaGuardia and the New York Medical Academy's findings."

White was yet to touch his drink as he crept to

catch up with his own conversation. President Puppé ploughed through George's fog.

"They'll naturally be some objections. Some of the more 'socialist minded' members of the AMA think Truman's health plan is a good idea."

"Well maybe they'll have to be reminded where the majority of the Association's funding comes from!" White proudly espoused.

"Speaking of which, a study of such importance will have to be somehow funded." Puppé nudged. White smiled.

"I think we might be able to work something out." White informed hm. Puppé finally took the chair adjoining White's.

"For it to be accepted on The Hill we'll have to be careful to 'scientifically' refute the NYMA and LaGuardia's findings." The Doctor assured.

"Then sounds like all you gotta do is make sure you pick the right man to head the research committee, ya follow?"

Dr. Puppé smiled and raised his glass and they toasted

†

It was twenty minutes later when Agent White left the AMA building and crossed over 39th Street to head up Madison Avenue.

With no way of knowing in which direction White would head when he came out of the building

The Wolves of Calabria

Doc, who had followed him there, took the precaution of stationing Louie across the street in the Chinese restaurant while he lingered outside the American Kennel Club building around the corner from the AMA on Madison.

White was in Doc's town now and thanks to a fifty dollar bill once a month the girl at Sunshine Cabs central dispatch took a call from a driver who recognized White from newspaper photos as he came out of Grand Central.

From inside the doorway of the Kennel Club's lobby McKeowen watched as White walked by. A half a block behind him on the other side of the avenue Doc spotted Mancino and waved him over. Dodging the traffic Louie jogged across the busy street and over to Doc.

"Run back around to the AMA and duck into reception. See if you can find out who White was visiting." Doc instructed.

"What are you gonna do?"

"I'm gonna stay on him. When you come back out catch up to me up the block."

"What about if he turns off, how'll I find you?"

"If he turns I'll stand on the corner till you catch up. Don't take all day! GO!" Mancino took off back around the corner and Doc waited until White was three or four hundred yards ahead. Doc was able to fade into the sparse crowd as he started tailing the unsuspecting agent.

McKeowen got lucky as White steered straight up Madison for the next four blocks. By the time they reached 43rd Doc looked back and saw Louie jogging after him about a block behind. It was a heavily panting Mancino who finally caught up.

"Well?" Doc asked keeping an eye on White who had turned right, crossed Madison and continued east.

"The skirt . . . at reception . . . said he was . . . there to see the . . . president of the . . . Association."

"Interesting. C'mon." They resumed the tail. Louie, covered in sweat and still struggling to catch his breath, was a bit slow to move.

"C'mon! How old are you? You need to join the Y!" Doc admonished.

"Fuck the Y! I need the B!"

"What the hell is the 'B'?"

"A BEER!"

"Look at it this way, you probably just worked off a couple of slices of pizza."

"So what you're tellin' me is now I gotta eat four slices later to get back up to fightin' weight?!"

They tailed White a little further Uptown to 42nd Street and over to the controlled chaos of Grand Central Terminal in Midtown where he made his way down to the lower level and the sprawling underground shopping plaza. It was approaching mid-day and the crowd wasn't that thick so they had to split up and drop back so as not to be noticed.

White perused the window of a jewelry shop, bought a package of cigarettes at a kiosk and leisurely pushed on. The open concourse afforded

The Wolves of Calabria

multiple vantage points for the two detectives to observe and so made this part of their task a little easier.

White checked his watch several times since entering the massive underground plaza and Doc began to worry that perhaps George suspected he was being shadowed.

Finally he walked into the Woolworth's, went to the lunch counter off to the left and took a seat in a booth in the back against the wall.

Doc and Louie were about 100 feet apart across the lower concourse from one another when Doc signaled Louie that White was there to eat. Louie shrugged, 'what to do?' and Doc waved him over.

"He's perusing the menu."

"Why don't he just read it?" Louie asked. Doc stared at him. Just then two rough looking mugs engaged in a conversation passed by and turned into the Woolworth's, looked around and made straight to White's table.

Doc raised his eyebrows at Mancino and nodded as the two took a place across the concourse but still able to see White who was eating.

"Hang out over by that kiosk." Doc nodded across the concourse to a news stand with a counter. "Grab a Nehi and a hot dog. I'm gonna see what I can see."

"Okay." Louie took off to get a grape drink and a dog while Doc removed his baseball cap and lowered the collar on his brown, leather bomber jacket. He entered the large department store and took the opposite direction of the lunch counter. Once a safe distance away he scanned the walls and ceiling above the shelves and racks of discount items. He found what he was looking for.

Though he was around the corner from the lunch counter, through one of the large, wall mounted anti-shoplifting mirrors he was able to keep an eye on the threesome while remaining out of sight and pretending to shop.

The two new arrivals were about ten years apart but dressed similarly, suits, overcoats and fedoras. He noticed, after the two sat, White did most of the talking and the only thing they ordered was coffee.

Doc leisurely drifted back outside into the busy mall and over to where Louie leaned on the counter of the kiosk.

"Hey Doc, I think I recognized one of them! The one in the grey hat, with the nose that points in three directions! Ain't that one'a them bastards we saw tailin' us down in -"

"Yeah it is Louie."

"Jesus, how many assholes does one guy need?"

"Besides White I don't know one of the others but interestingly, the other one is NYPD. He's out of the Second Precinct Downtown. And I think we just stumbled onto something."

They loitered around the soda fountain stand for the next twenty minutes when the two goons drifted back out of Woolworth's, turned left and headed down the concourse.

"Let's stay on these two." Doc decided.

"What about White?"

"We know he's a fed and we know that he works out of the Narcotics Bureau, so he's not going anywhere. Besides, I'm not ready to bring the Feds down on our heads yet. Not until we have more info on what's going on."

"Okay by me. What about Fric and Frac?" Louie asked.

"Let the cop go, for now. I'm interested in our old friend from Miami. But let's see where we go."

They watched as the two mugs stopped in the center of the lower concourse, exchanged a few brief words and split up. The NYPD headed up stairs but the other one headed towards the corner toilets. Doc inconspicuously followed.

"Where you goin'? You gonna hold his pecker while he takes a piss?" Louie cracked.

"Better than that!"

"What, what'a you gonna do?"

"Practice being an asshole. Wait here." Doc said over his shoulder as he headed for the toilet door. Louie shrugged and trailed behind.

Just outside the half dozen brass doors to the public toilets there was a negro maintenance worker mopping the floors. Doc approached him.

"Hey."

"Hey yo self." He brought his mop upright and leaned on it.

"Mind if I ask you a quick question?" The stout, late middle-aged man shrugged and shook his head.

"How much are the Vanderbilts paying you for

this job?"

"The Vanderbilts be real good folks. They pays us sixty cent per hour." He mockingly boasted.

"Twenty cents above minimum, very impressive. How would you like a dollar a minute for the next ten, fifteen minutes?"

"What for?!" He asked laced with suspicion.

"I've gotta have a quick chat with that fella just went in there, and I don't want anyone to wander in and disturb us." Doc held up a tenner.

The man deduced he wasn't a cop because of the bomber jacket and street shoes, but when his attention was caught by Doc's Negro League baseball cap, he had a gut feeling he could trust the strange white boy. He took the tenner and relocated himself and his mop in front of the double door entrance to the men's room after Doc entered.

Again the detective gods were with Doc as there was one young guy at the mirrors primping to get his duck tail just right and the only other guy in the toilet was the mark who was conveniently tucked away in the seventh stall from the left.

Docked wandered over to the urinals, the duck tail finished up and left and McKeowen formulated a plan.

As soon as he heard the toilet flush he walked over to stand in front of the stall door and as it cracked open he charged it as hard as possible causing the metal door to hit the mark in the face and slam him back against the wall where he banged his head and slumped down onto to the toilet.

With his blackjack already out Doc was on him before the door closed over and whacked him one or two times in rapid succession in the front of the head opening up a three inch gash across his scalp but stopped there. He wanted the guy dazed but conscious.

As the mark struggled to remain upright Doc wasted no time in searching him. He pulled the guy's Colt .45 from his shoulder holster.

"You shouldn't play with guns! Very dangerous!" He pocketed the weapon and systematically emptied the mark's pockets. He found just over a hundred bucks in small bills, some change, keys and a pocketknife. He took it all. But of most interest was the I.D. and badge.

"Gerard Klein, Special Agent Federal Bureau of Narcotics. Wery, wery interesting Mr. Chan!" Doc slapped him a couple of times to help him focus. "Look at me! LOOK AT ME! Now the sixty-four dollar question! What were you doin' tailin' me?"

Klein struggled to focus but slowly overcame the shock of the attack.

"Who . . . who the fuck . . . are you?"

"Santie Claus, and my elves tell me you been a baaaaad boy, asshole!" Doc slapped him in face. "Answer the question!"

"FUCK YOU PIG!"

"Ehhh! Wrong answer!" Doc administered two quick punches to the solar plexus knocking the wind out of him. He waited till Klein regained his breath and went at him again. "What was that meeting with White all about?!" Doc held him up with both hands by his collar.

"None'a yer . . . business Fuckhead!" Klein spat. Doc silently mouthed the word, 'fuckhead?' to himself.

"Okay potty mouth!" Doc produced Klein's handcuffs, cuffed his hands behind his back and around the toilet pipe then brandished his .45, coked it and pressed it against the agent's right knee. Klein's eyes widened. "OH, shit! Nearly forgot." Doc said as he eased the muzzle an inch or two away from Klein's leg. "These things can't fire when pressed against anything. Safety feature."

"It was about a meeting! What's it to you?!"

"Meeting about what?"

Klein weighed all the options he didn't have. Not knowing Doc from Adam he couldn't even guess what was happening. He quickly came to the conclusion that no cavalry were gonna arrive anytime soon.

"A meetin'."

"Where and when?!"

"FUCK YOU!" Klein narrowed his eyes and waited for the pain then had a brainstorm. 'HELP! HE-" It was lights out as Doc backhanded him with the .45.

The last thing Klein mumbled before passing out was "Saturday . . .ta see the monkeys."

Minutes later as Doc came back out through the front door the janitor was still there.

The Wolves of Calabria

"Mind if I ask you a quick question?" The janitor queried. Doc shook his head. "What was that all about?"

"That scumbag in there is part of a ring pushing heroin on young negroes up in Harlem."

"Is dat so?!"

"We needed the name of his contact."

"You ain't no cop?!"

"Not anymore brother!" Doc pasted by. "I seen the light, know what I mean?" As he walked away he turned and tossed the cuff keys to the man. "For when the cops show up." Doc called back.

"Halleluiah brother!" He glanced back at the toilet door then at Doc and Louie as they disappeared around the corner.

Still steaming from the little info Doc had given him, the janitor made his way back into the toilet and found the narcotics guy slumped over on the toilet, still unconscious.

He removed the agent's cuffs, shoes, tie, belt and mussed his clothes and hair. Then he removed a small hip flask and liberally doused Klein with bourbon.

The janitor made it to a nearby pay phone, dropped in a nickel and dialled.

"Dis da police?!"

Yes sir, what seems to be the problem? The female operator inquired.

"This the maintenance service at the Grand Central Terminal. I got's me a drunk man been in these here toilets all day! Been propositioning young white boys and I's too afraid to go near that crazy man!"

We'll notify the Transit Authority Police immediately sir.

"Thank you ma'am. You'll find him on the lower concourse."

A minute later a pair of Transit cops came through the door and the janitor waved them over.

"He ain't got no I.D. and by the looks of him this ain't his first arrest!" The janitor conscientiously pointed out.

"Thank you sir. We'll take it from here."

About that time Mancino and McKeowen were ascending the stairs up to the main concourse.

"D'ja get anything out of him?" Louie asked.

"The meeting with White was about a meeting on Saturday."

"You get where?"

"He mumbled something about seein' the monkeys?"

"Monkeys?"

"Yeah."

"Ringling Brothers in town?"

"No, they usually come in around May or June. Maybe the zoo?"

"I was gonna say, 'the zoo?'" Louie popped.

"Yeah, and I got date with Lauren Bacall."

"What about if he talks to the cops?" Louie pushed as they came out of the Park Avenue side of the station.

"Doesn't matter. With no I.D. they'll throw him

in the drunk tank. That means it will take two to three days to get prints back from D.C. so he's out of the game at least until Saturday. So we got two days to figure this out."

"Doc, why the hell'd you beat that guy so bad? Never seen you so aggressive."

"How do you know I beat him bad?"

"I know how pissed off you are and I can see your fists!"

"You know the old saying, 'If you can't join 'em, beat 'em'."

"You mean, 'If you can't beat 'em, join 'em'!"

"The hell with that! If you can't beat 'em, jack 'em up enough so they can never fight again! Because they'll be expecting you to join them, so you'll have the element of surprise."

"Can't argue with that! Let's get the hell outta here and find something to eat! Them two hot dogs made me hungry."

†

The Californian Restaurant
Corso Umberto
Naples, Italy

The same morning Harry Anslinger was putting a fire under his agent's asses Lucky Luciano was enjoying the fruits of the labor Anslinger et al were struggling to keep him from.

The hundred seat eatery overlooking the scenic port had been one of Charlie's investments shortly after being chased out of Rome by the local cops. A legit investment was necessary outside the capital city not because he was such a high profile gangster, but because the Roman cops had their own rackets going and didn't need a world-wise pro muscling in on their action.

Lucky, at his regular corner table, was relaxing with an afternoon espresso and a cannoli. His miniature pinscher Bambi sat in his lap.

Lucky's right hand man in the restaurant game was a late fifty something named Gino Kinelli. Gino was never part of the Mob, in fact he had very few dealings with the 'wrong' side of the law, which was in part why Luciano choose to work with him. Gino had a good rep for being trustworthy. This, however, did not mean that Signor Kinelli was not amenable to that old Neapolitan tradition, money laundering, which was why Lucky choose the restaurant business in which to invest. Lots of untraceable cash, on a daily basis.

By four that afternoon the place was less than half full with only a couple of them being locals as the location also attracted a good many tourists. Gino came across the floor and took a seat next to Lucky who, as always, sat facing the dining room.

"What's the word Boss?" Gino set his cappuccino on the table.

"The little lady's out shopping, we had our afternoon walk and now I'm just sitting here reminiscing."

"About?"

"New York, the old life." Lucky shrugged.

"You built a pretty good set up here." Gino commented as he casually sipped his coffee. "I mean, it ain't Angelo's, but then again this ain't Mulberry Street either."

Luciano glanced through the front picture window out into the Mediterranean.

"I suppose I can't complain. This time last year I was coolin' my heels in the can. So, all things considered . . ." He let the thought hang as he sipped his coffee.

A group of American sailors in their dress blues piled through the front door and scrambled over to the bar on the opposite side of the room.

As if to reinforce his melancholic nostalgia Lucky watched them. A smile crept across his face as he did.

He was snapped out of his stupor when he heard one of the sailors say his name. He looked up to see the half dozen swabbies in their dress blues drifting over to his table.

"Excuse me, Mr. Luciano."

"Yeah son, what can I do for you?" Lucky asked. The sailor extended his hand.

"My name is Petty Officer Cavallo. My mother lives in Manhattan now but she's originally from Palermo."

"Beautiful city Palermo. Lived there myself for a little while."

"Our ship's up in Rome but we came down here for a couple days R&R."

"You fellas see any action during the war?"

"Quite a bit sir. We were all stationed on board tin cans, I mean destroyers during Normandy, all except Jojo here. He was hit at Anzio."

Lucky glanced over at the blond haired sailor barely out of his teens. The kid had a partially healed over scar across his right cheek and two rows of ribbons on his chest. Lucky smiled at the kid.

"Got a couple of those myself." Pointing to his own scarred face he jokingly boasted.

Luciano was comforted by the American accents and the chance to engage in conversation with guys from what he considered his homeland.

"Mr. Luciano, can I ask you a question?"

"Call me Lucky, son. All my friends do."

"Can I get your autograph?"

Over the shoulder of one of the sailors Gino noticed a well-dressed stranger in a black fedora standing just inside the vestibule perusing the place. With his foot he tapped Luciano's and nodded towards the door. Lucky looked over but didn't show any reaction.

"Sure, why not? You got a pen?" The sailor fished a pen out from under his black silk neckerchief and passed it to Lucky.

The stranger spotted Luciano and Gino and with his hands in plain sight slowly made his way over.

Lucky grabbed several small drinks menus, signed them and passed them out to the navy men.

"You fellas will have to excuse me. I got some stuff to take care of."

"Sure thing Mr. Luci- Lucky!" They shook hands and left.

"Gino, buy the guys a drink on me, will ya?"

"Sure." Gino understood that Lucky wanted to be alone with the visitor.

The stranger, whose face Luciano had seen before but couldn't remember where, didn't stop at the table but brushed by it and surreptitiously slid a sealed envelope across the table top to Luciano as he passed by.

Lucky watched him turn back and head for the door. He watched the stranger leave then opened the envelope. It contained a note.

'Hotel Nacional December'

Charlie smiled and waved to Gino who was now over at the bar. Gino scurried back to the table.

"Gino, I need a favor." He tucked the note back into the envelope and stashed it in his breast pocket.

"Si Charlie."

"I need some papers, visas. I'll need them for Cuba, Mexico and see what other South American countries require papers to travel through."

"Sure, I'll drive over to the embassy first thing in the morning."

"And get them in the name of Lucania, not Luciano."

"Si Capo!"

Before leaving New York Lucky had given instructions to Meyer Lansky to pick a location and arrange for a meeting. But not just a meeting for a cup of coffee and some chit chat. A meeting of all the North American bosses, the Cuban associates and anyone else deemed necessary to bring to life a dream he had had back in Dannemora prison a decade ago.

With Lansky having established a firm foothold in Cuba, and their current venture in Vegas, he toyed with the idea of an international gambling racket to surpass all national efforts both in Europe and the U.S.

Luciano had decided it was time to go national.

So just as he had helped unite the New York Families, he would now attempt to unite all the major U.S. families. But first he would have to secure the loyalty of all the capos.

Such a substantial operation would of course require a head man. A head capo of all the head men.

A Capo di Tutti.

✝

The Wolves of Calabria

CHAPTER XVIII

**NBC Radio Studios
30 Rockefeller Plaza
New York City**

Doc and Louie stood behind a partition watching through the glass window of Studio 17 on the 37th floor of the G. E. Building in Rockefeller Plaza. The red light above the door to their left continually flashed:

ON THE AIR
DO NOT ENTER

Through the glass partition they could see a broadcast was in session as two groups of actors, three on one side of the large stage and four on the other were huddled around microphones, scripts in hand. A small orchestra occupied the music pit in front of the stage.

"HEY! Ain't that that guy that does that voice on that show?" Louie pointed to an actor who had just stepped into the mike.

"It's Orson Wells the voice of *The Shadow*." Doc explained. Louie scrunched his face and turned his head to one side.

"He looks different!" Mancino declared.

"It's radio! How'd ja think he was gonna look?!"

"I don't know! Taller."

Doc glanced down the hall and spotted an important looking guy in a suit purposefully striding in their direction. Doc elbowed Louie hard.

"Ow! What!"

"Act mournful." McKeowen directed.

"What?!"

"When we meet this guy, act mournful, depressed." Doc whispered.

"How?!"

"I dunno! Think of Doris' mother moving in with you!" Louie immediately assumed a maudlin demeanor.

The middle aged guy in the charcoal suit approached with a distinct air of confidence mixed with uninspired exuberance. He was topped with a bad rug that was two shades shy of matching what little hair clung to the sides of his head and looked like it might have been on backwards.

Brandishing a smile wide enough to span the East River, his extended hand out like a forward gun mount as he attacked, the guy appeared ready to sign, negotiate or nod, whatever it took to get the contract.

"Ed Maloney, Assistant Station Manager. What can I do for you fellas?"

"You got a bit player here, a contract guy, goes by the name of John Billinghouse."

"Jake! Yeah, why?"

"Friend of ours. Jimmy Moscawitz, said we could count on him for some help."

"Jimmy! How's Ol' Jimbo doing these days?"

"Not so good since his wife passed. But you know he's dealing." Doc informed.

"Yeah I heard, tough break." Maloney delivered with all the sincerity of a used car salesman. "What can I do for you fellas?"

"My friend here's in roughly the same position as Jimmy's wife." Doc put a hand on Louie's shoulder as Maloney shot a glance over at Louie who looked like his favorite dog just got hit by truck.

"Sorry to hear that!" Ed consoled.

"We were wondering if. . ." Doc continued.

"Wait here, I'll get Jake." Eddy disappeared back down the long corridor and ducked off to the left. A minute later a well preserved 60-something, playboy type, complete with ascot, came around the corner. It was Billinghouse.

Following preliminary introductions Jake indicated an unoccupied studio to their left.

"Please, let's talk in here."

Inside the empty, soundproof recording studio they took seats in the back row where Billinghouse suddenly metamorphosed into an RCA phonograph.

"Look, I told the last pair of cops came around here trying to shake me down that I QUIT THAT SHIT!"

Doc produced his I.D. and flashed it to the ranting actor.

"We're not cops and we're not here to shake you down, finger you or harass you in any way. Just that we got a problem and we need to address it." Jake calmed down a bit but still eyed them with suspicion.

"A good friend of ours, young good looking guy-" Louie started.

"Oh yeah? How good looking?"

"Forget it playboy." Doc interjected. "He iced himself while he was on the junk. That's why we want the guy who deals this shit." Doc quickly added.

"Oh, well, that's too bad."

"Yeah, I can see you're all broke up about it."

"No, seriously, that's the reason I got that monkey off my back! My lover - former lover, nice guy from Scarsdale, OD'd."

At the word 'guy' Louie became visibly repulsed.

"How long since -"

"Billy."

"Billy bought the farm?" Doc pushed.

"Just short of six months ago." Jake answered.

"So you'll help us out?" Doc pushed.

Billinghouse slowly produced a pack of Dutch Masters, methodically lit one of the filter tipped cigarillos and took a long slow drag as he perused the two.

"Anybody hears about this and I'm yesterday's news, you two understand that?!"

"Not an issue Jake. We've nothing to gain by bringing heat on you!" Doc promised.

"I've no idea of the current status of things however, if I was to hedge my bet I'd be particularly attracted to the Hoboken area. I believe I may have, at one time or another heard the name

The Wolves of Calabria

San Tung, whatever that may mean."

"I'm all ears." McKeowen encouraged.

"I think it's some sort of a Chinese restaurant supply place, just off of Court Street."

"I know the street. How is it you come to know about it?"

"A while before he OD'd Billy dropped the name once in conversation. I casually inquired and he said he was asked to meet a contact outside there once. I didn't pursue it, I was just happy to share the junk when he scored."

Doc and Louie exchanged glances.

"Of any help, Mr. McKeowen?" The P.I.'s stood to leave.

"I'm not sure Jake. Appreciate your trying anyway, we'll be in touch."

"Please don't bother!" He quipped, stubbed out his smoke and left. "All that's ancient history."

†

East Hoboken, New Jersey

Three blocks north of the rail station just off Court Street McKeowen looked around and across the two lane residential street in the run-down but quiet neighborhood.

On the corner of the intersection a gaggle of bums huddled around a large oil drum partially packed with burning scrap wood. They shared a quart bottle of Thunderbird while one of them was focused on busting up all that was left of a freight pallet by laying it across the curb and stomping on it.

Half of the dozen cars lining the street were missing hub caps, two others were up on blocks minus a wheel or two and all the basement windows along the block were protected by iron bars.

The cobblestone street, adorned with discarded White Castle burger boxes, Schlitz beer cans and the occasional crumpled cigarette packet as far as the nose could smell, would one day yield an archeologist's delight.

Looking up to read the addresses as he walked Doc accidently kicked a brown beer bottle which spun out of control and out into the street where the echo of the shattering glass reverberating down the street seamed to go completely unnoticed.

There were few shops, two that Doc could see, both roughly in the middle of a block which was otherwise lined with formerly well-kept Brownstone walk-ups. Dimly illuminated by the grey-white mercury vapor streetlamps he continued to peruse the addresses. All even numbers decreasing by twos which meant his place was on the other side of the street.

Following the lead he got from Jimmy's connection but not exactly sure what he was looking for, Doc pushed on down the sidewalk.

#214, #212, #210 . . . so it went until he was about mid-block where the address was #178.

From across the street Doc checked the address

of the store front. The numbers 177 had been hand painted on the glass of the single front door. He glanced up at the storefront's sign. Red lettering with gold trim on a white field labeled the place.

SAN TUNG IMPORTERS
CHINESE FOOD AND RESTAURANT SUPPLIES

Safely tucked in the lower right hand corner, in smaller black lettering, was a name. Doc read it.

"You have got to be shittin' me!" He quietly mumbled to himself.

Registered Acupuncturist
Foo Man Chu

Save for the bums on the corner, now a hundred yards away, he could see no one up and down the block so he casually crossed the street and approached the door. He was pleased to see the broken glass globe of the overhead streetlamp in front of the store front, which should have been illuminating the entrance. Probably not busted by accident he figured.

There was no bell but as he raised his hand to knock the door opened and a very old, Chinese woman, her snow white hair pinned up by several decorative combs, peeked her head around the door. She mumbled something in Chinese which McKeowen took to mean 'come in', so he did.

"You here for goo time?" She asked, locking the door behind him and raising the glasses dangling around her neck to her squinting eyes. Perplexed at how the bent over crone knew he was outside, all he could do was nod.

Inside, the dimly lit premises were arrayed with long, deep aisles of multiple varieties of dried and canned foods. There was an abacus and a turn-of-the-century, hand crank cash register rested on a small counter set off to the left.

They made their way down a very narrow aisle past boxed noodles, canned sauces and dozens of spices, cases of fortune cookies, take-out containers and chopsticks. She led him deep into the back of the place where in lieu of a wall there hung a heavy, black curtain. Doc happened to glance to his left and was instantly mesmerized.

He had seen them in *Buck Rogers* episodes, read about their development and about their demonstrations at the 1939 World's Fair before the war, but had never actually seen one in operation. The old woman noticed him noticing.

"Teri-vision!" She mumbled as Doc moved closer to the large, mahogany box on legs next to a table and chair. He continued to stare, genuine curiosity replacing wonderment.

The flickering, grey screen showed an overhead view of the front doorway out on the street where Doc had just come in through. A single, thick, black cable emanated from the back of the contraption and lead to the ceiling where it snaked its way along the overhead between the pipes and back out to the front of the shop.

"Come, come! We go." She tugged him by the sleeve, through the heavy black curtain to a formidable steel door on the right and to a stairway leading down to the basement.

In contrast to the dank, musty smell expected Doc detected a thick, sweetish odor as they descended the granite staircase and when he stepped through the door at the base of the stairs and looked up McKeowen got a look at his first opium den.

The floor, walls and ceiling were painted a dull black and the only available light was provided by sparsely distributed candles, one each on the low, small, bedside tables. Thin, worn and tattered mattresses which sat on the dirt floor served as beds and were spaced barley two feet apart, a row lining either wall.

Doc counted thirty beds in all, only a few of which were occupied by semiconscious to comatose clients.

Two, plainly dressed females, one young, one thirty-ish, carefully attended their patients, being careful to remove the smoldering, long pipes when it was obvious the smoker was incapable of further indulgences.

The younger of the two females smiled at Doc as she approached and extended a tiny hand. Doc looked back as he took her hand, the old woman had vanished.

The girl led him to an unoccupied place near the

back of the cellar and sat him down on the mattress. Next to the 'bed' was one of the small tables with a candle, a small dish of brown opium, a pipe and some matches.

She bent to remove Doc's shoes but he took her by the shoulders and shook his head no. She stopped and looked up. The other girl, now at the far end of the basement, ignored them.

"Speak English?" He whispered. She stared without answering. He pulled a sheaf of money from his pocket and brandished it. "You speakie English?"

The young girl cautiously peered back up the basement checking to see if it was safe to talk. Speaking to the clients was strongly discouraged.

"Oui, je comprends." She quietly answered.

"You're French?!"

"I from Viet Nam."

"Who brings your drugs here? I need to know who delivers your opium." Doc held up the wad of cash and she reached for it at once but he pulled back. "Who?" She looked back towards the stairs.

"No come here." She whispered back. "Go elsewhere to get. Bring here. One maybe two time each month." He peeled off a twenty and handed it to her.

"Anybody ever come here and not get hopped up? Not smoke pipe?" Still on her knees she squinted up at him. "Some man come, not smoke pipe?" He clarified.

"Yes. Two maybe three different man. Two not

look so nice, one look nice, act nice. Dress nice too, many money."

One of the clients across the room suddenly started yelling, apparently having a bad trip. The other woman scurried over and attended him.

"What day they come?"

"In beginning of month, sometime end of month-"

"All man white man? All man gwai-lo man come, no smoke?" Doc persisted.

"No! One man Spain man! You go now. Many danger here!" He slipped another twenty into her hand and rose to leave.

"You go now! Many danger!" She nodded towards a second basement exit off to the right of his mat. "Key in door. Turn two time on right, will open."

Instead of going back up through the front door McKeowen cautiously exited through the basement as the girl suggested and came up the sunken stairs the exterior of which dipped about eight feet below sidewalk level. Knowing the premise was likely under surveillance by local plain clothes cops of some variety, he peaked between the wrought iron railing before reaching the top of the stairs, saw nothing and slipped up the stairs and down the sidewalk.

Back upstairs, inside the restaurant supply house, a toilet flushed, a door opened and a steroid sized thug stepped out doing up his trousers.

"Who was here?" He mumbled past his unlit

cigar at the old woman.

"Man come but he change mind. No want pipe." The old woman answered avoiding eye contact. He glared down at her.

"What'a ya mean, 'change his mind' Why?"

"I no know! Maybe he scared! Never do before."

"He ask any questions?"

"NO! No ask questions! Leave me alone! I eat now!" She trudged off to another part of the premises. Had it not been for her snapping back at him his suspicions probably would have been allayed. As it happens, she did and they weren't.

At the first corner Doc noticed he had picked up a tail. Either it was a rank amateur or the tail didn't care if he was seen. Which further meant he wasn't afraid of Doc or he intended to make himself known. As he passed under a streetlamp Doc could see the upturned collar of a red flannel jacket.

Hoping it was the latter option Doc wandered for a few blocks south to First & Hudson then turned to walk up Newark Avenue. He looked up and saw the slow flashing red neon which outlined the giant pointing hand of a local landmark, The Clam Broth House.

†

Inside the turn-of-the-century restaurant a forty-something bleached blond went to the back bar, grabbed a bottle and poured a double and set it in front of McKeowen.

"I didn't order yet."

"Ya didn't have to." She nodded down the end of the fifty foot, mahogany bar. "It's from ya buddy. Guy in the red flannel jacket. Came in behind ya." Doc took his drink from the bar and headed down to his benefactor, a layer of broken clam shells crunching under his feet.

"I know you?" Doc challenged.

"You the guy askin' around about Vincent Rossini?" The stranger asked. Until that moment it had never occurred to Doc to use Rossini's name as a ticket in. He thought fast as he sized the guy up.

Cleanly dressed in a gabardine shirt, red flannel jacket, khaki work slacks and work boots. Dirty fingernails and callused hands as far as he could make out in the dim light testified to his working class status. Five shot glasses were lined up in front of his tall mug of lager. Two had been drained.

"You know me from somewhere?" Doc probed.

"Just because I'm a dock hand don't mean I'm illiterate. I read the papers, I know who you are."

"So you got something you wanna tell me or you such a fan of catchin' Feds gone bad that you were moved to buy me a drink?" The stranger took no pains to introduce himself only stared into his beer.

"This country's gone ta shit! Never knew no fuckin' judge to get it right or a prosecutor ta give a fuck about the truth!"

"If you're lookin' for an argument, ya got the wrong guy brother. You'll not get one from me on that topic. Far as I'm concerned half of them's the ones should be behind bars." Doc offered as he took up the topic and slipped right into the conversation.

The stranger did one of the shots, chased it with some beer then spoke down into the bar.

"Rossini didn't murder his wife." Doc nearly dropped his drink.

"How do you know that? You know him?"

"Knew him ya mean. They fried him this morning." In obvious anger he threw back a fourth shot. "Rossini was one'a Frankie Costello's boys. He would only work for Frankie on acount'a, like Frankie, he didn't believe in sellin' that white shit so many people seem so anxious to shoot into their veins." Doc suddenly became more attentive. "Didn't think the Mob needed it either. Cops come down especially hard on hop heads and dealers, the cops that are clean that is. It's a dirty business and Joe Public don't like it neither. 'It's dirty money!' he told me one time, 'Even niggers don't deserve ta die like that!' That's the kind'a guy Vinnie Rossini was. He didn't off his wife." He signaled for a refill of his beer. "Slapped her around a coupl'a times when he thought she was cattin' around on him, but he took care of her. She never wanted for anything. I'm telling ya as sure we're sittin' here he didn't off her!"

"You sound pretty sure of yourself."

"Somebody in the Mob did it because he was against having a snowfall."

"A snowfall?"

The Wolves of Calabria

"Flooding the streets with that white shit!"

"Rossini had no weight in the Mob! Frankie Costello's the top dog now. He'd a made the final decision." Doc challenged.

"Yeah, except Vinnie had his ear. He was Concierge. Costello trusted him straight across the board. Costello didn't know anything about it."

"So . . ."

"So what's the best way ta get somebody out'a the way short of puttin' a hit out on them?"

"That's easy, frame them!" Doc shrugged.

"Exactly! Let The Law do your dirty work. All you got'a do is get them into the courts, system'll do the rest. D.A.'s don't give two shits about the truth as long as they got a patsy ta take the dive. Long as they get the headlines sayin' they're doin' their job! Same as the judges."

"So they can get the votes when it comes time so they can keep prancing around in that black robe." Doc added and downed his whiskey. "So you reckon it was a contract hit on the wife?"

"Her name was Anna May!" He angrily corrected.

"Condolences about your buddy Rossini." Doc blurted. "Seriously."

"Costello's outfit doesn't normally put out contracts on civilians unless they did something particularly contrary. She never even knew Vinnie was with the Mob. I figure it was some low life, piece of shit wanted to impress his boss by getting Vinnie to change his mind and maybe even convince Costello to get involved with drugs. Probably one'a that scumbag Genovese's bastards." To keep the guy talking Doc motioned for another round.

"You don't mind me asking, what's your great interest in this case?"

"He was my brother-in-law." The stranger killed his last shot, and didn't wait for the next round. He hopped down off his bar stool and made for the door.

The blond brought the drinks and leaned into Doc as she watched the guy push through the swinging door.

"He looked really pissed off!" She said to Doc. "What'd ya say to him?"

"Nothing. I got a knack for making friends."

He did the two shots and left.

✝

"Dade County Sheriff's office, can I help you?"

Person-to-person, long distance for the Miami Sheriff calling. The nasal sounding operator relayed.

"Just a sec." The young deputy responded. There was a one to two minute pause before the sheriff picked up.

"Sheriff Kenny, who's speaking please?"

Go ahead for Sheriff Kenny New York. The operator directed.

"Thank you operator. Sheriff, this is Mike McKeowen in New York here. I had the pleasure of being your guest about a week ago in Miami."

"Oh yeah, how's your chubby little partner? Dry out yet?"

"Almost. Sorry about the ruckus in the harbor. We were on a case."

"I know. You two should'a stuck around. Two days after you left we had a quadruple homicide."

"Serial killer?"

"Nothing so exotic! Cuban gang wars kickin' up again. We mop up about half a dozen of them a week. What can I do for you?"

"The guy we were chasin', or should I say the guy who started out chasin' us, before we were chasing him but who got away across the bay in a stolen boat-"

"Oh yeah! Your 'uncle's boat' wasn't it?! Kenny sarcastically jibbed."

"Again, sorry about that. Did the owner get it back okay?"

"Yeah, no harm done. I told him not to leave the key on board anymore. What's up?"

"Any chance your guys nabbed him, the guy we were chasing?"

"As a matter of fact, we did and damn good thing you were gone before we picked him up too. You and your buddy might'a wound up in a Federal pen!

"Sheriff, I'm all ears!"

"Based on descriptions from a coupl'a people on the beach, we put out an APB, and about four hours later a coupl'a my guys picked him up at the rail station with a one way ticket to D.C."

"What happened?"

"We pulled him in for questioning, he flashed a federal I.D. and badge, claimed he was working for the Federal Bureau of Narcotics." As he listened Doc fought to retain his composure. "We held onto him, checked it out with D.C., and turned out he was on the level so, an hour later we let him go."

"Any chance I can get a name off ya? Might be a connect to an old murder case we're looking into." Doc was well aware that to cops 'murder case' was the magic word.

"Hold on." Through the phone Doc heard the Sheriff yell some orders for a file and a minute later come back on the line. "Heavy hitter, this suspect of yours." Kenny relayed.

"How so Sheriff?"

"Turns out he just started with the bureau as a federal agent with the Bureau of Narcotics, but was with the O.S.S. during the war. "Goes by the name of White, George H. White." Doc smiled as he remembered why he got into the P.I. game in the first place. "You still there McKeowen?"

"Yeah Sheriff, I'm here. Any contact details?"

"No but one'a my fellas overheard his phone conversation here. Apparently he rang the Bureau first then a number to the American Medical Association."

"Appreciate the info, very helpful. You're ever up in the City be sure to look me up. I'll buy ya a beer."

"Can't."

"Why not?"

"Wife made me quit. Said she'd leave me if I didn't. Hmm . . . come to think of it . . ."

†

CHAPTER XIX

Lindbergh Boulevard, Southwest Philadelphia

Jimmy Dugan had just woken up next to his latest girlfriend Marlene. Her apartment was on the first floor of a three story, Brownstone walk-up just off Lindbergh Boulevard in Southwest Philly.

Most guys judge the women they choose to keep company with by the color of their hair or the size of their breasts. Not Jimmy. His primary requirement to allow a girl to take him to bed was that she live near an airport. Hair color and curvature certainly played a role, but only a secondary one.

Usually rising around mid-morning they'd start the day off with a morning quickie followed by smoking a joint, having a light breakfast together then Jimmy would phone his message service. With nothing pressing on the board he and Marlene would spend the day wandering the city, shopping and taking in the latest films, sometimes popping home for a nooner.

At the end of the day they would have a quiet dinner, usually in a restaurant, then head back to the digs, share a joint and, following two or three hours of hot monkey love, retire.

In short Jimmy Dugan had been living 'The

Dream'.

And was completely and utterly bored out of his mind.

Then one Tuesday morning his service informed him that his Godfather called.

Carrying a small duffle bag and following their seventeenth final good-bye kiss, Jimmy caught a taxi just outside the apartment and headed for the airport only a few miles away.

He instructed the driver to drop him at the end of Terminal One but, as they approached, he readjusted himself in the back seat by sliding down out of sight and told the driver he made a mistake.

"Just keep going, you can drop me off over at the diner." The driver peered through the rear view mirror, decided maybe Jimmy had too much to drink that morning, shrugged and proceeded the extra two hundred yards ahead to the small, chrome festooned diner on the other side of the parking lot.

If the driver had any suspicions about Dugan they were quickly dissipated by the ten spot Jimmy handed over accompanied by a cabbie's favorite phrase: "Keep the change." The meter read $2.35 and all was right with the world by the driver as he disappeared around the corner.

Jimmy bounded up the steps of the diner and made for the thirty-something red head chewing gum seated behind the cash register.

"Ya got change for a buck Doll?" She smiled and traded his one dollar note for a fist full of silver. "Phone?" He asked.

"Sorry handsome." She shrugged. "I'm married." He smiled back and held his thumb and pinky to his ear mocking a phone receiver. She smiled. "There's a booth in the back, by the toilets." She informed.

"Appreciate it."

"But thanks for askin'!" She called after him as he headed to the back of the place.

Back in '43, when Dugan was tagged by the military police he only escaped by speed, sheer luck and balls. He never forgot the lesson and swore he'd never put himself in that position again.

Always on his toes he had been tipped off by the black 1946 Lincoln proudly boasting U.S. government plates sitting outside the two story control tower of the small airfield.

He pulled the bifold door of the phone booth closed, dropped a nickel in the wall mounted phone and dialed. A husky, male, negro voice came on the line.

Philadelphia Municipal how may I-

"DON'T say my name! You know who this is?"

Why yes sir Mr. –

"Regan."

Mr. Regan. How's you today?

"Looks like you got company." Jimmy ventured.

That's absolutely right sir, we do. We surely do.

Over in the control tower the tall, elderly negro behind the counter smiled across at the two black suited government agents sitting on the three seater couch leisurely perusing magazines near the picture window.

The Wolves of Calabria

"Pay attention and there's a hundred in it for you. You dig brother?" Jimmy promised.

Like Mike Mulligan's steam shovel Mr. Regan.

"I'm gonna hang up. You redial, count to three then give me the message that Mr. Regan wants to meet me in thirty minutes over at the Stag's Head. And that I should bring the stuff. Just 'the stuff'?"

I can do that sir. No problem.

"When they ask you, you tell those gentlemen in the black, shiny FBI shoes how to get to the Stag's Head, you savvy Old Crow?"

I'll do that directly Mr. R. Thank you sir, you have a nice day too sir. He hung up.

"Who was that, Old Timer?" The senior of the two agents seated opposite the tower's reception desk asked.

"Why that there sir was a Mr. Regan. Very important bidniz man around dees parts. He say fo' me ta call Mr. Dugan and have him meet him, Mr. Regan that is, over to the, the . . . ahh . . . Stag's Head! Yeah dat's it, da Stag's Head Lounge over on Woodland. That be up in the Squirrel Hill district, sirs."

"WHEN?!" Both agents rose to their feet.

"'Bout twenty, thirty minutes what he say." Without hesitation they were across the room, out the door and on their way out to the car.

"Old coon's dumber than a bag of hammers!" One of them commented as they climbed into the limo.

"If that clever!"

Back in the diner Jimmy sipped his complimentary cup of black coffee and watched out the window as the black Lincoln drove off in the opposite direction. He finished the coffee and headed for the exit past the register.

Still perched in front of the register the red head smiled widely as he approached.

"Hey, if you're still interested, I get off in an hour!"

"That's okay, I keep myself in pretty good shape!" He smiled and set his hand on hers. "Unfortunately I'm in kind of a rush just now, but I'm sure the wind will blow me back through here again. Maybe next time Doll." He threw a buck on the counter and left.

Five minutes later Jimmy waltzed into the ground floor of the control tower brandishing a crisp new Benjamin Franklin between his right forefinger and thumb.

"DAMN JIMMY!" The black man at the phone desk swore.

"What's wrong Crow?"

"You lost yo' mind young buck?"

"Crow, I got no idea who the hell those guys were, I swear!"

"I ain't talikin' about them honkies! I'm talkin' about that!" He nodded down to the hundred dollar bill. "Where the fuck in the entire state of Pennsylvania is a 76 year old black man gonna cash a hundred dolla bill without getting' heself throwed in jail for forgery, robbery and havin more money

The Wolves of Calabria

than a nigga's allowed?"

"I thought you told me you was Crow Indian?"

"Does my ass look red to you, you burnt out beatnik?! I told you I was 'a Crow man' damn it! Old Crow Whiskey! Dat's what I drink, Old Crow Bourbon Whiskey! Now help a brother out here Jimmy! Gimme some green I can spend."

Jimmy rummaged through his pockets and came up with a twenty, two tens a five and several ones. He wadded up the notes, took the old man by the hand and stuffed the wad into Crow's hand then snatched back the hundred.

"Those dapper, uptown gentlemen in that fine black Packard say what they wanted or who they was Crow?" Crow continued to stand behind the counter rummaging through and counting the crumpled bills.

"First they scoped out your ride out there . . ." He nodded out to the tarmac and to Jimmy's red and white, single engine DeHavilland Beaver.

"Then they come in here flashin' Bureau of Narcotics badges and said they was lookin' for some asshole calls himself Jimmy 'the Catman' Dugan. Prob'ly the same asshole who now owe me forty-seven dollas!" Crow nodded down to the laid out cash on the couter but quickly pocketed it as Jimmy kept moving to the back door which led out to the airfield.

"Better to owe it to ya then to cheat ya out of it Brother. Catch ya on the flip side!"

"Flipside my ass, you no account burnout!"

Crow mumbled.

Ten minutes later, as Dugan gently lifted off and banked south, he noted the controls felt sluggish and were responding slowly but saw no cause for alarm.

The weather was clear throughout the flight and just under three hours later he was touching down three nautical miles southwest of the central business district at Memorial Field Airport in Hot Springs, Garland County, deep in the hill country of Arkansas. It was a city owned, single airstrip, largely financed by the gangsters who used the town as a hub and retreat to do business.

Jimmy taxied to the hanger furthest from the small terminal and shut down. A tall, lanky mechanic, wiping his hands approached as Dugan climbed out.

"Lenny, have somebody check out the engine, maybe the hydraulics while you're at it."

"Probs Jimbo?" Lenny the Jew ventured between chomps of the wad of Wrigley's Spearmint in his mouth.

"She felt sluggish on take-off and the tac readings didn't jive with the air speed indicator. They were higher than usual, like she was pullin' a load."

"Will do Catman! Your man's in the upstairs lounge." Lenny informed him.

"Right, back in an hour. Get her some juice and oil too. Got a feeling I'm on a turn around."

Senator Francis Ignacious Woods on the face of it was an upfront, stalwart Commie hunter who in

The Wolves of Calabria

reality had his dirty little fingers in every piece of the public pie, especially the road construction pie.

Four different doctors were unable to diagnose Senator Frank Woods's arthritis. The fourth medical practitioner, an older doctor who had twice been cleared of performing illegal abortions at private homes, particularly delighted Woods by informing him, following a brief but concise phone conversation, that the good Senator would not even need to be inconvenienced by the trivialities of an actual physical examination. The former Manhattan doctor now based in Little Rock, Arkansas, informed the good senator that the requested medications could be prescribed as soon as the considerable fee required to obtain them had been arranged.

Suddenly everybody was happy. The self-proclaimed 'Arthrologist' even scribbled out a one year's recommendation to spend one weekend a month at the Hot Springs baths less than a half hour down the road from his clinic. At taxpayers' expense of course.

Jimmy made his way to the thirty seat, upstairs lounge and recognized the big guy, known as Mr. Paolini he had twice met before in the course of his 'delivery boy' duties for the Mob. The lounge was all but deserted. Paolini sat with an overweight, grey suited man wearing a white, straw fedora, easily fifty-ish.

"Jimmy Dugan, this is Senator Frank Woods. Jimmy works with us as a contractor Senator."

"Pleasure to meet ya Mista Dugan! Pleasure." Jimmy noted that Woods was slightly dull in the eyes and, by the state of the table, that they had just finished a sumptuous meal and several rounds of drinks.

"I was just about to 'scuse myself." The large man stood, polished off his final drink and made no pretence to reach for his wallet. "I leave you boys to it!" Woods waddled away.

"What's the mission Mr. P.?" He addressed the silver haired, goateed Paolini who looked as if he should have been an art dealer.

"We need you to fly up to Detroit. The coordinates of the airfield are in here along with your fee." Despite no one being in the immediate vicinity Paolini discreetly slid the letter sized envelope between the plates and across the table. Jimmy, now in the big leagues, knew to refrain from opening it. "The load is from our usual sources but due to some problems on their end they are using a new transporter, so as to stay on your toes as it were."

"I'm on the job Mr. P., never anywhere else." Paolini bristled at Jimmy's confidence. "See you next time." Dugan stood to leave.

"Oh, and Mr. Dugan, ever heard of such a thing as a Gooney Bird?"

"Yeah sure! Douglas C-47."

"Can you fly one?"

"Does a Pope shit in the woods? I used to fly 'em for cargo hauls late in the war."

The Wolves of Calabria

"I'm not supposed to say anything, but there's a very big job coming up in the near future. I'd leave myself available for the next few weeks if I were you. Maybe plan a place to lie low for . . . a while after." In his mind Jimmy had already accepted the job. He retook his seat at the table.

"Lay low, like for how long, oh distinguished prophet of my future?"

"A year, maybe two." Now it was Catman's turn to flash a bristling smile. A year or two easily equated to six digits, maybe seven.

Ten minutes and two drinks later Dugan was back out on the tarmac entering the hanger just as Lenny The Jew was wrestling something out from the rear of Jimmy's conical cargo bay. Whatever it was it didn't want to come out but Lenny finally let out one final, 'FUCK YOU BITCH!' and backed out of the narrow space ass-first dragging the thing behind him. Jimmy dropped what was left of his pastrami sandwich.

"HOLY SHIT DUDE!! Is that fuckin' thing what I think it is?!" Jimmy yelled as he pointed directly at the ovoid, metallic contraption which sported two blinking lights, a small set of dials and a row of screws encircling the perimeter.

"Not sure Jimmy, what do you think it is?"

"A GOD DAMNED BOMB!!" He declared as he backed away.

"No, it's not a bomb." Jimmy stepped closer. "At least, I don't think it is." Lenny said as he feigned dropping it causing Jimmy to scurry backwards and almost trip. "I'm just joshin' with ya!" He laughed.

"ASSHOLE!" Dugan yelled.

"Relax! It's called a homing device." Lenny The Jew answered as he lay the device on his roller bench next to the plane.

"Yo Dude, all I wanna know is . . . is it going to go boom?!"

"No. It's a homing device. It don't kill people. However, it does trace people for people who might want to kill people. You got anybody who might be looking forward to attending your funeral?"

"Just a couple a dozen. It's a what?!"

"A **homing** device. It pulses a constant radio signal at calculated intervals and by monitoring the pulse with radar the direction and distance of the target can be calculated."

"So now I'm a fucking target?"

"Jimmy-boy, who did you think you were getting into bed with when took this gig, Snow White and the Seven Dwarfs?"

Jimmy just shrugged.

The device, which required two hands to hold, was heavy, bulky, and about the size of a medium watermelon. Lenny applied a screwdriver and the contraption came apart in unequal halves. Inside it sported several sets of gears, servos and an electrical circuit board which lent it the appearance of an explosive device.

"What the fuck's it doin' in my bird?" Jimmy inquired as Lenny continued to probe the guts of the thing.

"Well, unless you got a rich, well connected, Soviet spy for a girlfriend Daddy-O, I'd say they's somebody . . . WOW!"

Jimmy jumped again as Lenny yelled.

"DON'T FUCKIN' DO THAT!" Dugan calmed down. "What, what's wrong?!" Jimmy asked.

"Who ever made this got Germans on the payroll!"

"You been smokin' sum'a that Hawaiian shit again?" Dugan asked.

"Not since lunch time. I seen these before when I was in the maintenance shack at Hereford in England. They must'a copied it out'a one of the V2's the Polish underground captured. It's a variation on the Young's Homing device. I read about these in *Science Magazine*. Jesus, clever little bastards!" Lenny perused the thing with great admiration.

"Okay, Buck Rogers, what'a we do with it now and how do I find out who the – NEVER MIND. I suddenly realized how it got there."

"Okay, what'a ya wanna do with it? Ya want me to take down the river and-" Lenny probed.

"No! No, don't. You got any rope around here? Rope or cargo strapping?" Lenny vanished into the rear of the hanger and returned with about twenty-five foot of one inch hemp hawser.

"Gimme that blanket." Jimmy directed. Lenny obliged and Dugan wrapped the device in the blanket, improvised a rope sling and lifted it from the tool trolley and wedged it behind the back seat of his plane along with the extra rope.

Once airborne and heading northeast he found what he was looking for, an unattended herd of cows in an open field.

†

The Alaskan Bush Company
Gentlemen's Club
Route 17, Paramus, New Jersey

Benson and Hernandez needed some place that Wednesday afternoon where they could relax, put the pieces together and come up with a viable plan of attack. The fact that The Chief was turning up the pressure and had given them a deadline forced them to accelerate their plans.

The Alaskan Bush Company had been like most of Benson's relationships for his entire adult life, an on again-off again emotional cushion where he could fall back onto when the shit got thick.

"Will there be anything else Mr. Benson?" The scantily clad cocktail waitress in heels asked. Sitting next to Benson, Hernandez leaned over and spoke in a hushed tone to his partner.

"Are you actually serious about this?"

Benson turned to the waitress from his stool in front of the stage. "I'm okay Doll but my friend could use a top up."

"I'm good!" An irritated Hernandez quickly

countered.

As she wiggled off back towards the bar Benson silently signaled her to bring another drink anyway.

"How you gonna get into the Treasury and steal a pair of printing plates?"

"Oh my little chimichanga! Do you forget with whom you are talking?"

They both went back to gawking at the slender, bikini clad brunette up on the stage in front of them working the pole.

"Mallakhamb, Agent Hernandez." Benson suddenly spouted.

"God bless you too!" Hernandez countered. Benson shook his head in exasperation at his partner.

"I've seen more cultured barn yard animals! The practice of Mallakhamb, the ancient Indian art of using vertical poles for gymnastic exercises. That's where Rachit got the idea to put a pole in this place for dancing. Probably the only place in the country that has one. But I'm bettin' sooner or later it's gonna catch on."

The dancer lifted herself onto the pole upside down and did a full split.

"I can see that!" Hernandez echoed. "Riveting history Agent Benson, will there be a quiz later?" Benson flipped him off. "Now if we may return to the original question. Stealing printing plates from the U.S. Treasury?"

"No need for stealing plates!"

Benson reached into his jacket breast pocket and produced a pair of one to one scale, mimeograph copies of the obverse and reverse of the new Federal Highways inspection sticker. Eyes still glued on the young dancer, he slid the opaque prints across the table to Hernandez. The dancer caught Benson gawking and realized she had a mark. She gyrated a little closer.

"That's the way it's supposed to happen but I got my own plans." Benson informed his partner.

"You gonna find somebody to make the plates?"

Benson waved the dancer over. "Always remember Number One son . . ." He affected a mock Charlie Chan accent. "If one wishes to run with big dogs, one must get off porch!" Benson downed his drink, grabbed a fiver off the stage in front of him and stuffed it into the bleached blonde's G-string smiling up at her as he took his time. "Already done. Already found somebody."

"Great, so let's do it! Why you still got a bug up your ass?" Hernandez was quickly tiring of his partner's sexual antics.

"Because I want to know exactly who that son-of-a-bitch down in Florida was and what business he had in Miami!"

"Why the fuck didn't you say so, ya dumb, honky redneck?!"

Hernandez fished a piece of note paper from his shirt pocket and handed it over to Benson.

"Here, don't stuff it down her panties!"

Benson was still drooling over the dancer but as he waved her back over he unfolded the paper and read it.

"1929 Christopher Street! Where the hell'd you get this?"

"What? Somebody fuck up and tell you were the only hot shot investigator workin' for the government?" Benson didn't answer. "White gave me the tags off the rental car. I verified it through the Miami P.D. Apparently your boy got himself popped stealing a boat."

"Well now I wanna know who he's workin' for and exactly what he wants!"

The dancer reached behind her back, her bikini top hit the stage floor a second later another fiver found its way into the G-string.

†

The chaos of the cramped market district which was Canal Street that morning was left behind as Benson and Hernandez turned and made their way down an alley off the main street.

"I told the Chief we needed an inter-office memo to the guys at the Treasury Department asking for a print of the new Interstate inspection stickers they were gonna issue. Told him it for was familiarization and training."

"Nice one. He didn't ask any questions?" Hernandez inquired.

"When you're the Golden Boy, people don't ask too many questions."

Near the end of the alley they descended a

couple of steps and entered a small shop. Inside they approached the narrow counter which ran the width of the minuscule premises. Benson placed the large manila envelope on the counter and rang the desk bell.

From the narrow curtain behind the counter an old, man, wearing a pair of glasses on his nose and another atop his head, shuffled out and greeted them. He spoke with a heavy Jewish accent.

"Got a job for ya Pops." Hernandez greeted.

"The name is Herschel, if you don't mind." The old man challenged.

"Okay, Herschel, if you don't mind making a quick five hundred bucks!" Benson jumped in.

"Show me." The man said.

Benson nodded down at the envelope and the old Jew opened it, dropped the second pair of spectacles down over the first and held the prints close to his magnified, fish eyeglasses.

"Yeah I can do it. I gotta make an emulsion-to-emulsion contact, transfer it to the plates then do a controlled exposure. Take about a day or so."

"Make it one day." Benson suggested as he threw five one hundred bills on the counter.

"Since it's a rush job and it's illegal, it'll cost ya seven fifty." Herschel pushed. Benson reached into another pocket and threw another five 100's on the counter. Herschel smiled.

"How's eight tomorrow night?" The old man asked.

"We'll be here with bells on, Herschel." They

turned to leave but he called after them.

"American Airlines!" Herschel blurted out. They stopped and turned.

"What?"

"American Airlines has had the *Air Travel Card* since back in early '34. Lots of other big firms are getting into them now too, folks are starting to call them 'credit cards'. Seems to be working pretty good for everyone. When you fellas come back, I got an idea you might be interested in. Plenty of room for jiggling cash around!"

"Credit cards, eh? Catchy Herschel. We'll let you know." Benson smiled and nodded.

Back out in the alley Hernandez posed a question.

"Where'd you come up with that old goat?"

"Pulled his record. He did three stretches for counterfeiting."

"Resourceful, Agent Benson."

"I consider it part of my one man rehabilitation program."

✝

South of Jackson
Bear Creek, Tennessee
The Ogilby Farm

Ma and Pa Ogilby were at supper when Pa pushed the curtains aside and peered out the front window and saw the cars racing down from the black top rural route which ran past their property.

At 60 miles per hour three black FBI sedan's tore down the one lane dirt road leading up to the eighty year old farmhouse. The lead car turned off at the first gate on the left, the Ogilby's place, and the rest followed. The cows and birds scattered as men poured from the vehicles and surrounded the two story, clapboard house.

Garbed in a dark suit, white shirt and black tie the senior agent in charge emerged from the lead car accompanied by another holding a box-like contraption the size of a restaurant serving tray and about twice as thick which was held by a strap looped over his neck. A red light blinked as the box emitted a steady beep which faded as they got closer to the house.

He slowly rotated it facing the contraption up towards the large barn and the light blinked faster. The other six agents had their weapons drawn and aimed at the house when the 72 year old Pa Ogilby opened the front door in his boxer shorts and open bath robe, his gums gnawing on a piece of toast.

"Can I help you fellas?"

"I don't see the airplane!" One of the identically dressed agents noted.

"Probably removed the device and hid the plane! You three, search the woods behind the house!" Three of the agents double timed into the forest.

They continued to ignore the old man who continued gumming his toast as he turned and slowly followed the agent with the gadget.

The Wolves of Calabria

They walked up the gentle rise and up into the barn, the FBI agent adjusting the dials on the device as he went.

Suddenly the light flashed quicker and the box beeped louder. The remaining agents quickly scurried inside, pistols at the ready. A minute later, inside the barn, the FBI's homing device had been located.

Dangling from the neck of a two year old Holstein who calmly stood chewing her cud next to old man Ogilby who stood chewing his toast.

"What in tarnation is that thing?"

†

Paddy Kelly

CHAPTER XX

**Bowl-A-Rama
36th Avenue, Astoria, Queens
Friday 28th, November**

During the war when money was tight so one of the less expansive and most popular pastimes was bowling. As a result a plethora of alleys had sprung up in and around the neighborhoods particularly in the residential areas throughout Brooklyn over in Queens and up in the Bronx.

Since Nikki and Katie weren't due to return to Manhattan from visiting Nikki's parents up in Worcester, Massachusetts until next Tuesday and Redbone's place was too small to accommodate everyone it was by Doris' invitation that Doc, Redbone and Harry had spent Thanksgiving dinner at the Mancino's with Louie and Doris.

The Friday afternoon following Thanksgiving, Doc, Louie and Harry had agreed to hop a cab Uptown and grab the N line subway up to Astoria to get out of Manhattan to avoid the maddest retail day of the year that some papers were starting to refer to as Black Friday.

The Bowl-A-Rama was the chosen rally point because, being owned by an Indian who fled Bombay after the forced partition by the British, it was one of the few non-retail businesses opened the day after Thanksgiving.

It was also the only bowling alley they knew of that served Jameson Irish whiskey.

The entire compact back bar area, as were all twelve lanes, was done out in Art Deco geometry highlighted by emerald green and bright red neon and save for lane number twelve which was occupied by an elderly couple, all the lanes were shut down.

Doc and Harry, who had arrived about a half an hour ago, were seated at one end of the bar, Shyam, the owner, who didn't drink, sat on a tall stool at the far end reading.

"Huh!" Harry grunted when he noticed Doc's mounting aggravation as McKeowen glanced up at the bar clock

"What's 'huh'?" Doc asked. Harry sipped his beer.

"Huh as in you didn't expect him to be on time did you, 'huh'?" Doc ignored Harry's badgering and sipped his drink.

As if on cue Mancino half walked half shuffled in the front door and up to the bar.

"Where the hell you been?! It's nearly half past two?!"

He limped over to the stool to the left of McKeowen's and plopped down carefully sitting to one side.

"Sorry I'm late but Doris wanted me to go with her all the hell the way up to Macy's then over to Gimbal's to look at some stuff for the house.

Couldn't get out of it." Harry signaled Shyam to bring Louie a drink. "Doris hasn't realized it yet that a 'bargain' is something you can't resist but don't need."

"Surprisingly clever." Doc quipped.

"Come on Doc, gimme a break, I learned a valuable lesson last night."

"Yeah, like that?"

"Never ever, under any circumstances, take a sleeping

pill and a laxative in the same night!"

"Shyam cancel that chocolate malt!" Harry called down the bar. With hardly a movement the owner casually glanced up immediately returning to his reading.

Behind them on lane twelve one of the elderly couple bowled another strike and mimed jumping up and down.

"You find anything out from the waitress?" Harry asked.

"Yes and no." Louie addressed Harry with a shrug. "She knew he was on the junk but they had an agreement: outta sight, outta mind. Apparently only suspicious person she knew of was some white guy who came around the apartment one time. Five six, five seven, slight build wore his hair in corn rolls."

"White guy with corn rolls?" Doc asked.

"I seen that before Doc." Harry interjected. "When I was in the joint. Some white guys from the south sometimes did it."

"She get the impression he was Leon's dealer?" Doc pushed.

"She didn't come out and say it but I got the idea she did."

"What else?"

"You know my cousin Guido, with the garbage truck?"

"Yeah, what about him?" Doc asked.

"Well he's got a guy on one'a his crews who's dating a gal who works at the Public Li-berry. She's what's ya call a 'Reference girl'. Know's where everything in the whole place is, even the toilets!"

"That's handy!" Harry declared.

"So I rang Guido, he rang Little Jimmy –"

"The guy on his crew?" Doc and Harry blurted simultaneously.

"Yeah, the guy on his crew. And Little Jimmy called Charlene at the li-berry."

Amongst the things Doc confiscated from Special Agent Klein after his little chat in the Grand Central Terminal toilet was his wallet inside of which was a piece of government memo paper upon which was scribbled in pencil, 'under the three pillars - Saturday'.

Heavily suspecting that there was a tie-in somewhere along the line between somebody in the Bureau of Narcotics or the Department of Foreign Affairs and The Mob, Doc had come to the realization this was much bigger than a random dealer selling bad junk to some innocent negro kid on the street.

Shyam set Louie's glass of beer and a whiskey shot in front of him and, having gotten reeled into the discussion, hung around.

"Didn't know the library was open today." Shyam interjected.

"Yeah, they're only closed about half a dozen days a year." Louie sipped his beer. "Any way, Charlene says she thinks there's a connection." Louie grabbed his beer and leisurely sipped his shot.

"So? Give already!" Doc prompted. Mancino reached into his jacket pocket and produced the sheet of government note paper with the handwritten note.

"First, it doesn't say **at** the three pillars, it says **under** the three pillars. Look see? That's a U and an N, fer 'under'." Louie proudly instructed.

"Okay, under the pillars. But what three pillars? Where? When?"

"All good questions Doc." Louie backed.

"Something with the three pillars of wisdom? Wisdom Strength and Beauty?" Shyam threw out.

"Only three pillars I know Doc are the three pillars outta the Bible, Faith, Hope and Charity." Harry suggested.

"There's more." Mancino continued. "Charlene says that buildings with that kind of symbolism are usually places like churches or public buildings with Leo-classical architecture." Doc shook his head and did his shot but didn't bother to correct Mancino.

"St. Patrick's, Uptown?" Harry suggested.

"Too central." Doc commented. "Trinity near

Wall Street?"

"Closed till the Christmas service. Renovations." Harry pointed out.

"The New York Public Library, The Museum of Natural History, all done by architects who almost exclusively used stone masons and sculptors who were members of the Masonic Temple!" Harry tossed his thoughts into the mix.

"The Mason's symbol has a triangle!" Louie contributed.

"Not really, it's a carpenter's square and it's just a crossed rule and compass beneath it." McKeowen corrected. "But we are assuming it's a building?" Doc inquired.

"Yeah." Mancino affirmed.

"Or a group, maybe a complex of buildings?" Harry added.

"They can only meet in one building at a time." Doc pointed out.

"True."

Their conjecture contest highlighted by trivial banter and several more drinks went on for the next half hour until Doc formulated a plan.

"Okay let's start diggin' through the *Yellow Pages*." Doc indicated the bank of six phone booths against the wall in the snack bar area, each of which routinely contained a yellow pages directory. "Harry, you take the Restaurants, taverns & hotels. Louie, private clubs –"

"SON-OF-A-BITCH!" Mancino loudly declared as he jumped from his bar stool, threw back the rest of his shot and chugged his beer.

"Did something bite you in the ass or did you just have an epiphany?" Doc probed.

"I don't know about that but I damn sure just had a thought!" The last two drinks, which had by now soaked in began to take their toll and Louie stared off into the distance.

"MANCINO!" Doc yelled.

"Yeah Doc?" Louie snapped out of it.

"Care to share with the others in class?"

"Leon's waitress! She said the creep that came to see Leon smelled like elephants!"

"Why in hell would he smell like elephants?"

"How the hell should I know Doc?! Maybe they're smuggling drugs into the country shoved up elephants' asses?"

"Okay, okay. I have no idea how, but maybe you're on a roll. Keep going, what else?" Doc encouraged.

"Where's the one place you can find elephants?" Mancino asked.

"India!" Shyam blurted as if on a game show.

"A little closer to home!" Louie prompted.

"Africa?" Harry guessed again.

"How in the hell is Africa closer than India?!" Doc chastised.

"I dunno! I got caught up in the excitement."

"Still no." Louie bragged.

"Barnum and Baily's!" Doc pushed.

The Wolves of Calabria

"EEEHHGGHH, wrong answer, but thank you for playing!" Louie mocked.

"Still no?" Doc protested.

"Besides Barnum and Baily's!" Louie prompted.

In a state of disgust, Doc finally hit it.

"We already talked about the circus which wasn't in town during the last half of the war anyways, so no circus. Animal imports were banned during the war so no private collections or traveling shows." Doc stood, threw a tenner on the bar and signalled for another round. "Okay my little Einsteins!" They both looked at him. "The meeting is going to be at the main pavilion in the Bronx Zoo!"

†

Jimmy had scored a short run from Hot Springs down to New Orleans ferrying a money man with a load of dirty cash to be laundered through some of the Mob's usual channels.

The novice recruit had no way to know it but he was still on probation with the Mob and the money run he was presently on was a test of sorts to see if he could be trusted around large amounts of cash.

Once airborne, along with the guy Jimmy had been introduced to only as 'Money Man' who was sitting in the back seat, riding shotgun next to Dugan was a tall pugnacious character who looked to be straight out of a Tex Avery cartoon, a guy Jimmy mentally named Trigger Man. He set their course due south by south east for the 450 mile trip.

Trigger Man impressively made no secret of the two pearl handled Colt .45's he was packing under his coat, .45's Jimmy knew full well were as much for him as anybody else who might have more balls then brains.

As they broke through a cloud formation into clear skies Dugan sought to pass the time until they approached the Arkansas state line.

"So you're the laundry man for the big boys?" Jimmy asked to the back seat.

"I transfer funds when required." Money Man tersely replied still careful to sit perfectly erect one large brief case on his lap, another on the seat next to him.

"Tell me about the money laundering game." Jimmy prompted as they climbed to 15,000 feet. The two passengers exchanged glances and Money Man shrugged then surprisingly opened right up.

"Well, you need cash intensive businesses to bury the funds. Small amounts can be run through diners, hotels, restaurants or strip joints."

"No wonder all them Italian cats dig restaurants!" Jimmy interjected.

"I prefer the strip joints!" Now that the atmosphere was loosening up Trigger Man joined in.

"You and me both Brother!" Jimmy reinforced.

"But for the larger amounts you need established corporations."

"Which is why we're heading down to the Fair Grounds?" Jimmy ventured.

"Bingo."

"Looks like you got near enough a million in here!" Jimmy declared.

"Mil and three quarters." Money Man corrected.

"Okay, a mil and three quarters, point is they ain't gonna be able to pass that much green off as one day's take at one track!"

"No need to, it'll be spread around. With big hauls along other parts of the country we use 'smurfing' or various other techniques to mix our paper with stuff that's legit. Later, through channels, we'll purchase various trade and bearer instruments, money orders, bearer bonds and so forth which will be deposited in legit accounts."

"Smooth!"

Both Money Man and Trigger man smirked at Jimmy's compliment.

"Smooth as a baby's bottom! Trigger man declared." Money Man continued the tutorial.

"Then you got your under-over . . . technique. That's where you do invoices or receipts for more or less than the . . . face value of whatever it is you're selling. The difference is made up in the dirty paper. Of course that has limits."

"Man, you ought'a do a fuckin' movie!" Jimmy blurted.

"Somebody probably will someday."

Dugan glanced in the back and noticed that Money Man was looking a little pale and glassy-eyed. "You cool back there man? You lookin' a little on the banana side, Daddy-O."

"Movie . . . wouldn't pay as . . . much." He gagged out. "How long . . . till we land?"

"'Bout thirty-five minutes." Jimmy answered as he pointed over to the passenger glove box in front of Trigger Man. "Reach in there and grab my man one of them air sickness bags would ya man?" Jimmy suggested. Trigger Man complied and when he thought Jimmy wasn't looking pulled one out for himself.

Built in 1852 the Manor Fair Grounds racecourse is one of the oldest operating horse racecourses in the U.S. It was here, on the south shore of Lake Ponchartrain, a little over half an hour later, Dugan skillfully landed on the unoccupied infield of the track and taxied up near the starting post just in front of the large pavilion.

Entering through a private back door as Dugan waited next to his plane in the nearby field, the two mobsters made their way up to the main office and handed over the two cash filled briefcases.

Two identical but empty cases were slid under the caged window, a docket was signed by Money Man and the cash was already being sorted by denomination to be run through counting machines and cataloged by the time they were outside heading back across the grassy field to the aircraft two empty cases in hand.

Due to the vastness of the open swamp land of the Everglades of southern Florida and the expanse of the Atlantic Ocean, the product now came in primarily through the panhandle, was shipped to,

The Wolves of Calabria

distributed and sold up in the New York/New Jersey area along with the dirty money then moved back down through New Orleans, across the south and as far out as L. A. to racetracks, and restaurants for laundering.

The rate of flow had become so constant that new businesses had to be 'recruited' into the, by now, nation-wide racket one way or the other.

Businesses were purchased, absorbed, forcibly franchised or, as in the case of the corner stone establishment which gave birth to Las Vegas, the Flamingo casino, were confiscated outright.

On a par with any of the corporate war profiteers, the Mob might have had to wait until after the war to re-establish itself, but now the profits exceeded even Lucky Luciano's wildest dreams.

So despite the fact that half the country was on strike with unions demanding war reparation money, wages having been restored to pre-inflation levels and ex-G.I's pouring into a flooded job market stilted by women who refused to give up their war time jobs, there was at least one U.S. corporate entity that was swimming in profits.

The New York Mob.

†

State House, Austin, Texas
District Office of Senator Woods

The magnificent domed structure which dominated the center of North Congress Avenue was almost an exact replica of the U.S. Capitol building. Complete with replica chambers, replica garden and replica neo-Classical architecture.

Up in a third floor office a young, blond secretary who could've been a former cheerleader or a Miss Texas Runner-up, set a silver, hand tooled tray of coffee on an over-sized, mahogany desk between the Senator and the impeccably groomed policeman seated in front of it. The high ranking police officer, in the starched blue uniform, highly polished Sam Brown belt and brown leather Jack boots sat ram rod straight

"Will there be anything else sir?" She asked.

"No Janeane, thank you." The secretary turned to leave. "And we'll only be ten or fifteen minutes so see that we're not disturbed."

"Yes Senator." She let herself out as Woods poured the coffee.

The man Woods was meeting with was the Texas State Chief of Police. More importantly, for the last seven years he had been the President of the Southeastern Policeman's Union, an organization which boasted a membership of better than 12,000 state, county and municipal cops.

"Chief, the reason I requested this meetin' was twofold." He passed a steaming cup on a saucer to the Chief who accepted but didn't move to drink it. "Firstly I was informed that you are a man who understands how our system of government works."

"I understand it's rooted in law, if that's what you mean."

"Good, that's good. He offered a Cubana from his desk top humidor. The cop took one and set it in his top pocket. "Additionally I am informed that you are a career oriented individual, that is-."

"No elaboration needed Senator." The cop interjected. Woods glanced sideways at him.

"Good. Then I take it you understand that on occasion it will be required, needed, necessarily convenient that is, if some'a your boys were a little more lax in their duties then might be otherwise required, especially with regards to the new interstate transport?" The cop set the steaming cup down, placed his elbows on his knees and leaned forward.

"Senator, work through me. Let me know when, let me know the route the trucks or other vehicles will be taking. We'll take care of the rest. Use the code word 'steak dinner'"

Woods sat back and smiled. The intercom rang through.

Senator, your ten o'clock is here. His secretary announced.

"I asked not to be disturbed! Who is it?"

Governor Stevenson, sir.

"Awright, one minute." Woods stood signaling the meet was over. The cop followed suit and, as they walked to the door Woods put his arm around the Chief.

"You and the wife ever been to Hollywood Chief?"

"No but, I hear Cypress Gardens is an interesting experience."

"Ahhh, the Water Ski Capital of the World! You let me know what dates you and the missus are available and we'll set somethin' up!"

"I'll have to talk with her Senator. Sounds like that could be an expensive trip."

"Did I neglect to mention they'd be plenty of spendin' money too?"

"Much appreciated Senator! And know that you can count on the union's backin' come September!"

"And you can count on my annual donation to the Policeman's Benevolent Fund!"

"Pleasure doin' bid'ness with you sir!"

"Give your personal contact details to my secretary on your way out." He ushered the chief out the door and in the same motion ushered Governor Stevenson back in.

"Governor Stevenson, sir, my pleasure as always!"

"Thank you senator."

"Come on in, come on in. I just poured you a cup of fresh coffee in anticipation of your visit!"

☦

The day after meeting with the State Chief of Police Woods was strolling down the marble corridor of the State Building to effect yet another meeting.

The Wolves of Calabria

He ducked into the men's toilet and after satisfying himself it was unoccupied entered the last stall on the right and took a seat.

Less than a minute later a second man, short and slightly balding dressed in a plain brown suit, plain shoes and Argyle socks, entered, checked for any other occupants and stepped to the row of sinks on the wall opposite the stalls.

He was a judge, judge Sidney Haro of the Fifty-seventh Circuit Court. As such he had jurisdiction, say-so or at least influence in most of the courts throughout the district.

He looked into a mirror to check the progress of his latest trial hair transplant. Peering under the stall door and sighting the yellow and green Argyle socks Woods came out through the door behind him and stepped to the right and up to a urinal over from where the judge was now feigning a piss.

"Let's keep this short." Woods proposed as he actually unzipped his fly and pissed.

"The shorter the better!" The nervous little judge countered.

"You understand what we are asking your honor?"

"Your man was very clear on the phone, Senator. I will arrange for any and all illegal contraband cases which come forth to be heard in my districts and in return, this account," Haro passed a slip of paper to Woods. ". . . will receive a monthly agreed upon telephonic transfer for said legal fees."

"It seems we are on the same sheet of music

judge." Woods agreed.

"Now the sticking point in the negotiations, Senator."

"I suspect you wanna know the all-important answer to the question men have sought through the ages?" Woods said. The judge smiled as he adjusted his trousers.

"How much?" Woods completed.

"Very astute Mr. Woods."

"My brokers are willing to start at one and a half points of the gross value of the product shipped and providing everything remains copasetic, are willing to raise it to two percent in six to eight months." Woods waited for an answer. "That should cover any and all 'legal' fees you may incur." Reluctant to verbalize Haro nodded his consent.

"Judge understand, the people we're dealing with-"

"The people **you** are dealing with Senator!"

"Won't be very patient if there are any foul-ups!"

"I'll see to it there won't be. I'll always be sure to err on the side of justice Senator." He preached as he feigned shaking his penis out and stepped back from the urinal to wash his hands again. "After all, we do have to follow the law."

✝

CHAPTER XXI

**Hotel Nacional
Havana, Cuba
Friday, December 20th**

In the winter of 1946 Havana was a hotbed of government nepotism, despots and drug dealers and rife with FBI and FBI informants.

Along with the appropriate supporting criminal empires and the competing political factions in the years before Castro staged the revolution none had any real desire for stability or social progress, only control. The slowly creeping, post war inflation in the United States and the ridiculously low prices of the Cuban depression combined to invite exploitation to rise to a new high on the island country. Anything that could be had for a price was. Essentially, Havana was Tijuana, on steroids.

In The United States one of the primary operating rules of la Cosa Nostra was to keep a low profile at all times. However, in Havana in December of '46 the rule seemed to be the louder the better. Like so many college kids in Fort Lauderdale, it was Spring Break for the Mafia in Cuba.

The long convoy of rented limos in route from the airport to the Hotel Nacional on the north shore, made the U.S. Presidential convoy look like the funeral possession of a moderately successful small businessman.

About forty minutes after leaving the airport the first of the collection of big, black Lincolns and Buicks arrived at the nine story, luxury hotel which overlooked the Bahia de la Habana. They queued up and coasted to a stop in front of the main hotel entrance where the highly attentive, hand-picked staff hopped to it collecting bags, registering guests and offering complimentary drinks.

As he entered the lobby of the Nacional flanked by bodyguards, something caught Frankie Costello's eye. Off to the side of the lobby area, with a vantage point that allowed them a panoramic vista of the check-in desk, were two Americans casually trying to nonchalantly fit in. Despite their lack of dark flannel suits and the fact that they wore flowered shirts and straw fedoras they still presented an amusing spectacle. Perhaps it was the haircuts and highly polished, black Oxfords.

Frankie nodded over to one of his guards and whispered something in his ear. The bodyguard glanced over at the men then mumbled to no one in particular.

"Fucking Feds!"

The fact that some of the biggest names in U.S. Gangland arrived in Havana alerted the FBI agents sent to keep track on the Mafia owned casinos.

The gang bosses staggered the arrival flights of the arrival of their flights so as not to arouse too much suspicion about the Gangland fest brewing south of the border which of course aroused more

The Wolves of Calabria

suspicion of the authorities.

The guest list for the upcoming week-long event read like a who's who of the top echelon of international organized crime. Counting the hangers-on there were numerous hoods involved but only a total of six recognized delegations.

Arranged and hosted by the New York delegation joined by a New Jersey delegation, who were in turn joined by a Chicago delegation, the Buffalo, New Orleans and Tampa delegations were there and finally a delegation from the Jewish arm of organized crime which had, save for full membership, now almost fully assimilated into the Syndicate as they were also based in New York City.

The paper thin premise for the whole get together was that they were there to see the future sweetheart of the New York Mafia, Frank Sinatra give a show for the Christmas holiday season.

Battling fading fame as a radio crooner Sinatra was staging a resurgence and with his debut album *The Voice of Frank Sinatra*, less than a year ago and his Hollywood career yet to leave the ground, Frankie needed the work.

Secondarily with the three Fischetti brothers, Rocco, Charlie and Joey, who formed the heart of the Chicago contingent, he had plans of sniffing around for some backing to boost his next assault on Tinsel Town.

As the press had given extensive coverage of Sinatra coming to Havana he was not disappointed as he and the Fischettis exited the limo into the hotel and found themselves being mobbed by young Cuban teens come wanna-be-American bobby-soxers.

Rocco and the boys however, hauling two briefcases with nearly a million dollars cash in each, weren't exactly thrilled at being surrounded by gaggles of screaming, teen-aged girls brandishing autograph books.

Nearly a hundred autographs and a half an hour later they made it across the ten yard driveway into the safety of the hotel lobby.

Charlie Luciano's arrival, however, was predictably more subdued. He purposely chose to arrive later in the day via a more circuitous route and employing the age old tactic of alternating between his Italian birth name, Salvatore Lucania and his adopted U.S. name, Charles Luciano, had come up and into Cuba through South America. Prepared for most situations he carried a pair of passports one in each name which had been easy enough to obtain through official channels in Italy.

Lucky, unlike most of the guys who came into the game behind him, still adhered to the low profile mentality and had travelled to Caracas, Venezuela through Mexico then over to Cuba.

A few months prior, and on Meyer Lansky's advice, Lansky had set it up for Lucky to buy a large number of shares in the Hotel Nacional in Havana thus ensuring President Batista's people could grease the skids for him to enter Cuba through Mexico and to reinforce the legitimacy of the grounds for his visa. He was officially a businessman.

By dinner time everyone was settled in for the evening, bosses were kibitzing, the casino was busier than a one legged man at an ass kicking contest and the hotel messenger boys were getting more tips than a Chicago bookie on race day.

✝

The next morning at around nine Lucky and Meyer walked past the breakfast buffet mobbed by overweight American tourists and sprinkled with screaming kids, then headed down the corridor to take their morning meal in the upscale Hatuey Dining Hall.

"Primarily the gambling interests." Meyer quietly replied as a middle-aged South American couple passed by their table.

"You think they'll go for the international investments angle with the drug trafficking I mean?" Lucky asked.

"I'm confident we'll get all the support we need." Meyer nodded and sipped his coffee. "Calò Vizzini has done very well since the war establishing the farming contacts, production connections and setting up the threads for the shipping routes. You saw his operation in Naples. He did that on a shoestring."

Lucky nodded in agreement as Meyer continued.

"With the backing we seek, I can see tripling our investment in the first year."

"Maybe we can get a Standard and Poor's rating?" Lucky joked. The waiter appeared and they placed their order. "Everybody get all the details and requirements of the meet?" Charlie asked.

"One advisor each, no torpedoes, everyone will have the chance to speak." Meyer reassured.

"What about the issue of Capo?" Lucky probed.

"A couple of Genovese's guys have already defected back." Meyer assured.

"Fuckin' rats desertin' a sinking ship! Told you not to worry about him. Lui e un cafone! That's why I think the time is right. There's fear in the ranks. Fuckin' Genovese never had any balls! Any hit he ever carried out was always by surprise, with a gang of guys or from behind!"

"Anything else?" Meyer inquired.

"You want me to bring up the Siegel situation?" Lucky offered as much to feel Lansky out as to get his opinion of the situation. Lansky stopped chewing on the croissant he held, sighed and looked down at the table.

"Handle it how you see fit. But if you don't mind, I may abstain from the vote." Lucky nodded and rested a hand on Lansky's shoulder.

"As you see fit Meyer. You'll get no grief from nobody."

Meyer leaned in, placed a hand on Lucky's arm and spoke in a more hushed tone.

"Just keep ya cool with Genovese, ya hear me!

The Wolves of Calabria

This is not the venue to air differences with the gun!" Lucky looked over at him and smiled.

"I'll be a good boy daddy. Cross my heart and hope to die." Meyer shook his head as Lucky laughed. Lucky drained his coffee cup and poured them both another. "When the time is right just introduce me and I'll take it from there."

The food arrived and they ate.

†

The conference proper launched off the Sunday afternoon of the twenty-second.

In cooperation with management and some local police in plain clothes, the entire wing of the hotel was cordoned off and the mandatory pat downs were confined to a closed off space just outside the meeting room. They would have been deemed unnecessary had it not been for the festering animosity between the recently organized Genovese faction of the Luciano family and those still loyal to Charlie Lucky.

Rocco Fischetti side stepped the line and brought a tribute/commission payment to Charlie of $2 million as his share of the earnings for the time Charlie had been exiled out of the country.

Suddenly a ruckus erupted at the head of the line.

"Hey! You was told, definitely no Roscoes!" One of the strong-arms manning the pat down station bellowed as he produced a Berretta from an ankle holster found on one of the Camardo gang.

"So sue me, I forgot I brung it!" He shrugged. The door guard confiscated and cleared the weapon then let him pass.

The "U" shaped banquet table in the spacious José Julian Pérez Banquet Room was immaculately set for a four course lunch and sat forty comfortably.

At the head sat Meyer Lansky and Lucky Luciano. Between them their esteemed Cuban host.

Although Lucky himself would initiate the business convention, it fell to Lansky, once all were inside and the door guards were posted, to open the proceedings. Someone tapped a butter knife several times against a water glass and the loud clamber filling the room quickly faded to silence. Meyer stood and surveyed the room.

"This is a landmark day in our history. As with all the great American corporations before us, Ford, U.S. Steel, Coca Cola, we have great things planned." A ripple of self-congratulations and muted applause quietly swept the room. "We have several events planned here and a few major topics to discuss but first I want to recall the words of a very wise man. 'True genius can be seen whenever all the elements of an endeavor join together to produce something greater than the sum of its parts'.

The primary purpose of this gathering, leave us not forget gentlemen, is to remind and bind us closer together as a family with mutual interests and goals, each one larger than any one of us."

Meyer raised his glass to a chorus of 'Salute!'

smiling when he heard a few 'L'Chaims!' thrown in.

Rapturous applause served to release some of the pent up catharsis which had, like a thick stew, been simmering since they had all been notified of the meeting some weeks ago.

Lansky held his hands up as a signal to restore order.

"Also let me start by saying that it is absolutely necessary to thank our distinguished host, a close personal friend to myself and Mr. Luciano." He glanced down and to his left to the forty-five year old well-dressed Cuban sitting there. "A good friend to our organization, and a staunch ally during the war years President of the great nation of Cuba, Colonel Fulgencio Batista y Zaldivar!"

To the last man the entire delegation rose and applauded with genuine enthusiasm.

The President soon-to-be-dictator, dressed appropriately in a three piece, pinstriped suit and sporting a red silk tie, stood from his place at the head table and modestly acknowledged the recognition smiling while signaling to restrain their applause.

"Gentlemen of the United Fruit Workers, the Fulton Fish Market Workers' Union, Teamsters and Longshoreman's Association and of the Temple Beth Israel in New York, honored guests, welcome to Cuba!" More applause followed and this time Batista let the enthusiasm run its course before speaking again. "It is little secret that the majority of investment in our small island comes from the generosity of the United States. It is also well known that the organizations represented here are amongst the most generous of investors in our fledgling economy."

"Our pleasure, Mr. President!" There was some laughter at Lucky's remark.

"It also gives me great pleasure to take the liberty to inform you at this time, that just last month, in my Waldorf suite in New York City, Mr. Lansky and myself concluded an initial agreement to pave the way for increased cooperation between your organizations and the government of Cuba."

Despite the elation of the meeting boosted by the Christmas season, which by all accounts was shaping up to be a bumper year, there was palatable confusion in the hall at this announcement.

Batista had only two years ago, been ousted as President. The fact that he raped the country, obstructed all progress of the duly elected Ramon Grau San Martin administration and sucked the treasury dry before fleeing the country in most cases would assume to be grounds for a trial and possible execution. However, the Boys from the Mob underestimated the mentality of the Latin Americans. A mentality that virtually every leader of virtually every Central American nation knew full well.

This mentality allowed that, no matter how bad a former leader screwed the job up, if the current circumstances of the citizenry were dire enough and the former political head could make the right promises to the right people, he could find himself back at the very lucrative helm of power.

Oft times stronger than before.

Batista had already set all the wheels in motion to slide back into power and had promised Meyer in their meeting last month that when back at the helm he would turn over the major gambling interests, casinos and the tracks, to the New York Mafia. Having already initiated events to undermine the next incoming government set to take over from the corrupt Grau who had apparently 'misplaced' over $175,000 of the worker's pension funds entrusted to the government, Batista was confident of his immediate future.

Little wonder the Colonel was comfortable traversing the same forests as the Mafia wolves.

Meyer spoke next saving Luciano to follow.

"The President assures me his return to Cuba is imminent where he intends to take back the leadership of his country."

Batista leaned in and whispered something to Meyer then didn't retake his seat but bowed and, flanked by his personal bodyguard, also in pinstriped suites, exited the room.

Waiting until he was clear of the hall Lansky again stood.

"I debated releasing this information at this convention but might as well. I have another meeting planned in New York City at Colonel Batista's suite in the Waldorf-Astoria next week to firm up details of control of the tracks and casinos once he's back in. Seems he doesn't trust his own people to run them. Too many crooks!" Laughter rippled through the room. "To the man who's brain storming gave birth to this whole thing-" He nodded towards Luciano's chair.

"Meyer! Let's see how this whole thing works out first before we go assigning blame!" Lucky chided from his seat next to where Lansky stood.

"Charlie Luciano!" With the ambiance of an Academy Awards dinner, the excitement seemed to reach fever pitch as the crowd once again stood and applauded wildly. Lucky signaled for calm and when the mob settled down he began to speak.

"It warms my heart to be back with my fellow entrepreneurs and colleagues. Brothers!" More applause followed.

"We have a lot to get through this afternoon so I'll keep it short, but there's something I must stress. As you listen to the proposition my good friend Mr. Lansky is going to put before you today, listen closely, and consider it carefully." He was careful to make eye contact with each of the three or four most influential of the attendees.

"And finally, I would be displaying the height of ignorance if I didn't thank all the people who were considerate and bestowed upon me numerous gifts of tribute upon my arrival."

Hidden by the low draping tablecloth, sitting at his feet under the table, were a collection of brief cases and various gifts given by various members to reaffirm their loyalty to him. To include a solid gold cigarette lighter with an inscription which read, 'To my good friend Lucky – Frank Sinatra'.

"Thank you, your generosity will not go unrewarded." Lucky concluded.

A final round of applause was given but died down quickly as everyone realized it was time to get down to business.

"Now, let's get on with the agenda."

From the time he arrived back in Italy Lucky had been helped by several people and friends of The Family. One of them was the Carlucci's from Messina, first cousins of the Gaglianos. Through casual but regular association with the late middle-aged couple he learned they had a son in America. A son it turned out who was on a crew in the Bronx working for the Lucchese Family. Discreet inquiries revealed the son to be a loyal, trustworthy crew member who had twice saved the lives of two different crew members and who was only modestly ambitious.

Before travelling to Cuba Luciano talked at length to Frank Costello who knew the young man. Costello's endorsement helped Luciano reach the decision to reward Carlucci.

"Mr. Umberto Anthony Carlucci step forward please." Luciano called out.

A young man, dark hair and light eyes about twentyish, rose from the back of the room and stepped forward into the center of the dance floor, between the tables and stood, hands folded in front as he had earlier been instructed.

At the same time Charlie Luciano rose from his seat, circumvented the table and met the well-dressed man in the center of the floor.

The young man extended his hand to kiss Charlie's signet ring and bowed politely as they greeted each other in Sicilian.

Dating back to the 15th and 16th Centuries as a means to combat Spanish oppression on the island, the Sicilians, and later the Italians of the southern regions such as Calabria, called on their ancient code of honor to help bind them together as an effective force against the foreign invaders. The parameters of the code are neatly contained in the sworn testimony of each new inductee.

A third man, slightly older, came forward with a small silver tray. On the tray was a lit votive candle, a 4" X 6" picture of Saint Genaro, a white, linen handkerchief and a straight razor.

Luciano turned to the room and spoke again in his native tongue.

"Who here speaks for Umberto Anthony Carlucci?"

To the left near the end of the table a mobster stood up.

"Capo, I Giuseppe Cassano of the Camardos speak for the purity and loyalty of Umberto Anthony Carlucci."

Luciano took Umberto's right hand, picked up the razor and drew a shallow slice across his index finger. Replacing the razor on the tray, he let the blood drip onto the saint's picture.

The Wolves of Calabria

"By this action, I Umberto Anthony Carlucci, do swear the oath of the Omertà." Luciano dictated.

"By this action, I Umberto Anthony Carlucci, do swear the oath of the Omertà." Carlucci echoed.

"I understand the code of Omertà to mean the categorical prohibition of cooperation with any state authority or its agents or reliance on its services even though I myself may be the victim of a wrongdoing." Carlucci repeated as Luciano dictated. "Further, I will not interfere in the business of others unless asked by a brother to invoke the vendetta."

The man holding the tray lifted the picture to the lit candle and as it caught fire handed it to Luciano who passed it to Carlucci who in turn held it up as he spoke.

"As this holy picture burns, so too may I burn in the fires of hell should I violate the sacred oath I take here today."

He dropped the picture onto the tray to burn out.

"Giuseppe Cassano, step forward." Lucky instructed and Cassano complied. "Give me your hand." Now Cassano complied. Lucky pulled the stick pin from his tie and lightly jabbed Cassano's trigger finger. He then set Umberto's bleeding index finger onto Giuseppe's and mixed their blood.

"Giuseppe is now your gumba. He will be responsible for you. If you have any questions, problems or if something is troubling you, go to him."

"Yes Don."

The slightly older man handed Umberto the handkerchief to wrap his finger.

Lucky hugged then kissed the new inductee on both cheeks and Cassano shook the young man's hand.

A restraind round of applause was followed by all around congratulations as Umberto was welcomed into The Family and to everyman in the room there could be no question, Umberto Anthony Carlucci understood that violation of the code meant death. Loyalty above all.

Formalities dispensed with, no time was wasted as Meyer once again rose to address the gathering.

"Now to the main order of business. Before arriving you have all been given a prospectus of the business arrangements along with details of expected returns and their respective time frames." Meyer reached over to a stack of plain blue folders and passed them across to his side of the table. Luciano did likewise on his side. They all opened and flipped through their folders.

"In these folders, which cannot leave this room, you will find a more detailed projection of the project. Based on this analysis it is our intention to invite you gentlemen to join with us to help form a . . . a cartel I suppose you could call it, of sorts to engage in large scale processing, refinement, shipping and distribution of our product from the Middle East."

For the better part of the next ten minutes Lansky and Luciano perused the room gauging reactions.

The Wolves of Calabria

After a while they exchanged glances and Luciano nodded. Meyer stood.

"Gentlemen, the floor is now open for discussion."

One of the Camardo's was the first to speak up.

"The way I see it, we don't do it somebody else will." This prompted someone across the table to jump in.

"The potential increased revenue will make them stronger. Strong enough one day, in five, ten years to either muscle us out or, God forbid, make a move on us." One of the Jersey delegation added.

"We get into this we're gonna haf'ta put on more soldiers and strong arms for security!" Someone else contributed.

"Go down to any street corner in any city to the unemployment line and throw a fucking stone! Ex-GI's up the ying yang!" Vito Genovese wise cracked.

"And they already know how to use a heater!" Another voice rang out.

"Which don't mean you take on any Tom, Dick or Harry that shows up on your doorstep claimin' to wanna job!" Lucky cautioned.

Meyer then chimed in.

"Each family will be responsible for their own security, any financial loss due to lost product or missing capital will be stood by that family and that family alone." There were no objections. "The way Charlie and I see it is we're providing a service to the everyday working man who fights with depression after bustn' his hump all day and not gettin' adequate compensation for it. He needs a little recreation. A little escapism."

"What exactly are you getting at?" Genovese blurted out. Meyer took up the challenge.

"All we're sayin' is, if this thing is gonna happen it's gotta be everyone in 100%, it's gotta be all or nothin' at all and it's gotta be now. 'Cause tomorrow's too late!" Lansky answered.

"We need to shit or get off the pot is what he's tryin' to say? Vito Genovese again spoke up.

"If there are no objections we'll adjourn for the day, enjoy our lunch and allow you some time to confer with your consigliores. When we reconvene tomorrow we'll put it to a vote." Meyer announced.

The folders were recollected, Meyer nodded at the door guards and one of them called out for lunch to be served.

†

The following afternoon, just after mid-day, Luciano and Lansky remained out in the hallway off to the side as everyone else shuffled back into the ball room to continue the convention.

"We just don't need another mess in the press like during the Greenberg trial, ya know what I'm sayin'?!" Lucky added.

Lansky was torn by what he knew would almost certainly be the outcome of the next bit of business at the convention following the investment vote.

"Yeah, no problem." Meyer nodded his agreement as he replied. "I just can't forget how well Benny did integrating the rackets and the construction crews." Meyer defended his lifelong buddy, Benny Siegel had been given the Vegas operation almost two years ago and now racing it towards bankruptcy.

"He did alright on that account." Charlie conceded. "But with all due respect Meyer, he did alright as long as Moe Sedway was his Lieutenant, the minute he decided to cut Moe loose and skip off to Hollywierd things fell apart. After all, it started out as a coupl'a million dollar operation, climbed to four million in the first six months then jumped to six million so far this year! Where's the limit, I mean where do we draw the line?" Luciano prompted. "I say turn the operations over to Moe and Gus and let them find a good front man."

"So, the question remains. What do we do about Benny?" Meyer innocently asked, staring at the floor and not wanting to hear the response.

Ten minutes later, behind closed doors the question was answered.

Lansky was clearly in charge at this point but what put himself and Luciano in a unique category and the reason they had enjoyed such a meteoric rise was they knew when to employ strong arm tactics as well as when to avoid them.

With both hands flat on the table Meyer looked up and spoke, hoping to grant his old Jewish friend one last reprieve while at the same time dealing with the reality that there was no chance of such a reprieve. After all, there was a reason Benny Siegel had not been invited to Havana.

"May I respectfully request our non-Syndicate members step outside for a brief moment?" The dozen or so associates, to include all the Jewish faction, quietly rose and filed out into the hallway. As they did, Lucky leaned over to Lansky and whispered to him.

"Meyer, I can take the vote if you like." Meyer smiled and put a hand on Luciano's knee.

"I sent him out there. I need to take responsibility for resolving this." Lansky looked over at the double doors to his left and over to their head of security, the pugnacious Albert Anastasia before Lucky began to again speak.

"We come now to a subject some of us may be reluctant to discuss, however by popular consensus it has been agreed that we must now address it, especially in light of the fact that we have our greatest representation of the organization gathered here. So-"

"If I may." Lucky was cut off by Lansky who rose from his seat and took the floor. Luciano naturally conceded.

"Gentlemen one of the cornerstones of manhood, indeed one of the cornerstones upon which we have founded our organization, is to know when you've made a mistake. To admit you were wrong." A respectful silence descended over the room. "It was

The Wolves of Calabria

I who first proposed Benjamin Siegel be sent out to Las Vegas to look after our interests in that part of the country. It was I who voted to support him when he came to us to back him in the takeover of the operation from the original owner, Mr. Wilkerson, and it was I who voted to give him a second chance when his big, grand opening turned into -"

"A pile of shit!" The uncomfortable sporadic laughter that followed was quickly stymied as both Luciano and Lansky shot stern looks at the offender near the end of the table. The perpetrator quickly realized his mistake.

"The situation is simply this. My faith in Benjamin Siegel appears to have been misplaced." Meyer slowly retook his seat in the now deadly silent ball room. Luciano stood and spoke.

"We will now proceed to vote on a resolution to the Las Vegas situation. As usual, I will only cast a vote in the unlikely event of a tie. Are there any objections from the floor if I propose that Mr. Lansky not be required to cast a vote?"

There were none.

"All in favor of issuing a contract signify by raising your hand." Save for two members the vote was unanimous. Meyer glanced over at Lucky.

As Meyer slowly perused the room, still reluctant to condemn one of their own, most of the convention looked up across the elaborately set table.

Lansky shrugged and raised his right hand. Luciano then nodded across to the doors and to

Anastasia, who nodded back.

"Mr. Lansky, when you deem it necessary, I'll make the arrangements." Anastasia quietly spoke up.

Benny 'Bugsy' Siegel, the blue eyed babe magnet and Mafia darling of Hollywood, had less than six months to live.

†

It was an hour and a half after dinner and Sinatra had just taken his last encore.

Earlier during the show Lucky was called aside by Meyer and informed that the feds had been tipped off that he was somewhere in Havana.

Although Luciano was technically only banned from entering the U.S. Anslinger and his branch of the Government Family had no intention of letting their Golden Goose, the corner stone of their careers, fade from the headlines and so had put out an edict that they would make life miserable for him anywhere, anyway they could. The fact that he had not been given the death penalty or was not still behind bars and had escaped Dewey's staged trial stuck heavily in their collective craws.

Temporarily suppressing his anger, a red flag immediately sprang up in Luciano's mind as to who had tipped the feds off.

On receiving the information Lucky instantly looked across the ball room to the bar where Vito

The Wolves of Calabria

Genovese sat laughing it up with a drink in one hand and two young Cubanera on either side of him.

Already having gotten wind earlier in the week that the U.S. authorities might suspect that he was in Cuba and further suspected he was planning an attempt to re-enter the U.S., Luciano was mentally plotting the best way to get Genovese out of the way. To that point in time, only his promise to Lansky not to cause a ruckus while in Cuba had kept him subdued.

Vito had no way to know Lucky suspected him and so was unsure how to cope with Luciano having been recognized as Capo di Tutti di Capi, the Boss of Bosses, by the entire convention the day before.

Vito had shown up at the convention harboring delusions of grandeur himself which he had hoped to unleash during the convention, but was outwitted by Lucky when Charlie called for an open vote and received unanimous support from all the others.

Now, on the last day of the conference and drained of confidence by the supporting vote Lucky had received, Genovese strategically plotted to get some time alone with Lucky in a lame attempt to mend fences and cover his own ass now that he was clearly outed as the enemy.

Vito Genovese may have had no clue about exactly where he stood but he was about to be enlightened.

It was up on the ninth floor of the hotel as he got off the elevator that Vito spotted Luciano down the end of the long hallway which led to the Capo's room. Luciano was unlocking the door to his suite.

"Lucky, can we talk?" Genovese called down the hall. Luciano eyed Vito with a measure of suspicion but was quick to note his suit jacket was open revealing no weapon and he had come alone, not his usual M.O. if he intended to make a move all the signs were not there.

Lucky opened the door and signaled for Vito to enter then closed the door behind them.

"What'a ya wanna talk about Vito?"

"Yeah Luck, look . . ." Genovese tried to appear relaxed but it was impossible. "Them rumors about me wantin' to take over the family, they ain't true. I was just feelin' out the territory, you now seein' where I stand with the guys."

"Uh huh." Luciano moved to the bar and poured himself a drink.

"Look Lucky, we known each other a long time, you and me. Let's face it. The reality of the situation is this, as long as Asslicker is in charge'a the drugs bureau you ain't never gettin' back into the States!"

Only half listening Lucky's mind was on fast forward as it ran through all the time and effort Genovese put in cozying up to Mussolini's relations before the war, the tricks he employed to weasel himself a position in the U.S. command in Italy after the Allies captured Sicily and the maneuvering he employed after the war to move in on the Lucchese Family and now the oldest and most established of the Five New York Families, the Luciano Family. Charlie's family.

When the droning of Genovese's voice died off Charlie spoke.

"I know you was in that room when they just voted to recognize me as Capo. Maybe you was distracted thinking about those pretty Cuban girls?" Lucky challenged.

"Okay, so you're Capo of the Capos! Even if you do get back into the country what good's that gonna get ya when they land ya back in the slammer or deport ya back to Italy?! Look, I helped set this whole thing up back during the war you know! I was my idea to hook up with Don Vizzini and use all that Army gear to move all that contraband which is where all the dough came from to finance the heroin operation. All I'm askin' for is what's rightfully mine!"

Lucky finished his drink and twirled the empty rocks glass in his hand as he stared at Vito.

"I Understand." He empathized as he moved closer to Genovese. "You just want what's comin' to ya, that it?"

"That's all I'm askin' Luck!"

In a rare display of physical violence Luciano slammed the rocks glass against Vito's left temple hard enough to crack it into several large shards cutting his hand in the process. He wasted no time in pinning Genovese's dazed body against the wall by the neck and proceeded to pummel him to within an inch of his life. Vito sank to the floor.

"Dirty rat bastard!" Luciano declared as he administered several vicious kicks to the abdomen.

Lucasia beat and pounded Vito's rib cage until he heard the crunch of bones and it was obvious Genovese was struggling to breath. He then bent and returned to punching his face until he determined the would-be-usurper was unconscious.

When there was no discernible movement from the crumpled lump on the floor against the wall, Lucky casually collected himself, strolled over to the bar, wrapped his hand in a cloth napkin and poured himself another scotch. When he felt himself back under control, he dragged Vito's unconscious body out into the hall and down in front of the elevator bank. Once back in his suite he phoned down to the desk.

How may I help you sir? The female desk clerk inquired.

"Front desk, there seems to be a drunkard passed on the floor up on nine. Could you see to that please? It's very unsightly."

We'll send someone right up sir. Sorry about the inconvenience sir.

"Oh, it's no inconvenience at all, Doll. Thank you."

Lucky had another drink then headed down to the casino.

It would be days after the convention was over before Genovese could travel and was able to return to New York.

†

The Wolves of Calabria

La Teja, Cuba
250 miles east of Havana

The open market in the small village of Marti in the north central district of Cuba was being set up as vendors prepared their stalls and kiosks for the day.

While the few farmers of the region guided their donkey carts into the square to deliver their vegetables, off in a secluded crevice of the old square two men, clearly not locales but definitely Cubans, sat in a black '36 Packard.

The driver, a surly looking forty-ish individual in cheap sunglasses, puffed on the stub of a cigar. Like the car, he had seen better days. The slightly younger passenger, feet up on the dash, flipped through a Spanish language girlie magazine.

"Those two!" The driver suddenly declared and pointed at two men unloading a small truck.

As the last sack of peppers was unloaded from the truck the Packard slowly drifted up alongside and with one arm perched on the window frame the driver nodded hello to the men. They nodded back.

"Muchachos, you are finished your work here?" The driver asked as the elder of the two men drifted over.

"Si senior, we are finished for now."

"I got some loading needs to be done."

"We have only one hour senior. We must be here at ten thirty to have our ride back to the farm."

"That's no problem, the work is only a little ways

from here. I will be finished with you in thirty or forty minutes." They looked reluctant to trust the stranger. "Did I mention I will pay in American dollars?" The two men exchanged glances, shook their heads and climbed into the back seat of the car.

He drove them east just over fifteen miles along the Circuito Itabo to the open fields of central La Teja then turned north to the sea.

Ten minutes later they came on an open field about fifty yards in from the ocean where Jimmy Dugan was doing a final engine check on his custom DeHavilland Beaver.

Jimmy didn't know the two Cubans but was briefed that they would stay behind and see to the loading after the latest shipment had been delivered for him to collect. He knew better than to ask questions regarding the two coolies.

Over by the Packard everyone got out and a short conversation took place. A stack of crates of canned tomatoes lay under a tarp off to the side of the plane.

Finished with his walk around and checks, Jimmy ambled over to the rubble of what used to be a farm building of some sort, grabbed a seat and lit up a joint. He nodded to the driver who instructed the two locals to load the plane.

The driver got back into the car while his colleague supervised the load up of the cases into the cargo hold.

Jimmy polished off his joint and when the plane was packed full to the limit he drifted back over. He checked that the hatch was secure and with a nod to the men he climbed back into the cockpit, fired up the engine and taxied off into the center of the field to launch his take off.

From near the car the Cubans watched as Dugan softly lifted off and banked out over the beach then headed north into the clouds.

From the open field in the La Teja spur east of Havana it was two hundred and fifty miles north to West Palm Beach, Florida, Catman Dugan's first stop.

Using predesigned, private airfields all along the Eastern Seaboard he would refuel and take short rests along the route as he worked his way to the drop off point just outside New York City. With a total trip of about 1500 miles plus, and allowing for windage, Catman prepared himself for a twelve to fourteen hour trip.

Back on the ground the driver signaled the two locales to come over to the car for payment.

"You and your friend did a fine job!" The driver complimented as he passed a handful of U.S. one dollar bills to the men.

"Mucho gracias senior! Thank you for choosing us." The older one related. They began to divvy up the money between them.

"Don't thank me just yet!" The driver warned as he produced a .38 revolver and emptied two rounds into the back of the older one's head and two more into the face of the younger one as he spun around.

"ENRIQUE! WHAT THE HELL YOU DOING MAN?!" His partner asked.

The driver climbed out of the car, reloaded his pistol into the corpses and collected the dollar bills from the two.

"Mr. B. say to leave no trail." He casually wiped some blood from one of the notes as he answered.

At ten thousand feet over the Bay of Santa Clara Jimmy gently turned east and flew out over the Caribbean.

✝

The Wolves of Calabria

CHAPTER XXII

M&M Private Investigations
Christopher Street

Late that afternoon back at the office, McKeowen and Mancino were getting ready to head up to the Bronx.

"Remind me again why we ain't bringing any guns? Ya think we ain't gonna need 'em?" Louie asked as they started to gather their things for the hour train ride.

After carrying one for four years as a beat cop Doc never adjusted to the idea of carrying a gun as a P.I. In his experience a gun was no deterrent to people who carried guns, to include other cops. Not that he was beyond engaging in physical violence when required but, as his father found out there was an irreversible finality about guns that didn't sit well.

Louie threw his coat on over his black and blue bowling shirt and Doc grabbed his bomber jacket and ball cap off the King Edward coat rack next to the door as he explained.

"We're just going up there to take a snoop around. Besides, there's a precinct house over on Morris Avenue and call boxes all around the zoo area. Cops can be there in five minutes. Shit gets heavy we'll bail and call in the cavalry."

"So I'll just pack the Bat Signal and before we

leave we'll just call Commissioner Gordon and say, 'Hey Gordo! Watch for the Bat Signal, out by the Zoo. Around twelve.'"

"Awright asshole!" Doc went back over to his desk, reached in the center drawer and retrieved a snub nosed .38 and a box of rounds and handed them to Louie who took them with a smile. "You been going over to the Fourteenth Street range I like told ya?"

"Yeah! Good thing too, cause now I got a sure fire way to hit whatever I'm shooting at."

"Yeah, what's that?"

"Shoot first and call whatever you hit the target."

"Great." Doc responded as he fished his Tokarev TT-33 out of another drawer with some ammo and started to load a couple of magazines as they spoke.

Although by preference he never carried a weapon Louie's prompting reinforced Doc's sneaking suspicion that if this did turn out to be mob or government related things could go south very quickly.

The TT-33 was an impulse buy from a hock shop nestled amongst the Chinese markets along Canal Street back during the war.

"You get trapped a couple of hundred feet in the air on a church steeple by some vicious killers with guns looking to kill ya one time and ya start getting spooked at the least little thing!"

"Very funny! Like you said about keeping my ass safe, I got Doris and possibly a little Mancinoette to look after. I'm bringing a piece!" Doc glanced up at him with a puzzled expression. Louie shrugged back. "Yeah, that's right, Doris is tryin' to get pregos." Doc continued to stare. "What?! You know, pregos! To be with child. To have a bun in the oven. Pregnant. Get it?"

"I didn't say anything!"

"No but you were gonna!"

"Congratulations! That's all I was gonna say! Why you always get so defensive?"

"Cause in the four years I'm with you I know you! You never take nothin' serious!" Louie finished loading the .38 and holstered it under his wool overcoat.

"Alright already I'll be serious." Doc declared.

"That's better. That's all I'm askin', is fer ya to be serious fer once! This is my kid we're talkin' about." Louie pushed. Doc finished loading his three mags, thought for a moment then loaded a fourth.

"Okay, so I'll be serious." He pocketed the extra magazines and holstered his weapon. They left the office and headed down the hall to the stairs adjacent to the broken elevator.

"One question." Doc paused on the landing.

"What is it?"

"Any idea who the father is?" Doc continued down as Louie stopped dead, stamped his foot and yelled.

"NOW GOD DAMN IT DOC, THAT'S EXACTLY WHAT I MEAN! THAT SHIT AIN'T FUNNY!"

Paddy Kelly

✝

As the trains were on a holiday schedule the guys had to wait a little longer than usual at the Manhattan station and it was just over an hour up to the Bronx after they caught their afternoon connect from Midtown. Forty-five minutes after leaving Grand Central the subway pulled up to the Tremont Avenue platform and they disembarked.

"From here we'll walk up to the park, it's only about quarter mile."

"Quarter mile through the Bronx! I'm already feelin' better about bringing the hardware!" Louie tapped his holster.

The thirty-eight square miles of the New York Zoological Park dominate more than half the New York City suburb of Belmont in the borough of the Bronx. The large parcel of land was sold for a mere $1,000, the idea was to establish a buffer to the steadily encroaching urbanization of the then exponential growth of the city. It was later decided that a dual purpose for the land would be the establishment of what was to become the nation's largest zoo, and eventually one of the largest in the world.

The park is an elongated hourglass shape which straddles the winding and rapidly flowing Bronx River.

As they made their way towards the park Doc

laid out the plan to Louie, who had never been north of 125th Street.

"The river runs north-south through the entire length of the grounds. It's pretty windy this time of year and flows pretty fast but is good for navigating around the place and forms a lake in the southern third just east of the main zoo."

"Okay."

"Aside from freezing cold water, it runs at a pretty rapid pace, with very muddy banks, so try to stay away from the riverbanks."

"So, no swimming at night s what you're sayin'?"

"Not unless you want to win up in the East River!"

They walked over to Grote Street, bought two tickets to the zoo and went in through the Fordham Road gate.

"If we're right and they're here, I doubt they'll meet anywhere too far into the zoo so I'm banking on the Court." Doc theorized.

"Doc how do we know the meet wasn't earlier in the day?"

"We don't but, I'm bettin' heavily they don't trust each other so it's my guess they don't want to chance any gun play around a crowd. Hence the meeting in an isolated place at night, after hours."

They moved through the heavily foliated and narrow path which led to a huge fountain which in turn opened out into the massive complex of the ornate esplanade known as Baird Court.

Baird Court in the New York Zoological Park is

the center piece of the zoo. With raised terraces, ornate floral arrangements and some of the finest artistic limestone and terra cotta carvings in the world, it featured six detached and purpose built neo-classical buildings arranged around what was known as the Central Sea Lion Pool.

Moving under the shadow of a large domed entrance they came out into an expansive, well-manicured open area.

Here were the world famous, red brick and smoke grey limestone, free standing buildings embellished with elaborate terra cotta carvings of the respective species they housed.

Above each of the entrances to the buildings were larger-than-life Oran-o-tangs for the primate house, royal lions for the cat house, majestic birds of prey for the avian house and slithery looking snakes and iguanas for the reptile house.

They had arrived just after four o'clock in the afternoon, about an hour before closing so they strolled leisurely as if enjoying a day off but in reality getting the lay of the land.

"Like I said, there's police call boxes all along the main paths." He said as pointed to a call box off to the side of the path while they headed for the main esplanade of the court.

They wandered the zoo grounds of the esplanade's perimeter for a bit then took a seat near the lion house on the south side of the ornate plaza.

Still pissed off about Doc's ribbing him Louie couldn't find it within himself to let it go.

The Wolves of Calabria

"Do you have ANY clue how much of a pain in the ass it is to work with you sometimes Doc?" Mancino complained as they sat on the bench.

"Louie, last time I checked, garbage day was still Thursdays." Doc subtly relayed. Having worked with his cousin, a career garbage collector, before working with Doc, Mancino seemed to get the hint. "Now focus! The meet will be small or big. If small it could be anywhere, but if there's more than two main parties interested they aren't going to come alone. They'll bring back-up. Probably more than one guy each, torpedoes like to work in pairs. That being the case they'll almost certainly have to meet somewhere in or around this esplanade."

"Doc, why the zoo?"

"Who knows? Maybe one of the gangsters has childhood memories of this place. Hell, if you grew up in New York City who doesn't?"

"I doesn't!" Louie snapped.

"I'm talkin' about normal people." Louie didn't respond. Doc continued. "Whatever they got going on it requires absolute secrecy and there's no place in The City they can meet without being spotted. I'm bettin' the meet is set for near closing time when most people have cleared out. If that is the case, like I think it is, they'll have plenty of privacy here after hours."

In reality McKeowen wasn't really explaining his thought process to Mancino, he was actually just thinking out loud while hoping this wasn't as long a long shot as he felt it might be while at the same time suppressing the thought that he had no idea what the hell to do next if things didn't evolve as he predicted.

"Makes sense." Louie agreed.

"Even with the 'hide in plain sight' theory of doing things, you can only have so much privacy on the streets of Manhattan. More importantly, here its wide open, they'll be able to keep an eye on one another."

"There's parks in the city!" Mancino argued.

"Yeah but a place like Central Park would be too obvious and, ever since the Rossini case, there's too many cops around there."

"Doc?"

"Yeah?"

"Sorry I got sore at you."

"Ferget it."

"No, seriously, thanks for givin' a fuck. I'd still be slinging garbage if it wasn't for you."

"If we can stop these assholes from getting their junk out on the street and get them to the cops, in a sense you'll still be picking up the city's garbage, only now it's more dangerous garbage and you'll have left the place better off for your kid."

A sudden swell of pride filled Louie.

"Now, get your head in the game!"

"Right Doc, will do."

Doc scanned the area, calculating distances and locations of cover and concealment around the esplanade.

"Hey Louie."

The Wolves of Calabria

"Yeah?"

"Who said I gave a fuck?"

Mancino quietly smirked.

Both of them sat silently on the bench, temporarily lost in the serenity of the holiday crowd now rapidly thinning as dusk began to set in.

Parents with kids in tow who in return were too pre-occupied with their balloons to pay attention to where they were heading. Moms pushing baby carriages and couples at kiosk stands and push carts selling peanuts or hot dogs.

"Place is big enough to get at least half dozen people killed if the shootin' starts!" Louie observed.

"That's the reason I'm banking on them showing up after closing."

"Doc, you do know that the zoo is closed at night, and it's dark? Darker than now. I mean, how they gonna get in?"

"The animals don't know the zoo is closed and they still need looking after. There's service gates somewhere."

"So what'a we gonna do?"

"We're going to conveniently, accidently on purpose get ourselves locked in somewhere until everybody's gone home, come back here, hang out around the esplanade and hope that these Jamokes show up before it freezes out here!"

"Yeah but, how are **they** gonna get in?"

"They get into bank vaults all the time, they're clever little boys. They'll figure something out." Doc stood. "C'mon. Let's take a walk around, scout the place out one more time."

"Good idea! I'm already startin' ta freeze my cahones off!"

†

Following the Havana Convention Lucky, happy to be out of Italy, decided to stay in Cuba for a while and look after the casino and betting operations and quite possibly explore other ways back into his adopted homeland. To this end he took up residence at the Quinta Avinida in Miramar.

As the true motives of the head of the Luciano Family in Havana were suspected by the head of the Anslinger Family in D.C. hardly an hour passed when Anslinger's agents were not following Luciano around Havana taking notes and increasingly making no effort to conceal themselves.

Through connections in the government Lucky found out the U.S. agents were not only reporting directly to D.C but were doing so by trunk call using a secret police office right there in the capital.

To the casual observer it would have seemed that the Cuban officials were playing both sides of the fence.

However, unbeknownst to Anslinger's agents, the police phones were bugged and regular reports were being sent to Chief Inspector Señor Colonel Alfredo Requeno then passed onto the Minister for the Interior, Nicolas Hdalgo Torrado. Both of whom, on the advice of Meyer Lansky, were on the Luciano's payroll.

After copious amounts of pressure from the U.S. State Department's office in Havana, Requeno and his people were ordered to initiate an investigation. At the behest of the U.S. authorities, Requeno was issued with strict orders that if it was determined that Luciano had entered Cuba illegally, he would be deported.

Unfortunately for the Capo Anslinger, as Lansky had gotten Lucky to invest in the casinos, he was a bone fide businessman and clearly legitimately permitted in Havana.

As in the American governmental model Lucky had long ago learned that to get things done you had to grease palms. Not just any palms but the right palms and so, several weeks later, Havana's answer to Washington was a polite reply in the form of a written statement to Anslinger's office in D.C. that Mr. Luciano was in no way in violation of Cuban law.

Anslinger had no sense of humor about Havana ignoring His Royal Highnesses' edict to evict Luciano and so made his next move.

With chest thrust out and head held high, in a daring bid to solidify his place in history and his rightful seat on the thrown as America's royal guardian of morality, right beside J. Edgar Himself, Harry gained an audience with President Truman to plead his case.

The former haberdasher behind the desk in the Oval Office accepted Anslinger's wildly overblown estimate of the grave danger Luciano posed to the United States as long as he remained in the Western Hemisphere and gave Anslinger carte blanch to do what he deemed necessary to force the Cuban government to deport Luciano regardless of the fact that he had a legitimate visa, valid passport and a legitimate business interest in the country.

Harry A. promptly thanked Harry T. and went to work firing up his Rube Goldberg machine-like chain of command at the Bureau of Narcotics.

He quickly discovered that with little or no capability to produce their own medicinal drugs domestically the tiny island nation was compelled to import them, largely from the United States. Anslinger had hit on a sure–fire way to pressure the Cuban government to bend to his will.

As with Dewey and his masterful framing of Lucky ten years earlier, Anslinger, despite international treaties and legal agreements, in short the law, abruptly ordered the shipment of all pain drugs to Cuba halted. Despite the fact that he didn't actually have the power to do so, he did it and then took it one step further.

Through Colonel Garland Williams, Director of Narcotics Enforcement for the Department of the Treasury, Anslinger ordered a complete embargo of medicinal drugs to Cuba. Attempting to justify their blanket punishment of the Cuban people, Williams issued a public statement.

The Wolves of Calabria

"In a supposed deal with the future presidential candidate, Thomas E. Dewey, Luciano's lawyer claimed a deal was struck for early parole based on his 'invaluable' contribution to the war effort." Williams further went on to make the dubious claim that he had made a 'diligent' investigation of 'various government departments' and was unable to substantiate any such claim.

As always in such situations, he was never pressed for details.

Based on this and other bravado laden speeches, Williams had garnered his eagerly sought after notoriety by claiming that he had ruined the careers of no less than 15,000 criminals, pimps and racketeers, (curiously more than existed in the entire Mafia at the time), and who collectively had amassed an estimated empire of $150,000 a year.

The fact that this averaged out to $10.00 per criminal was apparently lost on the popular press and never came up.

On this, as with most other counts, Williams, like Anslinger, wasn't even in the ballpark. The actual dollar figure more probably exceeded ten times that, easily into the millions.

The point is he was only too happy to carry out Anslinger's bidding and the people of Cuba bolstered both Anslinger and Williams' careers by suffering without much needed antibiotics and pain meds for the better part of two weeks.

Paddy Kelly

✝

Although Vito Genovese had earned his well-deserved beating by pushing his double cross technique one gangster too far, Lucky would never know, until it was too late, that it wasn't Vito Genovese who ratted him out to the world through the U.S. papers.

It was early one *evening when Henry Wallace, a freelance 'journalist' who in realty was a paparazzi before the term was popularized, spotted Luciano in a night club, doing what he did best charming some admirers who had gathered around his corner table.

The financially strapped Henry, knowing Lucky was not fond of headlines and sought to keep his whereabouts quiet, was struck with a brainstorm. Why not shakedown the master of shakedowns?

Wallace approached the table, introduced himself as a 'friend' and whispered into Luciano's ear.

"If you are wise, you will do whatever is necessary to keep your whereabouts here in Havana out of the headlines."

Lucky smiled, thanked Wallace for his advice and signaled to a pair of torpedoes across the room. A couple of minutes later Henry was sitting on a sore ass outside the evening hotspot next to his broken camera being side stepped by the well-dressed guests as they entered.

Wallace, having no sense of humor, waited outside the club in the parking lot that evening and

The Wolves of Calabria

tailed Lucky to his Miramar apartment.

The next morning Wallace was in the office of his friend, the Minister for the Interior.

Bureau of Narcotics agents were dispatched the next day and the day after that New York City papers brandished the headlines that Lucky Luciano, the undisputed 'King of Crime' was doing the business of crime right on the America's doorstep, in Cuba.

Meyer Lansky immediately caught a plane north and made a visit to Batista's home in Miami. Over afternoon drinks in the sun room, Batista reiterated to Meyer what everybody already knew about Cuban law and international treaties regarding external interference in Cuba's internal matters.

"Meyer, Senior Luciano is safe as long as he has a legitimate passport, a Cuban Visa and a legitimate business interest, which he does. He has a majority interest in the casino of the Hotel National." A servant poured them a refill. "Besides, Senior Lansky, Governor Dewey's election to the presidency is inevitable as is my return as the rightful leader of the Cuban people. Dewey knows as much about foreign policy as he does rolling cigars."

"What are you trying to say?"

"After he is president he would look very foolish bothering with a has-been gangster whom he gave parole to only a short time ago, especially when the communists are planning world domination and he will be seen, as the President of the most powerful nation in the world, the only one who can stop them. Do you see my point?"

Meyer smiled at Batista's logic.

"Yes I do. Thank you el Presidente."

Afterwards, back in Havana, Lucky met with Meyer and Frankie Costello to receive this news but, having been on the receiving end of the U.S. legal system, was not encouraged. Both Luciano and Costello had dealt with the Boys in D.C. before. So they did all he could do. They waited.

It didn't take long. In February Anslinger attacked.

Bowing to further terroristic threats from the D.C. Don, Pequeno back tracked on his earlier stance not to pursue the Luciano matter. Batista and Meyer met again but el Presidente, needing American funding to stage his comeback, merely suggested that Lucky make the first move and send word to the authorities that Lucky would leave Cuba voluntarily.

It was explained to Luciano that with Dewey's impending presidential win in the U.S. and Batista's impending return to Havana as president after the defeat of Ramon Grau San Martin, Lucky would be able to return to Havana the following year.

It was in the middle of the afternoon during these protracted negotiations that Charlie was arrested in a restaurant while eating lunch.

Trying to walk a tightrope between the guys who brought in a large chunk of their personal income and the guys who had an axe to grind with those guys the Cuban authorities tried to strike a negotiation with Anslinger after they had secured permission for Lucky to go to Caracas, Venezuela.

However, as the U.S. has no friends only partners, Anslinger and Williams wanted the P.R. more than they needed diplomatic relations with a tiny third world country.

With critical medical supplies now all but exhausted, the Cubans proposed several other countries and each time the answer was the same: "Deportation to Italy or the embargo continues."

A short time later Charlie 'Lucky' Luciano's luck ran out and he was officially deported back to Italy, for the second time, where he was again arrested by the Roman police, duely released and again diligently followed by Harry A's stalwart agents.

Harry had no intention of losing track of his cash cow.

In April of that year Luciano sailed out on the S.S. Bakir, ironically a Turkish ship bound for Rome. Turkey being the major supplier of the growing cartel's raw material.

The junior, wanna-be politicians up in D.C. were bound and determined to soak the Luciano headlines for all they were worth and Harry Anslinger was not late to the party when he realized he could further solidify his power by exerting more political pressure on yet another foreign government, this time the Italian government.

Charlie was arrested in Italy when he landed and, under heavy guard was escorted to Palermo for an 'inquiry' as to how he got to Cuba. Once again

Washington proved that the law applies equally to everyone. As long as the Boys on the Hill could further their political interests and careers by applying it.

Leaning over the rail on the way out of port Charlie produced a news clipping someone had given him as he boarded the ship. The small clipping was a public service notice which was torn from page seven of the *Havana Tribune*:

> 'Henry Wallace, an American freelance journalist has been reported as missing. Anyone with information as to his whereabouts is requested to notify the local authorities.'

Charlie may have once again been heading back to Italy but, the phenomenon which would provide work for millions of law enforcement officials in dozens of countries in the years to come had been spawned by what would become to be known as: The International Drug Cartel

✝

Bureau of Narcotics
New York Branch Office
Midtown Manhattan

The Wolves of Calabria

Benson, Hernandez, Agent White and a second B.O.N. agent stood around a desk completing functions checks and loading magazines for their military issue Colt .45's. A map of the southern sector of the zoo was spread across the desktop.

"They've designated the monkey house as the meet point. That means they've scoped it out and no doubt will have back up in the most strategic locations. We'll go in through the small service gate just south of the Fordham gate and split up there. Hernandez and I will run the exchange, White you and . . ."

"Johnston."

"Johnston, will stand security." Benson scanned the group for questions. There were none. "After the deal goes down, none of them walks away alive, clear?" Benson dictated. White suddenly looked a little nervous.

"You said it was a clean exchange. We were here to get the drug sample and find out when the big shipment's coming in!"

"You gettin' cold feet Agent White? Because if you are there's the door." Benson offered.

"I ain't gettin' cold feet! I just wanna be clear on what we're doin! First it was a simple exchange, no busts, no bullets. Now you wanna make a Jimmy Cagney movie, okay, fuck it! Let's make a Cagney movie!"

Hernandez took up the challenge.

"These scumbags are bringing massive amounts of drugs into this country which are going to do two things, make criminals rich and kill people! We've been entrusted and empowered by the government to defend the people at all costs! Questions?"

"Save the flag wavin' routine Hernandez! Let's just light this fuckin' candle!" White demanded.

Satisfied they were appropriately armed and all on the same sheet of music they went downstairs to their respective government vehicles and headed over to the East Side and up the FDR Drive.

"You trust that little asshole?" Hernandez asked Benson concerning White as they pulled out into the sporadic evening traffic.

"Don't need to. Best case scenario he gets whacked, worst case scenario he survives. If the shit goes south altogether he, Anslinger and the B.O.N. take the heat."

"I kind'a like scenario number one." Hernandez cracked.

"So do I." They continued to follow the FDR Drive north to Harlem River Drive and then crossed into the West Bronx over the Harlem River north of Yankee Stadium via the Washington Bridge.

The zoo was a mere fifteen minutes further on.

†

Meanwhile, Jimmy Dugan was just clearing the airspace over Wilmington, N.C., marking the halfway point to his final destination and a leisurely year or two on a Caribbean island.

The Wolves of Calabria

CHAPTER XXIII

It was twenty minutes to five, nearly closing time, when several zoo employees were making their rounds politely shepherding visitors to the exits while a pair of grounds keepers had started at the far, north end of the park and were systematically checking the snack bars, restaurant and toilets for stragglers before locking up for the night.

After nearly two complete rounds of the zoo's grounds, aided by their complimentary visitor's map to orient themselves, Doc and Louie had made their way to the small set of toilets furthest out from the main gates and hid out in a small men's room.

Less than five minutes after Doc and Louie entered the single door flew open and an employee poked his head in the small rest room and peered around.

"Anybody in here?! We're closing up, time to go home!" Without venturing inside and receiving no answer the teen worker pulled the door over and locked it from the outside.

After a minute or so the two P.I.'s deemed it safe and stepping down from the toilet bowls they had been standing on, ventured out into the tiled room.

"We'll still need to hold off for another half hour or so to give the workers time to clear out." Doc said to Louie as they both emerged from their respective stalls.

"Can we at least relocate outside? This place smells like a chemical weapons dump!"

"I would think that with planning a kid on the way you'd want to acclimate yourself to the smell of . . . poo poo, Daaaddy!" Doc quipped as he made his way to the door.

"Ha ha! Just so happens we have an agreement, Doris and me. She's on diaper duty and I get the kid after he can walk!"

Doc used his pocketknife to jimmy the lock away from the frame enough to slide the thin dead bolt back.

"Doris know that?" He opened the door and popped his head outside.

"Yeah! Kind'a." Louie answered.

"All clear." Doc whispered. They closed up their coats as they took a seat on a bench in a gazebo in front of the camel enclosure a short distance north of the esplanade.

After a moment Louie reached into his coat and produced a foot long hoagie wrapped in wax paper. Doc stared.

"That why you were adamant about bringing hardware? In case somebody wanted to steal your hoagie?"

"I always come prepared!" With his wide open mouth Louie ferociously ripped off a bite, looked over at Doc and offered him a bite.

"No thanks, I'm on duty." Doc declined. "I saw an employee's locker room down the path. I'm gonna see if it's unlocked. Stay here. I'll be right back."

As night set in Doc strolled down the heavily foliated path. He returned a short time later carrying two pair of zookeeper's green coveralls, two green, embroidered dress shirts & khaki trousers plus a pair of Bronx Zoo baseball caps.

Louie, finishing up his sandwich, grabbed one of the ball caps, slapped it on his head and took a shirt. He dropped his coat on the bench and held the shirt out in front of him, glanced down at his purple and black bowling shirt he had worn under his coat and shook his head.

"It's no good!" He commented about the shirt.

"Why not?" Doc asked.

"It's all one color!" Louie objected. That decision being made, Doc tossed the rest of the clothes into the bushes behind the bench.

It was nearly seven when they quietly made their way down into the center of the park but, at about 200 yards from the toilet they found there was a high, chain link fence that had been gated and locked after they hid out up in the north end of the park.

The barbed wire crowning on the eight foot tall chain link fence had seen better days and so presented no major problem to Doc but Louie, given his athletic limits, negotiating the top of the fence was challenge. He snagged his jacket and tore a pocket.

As they came over the last line of fencing onto the foot path on the other side they saw why the gate was closed over and locked. A sign on the other side read:

> Extreme Danger: Wolf Enclosure
> KEEP OUT!

Doc pointed at the sign and Louie panicked.

"Now they tell us!" Mancino declared fumbling to pull out his pistol.

Doc was the first one over the second, lower barrier but as the two scampered down the fifteen foot embankment, half sliding half stumbling, Louie fell further behind. Doc finally came across the paved footpath in the dark by the time Louie caught up.

"It's not likely they'll meet very deep up in the zoo and they're definitely gonna want to keep an eye on one another that means an open place. The Promenade is the only wide open place. If we get back up by the fountain there's high ground that will let us see the whole promenade."

"Doris is gonna kill me!"

"What'd ya do now?"

"Tore my jacket!" Doc shook his head.

"Hey Louie."

"Yeah Doc?"

"Go stand off to the side of that information board and keep ya ears open will ya?! I'm gonna walk the perimeter and see if there's anybody else snooping around. Meet ya over there."

"Okay. I'll be by the board."

"Good idea. When I get back I'll look for ya by the board."

McKeowen's frustration was assuaged by constantly reminding himself that, above all else, Mancino was at least loyal. And reliable. Most of the time.

As Louie moved to his assigned position Doc crossed behind the fountain and went around behind the Lion house staying out of the little available light provided by the lampposts lining the promenade.

As he looped back around to the Fordham Road gate area and finished his short recon he headed back to where he left his partner. It wasn't long before he came within earshot of Mancino, apparently talking to himself.

"Baird Court Promenade is the ten acre central attraction of the zoo featuring gardens, pathways, grottos and fountains." Louie read partially to himself and partially to the sign in a muffled whisper.

Doc emerged quietly from the bushes.

"What are you doin'?"

"I'm learnin' stuff. Hey Doc, what's an acre?" Louie asked.

"It's a parcel of land, four rods by one furlong, about an eighth of a mile." Doc answered as he scanned the footpaths bordering the esplanade.

"What's a rod besides something ya fish with?"

"It's a measure of land, it's about forty perches."

"Okay, Perfessor, what's a perch?"

"It's also a measure of . . . it's a kind of fish! When you're finished reading the god damned sign can we get back to work?"

"I'm tryin' ta learn sumthin' here, don't get so touchy!" Louie read slowly and with great respect.

"The buildings of the court were constructed between 1899 and 1910 and include richly embellished detailed sculptures of realistic, terra cotta animals created by Eli Harvey, Charles Knight and Alexander Phimster. Huh! Not one Italian!" Louie didn't notice but Doc had disappeared.

"Hey Doc, I still don't get how . . ." He looked around for McKeowen but didn't see him. "Doc?" Doc suddenly popped out from behind a large shrubbery ten feet down the path.

"Hey Mancino! Any time today!"

"Yeah, Doc. Coming!" He scurried down the slate path to catch up. "Over five million visitors a year! Do you realize-"

"SHHH!" He pulled Louie in between the bushes as he pointed out a group of four men casually assembling down by the south façade of the monkey house about 100 yards away. As two of them drifted under a lamp post Doc and Louie could see they were doing functions checks on their pistols. Louie leaned into Doc and whispered.

"And you didn't wanna bring heaters!"

"Can it! Those mugs aren't government!"

"How do you know?"

"The clothes. Their shoes! The tall guy, crocodile Oxfords for Christ's sake!

"Then who they with?"

"No idea, probably Mob guys. But whoever they are, they're not G-men!"

"What'a we do?"

"We wait until the other guys show up then try and see if we can figure out who they are and why they're all meeting in the middle of the night in the Bronx Zoo with guys from the Mob."

"How do you now they're Mob guys?"

"I don't for sure but they're at least not NYPD."

Although a near symmetrical rectangle the South façade of the main entrance to the primate house sported a larger more elaborate entrance.

"Doc, look!"

"What?"

"This is the south side we're on yeah?"

"Yeah, so?"

"Look at the carvings above the entrance, up there on the peppermint!"

"The peppermint?!"

"The triangle part of the over the door!"

"Pediment Einstein!"

"Whatever! Threes! The triangle, three monkeys! Three pillars! Everything's in sets of threes!"

Doc stared out across the grounds, at the main entrance to the monkey house then over at several of the other entrances.

"Son-of-a-bitch! Good eyes Louie. Remind me to buy you a beer!"

"I could be a liberrian, huh?!" Mancino boasted.

"Louie?"

Paddy Kelly

"Yeah Doc?"

"Stick with detective work!"

They sat in the cold for the next twenty minutes until they saw four more individuals stroll in from the left onto the esplanade in plain sight and then meander over to the monkey house. After a short consult four of them spread into a strategic formation and waited. The other four disappeared behind the building.

"Reinforcements!" Doc declared. This is not gonna end well!"

By the size of the guy giving directions and the way he walked Doc figured it was probably Jimmy Camargo leading some of Genovese's boys. Doc was right.

At the same time as the mobsters were getting into position, Hernandez and Benson pulled up outside the zoo next to a side gate reserved for service and maintenance personnel. White and his sidekick pulled in right behind them. Benson wet over to the pair as they got out of their car.

"We're going into the Promenade. White, take your guy, skirt the perimeter and come up behind the monkey house." Benson directed. Using a pair of bolt cutters Hernandez cut the chain on the personnel gate and kicked it open.

"Right!" White enthusiastically answered.

"Don't show yourselves until I signal."

"What signal?" White asked.

"Gun fire! Get going."

The Wolves of Calabria

The two Narcotics agents passed through the gate and took off to the left. Once they were out of sight Hernandez stepped around to the trunk of the car, unlocked it and opened a large black case to reveal a pair of standard FBI issued Thompson sub-machine guns. The .45 caliber weapons had been modified with folding stocks and rudimentary, two point slings.

He passed one to Benson along with four fully loaded pistol clips of Colt .45 ammo and, after a basic functions check they both loaded a drum of ammo into the Thompson's, slung the weapons so they hung to the side and slid their long over coats on concealing the heavy hardware but rendering the weapons readily available,

Hernandez locked the trunk and they headed in through the open gate.

Having reconnoitered the park by map earlier they made their way to the fountain and across the esplanade.

Benson slowly approached the mobsters only four of whom stood in plain sight. When he thought White and his sidekick were in position behind the gangsters, he stepped out into the light of the esplanade about fifty feet in front of the monkey house in plain sight of the hoods, hands up.

"What is this? A fucking Wop convention?" Benson quipped as he carefully perused the grounds his left hand in his coat pocket, the arm keeping his coat flap over his weapon.

"Pardon us if we don't trust a Fed." Camardo answered from just in front of the steps of the monkey house, cautiously maintaining his distance.

"I don't blame you. Let's get this show on the road, I got a hot date." Benson snapped as he started towards the steps of the entrance.

Doc, off in the perimeter foliage, didn't recognize Benson but he could also make out Hernandez off to the side but he was in no position to detect the two others, White and Johnston, nor could he determine exactly where the other four mobsters had posted themselves.

Benson and Hernandez spread out as they approached the first group of four, two of which had their hands inside the breasts of their overcoats. Benson held his hands open to show he was clean, but kept the middle button on his overcoat done up to conceal the Thompson under his right arm. He approached the big guy in front of the group of mobsters.

"We said two men! One torpedo and the delivery boy!" Benson challenged.

"Guess you didn't get that memo either, didj'a?" Jimmy Camardo shot back. "It's okay. They're just a couple of new guys, we're breakin' them in."

Eyeing behind him as he sensed White and the other guy both of which had disregarded Benson's instructions. Camardo smirked.

"You got the location?" Benson asked.

"You got the plates?" Camardo challenged.

Doc and Louie watched as they split into two

The Wolves of Calabria

groups, Benson leading Jimmy Camardo and one torpedo while Hernandez remained with the other two.

Benson led them across the paths and over to the steps of the monkey house where he skirted to the right of the granite steps and made for one of the large terra cotta pots housing a giant areca palm. He pulled a knife out of his pocket and began to dig.

Less than a foot and a half under the loose soil he struck something hard. It was a standard five and dime store, stamped metal cash box like the kind used by carnival cashiers and cinema ticket booth workers. He shook the residual dirt and mulch off it and opened it to show Camardo.

"Clever little fuck, ain't ya?" The hood quipped.

Inside, wrapped in a piece of heavy cheese cloth were two metal plates, one reverse one the obverse of a federal road inspection sticker meant for long distance haulage trucks. He allowed Jimmy to remove them for examination.

From between the shrubbery in their distant perch Doc and Louie watched carefully.

Camardo set the plates on the pedestal near the base of the column beside the stairs and reached into his overcoat pocket to produce a jeweler's glass and a hand mirror. He held the mirror at an angle to reflect the light over one plate at a time and, using the jeweler's glass to examine the workmanship and looked for defects while checking the wording.

"Genuine steel, dry point, hand cut plates. Your very own *Operation Bernhard*. You can succeed where Hitler failed." Benson prompted.

"Fuck you Fed, we ain't no Nazis!" The gangster snapped back.

Camardo seemed satisfied and re-wrapped the print plates and reset them in the cash box.

"I showed you mine, now you show me yours!" Benson prodded. Jimmy didn't smile as he handed the box off to one of his men who walked towards Hernandez where the man handed the Fed a sealed envelope as he continued to walk past him and out towards the esplanade. Jimmy, who had already started to follow his man, continued on down the path with his other two men following suite.

Hernandez pocketed his .45 and ripped open the envelope.

"What's it say?" Benson called over to Hernandez maintaining his position to afford distance between them.

"I don't know, some kind'a code! I can't read the fucking thing! 40 degrees, 48 minutes, 57 seconds North by 74 degrees, 02 minutes, 23 seconds West. What the fuck is this?!"

"They're map coordinates! Hey Asshole!" Benson called after Camardo. "I didn't come here for fucking map coordinates! Where the hell is this?" Jimmy was part way down the path walking towards the gate but yelled back as he continued on.

"Fer-get-about-it! It's close. By the time you figure it out we'll be back home havin' a beer."

Benson wasted no time in producing the Thompson from under his overcoat. Hernandez, still off to Benson's right about 100 feet away, was right with him.

Jimmy heard the weapons being cocked, stopped in his tracks and slowly turned to face back up across the esplanade at the two.

"You sure that's the card you wanna play at this particular time, John Wayne?" Just as Camardo spoke, the other four mobsters appeared from around the sides of the buildings, well disbursed and each brandishing a U.S. Army issue, M3 .45 caliber Grease Gun.

The fact that they were Army issued weapons meant that the Grease Guns were fitted with 30 round clips and tooled to take the same .45 round as the Thompson. However with superior accuracy and an increased rate of fire, Benson knew he was out gunned. Not to mention outnumbered two to one, even with his single fifty round drum ammo.

Now exposed on the edge of the esplanade with four mobsters in front of them with drawn handguns and four more flanking his rear with machine guns, Benson and Hernandez knew their plan had gone south. Suddenly a voice rang out across the open grounds.

"ALRIGHT! DROP YOUR WEAPONS, RAISE YOUR HANDS THIS IS THE UITED STATES GOVERMENT!" All heads turned as the shouting came from the left of the monkey house behind the two gangsters on that side. It was Agent White to the rescue.

For about two seconds. Then the shit hit the fan.

White and his partner stood nearly side by side and the first to fall was a gangster who stood about twenty feet directly in front White's partner as the partner shot from the hip several times. The second mob man responded instantly with his Grease Gun and erased the agent's face and right shoulder.

White blindly emptied his clip, hitting the gangster twice then dropped his piece and broke the land speed record for the low crawl as he took fire and scurried off into the high bushes along the side of the path, bullets biting off chunks of flying turf chasing after him into the shrubbery. By the time the tufts of dirt and grass settled White had done a Houdini. Though unscathed he was not seen again that night.

Benson and Hernandez were well coordinated as Benson sprayed Camardo and his three while Hernandez laid down suppressive fire back up across the sides and front of the monkey house to occupy the remaining three.

Benson scored one direct kill and got Jimmy Camardo in the left thigh, while Hernandez took out two thugs in the rear guard and possibly wounded the third.

Jimmy dropped the plates when he was hit but crawled back over to them as the remaining Mob man gave him cover fire. By the time Benson recovered the two were nowhere to be seen.

Ignoring the constant bursts of fire directed at him, Benson made it over to where Camardo had been but found no plates.

The Wolves of Calabria

Hernandez took cover, reloaded then fired and maneuvered clearing the perimeter around the monkey house of any possible remaining mobsters who might have disappeared after the initial volley of fire.

Over on the sidelines, from the prone position in the bushes, Doc and Louie stared in disbelief.

"I thought the O.K. Corral was in Tombstone!" Doc declared.

"Fucking Anzio Beach all over again! And you didn't wanna bring firearms!" Louie gloated.

"Yeah, yeah. I don't know what they were exchanging for those coordinates but whatever it was it must'a been important."

Suddenly a burst of fire ripped across the foliage just above their heads. They hit the ground hard and low crawled to the base of the large elm tree centered at the fork of the paths.

"That wasn't no God damned pistol!" Louie observed.

"Sounded like a Grease Gun!" Doc affirmed as a second short burst came in, this time lower to the ground. McKeowen cursed, rolled over onto his back and grabbed his left shoulder.

"Genovese's goons must think we're Feds!" He peered out through the bushes and saw a thug, now only 50 or so yards away, reloading his Grease Gun.

"There's a police call box opposite the bird house! Tell them there's a fire fight in progress at the zoo, Fordham Road Gate." Doc ordered Louie. "Tell them it's a silent alarm, two P.I's on the scene! Meet me back at the sign!" Doc ordered.

"Can you still shoot?" Louie asked.

"Yeah! Why!?"

Without warning Mancino ran out and up the path yelling like a mad man and waving his arms.

"THE GERMANS HAVE LANDED IN JERSEY!! THE GERMANS HAVE LANDED IN JERSEY!! WE'RE ALL GONNA DIE!!"

Doc rolled back over and drew a bead on the remaining thug. The gangster managed to get off a three round burst at Louie just before the right side of the thug's face was ripped from his head. He collapsed in a heap where he stood. As he fell the Grease Gun continued firing into the ground until the mag was empty.

Louie threw a thumbs up back at Doc as he took off around back of the pavilions out of the line of fire.

"Mancino, you're a fucking maniac!" Doc mumbled as he reloaded.

Things went quiet and McKeowen decided to check the damage on his shoulder.

Laying supine behind the tree, he set his TT-33 on the ground and twisted his head around to examine his wound.

He opened his brown bomber jacket and gingerly slid the sleeve down off his left shoulder.

He had enough basic first aid to know it wasn't bad enough to pull up stakes and get out and nowhere near as bad as the broken arm that prick cop gave him in the museum back in '42, but it would need medical attention.

He stuffed his hanky between his flannel shirt and the wound and stemmed what little bleeding there was reasoning that the heat of the round must have partially cauterized the surface flesh wound. He cursed when he saw the tear in his brown bomber jacket.

"Son-of-a-bitch! Third god damned jacket in four years!"

Suddenly, still obscured by the bushes, from across the esplanade, Doc perceived a slow, but distinct movement. Grabbing his weapon he rolled over back into the prone position, cocked his pistol and took aim but held his fire. His patience paid off.

It was a mobster carrying a pistol who had decided to chance it and dash across a nearby path. Doc again took aim and three shots in rapid succession caused the guy to hit the macadam path, his pistol flying into the air, bouncing twice until it slid a few yards before coming to rest near the water fountain the thug apparently thought would provide cover.

Doc had the good sense, after revealing his position, to not remain static. Low crawling backwards until he was once again back across the footpath he rolled across it and crawled behind a large oak next to some kind of small shed.

Meanwhile, a couple of hundred yards away Louie, attempting to maneuver to the bird house and reach the call box, heard rustling in the bushes near the lion house and called out in a loud whisper from the main path.

"Doc?!" He realized it wasn't Doc when a short burst of automatic weapons fire ripped through the bushes and tore into the information booth off to his right.

Louie made for the other end of the lion house and franticly concocted a plan. He spotted a service ladder up to the roof just as Hernandez emerged from out of the bushes and onto the path brandishing his Thompson.

Based on the direction he fled in after tagging Camardo, and the direction of the footprints in the soft sod of the esplanade, Doc had been able to track Benson to the west side of the park. The path dried up a hundred yards on the other side of the monkey house just across from the buffalo enclosure.

There was only one path running north south on that side of the zoo and they had had a pretty good view of the south end of the path so Doc guessed Benson had gone north. Stalking carefully through the decorative but heavy brush, he heard a noise, raised his TT-33 and slowly scanned 180 degrees.

Suddenly there was a 2000 pound, African water buffalo bearing down on him at full speed from across the paddock. He momentarily froze and took aim until he peered through the shadows and saw there was a ten foot wide very deep ditch behind the flimsy looking wrought iron fence in front of him. He lowered his pistol, took a breath and moved on.

"What to do when being charged by a pissed off

bull?! Things they never taught you at the police academy." He mumbled.

Back down at the esplanade Hernandez fired two short bursts in rapid succession but, toying with Louie, only hit the granite edge of the eaves as Mancino scrambled up off the ladder and onto the large roof gable. Hernandez wasted no time in pursuing Mancino up and over the kiosk and onto the roof.

Struggling up onto the main roof Mancino scurried along the shallow peak. He quickly came to a two foot wide ventilation transom which ran down the center of the peak and looked back to see a smirking Hernandez nonchalantly stepping up onto the roof top and strolling towards him. Mancino carefully stepped around a two foot square sun window and stumbled.

After firing off two clumsy shots, which didn't even cause Hernandez to flinch Mancino reached the end of the roof where there was a raised wall blocking any quick escape or chance to jump.

Louie stopped running and turned to face his pursuer.

The Fed was just past the midway of the long roof when he stopped, about seventy-five foot away, and fired again this time purposely too high.

"DON'T SHOOT! DON'T SHOOT! I ain't with the Mob, I'm on your side!" Hernandez, now a good fifty feet away, hesitated as Louie threw down his gun and produced his P.I. badge and I.D.

"I know who you are! And if you're with the

law . . ." Hernandez casually ejected his magazine, quickly slapped another one in and cocked back the bolt. ". . . then you ain't on my side, cabrón!"

"Wait! That fake window you're standing on -" Louie pointed. Hernandez looked down.

"It's called 'plastic', Germans invented it!" To reinforce his point he stomped one foot on the skylight once or twice to demonstrate. He leveled the gun's muzzle at Mancino. It would be the last mistake future, former Department of Foreign Affairs Agent Hernandez would make.

Unbeknownst to Louie, Hernandez or anyone else involved in the deadly game of gun tag that night, the meat ration schedule from the war still hadn't been adjusted and so the large male Siberian tiger named Jaipur weighing in at over a 1,000 pounds, now prowling a mere three yards under them, hadn't been fed that afternoon.

Raising his foot up for the definitive stomp the seam of the window joint gave way and when Hernandez came down he, his weapon, the entire window seam and the Jet Age plastic window kept going, down.

Down into Jaipur's spacious cage. But not spacious enough.

Louie fell flat on his stomach and quickly crawled to the edge of the opening to look down into the cage just in time to see Hernandez's right arm, still clutching the Thompson, get torn off and go flying across the cage. As Jaipur took a giant swipe at Hernandez's belly and tore open his abdomen the screaming was so intense that Mancino, although he couldn't look away, was compelled to cover his ears and yell.

"JESUS CHRIST!"

Aside from having seen his cousin Guido cut his hand on a bent garbage can one time, this was the most gruesome thing Louie Mancino had ever witnessed.

Mancino rolled over onto his back and stared up at the stars to compose himself. He took a few deep breaths trying to block out Hernandez's mind splintering screams punctuated by the bone shattering roars of the Jaipur's anger and as the tiger finished the job.

The screaming finally stopped but the sound of tearing meat made Mancino quickly re-cover his ears, struggle to his feet and make the decision to get the hell out of there.

It was a good five minutes later before a pale faced Louie was able to get up and traverse back across the peak of the long roof. Jaipur's roars of dominance echoed in the distance as Louie climbed down the rear fire ladder then down the pitched and layered gables to get down onto the top of a snacks kiosk and finally back onto terra firma.

"Guess the Germans weren't done testing that plastic stuff before the war ended!" Louie mumbled to himself.

He took a deep breath as he considered which direction to head in. Jogging, he made his way back around to the Esplanade

With all the gangsters and feds now cleared out Doc and Louie met back up near the bird house.

"Doc! Am I glad to see you!"

"You look like shit! You alright?"

"Yeah, yeah I'm okay." A glass-eyed Louie half mumbled.

"Well at least we know we're dealing with the Mob and the Feds!" Doc confirmed. Louie remained silent. "Com'on then, we gotta catch that guy Benson. He finds a way into the City we'll never see him again."

They headed out on foot in the direction of the Fordham Road gate and as they jogged away Doc noticed Louie's glazed over eyes.

"What happened to the other guy, the one chasing you?" Doc asked.

"You're not gonna believe this one Doc!" He maintained his forward stare as he answered.

"Try me."

"Ate by a fucking tiger!"

"Get the fuck out'a here!"

"A big fuckin' tiger!"

"You're serious!"

"Serious as a heart attack, it was discusstin'! Guts all over the place . . ."

"I guess it's been that kind'a night!" Doc shook his head.

"I nearly tossed my cookies!" Louie confessed.

"You trying to say it was . . . emetic?"

"No, it was repulsive!"

"As in repellent?"

The Wolves of Calabria

"As in repugnant." Louie added, his intense fear dissipating as they spoke.

"Probably beastly too."

"But that's not the worst of it!" Louie volunteered.

"How do you mean?"

"I ripped my bowling shirt!" Like a child showing mommy his boo-boo he displayed the ripped shirt tail.

"Bastards!" Doc declared.

"Tell me about it! It's a Brunswick!"

They slowed to a shuffle as the exit came into sight.

"What a shit way to die!" Louie unexpectedly let out. Despite Hernandez's efforts at trying to kill him, Mancino stull sympathized.

"Maybe, but I feel bad for the tiger." Doc quipped.

"How'd ya figure?"

"Probably still suffering from indigestion."

"What the hell you talkin' about?" Louie pushed.

"He's from Siberia. Probably first time he ever ate Mexican." Doc whispered.

"That's sick Doc. Funny, but sick." Louie smirked as he whispered back. "You are a sick puppy Doc!"

Suddenly they heard somebody rustling around in the bushes behind them. They froze and ducked behind a tree. At the same time The distant wail of screaming police sirens seeped through the silence.

"Finally, the cavalry!" Doc declared before they

heard a second siren. "Did you tell those assholes silent alarm like I said?" Doc cursed.

"No, never made it to the police box. Must'a been somebody else heard the shots."

"Well then let's not be here when they show up!"

Once outside the Fordham gate it took less than a minute to locate Benson. He was the guy in the late model Buick hurdling up the side-walk at sixty miles per hour, heading straight at them.

Doc, too far from the gate to dive back in, waited till the last minute and vaulted up onto the wrought iron fencing as Louie dove back in through the gate way and ducked behind a small one stall toilet just inside the gate while 3,000 pounds of Detroit steel went barrelling by missing them by inches.

They watched as the car sped down the road then suddenly became aware of more rustling up the road behind them. They quickly ducked back into the entranceway.

Carefully peering out around the gate Doc watched as one of Genovese's men awkwardly climbed over the top of the iron rail fencing, brushing away the low hanging tree branches in his way and dropped down to the side-walk outside the zoo grounds. The thug paused and took time to brush his Armani suit off and wipe his shoes with a hanky.

Doc quickly reached over and turned up Mancino's jacket collar and mused his hair.

"Call out to him in Italian!"

"Call out for what?!"

The Wolves of Calabria

"For help moron! Duck down and call!"

"Aiuto! Aiuto, bisogo . . . di aiuto!" Louie called out in muffled Sicilian as he feigned injury.

The Mafioso took the bait and, gun drawn, ran down the side-walk along the fence line towards them.

Louie bent down with his back to the street and, when the torpedo ran up to him Doc came out of the shadows, blackjack in hand.

A moment later Doc was pulling the mobster's car up to the curb while Mancino dragged the thug into the nearby toilet. As he left Mancino looked back and smiled at the big guy sitting on the crapper, slumped over, pants around his ankles.

"Where's a camera when ya need one?" Louie pocketed the mobster's roscoe and joined Doc out in the car.

☦

CHAPTER XXIV

East of Newark, New Jersey
75 Miles from the Jersey Meadowlands

"What the hell was that all about?" Mancino asked as they lit out after Benson.

"What was what all about? Mob guys givin' the Feds map coordinates instead of money for those counterfeit money plates?"

"I don't think they were givin' the Mob counterfeit money plates."

"What then?"

"Not sure but whatever that fed Benson gave Camardo must be pretty important and those coordinates must be where our boy is now headed and wherever it is he's headin' to collect must be pretty God damned important! Plus the fact that he's headin' there like a bat out of hell must mean there's some kind'a deadline for the pick-up. Too bad we don't when that is!"

"Thanks Doc! That just about clears that all up." Louie quipped.

While the two had no way of knowing what the geo-coordinates Camardo gave Benson meant there was another man who not only knew better than anyone exactly what they meant but knew exactly what was there. Or at least exactly what would be there in a very short time.

The Wolves of Calabria

As he confirmed the current heading of his brand new DeHavilland Beaver, descending from an altitude of 15,000 feet over Elizabeth, New Jersey, Jimmy Dugan, accompanied by a Mafia appointed babysitter affectionately named Icepick Lou, were coming up the Hudson enroute to the New Jersey Meadowlands.

It would be a dodgy enough landing in an area like the open, marshy, reed-strewn Meadowlands in daylight hours but a night landing guided by a dozen battery operated flashlights on either side would be considered by most pilots the dodgiest dodge of all dodges.

Jimmy Dugan wasn't most pilots.

The 10,000 acre area had, during the war, been used as a dumping ground for rubble from the London blitz as ships, using the rubble from the bombed out East End as ballast, returned across the turbulent trans-Atlantic after delivering food, ammo and equipment.

By now most of the London rubble had been cleared away and relocated and the New Jersey State Highway Department were merging State Highways #100 and #300 christening the huge construction project the New Jersey Turnpike.

Now, using the historic, well lit three and a half mile long Pulaski Skyway, America's first 'superhighway', as a guide, Jimmy the Daredevil Catman slowly descended to 500 feet and gently banked left to execute a slow flyover of the marshy Meadows before landing. As he did he spotted the small battery operated lights as they began to light up along an 800 foot strip of roadbed which had been laid down for the new turnpike project just two weeks prior.

On the cautionary loop around he decided to line up with a small arm of the Passaic River, which ran roughly parallel to the road strip, as a guide. Coming in for his final approach he brought the bird in low through the sporadic patches of fog, between two huge stanchions under the 135 foot high roadbed on the Pulaski, which also helped the Jimmy line up the aircraft.

As a gust of wind struck he barely missed one of the bridge's massive pylons but quickly recovered control. However he instantly faced a new problem.

The warm, brackish waters of the swamps converged with the cold night's air to suddenly create a thick fog which reduced visibility to less than ten feet ahead around the improvised runway.

As Jimmy brought the plane in he was forced to make multiple corrections as the lighted area between the two short rows of lamps faded then appeared again as the fog bank drifted through the area.

Tall reeds on either side slapped against the leading edges of the wings as they came in.

By now Icepick was about to rip the grab bar from the plane's bulkhead and was on his second air sickness bag.

Finally they felt the wheels hit the concrete slab, bounce twice then remain down. Jimmy pulled back hard on the throttle, adjusted the flaps and peddled the rudder hard right to come about only a yard from the edge of the roadbed.

"God bless Alfred E. Driscoll!" Jimmy tapped the dashboard as he praised the New Jersey governor.

"And . . . local 837 of the . . . United Steel Workers!" A green-faced Icepick added.

"Yeah, them cats too!" Jimmy seconded.

As per Catman's previous orders the industrial flashlights were extinguished as soon as he taxied the plane around and shut it down alongside three dark sedans and a 1944 Studebaker box truck lettered, 'Grossman's Haulage' along both sides.

Large road machinery, bundles of steel reinforcement rods and hundreds of tarp covered bags of cement lay strewn about the area.

Once the engine died down Jimmy dismounted the aircraft and made his way over to the guy who clearly looked to be in charge.

"You Dugan?" The well-dressed big man asked.

"In the flesh brother!" Jimmy extended a hand as half a dozen men, two brandishing Grease Guns, scurried from the warmth of their vehicles. The New York skyline blazed in the distance.

"Good flight?" Big Man asked as they moved towards the opposite side of the plane and to the cargo hold.

"No hairier than usual. But I'll tell you cats somethin', this is about the max capacity this little bird will handle, you dig where I'm coming from?"

The big man smiled and patted Dugan on the shoulder.

"Don't sweat it Dugan! After this load hits the streets you tell us which plane you want and you got it!"

Jimmy threw open the hold to reveal sixty-four cases of tightly packed canned tomatoes.

"As per order Daddy-O!" Jimmy presented, proudly indicating the cargo of his DeHavilland. "Twenty-four, fifteen ounce cans per case."

"Powdered gold my good man. Powdered gold!" The boss declared.

With sixty-four cases aboard and the going street price of $75.00 per gram, or over $2,000 an ounce, Jimmy had just brought the Mob a cool $48 and half mil in product.

☦

Mancino had jogged through the gate just as Doc unsteadily pulled up in the mobster's 'borrowed' '46 Hudson and vaulted over the passenger's door into the seat.

It was a tan convertible with, for whatever reason the top was down and Doc had no inclination to put it up, even if he could figure out how.

"He's no doubt heading south!" McKeowen predicted as he floored it and pulled out. In the rear view mirror he could see two squad cars come around the corner, cherry roof lights flashing and sirens screaming.

"Best way south is the FDR!" Mancino added.

"Yeah but which way'll he take to go west?" Doc gestured ahead to the five point intersection. After they turned the first corner he checked the rear view again but didn't see any cops in pursuit.

Just as the words left his mouth they heard the screeching of tires and what sounded like a collision off to their right.

"There he is!"

When they reached the end of Royalston Avenue, up ahead they could see the chrome festooned tail end of Benson's Buick vanishing left around the next corner and a guy trapped in a black Chrysler crunched against a telephone pole trying to kick the passenger side door open from the inside.

They sped west past the wreck and in the all but deserted, late night streets it was easy enough to pick up the Buick again as it continued straight west along Tremont heading towards the river. As Doc fought the wheel Louie suddenly piped up.

"This is a Hudson Super Six! Over 61,000 rolled off the line between late 1945 and late 1946. Although there are several new features in the '46 model it has the same pre-war body style." Doc, keeping his eye out for any signs of Benson, cops or traffic while focusing on the road assumed a puzzled look as Louie continued his automotive history lesson. "The transmission was offered in three different options, Drive Master, Over drive and —"

"Louie?!"

"What?!" With his eyes still glued to the road Doc didn't look over at Louie.

"How the hell do you know that?!"

"It's right here in this little book. Was in the glove compartment." Louie brandished an owner's manual.

"Asshole!" Doc muttered as they were now a solid two blocks behind Benson.

"Doc, what if he cuts back north and heads Upstate?"

"Then we're gonna be late getting' home!"

The mystery was cleared up when they reached the Washington Bridge a few blocks ahead. Still speeding at over seventy miles an hour, Benson crossed the Harlem River and turned south down Harlem River Drive.

The exit ramp was still under construction so Benson's Buick was forced to crash through several wooden barriers to reach the main four lane blacktop. Now closer behind him Doc had to swerve the Hudson around the debris.

"Governor's Island is a federal reservation, maybe he's heading down there?" Mancino suggested.

"Could bee but I don't think so, he doesn't strike me as the kind'a guy who quits that easy. I think he's still gonna try and make the meet."

"Whatever he's after it must be pretty God-damned important!"

"You can say that again!"

"Whatever he's after-"
"Don't even!" Doc ordered.
They continued speeding south through Manhattan and onto the FDR when Louie's mind stumbled onto a thought.
"Doc, lemme ask you something."
"Yeah?"
"Why would anybody with a good government job, and a pension go and screw it all up by goin' crooked?"
"Because some people see the system as being founded on the corporate model of profit, profit, profit. Profit at all costs. Everything else is secondary. Getting a job like one with the government is just getting your foot in the door for some people."
"That's a given." Louie shrugged
"A foot in the door can lead to little politics which can-"
"Lead to big politics!" Louie blurted out.
"Exactly. And in big politics there's a heavily defined code, a set of rules. Breaking the rules is encouraged. The more you understand the system the more you can cheat, lie and steal, like all the Wall Street scams and scandals that pop up every couple of years. Essentially the people involved in big politics have more brains than balls."
"Okay."
"In organized crime there is also a clearly defined code of conduct and hierarchy. The distinguishing difference in the two is, in one you

break the rules you maybe do a little jail time you may not, you get out, write a How-To book, get another job and plan the next scam. Break the rules in the organized crime game and you die."

"So what you're tryin' to say is the mob system is a helluv'a lot more honest system?"

"Well, more straight forward anyways."

"Yeah but loads of politicians commit really big crimes and get away with them!" Louie challenged.

"So do lots of gang bosses."

"HUH! Never thought about it that way."

"People who are good at either career field soon realize they have a half-life of about the same length with the similar retirement benefits."

"I see." And he did as Mancino genuinely appreciated Doc's insights. "But I still hate those gangster bastards!" He unreservedly declared.

"Which ones?"

Doc watched the shadowy, empty lanes far ahead as, without warning, about a half mile up an NYPD patrol car pulled out in front of Benson's speeding Buick. In an apparent attempt to stop him, the cop pulled his cruiser across both lanes.

Doc and Louie watched as the Buick accelerated and ploughed straight into the left rear quarter panel of the black and dark green Plymouth causing it to spin a full 360 twice before coming to rest halfway up on the side of the road.

Doc pulled up and yelled over to the patrolman who was climbing through the busted out window of the wrecked cruiser.

"You okay?"

"When I catch that son-of-a-bitch he's gonna wish he was never born!"

"We think he's probably heading towards The Battery! Call in and get some units down there!"

"Right!"

"And alert the tunnel and the G.W. just in case!" He yelled back as he pulled away. The cop reached back in through the window of his cruiser and manned the handset hanging from the crumpled dashboard.

"Doc, what if the meet is not on this side of the river but over in Jersey?"

"What's the matter? Forgot your passport?!"

Doc decided to take a chance and drifted over into the right hand lane to exit across the Bowery north of The Battery. "Where the hell are all the cops?!"

"You can never find one when you need one!" Louie added.

"With any luck if he heads into Jersey they'll trap him in the tunnel!"

As they rapidly approached the Holland Tunnel, there were two separate tubes with two car lanes each. One tube ran west to east from Jersey City, N.J. into Manhattan and the other east to west from Lower Manhattan back over to Jersey.

As he approached the long, winding entrance ramp to the mile and a half long tunnel at St. John's Park freight terminal, Benson spotted police patrol cars guarding the entrance.

Paddy Kelly

The street ramp was elevated enough at the base of Canal Street so that he spotted the pair of police cars, red roof lamps flashing set around the ramp to the toll booths with the tunnel entrance below and beyond.

He cautiously cruised past the turn off to the tunnel and pulled over and parked just off Spring Street. Controlled but with a sense of urgency Benson's mind raced for solutions.

That's when he spotted a lone car on its way over to the Jersey docks casually driving around the corner and up Spring Street. Benson carpe-ed the diem by popping his hood and stepping out in front of the oncoming vehicle while waving.

The car slowed to a halt and Benson approached the driver's side as the man rolled down his window.

"What's the problem?" The driver asked.

"There's something going on down at the tunnel. Loads of cops. Looks like your left rear running light is out. I noticed it when you came around the corner. Coppers see that they'll slap ya with a summons!"

"What's wrong with your jalopy?"

"Ahh! Bonehead move on my part. Outta gas. Wife keeps telling me to fill it p but . . . you know."

The guy put it in park and got out. As he walked around in back of his vehicle to the passenger's side Benson followed close behind reaching for a blackjack he slid from his hip pocket.

Less than a minute later Benson had the weapons from the stolen Buick in the back seat of the stolen

Chrysler and was cruising towards the tunnel entrance.

The ferry operator didn't make it to work that night.

As Doc and Louie were heading cross town Benson was slowly rolling up to the police roadblock 100 yards in front of the tunnel. The two black and white patrol cars were arranged at 45 degree angles to the retaining walls of the four lane entrance ramp just forward of the four toll booths. The sole, on-duty toll collector sat comfortably sipping coffee from a Thermos in the back seat of one of the cruisers.

Benson slowed to a coast pointing his car at the narrow space between the two squad cars as a middle-aged cop approached.

By now Doc had exited the FDR, was cutting across the Bowery and heading for the tunnel on a hunch. At the entrance down to the ramp just off Canal Street, his attention was caught by what appeared to be a ruckus down by the toll booths at the tunnel entrance.

"SHIT!"

"What?!" Louie questioned.

"That's probably him down there in the Chrysler!"

Benson flashed his badge through the glass of the closed window. The cop perused it then tapped the window with his wedding ring and signalled to roll it down.

"Sorry Agent but we got strict orders about lettin'

people through here."

"I'm a Special Agent with the Department-."

"Like I said, we got strict orders about -"

"You're here because you got word about a shoot-out up in the Bronx!" Benson's belligerence took the veteran cop completely off guard.

"Yeah, how'd you know?" The cop defended.

"Because it was one'a our guys was up there to meet an informant about a possible spy ring and the bastard opened up on him! That's how I KNOW! AND FOR ALL I KNOW MY PARTNER COULD BE LYING IN A POOL OF HIS OWN BLOOD OVER IN JERSEY AS WE SPEAK!"

"Shit, I'm sorry! What'a ya need us to do?"

"The asshole we're lookin' for goes under the name of McKeowen, probably an alias. Truckin' around with a short, chubby guy looks like Lou Costello."

"Gotch'a."

"They were last seen speeding down the FDR about ten minutes ago, maybe headin' this way, maybe not. I need two things from you guys."

"Name it!" The uniform's excitement at the prospect of playing with the Big Boys was obvious.

"Follow your orders and don't let ANYBODY else through here! Then radio over to the Jersey side and tell them there's a Federal agent coming through in a hurry. Ya got that?"

As he spoke the cop noticed the military grade weapons in the back seat.

"What's with all the hardware?" The cop asked.

The Wolves of Calabria

"Told ya, these guys are dangerous! Especially the little fat one! We suspect he could be with the Soviets!"

"Mother of God!"

The cop signalled for his younger partner to open the roadblock which he did by backing one of the cars away from the other.

Benson put it in drive, floored it and with a quarter inch of rubber burned into the pavement he released the break and sped between the two cars.

While Benson was bullshitting his way through the roadblock Doc, seeing the cop cars at the tunnel, had wasted no time in determining there was no way through the tunnel and so sped off in the direction of the river, less than seventy-five yards away.

He skidded the car to a halt on the very edge of a pier where a police boat was moored, jumped out of the car and dashed to the pier, Mancino close behind. The large Jon boat sported an open cabin and was moored bow out along side of the pier.

"Doc, tell me you're not thinkin' about-"

"Not thinkin' about it Louie. Thought about it!" One hand on the creosote soaked piling he hopped from the pier into the police boat and began quickly searching for the start button. Louie got to work on the mooring lines.

"We're gonna die! Thank God for my last Thanksgiving dinner with Doris, because we're gonna miss Christmas cause we're gonna be dead!"

"It's okay, I had a lesson once, down in Florida."

Doc said.

"Yeah, I was there! You can drive a boat okay but your parking needs a little work!"

"I didn't crash the boat, did I?!" Doc quickly retorted. Seeing there was a standard ignition on the dash he quickly realized cops were not likely to leave the key on board.

He produced the key to his apartment, jammed it into the ignition as far as it would go and twisted. The key snapped off but the motor kicked over and they were in business.

"I purposely ran it aground." McKeowen slammed the throttle all the way forward and the former Army patrol boat come NYPD river patrol craft bucked out of the slip and rooster tailed towards the Jersey docks directly across the river.

A reflection of the Manhattan skyline only partially illuminated the near dark of the open Hudson as the boat raced over the choppy waters. Standing next to Doc, Louie braced himself against the cold of the open cabin and the hard ricochet of the hull as it careened against the river's surface.

"Doc he'll be through that roadblock any minute now and a car is a helluva lot faster than a boat!"

Through the murky air McKeowen maintained focus on the swiftly approaching piers ahead.

"The tunnel is over a mile and a half long. It's only about a half a mile straight across to the pier at River Drive! But I got another idea." Doc manned the radio and switched to channel 9, the emergency channel.

The Wolves of Calabria

"Central Dispatch, Central Dispatch, this is Hudson River Patrol 186."

At Doc's phoney I.D. radio call Louie's face dropped into his hand and shook his head.

"Message to all units, all units, be advised, currently in pursuit perpetrator has been identified as a rogue Federal agent. Goes by the name of Benson. I repeat, rogue federal agent! Suspect is currently heading west through the Holland Tunnel into Jersey City. He is armed and extremely dangerous!"

"Hudson River Patrol 186?" Louie challenged.

"At least it'll wake 'em up." Doc countered.

The cordon of four New Jersey State Troopers and their two blue and white vehicles already in front of the tunnel's exit across the river on the Jersey side all picked up on Doc's transmission and drew their weapons preparing themselves for a felony stop.

Who is this?! This is an official police band, identify yourself or you will be charged with-

"That sounded a lot like Chief Sullivan?!" Mancino declared. Doc shrugged.

"Maybe. Could'a been. Or could'a been some other asshole."

Meanwhile Benson was approaching the thick blue stripe on the tunnel's wall which designated he was about to cross state lines. He slowed a bit and steered with his knees while he continued to load a new mag into the Thompson then reached into the back seat and retrieved a Grease Gun he had confiscated from Genovese's' boys. He then rolled down the driver's side window and slowed to just below the speed limit.

Back at the New York entrance, upon hearing Doc's call the middle-aged cop who waved Benson through cursed himself.

"Should'a freakin' known!" He quickly yelled over to his partner to fire up his cruiser as he followed suit. Manning his radio as they drove into the tunnel, he reaffirmed Benson's 10-20 with an APB.

By now Doc and Louie were about a hundred yards out from the Jersey shore and, peering through the grey shadows McKeowen perused the shoreline ahead and decided on the south side of a 300 yard long pier which jutted out into the black of the Hudson.

Their course had taken them in a straight line across the expansive river so they were essentially on top of the tunnel most of the way across.

"You gonna crash the boat again?" Mancino chided as they drifted into pier side only yards from the shore on the Riverfront Walkway. Doc cut the engines and drifted in. Louie hastily lassoed a piling and they scurried up onto the creosote soaked pier and they ran for all they were worth.

"There, happy?! No crashed boat!"

"Okay, maybe we're not gonna die. Yet." Louie echoed as they jogged off the pier and across the abandoned lot.

The Terminal Tower clock over on the Hoboken

The Wolves of Calabria

docks read nearly half past one.

Underneath them, down in the tunnel, with the New York State line well behind him, Benson glanced in his rear view mirror and spotted the two NYPD vehicles closing the distance between them. Not the kind of guy to panic he just smiled.

The gentle curve in the tunnel ahead was just what he needed and he slowed the stolen Chrysler, turned it forty-five degrees to the wall, put it in park and stepped out brandishing the Grease Gun. The first patrol car, driven by the very angry middle-aged cop, didn't stand a chance.

By the time Benson's image crept into the cop's field of vision, at about seventy-five yards out, the weapon was already firing and Benson emptied the thirty round clip into the grill and up across the wind shield.

The green and black unit swerved left, smacked into the wall, nose first and, carried by its forward momentum, rolled over onto the roof. Spitting sparks as it skidded across the roadbed and its windows blew out as it spun until it slowed to a halt, less than fifty feet from the Fed.

The second patrol car screeched to a halt well behind and the rookie cop jumped out and scrambled to help his partner.

Benson nonchalantly reloaded and waited to see what the rookie would do. The young cop ran to his injured partner and Benson, satisfied he was out of the game, climbed back into his car and drove off.

Up on the surface, backlit by the lights of the

Manhattan skyscrapers, Doc and Louie raced towards the tunnel entrance until they arrived at a fenced off ledge right over the tunnel's mouth about fifty feet back from and above the row of toll booths. The few vehicles out that night were being held up at the gate by the toll attendant.

Down in the tunnel Benson's Chrysler had slowed to 15 mph to assess what was ahead of him. As he approached the exit the flood lights illuminating the tunnel's exit ramp clearly revealed the silhouettes of the Jersey State Troopers lying in wait, bent forward over their cruisers, weapons drawn.

He set his .45 on the seat next to him and steering with his right hand, used his left to steady the Grease Gun out the window, resting it on the side view mirror.

The four troopers, taking cover behind their two toned cruisers, stood ready, pistols aimed as the Chrysler crept forward.

Back outside and above the tunnel entrance, the sudden sound of a short volley of pistol fire peeled through the night air and was quickly answered by automatic weapons fire. Doc and Louie instinctively flinched as the fire fight below them ensued.

"Okay, maybe we are gonna die!" Louie reaffirmed.

In and around the entrance deafening cracks of weapons fire continued to ring out as the troopers fruitlessly traded volleys with the on rushing Benson. Bullets ricocheted off the white tiled walls, the concrete roadbed and Benson's angled windshield as the .38 rounds of the troopers proved ineffective against the thick, tilted glass.

The .45 rounds of Benson's M3 Grease Gun however chewed at everything they hit including three of the four troopers.

By the time he emptied his second clip of ammo in as many minutes Benson's only slightly damaged Chrysler ploughed through the second roadblock. The remaining policeman's feeble pistol shots at the rear of the Chrysler, though on target, were even less effective than before.

Benson, now up between the toll booths where the handful of drivers had abandoned their vehicles and sought cover wherever they could, stopped and stepped partially out of the car.

Now some seventy-five yards or so past the wreck of the roadblock, he produced his Thompson and raked fire back at the remaining trooper. The cop was able to dive for cover and escaped injury.

Benson glanced up to the portico, spotted Doc and waved. Doc just stared back as Benson smirked, tossed a dime into the toll booth and drove off up into Jersey City.

"He seems really pissed off!" Louie observed from the safety of their elevated perch. Doc was already en route down the embankment heading for the toll booths.

"He's a fuckin' psychotic asshole is what he is!" Doc called back.

Unsure if the shoot-out was over or not, the four

or five civilian drivers were still behind a cluster of trees and some benches well off to the side as Doc dashed up to the toll booths.

Amongst the dribble of vehicles being held at the east bound booths was a pair of cars, a small delivery van and a red Indian motorcycle now laying on its side.

From inside one of the booths the toll booth operator popped his head up from the floor and caught Doc mounting the bike.

"Hey mista', that ain't yours!" The soon-to-be completely bald man challenged.

"It's okay, the guy who owns it and me, we're old Army buddies."

After yelling at Louie to find the owner of the bike, Doc was off on the Indian up Route 9 and into Jersey City.

Louie didn't have to look far as the bike's irate owner came out from behind the trees screaming after Doc.

✝

Meanwhile, back in the tunnel, Assistant Chief Sullivan, alerted by the team investigating the mess Benson and Hernandez left up at the zoo, had been following the action from Downtown by radio and had arrived at the scene of the tunnel crash pretending to take charge.

He watched grimly as the white garbed

ambulance crew loaded the dead body of the older NYPD policeman into the Cadillac ambulance.

"You get a good look at this bastard, Carnes?" He asked the younger patrolman who had run back-up for the older officer.

"Yes Chief. He stopped at the entrance and told officer Kazinski that he was a federal agent in pursuit of a suspect. We let him though and a minute later we got the call." The rookie informed him. Sullivan turned to question the other cop standing beside him, a tall negro who looked to be in his early forties.

"This guy who called from the police radio, we got any idea where he called from or who the hell he was?" He asked.

"Not yet Chief, but he signed off with a badge number and a Jersey river unit found the stolen NYPD patrol boat abandoned next to the River Side pier in Jersey City."

"Morris you still a cop?"

"Yeah Chief, why?"

"What badge number and WHO DOES IT BELONG TO, FER CHRIST'S SAKE?!"

"That's just it chief! We got a badge number but it doesn't belong to anybody. At least not anybody on the force now."

"The River Side pier? That's a straight line from Manhattan over the tunnel." The rookie Carnes observed. "Perhaps somebody was giving chase at the same time we were?"

"Or could mean he had back-up." Morris

suggested.

"Nah, they would'a been riding together. Trace that badge number. I don't think the caller just pulled it outta thin air. I wanna know who had it before."

Checking his notes Morris related another bit of info.

"Also the radio transceiver was found on the deck of the pilot house of the police boat, not on the hook."

"So our mystery man stole the boat and called in from there!" Carnes surmised.

"Looks like." Sullivan grunted.

✝

In a little over four hours the sun would rise over the Jersey Meadowlands leaving no question that the rest of Camardo's crew over in the Meadowlands had to get things moving.

"Awright, let's get this shit in the truck and let's get the hell outta here!" The crew leader called to his men who were all dressed in Grossman's Haulage uniforms. Four attacked the cargo while the other two, with Grease Guns at the ready, stationed themselves at either end of the roadbed facing out board.

"I assume everything is copacetic my good man?" Dugan queried standing next to the crew boss, both watching the unloading operation.

The Wolves of Calabria

"Looks like it." Big Man confirmed as he handed Jimmy an envelope so fat it required several thick rubber bands to hold it closed over.

"What you cats need me to do now?" Jimmy asked taking the overstuffed envelope.

"The Camardos give you follow-on instructions?"

"Negatory!"

"Camardo or somebody was supposed to tell you."

"We'll be all clear in fifteen to twenty minutes Boss!" A gang member yelled over.

"Alright, when you're done get outta here! I'll meet you back in The City." He turned back to Jimmy who shrugged.

"Well Dude, I don't know nuthin' about that. I'm just the guy in charge of flyin' the Friendly Skies, you dig? But I'd be happy to make a quick long distance call if it'll help."

"We're in the middle of the fuckin' Meadowlands! Where the hell you gonna find a god-damned phone way the fuck out here?"

"Follow me!" Jimmy smirked as he led the boss around to the passenger's side of the De Havilland, grabbed the wing strut and swung the door open and took a seat. There, bolted underneath the dashboard, was a U.S. military radio transmitter.

"ART-13, Navy issue." Dugan proudly presented as he climbed up into the passenger's seat and fired up the radio. "Gives you an open shot across the Meadowlands and the Hudson River straight into

NYC. Capable of operating CW, MCW, AM, LF or HF up to 18 Megahertz!"

"I guess I'm impressed Mr. Dugan!" Jimmy keyed the hand mike.

"Captain Midnight, Captain Midnight, this is the Catman, how copy? Over." Static filled the cabin.

"What about the coppers listening in?" The Big Man asked.

"Police bands are usually on one of the lower frequencies but when I'm in the proximity I switch to MCW at 40 megahertz or below. We call it black band, technically illegal! But, shhh! Don't tell nobody. Wouldn't wanna break the law!" If the gang boss wasn't truly impressed before he was now."

"Captain Midnight, Captain Midnight, this is the Catman, how copy? Over." A few seconds later the small dashboard speaker crackled to life as a voice broke in.

Catman, Catman this is Captain Midnight! You still breathin' brother?!

"Breathn', fightin' and fuckin' amigo! Hey buddy, we gotta get a landline message to a . . ."

"Camardo, Frankie Camardo." The crew boss relayed.

". . . to Mr. Frankie Camardo, regarding a delivery. Can you help us out brother?"

With the appropriate connections made by telephone, the gang boss informed the New York boss that shipment had been received, payment had been made and requested future rendezvous details for Catman.

The Wolves of Calabria

By the time all the necessary commo was complete the cargo had been unloaded and the Studebaker truck and two of the cars started up and pulled away north to head out of the Meadowlands and back over Manhattan.

"On a clear day you can talk to Pismo Beach!" Catman was cheerfully informing the Mafioso when his attention was distracted by a commotion approximately 300 yards across the reed beds, out near the main four lane blacktop. A few seconds later shots rang out through the darkness and within seconds it erupted into a full blown fire fight.

"Well, that's my cue!" Jimmy stuffed the envelope into his jacket and was already shifting over into the pilot's seat.

"It's dark as hell out here! How you gonna take off?!" Big Man challenged.

"That a Packard you got over there?" Jimmy asked as he fired up the DeHavilland.

"Yeah why?"

"Get her revved up, pull her around to the far end of the roadbed as possible and pop on your high beams!"

"Then what?!"

"Look up and as soon as you see the belly of my Beaver get the hell outta Dodge Daddy-o! Nice meetin' ya, don't forget to write!" He slammed the door behind the boss and fired up the engine.

Less than a minute later Jimmy Dugan came within six inches of leaving tire marks on the roof of that '46 Packard as the big man dove from the driver's seat onto the floor.

No sooner was he airborne and the radio again crackled to life.

Catman, Catman, Midnight here. You read me man?

"Ahh Midnight, Catman here. Looks like we gonna havt'a get that drink a little later Daddy-O! I've some Enemy in the A.O. and am about to bug out. Have a good one. Out!"

Jimmy banked out hard left and using the road lights to navigate, turned the nose 180 and headed south as muzzle flashes twinkled below him in the inky dark of the Meadowlands.

"Ahhh! The good old days!" He sighed.

☦

While Jimmy and the Jersey crew had been unloading the plane Doc and Benson were engaged in a high speed game of car tag.

They came out curving to the left of the tunnel's toll booths at the intersection of Jersey Avenue and Marin Boulevard in lower Jersey City, which tied into Route 1-9 then headed west through Jersey City.

The normally hectic New York City suburb was quiet at the hour of two in the morning and so, Doc mentally noted, posed minimal danger to civilians.

In an attempt to lose the motorcycle, Benson jumped a median and headed the wrong way down a one way street. Seeing an oncoming set of

The Wolves of Calabria

headlights he decided to play a quick game of chicken and although he didn't accelerate any faster he refused to move over.

The car, full of drunk teenagers suddenly sobered up as they realized there was a mad man in the other car. Their driver swerved into a row of parked cars and Benson shot passed.

McKeowen on the motorcycle was now a block behind.

Where the hell is this asshole heading! Doc's mind raced to work out.

Easily able to keep up and outmaneuver the car Doc held back so as not to force an accident as he chased Benson up onto Palisades Avenue past William Dickinson High built from the original blueprints from Buckingham Palace, on through Journal Square and onto Sip Avenue. Benson turned right back onto Route 9 and headed north.

A mile down Route 9 Doc saw the approaching overhead sign: Pulaski Skyway- Keep Left

He's heading out to the Meadowlands! Doc surmised!

✝

Back at the tunnel when McKeowen sped off, Louie glanced over at the tunnel's entrance.

"Fangulo!" He cursed.

Having heard the exchange of gun fire at the Jersey entrance Chief Sullivan and Patrolman

Morris appeared from the tunnel in their black Plymouth fastback cruiser. They pulled right up to Mancino.

"Who the hell are you?"

"Louie Mancino. Who the hell are you?"

"None'a your fuckin' business!" Sullivan snapped. "Morris, follow that motorcycle God damn it!" He ordered.

"Chief, this is Jersey, we ain't got no jurisdiction here!" Morris protested.

"I know we're in Jersey! DON'T YOU THINK I KNOW WE'RE IN JERSEY?! I'm gonna nail that son-of-a-bitch on a federal rap! Follow him God damn it!"

"What federal rap?" Louie asked.

"Committing a crime then crossing across state lines!" Uninvited Louie threw open the back door of the sedan and jumped in.

"Hey asshole, this look like a fuckin' taxi to you?!" Sullivan barked.

"You wanna know what's going on here?" Mancino countered. "Then drive. Morris follow that motorcycle!"

As they continued west into the city the questions Sullivan were throwing at Louie were cut short by an intercepted radio dispatch.

Unit three-four, unit three-four this is dispatch. Come in.

Dispatch go for three-four.

Three-four high speed pursuit reported along Route 9 north. One late model vehicle and one motorcycle reported involved. Please respond.

Roger dispatch, three-four enroute. ETA three to four minutes.

"OH SHIT! OH SHIT! Gimme a map, gimme a map!" Louie insisted from the back seat. Sullivan turned in his seat and stared as Morris reached into the glove box and retrieved a map of the bi-city area and passed it back to Louie.

"What'a you got Barret's syndrone or something?" Sully sarcastically asked. Louie quickly unfolded and oriented the map.

"It's called Turret's and it's a syndrome, not syn**drone.** Buy a dictionary fer Christ's sake!" Louie smoothly corrected.

"Fuck you!"

"Snappy come back Chief!" Morris said. "What'a you want with the map? What'a you looking for?" Morris asked.

"Doc and I were talking-"

"WHAT'D YOU SAY?! YOU AND WHO?!" Sullivan twisted around in his seat and demanded.

"Doc and I -"

"THAT PHONEY PAIN IN THE ASS MCKEOWEN DOC MCKEOWEN?! THAT 'DOC'?!"

"A little harsh don't ya think, Chief?" Louie asked as he perused the map.

"SHUT IT LUMPY!" Louie looked over at Morris and mouthed 'Lumpy' as if insulted.

"What'a you and that phoney pain in my ass doin' chasin' Mobsters?" Sullivan demanded.

577

"I'm not sure about the phoney part but I agree, he can be a pain the ass sometimes-"

"Don't get cute with me! Answer the question!"

"They are, he is not a mobster Chief."

"Then what the hell is he, a J-walker?!"

"He's a Department of Foreign Affairs agent."

"You expect me to believe you and McKeowen uncovered a crooked Federal agent again, foiled his plans and now are chasing him through the streets of New Jersey?!"

"Actually Chief Sullivan, there are, were, two federal agents."

"Two?! Where the hell's the other one?"

"He a . . . he got ate by a tiger."

Unsure how to react Sullivan fell back in his seat and stared at Mancino.

"Soon as this is over you're gettin' a drunk test!" The Chief demanded.

†

Once off the Route 9 by-pass and up into the Meadowlands which ran north of the Pulaski and up the Hackensack River, Benson pulled off the main road and steered over to the Turnpike construction site closest to the exit.

He pulled onto the dirt service road where he spotted the small convoy of cars escorting the haulage truck.

Suspecting there might be trouble with what he

was about to pull, he parked the Chrysler adjacent to a large John Deere articulated loader across the road.

The Grossman's Haulage truck, led by one of the two black limos was just turning onto the road.

Benson quickly checked his .45 and waving his arms ran to the middle of the road to flag the convoy down.

The truck driver slowed to a halt and the men in the lead car hopped out and approached him. On seeing the .45 they went for their roscoes but Benson held his hands up in surrender and they backed off.

"What's the problem?!" The lead car driver asked as he got out.

"Change of plans." Benson yelled over.

"Says who?"

Benson flashed his badge and Federal I.D.

"You the Fed we're supposed to meet?!"

"Very astute!"

The mobster mentally debated whether or not to take offence at the word.

"You was supposed to be here half hour ago!"

"The tunnel was backed up. Where's your crew boss?" The driver sized him up and called over his shoulder.

"Get Ernie up here!"

Only three or four minutes behind Benson McKeowen arrived at the construction site. However, spotting the gaggle of gangsters from down the road he thought it prudent to lay low and assess the situation. He shut the bike down and wheeled it off to the side of the road behind a stack of drainage pipes.

From behind a dozen bundles of reinforcement rods, standing in the glare of the trucks' headlamps he could see Benson talking with one of the men who was not in uniform. Both stood almost directly in front of the haulage vehicle, surrounded by three others in uniforms.

As they waited for Ernie, Benson made a mental note of how many men he could see and where each stood. Two to the right, the driver in front of him. The two in the truck stayed put likewise the few he could see in the car at their six o'clock. A minute later Ernie's car drove up and he got out.

"You Benson?"

"Yeah." Again he flashed his I.D.

"You're late!"

"I know."

"What happened, traffic in the tunnel?" There was sporadic laughter.

"The Bronx drop point's been compromised to the NYPD." Benson explained. Ernie looked suspicious.

"Yeah? Where's the new drop?"

"Long Island."

"How come we didn't know nothin' about that? We didn't get no word about a back-up drop location."

Ernie wasn't about to reveal and Benson had no way to know that he just got off the radio with his

The Wolves of Calabria

contacts in Manhattan.

"Just found out this afternoon. The backer notified me by phone from D.C. and asked me to get word to you." Ernie mentally juggled what to do about this poor bullshitter.

"Well we deeply appreciate your going through all the bother Agent Benson, but I think we'll just take the stuff into The City, contact Mr. Costello and take it from there."

"Have it your way." Benson, not having had a good night so far, probably wasn't thinking straight when he drew down on Ernie with his .45

Ernie didn't even flinch at Benson's threat as a half dozen gun hammers were heard cocking back as the rest of the crew drew down on agent. Ernie casually reached over and relieved Benson of his .45.

"Ever heard the expression, 'born during the day but it wasn't yesterday'?" Ernie taunted. "Get the fuck out'a here, Bush League!" Benson, realizing it was only due to his badge that he was still breathing and seething with anger, made his way back to the Chrysler.

"LET'S GO!" Ernie yelled and the mobsters remounted their vehicles and moved out.

Not the kind of guy to handle humiliation very well Benson scurried into the driver's seat of his newly acquired Chrysler, started it up and reached for the Thompson.

He stood halfway out the door and, as the convoy started back up the road, he let rip a burst at the lead car and on into the Studebaker box truck behind it.

The convoy, now thirty or forty yards up the road, stopped and immediately returned fire. Clearly out gunned the Fed took cover.

The firing halted as Jimmy Dugan's DeHavilland soared overhead less than 300 feet off the deck, banked hard left and climbed south.

Suddenly the wail of police sirens broke over the horizon, the flash of multiple red lights could be seen in the distance and the Mafiosi lost their appetite for the fire fight. Their vehicles spat dirt and gravel as they vacated the area.

Coming back out from behind the rear of the car smiling Benson climbed in and prepared to vacate the area himself.

He started the car and as he put it in gear he frantically struggled to make sense of the loud bang which rocked the entire vehicle. He grabbed at the wheel and spun to see what was happening when he realized the bucket on the front of the articulated loader he had parked next to was creeping underneath the chassis and starting to lift the driver's side of the vehicle off the road. Through the side window he could see McKeowen at the wheel of the loader.

"Knock, knock, ass-hole!" Doc called out.

The Chrysler's wind-shield was suddenly at a 45 degree angle to the earth and then completely perpendicular as the car was on its side.

Realizing there was no chance to lift the heavy door to escape Benson scrambled to roll down the window and climb out instead.

Doc backed the machine up a few feet, readjusted the bucket and rammed into the undercarriage knocking the car over onto its roof.

Just as the bucket hit again, Benson squirted out of the driver's side window and rolled out into the dirt.

Scrambling for the Thompson he cocked aimed and fired. Doc ducked down but there were only two rounds left in the mag both hitting and smashing the wind-shield of the loader.

With his left hand Doc reached around the driver's compartment and fired until his mag was empty.

Rather than fumble for his back-up pistol while under fire, Benson ran for all he was worth up the road, past a pile of drainage pipe and into the reeds.

☦

En route across the bridge spanning the Hackensack River Louie had filled Sullivan in on what he and Doc had figured out to that point and, using the road map Morris had dug out of the glove box they made their way to where Mancino believed the drug drop would be. Although his deductions were right they were about ten minutes too late.

By the time they reached the Turnpike construction site the New Jersey State troopers had found the wrecked Chrysler, had the area cordoned off and had Benson's Thompson and Grease Gun in custody. There were several officers at work planting evidence flags and collecting shell casings.

✝

A mere three hundred yards away Benson, quietly sat behind a large pile of timbers, his coat and jacket off, as he improvised a bandage from his shirt tails. He winched but was careful to remain silent as he wound the white, linen material tightly around his left upper bicep where one of McKeowen's rounds had ripped through it.

Doc slowly crept through the reeds around the crime scene as a small passenger plane flew overhead. It was then that he realized that was the second plane that had seen flying by at low altitude headed in the same direction.

Also keeping a low profile to avoid the troopers Doc scanned the darkness for some sign of Benson.

He's probably trying to make it over to the airport! Doc guessed.

Less than a mile away laid Newark Metropolitan, opened by Amelia Earhart in 1934. Less than 15 miles outside of Manhattan it was the busiest airport in the world.

Doc spotted Benson about three hundred yards away scurrying up the road back towards the Pulaski Skyway and cautiously moved to follow.

The Wolves of Calabria

Once at the base of one of the massive caissons Benson found a service ladder and began to climb. With his wounded arm it was a struggle but he made it up to the roadbed on the bridge.

As he crested the top of the ladder and climbed up onto the roadbed Benson glanced down and was not a happy camper at what he saw. McKeowen was past the halfway point up the ladder, hanging by one hand while attempting to get a bead on the agent who quickly pulled back as Doc squeezed off a single round.

Too exhausted to run and with his improvised bandage loosening, Benson calculated his best bet was to ambush Doc as he came up the ladder. From across the road he spotted a roadside salt box which would afford him cover as well as a clear field of fire to the point where the ladder let off onto the bridge and so made for that. He drew his back-up piece and hunkered down behind the large saltbox.

Just as he reached the top of the ladder Doc became suspicious and stopped. Backtracking down a couple of rungs he peered under the bridge and spied an unprotected catwalk to the other side. Holstering his weapon he climbed off the ladder onto the narrow walk and headed across the 30 yard span. The wind only came in gusts but he was able to steady himself by holding onto an adjoining guide cable.

At the point where the roadbed crossed the Hackensack River there were three foot high iron crash barriers on the side of each of the outer traffic lanes as well as one down the center of the road acting as a median to prevent head-ons. Doc's plan was to take Benson from behind using the barriers behind him as cover.

Meanwhile Doc's pot shot from the ladder at Benson attracted the attention of Mancino and company down in the Meadowlands a half mile away.

"You hear that?" Sullivan asked to no one in particular as he was poised to re-enter his squad car.

"Came from the direction of the bridge." Morris affirmed.

"Let's go!" Mancino was first back into the squad car and they were away.

Back up on the Skyway Doc got a nasty surprise as he eased his head up above the foot rail to peruse the roadbed on Benson's side of the bridge.

Benson also had become suspicious when, after a few minutes time Doc hadn't materialised from the ladder and so deduced he was trying to outflank him.

Two rounds in rapid succession ricocheted off the girder right next to McKeowen's left ear rendering him temporarily deaf but he was able to return fire with enough effect to cause Benson to dive for cover and allow himself to scramble back across to the other side of the road.

"Did I get you with that one, McKeowen?" Doc discerned Benson's quip through the ringing in his ears.

With a mere four lanes now separating them and very little early morning traffic they were easily able to shout from behind the safety of the crash barriers on either side of the roadbed.

"Hey Asshole, your girlfriend's name was Hernandez, wasn't it?" Echoed across the road.

"What do you mean 'was'? What about him, tough guy? Where is he?" Judging by Benson's tone Doc knew he struck a nerve.

"I don't think you're gonna make the funeral, but lemme put it to you this way dumbshit, when it comes time for ya buddy's memorial service, after they I.D. his teeth, they're probably gonna bury him in a sandwich bag."

"What'd you do to him fuck-face?!"

"Not me! My partner, Mancino."

"The little fat guy?"

"One and the same."

"What happened? Where is he?!"

"Ate by a tiger!"

"Get the fuck out'a here!" There was a pause. "You shittin' me?"

"Swear to God! No lie."

"Son-of-a-bitch!" Benson momentarily lost concentration as he contemplated Hernandez's death. "Bastard always said he wanted to go out with a fight!"

"Well, I don't know about a fight, but he sure went out with a bite!"

"Funny McKeowen, not too clever, but funny. I'll try and remember that when I put a bullet in your fuckin' head!"

"So you and Hernandez were hired to babysit the

operation but you had plans of your own?"

"What'a you?! Dick Tracey? Here to keep the streets of the city clean for 'da decent folk'?!" As the fed launched into his self-absorbed conjecture Doc quietly changed location by crawling along the walkway on his own side of the barrier. "The kind of guy who could only be found outside the ranks of the established judiciary?" Benson finished and decided to move.

Without revealing his exact position while carefully listening for Benson's footsteps on the macadam roadbed Doc guestimated the fed's location and took a chance. He sprang up from behind the guard rail, fired two quick rounds and ducked back down. Benson was up and moving but was caught off balance as he attempted to charge Doc got two rounds off also, but he was too late and caught one of the TT-33's 7.62 rounds in the right upper shoulder. The force of impact spun him around and he stumbled back onto the road and fell face down.

Not hearing any return fire or any more footsteps Doc cautiously peeked over his side of the barrier in time to see an over-sized delivery truck bearing down on Benson. The fed desperately clawed to crawl to the side of the road but was not quite fast enough.

The truck ripped across both lower legs before the driver realized what was happening. The truck screeched and skidded to a halt about a hundred yards up the road as McKeowen, maintaining a bead on Benson the entire time, approached the legless, mildly convulsing criminal. As the crush injury had temporarily pinched off his leg stumps the blood only slowly pooled from the mess his lower legs had become.

Doc approached, stood over him, weapon pointed down and fought back a surge of pity.

"Why'd you have Rossini's wife killed?" Doc asked.

"'Have' her . . . killed? You are . . . behind the power curve!" Benson choked out between coughs. "I didn't have her killed."

"I know Rossini didn't do it."

Despite Rossini's now obvious frame-up, Doc fought back his guilt at having played a hand in his conviction.

"Ahh, the wonderful science . . . of forensics! Door swings both ways, 'Doc'! You don't . . . don't just catch criminals with it, you can make 'em too!"

"After all, we can't let an insignificant thing like moral consciousness get in the way of business and politics, can we now? Where would this country be?" Doc lowered his pistol but only slightly. "I killed her you idiot!"

Doc flinched slightly when Benson raised his .45 but was taken off guard when the fed put the gun to his own temple.

"Who's your backer?"

Benson was breathing more rapidly now as the pool of blood around his lower legs slowly widened. "Who was it, Anslinger?"

"Asslicker is a fucking marionette!" He choked out. "The Bureau pulls . . . his strings! Him and that bleeding heart, suffragette he married . . ." Benson boasted.

"Then who was your backer? Who fronted the money for the buy?" Doc took one step closer and readjusted his aim.

The young black, heavily panting, truck driver came up to the two at a full run but slammed on the brakes and raised his hands as soon as he saw the guns.

Benson smiled and pulled the trigger of his .45.

Doc and the driver just stared. Doc lowered his weapon.

"Who was he?" The driver asked as he moved up next to

"Just another retired government worker." Doc mumbled half to himself.

†

CHAPTER XXV

As the burning sun crested the harbor from behind the Manhattan skyline and climbed above Hudson Bay, the last of the emergency vehicles up on the bridge pulled away from the police traffic barriers that had been erected and the Pulaski Skyway was once again open.

"Benson killed Rossini's wife to persuade Rossini to get Costello to get with the programme, the drug programme that is." Doc briefed Sullivan as they sat to the side of the cordoned off road in Sully's squad car. Sully sat and stared.

"A fuckin' tiger?" Sully again asked in disbelief. "You know what this means, don't ya?"

"Yeah, now you can't arrest Detective Mancino for murder." Doc quipped.

"It means I got paperwork until Christmas!" A dejected Sullivan snapped. "Alright, you two can go." Sullivan eventually declared. "We need anything else I know where to find ya."

Doc and Louie climbed out of the black fastback and started down the bridge's pedestrian path to the Jersey City side of the bridge.

"Why'd you let Sully get credit for the take down?" Louie probed.

"To avoid future headaches."

"You think he'd go that far? Try to prosecute us?"

"Probably even try and arrest the tiger if he

thought he could make it stick!"

"I'd pay to see that." Louie looked back up the bridge as they walked. "Maybe it'll make the peace with that fat assed gavone!" Louie conjectured.

"Not likely, but anything's possible." Doc added.

Just as they hit the sidewalk on the shoreline and were off the bridge Morris the cop pulled up and rolled down his window.

"You fella's want a lift back over? Or I'lldop ya at Journal Square, you can get the tube over to The City."

"Nah, thanks pal. I think we're just gonna walk for a while." Mancino replied.

"Suit yerselfs"

"Hey Morris."

"Yeah Louie?"

"Nice drivin' man!"

"Hope so. I used to be a car thief." Morris smiled and drove off.

"I don't think he was kidding!" Louie added.

"Neither do I."

"How's the arm?"

"It's the shoulder."

"How's the shoulder?"

"It hurts."

They walked for a ways in silence. The sun slowly begun to burn off the residual chill of the night air and it was a good fifteen to twenty minutes that they walked in silence, digesting the night's events. With a suggestion Mancino rekindled the conversation.

"There used to be an all night joint up on Duncan Avenue. Jimmy's Tavern. Probably got something for the pain. Might be able to coax some bacon and eggs of 'em too."

"Louie?"

"Yeah Doc?"

"Ya did good tonight."

"Thanks Doc! That really means a lot ya know. I was thinking-."

"Don't get a big head!" Doc kept walking as Mancino stopped in his tracks.

"There's always a price with you, ain't there?" Louie jogged to catch up. "Why can't you ever just pay somebody a compliment and let go with that?!"

Doc smirked.

✝

CHAPTER XXVI

It was 11:07 and Doc was waiting to meet Nikki & Katie at Grand Central Terminal. Nikki had phoned the day before and told him they would be arriving at the station on the 11:15 from Boston that morning.

They arrived on time and Doc suggested they stop and have an early lunch.

"It's called 'brunch'." Katie corrected and informed him.

"Okay then, let's have 'brunch'!" McKeowen mocked.

After collecting their bags they made their way up to the main concourse to catch a cab Downtown. The front page of the *New York Daily News* on the kiosk next to the taxi rank outside the station caught Doc's eye.

The headline story blared:

ANSLINGER'S OFFICE REPORTS $100
MILLION IN HEROIN VANISHES
FROM B'LYN EVIDENCE WAREHOUSE

Doc plucked the paper from the stand and read on.

According to authorities the record breaking catch was scheduled to be transported to a federal warehouse in Brooklyn on Water Street where it was to await a court order to be destroyed when it vanished. The haul had been confiscated in a joint operation between N.J. State Troopers and the NYPD. A protracted court battle ensued before it was transferred to the Federal Bureau of Narcotics and eventually remanded to the custody of the Department of Foreign Affairs.

McKeowen tossed a nickel on the counter, took the paper and read as they walked.

"Son-of-a-bitch!"

"Mind your mouth!" Nikki scolded.

"Yes dear!"

"I forgot how much I miss your manners." She countered.

"Yes dear."

Katie shook her head and giggled.

"You guys should be married!" She quietly declared.

✝

As Commissioner Anslinger continued his conniving to the top and White faded back into government induced obscurity, Senator Woods stood at his desk in a prestigious front section of the floor of the Congress.

Two junior senators in the rear of the auditorium watched the congressional stage as Woods proceeded to steal the show.

"Can't believe the crusty old bastard's been re-elected for a record fourth term!" One whispered to the other.

"What'a ya suppose the old boy's secret is?" The other asked.

"No doubt it's how he picks the cornerstone of what he builds the foundation of his public platform on!"

"Get involved in the war, don't get involved in the war. Help the poor, don't help the poor. What is it this time around?"

"His widely publicized, well-known anti-drugs stance."

Out on the floor Wood launched into his thank you speech.

". . . in full support of Commissioner Anslinger's aggressive anti-drug program, being made into law by the passage of this bill I am about to introduce, a bill which will garner another fifteen million dollars in this crucial fight against the evils of illegal narcotics!" Woods declared amongst enthusiastic applause.

Meanwhile two men a half a world apart, one in Washington D.C., and one in Naples, Italy were planning their next scheme to launch yet another attack on the American economy.

☦

CHAPTER XXVII

Playa Vista de Nada
3 Miles East of Havana

He set the empty glass on the small, bamboo glass-topped table next to him as he lounged beneath the huge, multi-colored, beach umbrella.

On a small private beach a few miles from the capital, living in a small, thatched hacienda adjoining the *Sand & Surf* puestito on the beach, Jimmy Dugan, war hero, drug runner, ace pilot and lover, stretched out on his palm shaded, chaise lounge killing time before dark when he would take his brand new, 1947 Kurtis-Omohundro into the city and hit the clubs to make the most of the Havana night life.

"Waiter!"
"Si señor Dugan?"
"Another Cuba Libre please."
"Coming right up Mr. Dugan!"

The pristine beach softly vignetted into the sparkling, azure ocean as it stretched out across the Caribbean. Jimmy mused; *Life is good!*

✝

THE END

Paddy Kelly

Also by Paddy Kelly

Ghost Story
(A play)

Operation Underworld

The American Way

Politically Erect

Kelly's Full House

American Rhetoric

The Wolves of Calabria

Children of the Nuclear Gods

The Galileo Project

Synopsis or option information available online at:
www.paddykellywriter.com or from
Fiction4All
https://fiction4all.com

Lightning Source UK Ltd.
Milton Keynes UK
UKHW021957080819
347643UK00010B/371/P